New TOEIC 990

新多益

高分關鍵字彙

目 錄 Contents

序

　　TOEIC（Test of English for International Communication）是一項針對母語為非英語的人士所做的溝通測驗，自1979年研發至今，可說是最受國際肯定、最具公信力的職場應與測驗。

　　目前在台灣，已有許多企業在徵才時將TOEIC成績列入考量，並做為公司內部升遷的依據，因此許多高等學府為提高學生就業競爭力，均會要求學生畢業前通過TOEIC測驗。

　　TOEIC不同於留學英語測驗如TOEFL之處，在於生活實用性很高，不會考驗艱澀的字彙及句型文法，目的在於確定一個人工作職場上順利閱讀及溝通的能力，尤其閱讀部分題目多、篇幅大，極度考驗考生的閱讀速度。

　　近年新推出的New TOEIC最大特色，是在原本的「聽力」及「閱讀」測驗之外，加入選擇性參加的第二階段「口說」及「寫作」，以測試考生靈活運用字彙及文法的能力（也因此New TOEIC紙筆測驗將紙筆測驗的文法考題「挑錯」部分全部刪除）。「口說」與「寫作」的考試方式，均為文字及錄音題目的搭配，大幅提高「聽力」在這項考試中的重要性。

　　除了大幅提高聽力的重要性，New TOEIC的錄音題還加入了北美腔之外的其他英語腔調（英國、加拿大、紐、澳），以期更符合實際英語工作環境的情況。

　　為了讓讀者得到最好的閱讀、聽力訓練效果，《New TOEIC 990 新多益高分關鍵字彙》除了分析歷年TOEIC考題及主題範圍，精選必考字彙，並針對New TOEIC修訂最新字表，本書還聘請英、美籍教師比照TOEIC主題及常考句型撰寫例句，絕非一般輕鬆寫就的簡短句子。有聲品錄製亦比照New TOEIC測驗，分別以男、女北美腔及男、女英式腔發音。

　　考試並非學習英文的目的，《New TOEIC 990 新多益高分關鍵字彙》在編輯撰寫上格外的設計及用心，是希望讀者能在閱讀本書的過程中，實際增進職場閱讀、溝通能力，在考試得到高分的同時，也能真正習得實用的英語資訊，這正是EZ talk對英語學習一貫的信念。

EZ叢書館總編輯　陳思容

如何使用本書

為了方便讀者查閱，本書依照A-Z字母排列。各單元學習設計如下：

1. MP3序號

2. 字彙
3. KK音標
7. 相關補充
4. 英文例句
5. 詞性及中文定義
6. 中文翻譯

英文關鍵字

.0055

agree
[əˋgri]

必
同 concur, consent
反 differ, dissent
形 agreeable
副 agreeably
名 agreement 同 accord
反 disagreement, dissonance
片 agree on/to something
agree with someone

After extensive negotiations, the two companies **agreed** to form a partnership.

(v.) 同意
在廣泛的協商過後，這兩家公司同意合夥。

1. MP3序號
　北美腔（Disc 1）、英式腔（Disc 2）共用相同序號搜尋方便。

2. 字彙
3. KK音標
4. 英文例句
5. 詞性及中文定義
6. 中文翻譯

7. 相關補充
　必　必考字彙
　聽　聽力高頻字彙
　讀　閱讀高頻字彙
　名　相關名詞形式
　動　相關動詞形式
　形　相關形容詞形式
　副　相關副詞形式
　同　同義字
　反　反義字
　片　常考片語

New
TOEIC
新多益高分關鍵字彙
990

A
Group

0001

abide by
[əˋbaɪd baɪ]
必

The CEO must **abide by** the rules set forth by the board of directors in order to protect the interests of shareholders.

(v.) 遵守
執行長必須遵守董事會所訂定的規則，以保護股東的利益。

0002

ability
[əˋbɪlətɪ]
必
反 disability
動 enable　反 prevent
形 able　反 unable
副 ably

The driver's **ability** to find the quickest route to reach a destination made him well-liked by his employers.

(n.) 能力
這司機有能力快速找到通往目的地的最快路線，讓他深受雇主喜愛。

0003

aboard
[əˋbord]
同 on board

Once the entire crew was **aboard** the ship, the vessel cast off and sailed away from the dock.

(prep., adv.) 在（船、飛機）上
一等全體組員都上船，這艘船便離岸，駛離碼頭。

0004

abolition
[͵æbəˋlɪʃən]
同 abolishment
動 abolish　反 establish
名 abolitionist
名 abolitionism

Business leaders worked together at the national level for the **abolition** of unfair taxes.

(n.) 廢除
企業領袖全國性大規模共同合作，以廢除不公的稅賦。

0005

abstract

[ˋæbstrækt]

反 concrete

名 abstraction

The challenge for MBA graduates is to apply **abstract** knowledge in the real world of business.

(a.) 抽象的

企業管理碩士畢業生的挑戰，在於把抽象的知識應用於真實的商業世界。

0006

abundant

[əˋbʌndənt]

必

同 plentiful

反 sparse

Karen's **abundant** experience in the marketing field made it easy for her to find a well-paying position.

(a.) 充沛的，豐富的

凱倫在行銷領域的經驗豐富，很容易找到高薪職位。

0007

accept

[əkˋsɛpt]

必

同 take

反 reject

I believe Albert will **accept** the terms you have laid out, but you may find that he will still request an increase in salary.

(v.) 接受，接納

我相信艾伯特將接受你開出的條件，但你可能會發現他還是會要求加薪。

0008

acceptance

[əkˋsɛptəns]

必

反 rejection

Although the product is well-designed, it has not yet gained **acceptance** in the marketplace.

(n.) 接受，接納

雖然這產品設計得很好，但尚未獲得市場的接受。

0009

access
[ˈæksɛs]
必 聽
形 **accessible**
　同 attainable, available
名 **accessibility**

If you really want to **access** the information on your frozen computer, you'll need to leave it with the technician.

(v.) 存取，使用
若你真想存取當機電腦裡的資訊，你得把電腦交給技術人員才行。

0010

access
[ˈæksɛs]
必 聽
同 **admission**

Only employees with security clearance have **access** to the top-secret files.

(n.)（電腦檔案）存取，進入使用權
唯有通過安全查核的員工，才能存取最高機密檔案。

0011

accommodate
[əˈkɑməˌdet]
必 讀
同 **oblidge, indulge**
名 **accommodation**

The hotel makes every attempt to **accommodate** guests by making sure it pays attention to even the smallest details.

(v.) 滿足需求
這家飯店連最小的細節都注意到，極力照顧客人膳宿的所有需求。

0012

accommodation
[əˌkɑməˈdeʃən]
必
同 **lodging**

The businessman's **accommodations** left him less than impressed, and he complained to the hotel manager before checking out.

(n.) 膳宿，適應
這個生意人對於膳宿不盡滿意，在退房前向飯店經理抱怨了一番。

0013

accompany

[ə`kʌmpənɪ]

同 go with
片 be accompanied by

When attending meetings, the company president is often **accompanied** by his personal assistant.

(v.) 陪伴
公司總裁參加會議時，常有私人助理陪同。

0014

accomplish

[ə`kɑmplɪʃ]

必
同 fulfill
形 accomplished
名 accomplishment
　同 achievement

Start working on the report now and see what you can get **accomplished** by Monday morning.

(v.) 完成，達成
現在就開始寫報告，看你到週一早上能完成多少。

0015

accomplishment

[ə`kɑmplɪʃmənt]

必
同 achievement

The young mayor felt it was a real **accomplishment** when his attempt to earn a seat in the House of Representatives was successful.

(n.) 成就，完成
這年輕市長成功在眾議院拿下一席，感覺這是一項真正的成就。

0016

accordance

[ə`kɔrdəns]

片 in accordance with

This product should be used in **accordance** with the guidelines in the enclosed User's Manual.

(n.) 符合，授予
這產品應依隨附的說明書裡的準則來使用。

0017

according to
[əˈkɔrdɪŋ tə]

According to most surveys out on the market, this computer is the top of the line.

根據

根據市場上最新的調查，這部電腦是這系列最頂級的機種。

0018

account
[əˈkaʊnt]

同 client
動 account

Mark was promoted to Sales Manager because of his success in winning new **accounts**.

(n.) 客戶

馬克因為成功爭取到新客戶，被擢升為業務經理。

0019

accounts payable
[əˈkaʊnts ˈpeəbl]

The bookkeeper used her new accounting software to keep track of **accounts payable**.

應付帳款

簿記人員用她新的會計軟體來記錄應付帳款。

0020

accounts receivable
[əˈkaʊnts rɪˈsivəbl]

The company went into bankruptcy because of its failure to collect on **accounts receivable**.

應收帳款

這家公司因為收不到應收帳款而倒閉。

0021

accountability

[əˌkaʊntəˈbɪlətɪ]

同 responsibility
形 accountable

In our company's management training program, trainees are taught the importance of **accountability** and integrity.

(n.) 負有責任

在我們公司的管理訓練計畫中，受訓者被教導負責任和正直的重要性。

0022

accountant

[əˈkaʊntənt]

必 聽
同 auditor, bookkeeper

The **accountant** at the large firm made sure the daily expenses of each employee did not exceed the set amount.

(n.) 會計師

這家大公司的會計確保每名員工每天的支出均未超過規定金額。

0023

accounting

[əˈkaʊntɪŋ]

必

An **accounting** agency was hired to handle all the money matters for the up-and-coming young model.

(n.) 會計（學）

一家會計公司受雇替這年輕的模特兒新秀，處理所有財務問題。

0024

accumulate

[əˈkjumjəˌlet]

必
同 amass
名 accumulation
   accretion

After **accumulating** sufficient funds, the lawyer decided to leave the firm and start his own law office.

(v.) 累積

累積到足夠資金後，這律師決定離開事務所，自己開業。

0025

accumulation
[əˌkjumjəˈleʃən]

必
同 accretion, build-up

The **accumulation** of papers on Mr. Johnson's desk made it difficult to find the important file.

(n.) 累積，堆積
強森先生桌上堆積如山的公文，讓他很難找出重要的資料。

0026

accuracy
[ˈækjərəsɪ]

必
反 inaccuracy

Accuracy is very important in the translation of contracts and other legal documents.

(n.) 精確
翻譯合約等法律文件時，精確性是很重要的。

0027

accurate
[ˈækjərɪt]

必
同 exact, precise
反 inaccurate
副 accurately
名 accuracy 反 inaccuracy

If marketing research figures are to be useful, they must be both **accurate** and timely.

(a.) 精確的
行銷研究數據若要有用，就必須精確又及時。

0028

accuse
[əˈkjuz]

同 charge
名 accusation
　　同 charge

During the court case, the defendant was **accused** of several additional crimes that fell outside the scope of the trial.

(v.) 指控
在庭訊過程中，被告額外被控本案之外的幾條罪狀。

0029

accustomed to…
[əˋkʌstəmd tə]
必

It usually takes companies setting up offices in China several years to become **accustomed to** the local business environment.

習慣於…
在中國設立辦公室的公司，通常要花好幾年才能習慣當地的商業環境。

0030

achieve
[əˋtʃiv]
必
反 fail, lose
名 achievement
　　反 failure
形 achievable

If we do well in the fourth quarter, we should have no trouble **achieving** our sales target.

(v.) 達成
若我們在第四季有好表現，達成業績目標應該是沒問題的。

0031

achievement
[əˋtʃivmənt]
必

The executive's lifetime of **achievement** was recognized at the annual dinner when he was awarded a BMW.

(n.) 成就
這位主管在年度晚宴上獲贈一部寶馬汽車，表彰他一生的成就。

0032

acknowledge
[əkˋnɑlɪdʒ]
讀
同 recognize
名 acknowledgement

The secretary was asked to send a letter to **acknowledge** receipt of payment once the funds were received.

(v.) 告知收到，表示謝忱
這祕書被要求收到資金時，要寄信告知已接獲款項。

0033

acquire
[əˋkwaɪr]

必
同 get, obtain
名 acquisition
形 acquisitive
　同 avaricious, greedy

In an attempt to **acquire** a stronger market share, the company decided to lower prices on all its products.

(v.) 取得，養成

這家公司為了嘗試取得更高的市占率，決定降低所有產品的售價。

0034

acquisition
[ˌækwəˋzɪʃən]

讀
同 purchase

The **acquisition** of two companies last year left the real estate company heavily in debt.

(n.) 收購

去年收購了兩家公司，造成這家房地產公司負債纍纍。

0035

acting
[ˋæktɪŋ]

必
同 temporary, interim

The **acting** head of the department made sure everything was working smoothly while the department head underwent an operation.

(a.) 代理的，臨時的

代理的部門主管確保在部門主管去動手術時，一切運作都很順利。

0036

adapt
[əˋdæpt]

聽
反 unfit
名 adaptability
　反 inadaptability
形 adaptable
　反 unadaptable
副 adaptively

In order to survive in today's competitive business world, a company must always be ready to **adapt** to new market trends.

(v.) 適應，改良

為了在今日競爭激烈的商業世界中存活，公司必須隨時準備適應新的市場潮流。

0037

address
[əˋdrɛs]
必
同 **handle, discuss**

At the next meeting, I would like to **address** the need for more parking spaces for company employees.

(v.) 處理（問題），討論
在下次會議中，我想要處理公司同仁需要更多停車位的問題。

0038

address
[əˋdrɛs]
必
同 **speech, lecture**

The CEO's **address** to shareholders was posted on the company website.

(n.) 致詞，演說
執行長對股東的致詞內容張貼在公司網站上。

0039

adhere to
[ədˋhɪr tə]
必

The lawyer asked that both parties **adhere to** the terms of the partnership agreement.

遵守，支持，堅持
這位律師要求雙方遵守合夥協議的條款。

0040

adjacent
[əˋdʒesənt]
必
同 **close**
名 **adjacency**

I often have lunch at a small Thai restaurant that is **adjacent** to my office.

(a.) 鄰近的
我常在辦公室附近一家泰國小餐館吃午飯。

0041

adjust
[əˋdʒʌst]

必　聽
同　adapt
名　adjustment
　　同 modification
形　adjustable
　　同 adaptable, flexible

Daylight Savings Time starts tomorrow, so please make sure to **adjust** your clocks tonight.

(v.) 調整，適應
明天開始就是日光節約時間，所以今晚請務必要調整時鐘。

0042

adjustment
[əˋdʒʌstmənt]

必

After the manufacturer's poor results last year, **adjustments** were made to the management team.

(n.) 調整，適應
這家廠商去年業績不佳，隨後調整了經營團隊。

0043

administrator
[ədˋmɪnəˌstretə]

同　executive, manager
名　administration
動　administrate
　　同 administer
形　administrative
　　同 executive

The site **administrator** was online last night making sure the information about all user accounts was up-to-date and correct.

(n.) 管理人，行政官員
網管人員昨晚上線，確保使用者帳戶的資料都是最新且正確的。

0044

admire
[ədˋmaɪr]

必
同　respect, adore
名　admiration
　　同 appreciation
形　admirable
副　admiringly, admirably

I really **admire** the way our manager handles himself in business meetings; he has excellent communication skills.

(v.) 欣賞，仰慕
我很欣賞我們經理在業務會議上的應對；他的溝通技巧很優異。

0045

admit
[əˈmɪt]
必 聽
形 admitted
副 admittedly

The airline finally **admitted** that the recent flight delays were their fault, and not the fault of the airport.

(v.) 承認
這家航空公司終於承認最近的班機誤點是他們的錯，並不是機場的錯。

0046

admittance
[əˈmɪtəns]
必
同 access, admission

Members of the press fought for days to gain **admittance** to the international business summit.

(n.) 入場許可，進入
媒體成員為了取得國際商業高峰會的入場許可，爭取了好幾天。

0047

advance
[əˈvæns]
必
同 beforehand
動 advance 同 proceed
名 advance 同 progress
片 in advance

Advance purchase of tickets was required to guarantee a seat at the rock concert in the small arena.

(a.) 預先的
需要預先購票才能保證在這場搖滾演唱會的小場地中，有位置可坐。

0048

advisory
[əˈvaɪzərɪ]
同 announcement
名 advice 同 recommendation
動 advise
形 advisory 同 consultative
副 advisedly

A travel **advisory** was issued last week for certain areas of the Philippines where political unrest has made travel potentially dangerous.

(n.) 公告，報告
上週針對菲律賓某些地區發布了旅遊警告，當地的政治動盪造成旅遊可能發生危險。

0049

affiliate

[əˋfɪlɪˌet]

讀
同 branch, subsidiary

We do business with France through our **affiliate** in Paris.

(n.) 分支機構

我們透過我們在巴黎的分支機構和法國做生意。

0050

affordable

[əˋfɔrdəbl]

必
同 inexpensive
反 unaffordable, expensive
動 afford

The company's top engineer was not looking for the most **affordable** car; instead, he bought the fastest.

(a.) 負擔得起的

這家公司的總工程師不是要找最符合預算的車；反倒買了性能最好的車。

0051

agency

[ˋedʒənsɪ]

必
同 bureau

Which advertising **agency** was chosen to manage our new advertising campaign?

(n.) 代辦處，專責行政機構

哪家廣告公司獲選來經手我們新的廣告宣傳？

0052

agenda

[əˋdʒɛndə]

必 聽
同 schedule

The CEO's weekly **agenda** was filled with conference calls and meetings with the Board of Directors.

(n.) 待辦事項，議程

這位執行長每週的行程，滿是和董事會進行電話會議和開會。

0053

agent
[`edʒənt]
名 agency

The export company's new Asia-Pacific **agent** spent six months at the home office in California learning about the company's products.

(n.) 仲介，代表
這家出口公司新任的亞太代表，在加州母公司花了六個月學習公司的產品。

0054

aggressive
[ə`grɛsɪv]
必
同 assertive
副 aggressively
名 aggressiveness, aggression

The sales representative's **aggressive** style made it easy for her to meet her quarterly sales quotas.

(a.) 有幹勁的，侵略的
這個業務代表充滿幹勁的風格，輕易就讓她達成季銷售業績。

0055

agree
[ə`gri]
必
同 concur, consent
反 differ, dissent
形 agreeable
副 agreeably
名 agreement 同 accord
　　反 disagreement, dissonance
片 agree on/to something
　 agree with someone

After extensive negotiations, the two companies **agreed** to form a partnership.

(v.) 同意
在廣泛的協商過後，這兩家公司同意合夥。

0056

agreement
[ə`grimənt]
必
同 accord, contract

Our office will have a tentative joint venture **agreement** on your desk by the end of the week.

(n.) 協議
我們公司將在本週結束前，把一分暫時的合資企業協議送到你的辦公桌。

0057

air parcel
[ɛr `pɑrsl]

To ensure that the **air parcel** would reach its destination, the secretary sent it by registered mail.

空運包裹
為了確保那個空運包裹能送達目的地，祕書用掛號交寄。

0058

aligned
[ə`laɪnd]

動 **align**　　　同 **line up**
名 **alignment**
反 **unaligned**

It took months for the territory manager to get his agent's sales presentations **aligned** with the company style, but the end result was very impressive.

(a.) 與…一致的，排成直線的
區經理花了幾個月才讓代理商的銷售提案報告符合公司的風格，但是最後的結果相當耀眼。

0059

alleviate
[ə`livɪ͵et]

讀
同 **relieve, assuage**
名 **alleviation**
　　同 **relief, assuagement**

Our hope is that a slight increase in product prices will enable us to **alleviate** the losses sustained due to currency fluctuations.

(v.) 減輕，舒緩
我們希望，微幅提高產品售價能幫助我們減輕匯率波動所蒙受的損失。

0060

allocate
[`ælə͵ket]

必 聽
同 **apportion**
名 **allocation**　　同 **allotment**

During the annual meeting, the Vice President of Marketing suggested that more funds be **allocated** to television ads.

(v.) 配置，分配
在年度會議期間，行銷副總建議應該把更多資金分配給電視廣告。

0061

allowance
[ə`lauəns]

必
同 stipend

The company provided each employee with a monthly food **allowance** to offset lunch costs.

(n.) 零用金，容忍
這家公司提供每名員工月伙食金，以貼補午餐花費。

0062

alternate
[`ɔltənɪt]

必
同 alternative, substitute
名 alternate 同 replacement
副 alternately
名 alternation
　　同 variation

The sales team spent the last week developing an **alternate** sales plan to improve sales in the region.

(a.) 替代性的，輪替的
業務團隊上週都在開發一個替代銷售計畫，以提高該區的業績。

0063

alternative
[ɔl`tɜnətɪv]

必
同 option, recourse
形 alternative
　　同 alternate, substitute
副 alternatively
　　同 instead

If that sales manager doesn't improve his sales record, the boss will have no **alternative** but to fire him.

(n.)（替代）選擇
如果那個業務經理無法改善他的銷售紀錄，老闆將別無選擇，只能解雇他。

0064

ambitious
[æm`bɪʃəs]

同 enterprising
反 content,
　　unambitious
名 ambition

An **ambitious** employee is sure to advance in the company much faster than one who shows no initiative.

(a.) 有企圖心的，有野心的
有企圖心的員工比起不主動進取的同事，在公司的升遷一定更快。

0065

amputate
[ˈæmpjəˌtet]
同 cut off
名 amputation, amputee

If the bacterial infection in the man's leg does not subside with the intake of antibiotics, the doctor would have to **amputate** to save the man's life.

(v.) 截肢
若這男子腿部的細菌感染在投以抗生素後並未減緩，醫生就得截肢才能救他一命。

0066

animated
[ˈænəˌmetɪd]
同 lively, spirited
反 unanimated
動 animate

The young employee's **animated** presentation caught the manager's eye, and the man was soon given a promotion.

(a.) 生動活潑的，動畫的
這年輕員工生動的提案報告博得經理的青睞，他很快就被拔擢。

0067

annihilation
[əˌnaɪəˈleʃən]
同 eradication, destruction
名 annihilationist, annihilationism
動 annihilate
　同 eradicate, decimate

Researchers worked day and night to prevent the spread of the disease from causing the complete **annihilation** of the honeybee species.

(n.) 殲滅，消滅
研究人員日夜努力防止這疾病的擴散，以免蜜蜂族群全數被滅絕。

0068

announce
[əˈnauns]
必
同 declare, proclaim
名 announcement
　同 proclamation, declaration

The company's head of accounting will **announce** the quarterly sales results at the upcoming meeting.

(v.) 宣布
公司的會計主管將在即將到來的會議中，宣布季銷售的業績。

announcement

[ə`naʊnsmənt]

必
同 proclamation, declaration

The **announcement** of the merger will not be made to the press until the deal is signed.

(n.) 宣布
併購案將待合約簽署過後才會向媒體宣布。

annual

[`ænjʊəl]

必
同 yearly
副 annually

An **annual** review is performed to make sure that quality levels are maintained in the production facility.

(a.) 年度的
進行年度檢查是為了確保能維持生產設備的品質水準。

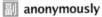

anonymous

[ə`nɑnəməs]

同 unknown
反 known, identified
副 anonymously
名 anonymity

An **anonymous** tip led many stockholders to sell off their shares just before the company declared bankruptcy.

(a.) 匿名的
一則匿名線報讓許多股東在該公司宣布破產前賣掉了持股。

anticipate

[æn`tɪsə‚pet]

聽
同 expect, forecast, predict
名 anticipation

The chairman had no way to **anticipate** that the chief financial officer would quit on such short notice.

(v.) 預料，搶先行動，預支（薪水）
董事長無法預料財務長會突然辭職。

0073

anxiety
[æŋˋzaɪətɪ]

必
同 anxiousness, worry
形 anxious　同 uneasy

Job **anxiety** seems to be one of the leading causes of stress in our society at the present time.

(n.) 焦慮

工作焦慮似乎是現下在我們的社會中，造成壓力的一大主要原因。

0074

anxious
[ˋæŋkʃəs]

必
同 uneasy
反 unconcerned

The man was very **anxious** to receive a phone call from the company after his job interview.

(a.) 焦慮的

這位男士在面試過後，急著想要接到那家公司來電。

0075

apart
[əˋpɑrt]

形 apart　同 separate
片 apart from　除了…

Our R&D department took **apart** the competitor's product to see how it worked.

(adv.) 分開地

我們的研發部門拆開對手的產品來一探究竟。

0076

apologize
[əˋpɑləˏdʒaɪz]

讀
形 apologetic
　同 contrite, regretful
　反 unapologetic
名 apology
片 apologize to sb. for sth.

I'm afraid I have to **apologize** for my colleague's absence today; he was called away on an emergency.

(v.) 道歉

恐怕我得為我同事今日缺席而致歉；他被緊急叫走了。

apparent
[ə`pærənt]

讀
同 obvious, evident, seeming
副 apparently

It was **apparent** that the new product would not be finished in time for the upcoming trade show.

(a.) 顯而易見的，表面上的（但未必為真）
那個新產品顯然趕不上在即將來臨的商展前完成。

appeal
[ə`pil]

必
同 attract
名 appeal 同 allure, attraction
形 appealing 同 attractive
反 unappealing
副 appealingly
片 appeal to 同 attract

The advertising head asked her department to find a way to make the product **appeal** to a younger audience.

(v.) 有吸引力
廣告頭頭要她的部門找出方法，讓產品能吸引到更年輕的族群。

applicant
[`æpləkənt]

必
同 candidate, seeker

Many of the **applicants** we saw today had strong academic backgrounds, but were lacking in practical experience.

(n.) 申請者，應徵者
我們今天看到的應徵者許多都有深厚的學術背景，但缺乏實務經驗。

apply
[ə`plaɪ]

必
名 application
同 petition
形 applied 反 theoretical
副 applicably

In order to find a position that really suits you, you may find it necessary to **apply** to a number of different companies.

(v.) 應徵，申請，應徵者
為了找到真正適合你的職位，可能必須去應徵多家不同公司。

0081

appoint
[əˋpɔɪnt]

聽
同 assign, name
形 appointed　　圓 appointive
名 appointment　圓 designation
片 appoint... to,
　be appointed to...

In order to make the planning process go more smoothly, I'm going to **appoint** you leader of the planning team.

(v.) 任命
為了讓規畫的過程更順利，我要任命你擔任領導規畫小組的領導人。

0082

appointment
[əˋpɔɪntmənt]

必
同 engagement, date

Martin scheduled an **appointment** with the bank's loan officer for next Tuesday.

(n.) 約定會面，任命
馬丁下週二和銀行的貸款專員約了要見面。

0083

appreciate
[əˋpriʃɪ‚et]

必 聽
反 depreciate
名 appreciation

Our boss **appreciates** the support you've shown towards our company over the years and would like to offer you a special deal.

(v.) 感謝，欣賞
我們老闆很感激你多年來對本公司所展現出的支持，想要提供你一個特惠方案。

0084

appreciation
[ə‚priʃɪˋeʃən]

必
同 increase, rise, gain
反 depreciation

The **appreciation** of the euro has made travel in the United States cheap for European tourists.

(n.) 升值，鑑賞力
歐元升值已經讓歐洲觀光客來美國旅遊很便宜。

0085

appreciative
[ə`priʃɪˌetɪv]
同 grateful

While we are **appreciative** of your contributions to the company, we are unable to give you a raise at this time.

(a.) 心懷感激的，懂得欣賞的
儘管我們感激你對公司的貢獻，但我們此時無法給你加薪。

0086

apprehend
[ˌæprɪ`hɛnd]
必
同 arrest, capture
名 apprehension

The former executive accused of stealing company secrets was **apprehended** by the police last week.

(v.) 逮捕
被控竊取公司機密的前主管，上週遭警方逮捕。

0087

apprehensive
[ˌæprɪ`hɛnsɪv]
必
同 anxious
名 apprehension
　同 anxiety
　反 calmness, ease

While your company might be **apprehensive** at the idea of collaborating with a small, new business, I believe our relationship will be mutually beneficial.

(a.) 感到戒慎恐懼的
儘管貴公司或許會擔心和一家新成立的小公司合作，但我相信我們的關係將是互惠的。

0088

apprentice
[ə`prɛntɪs]
必
同 trainee

The plumber received so many job referrals that he found it necessary to hire an **apprentice**.

(n.) 學徒
這位水管工接獲很多工作介紹，他認為有必要雇用一個學徒。

0089

apprenticeship
[ə`prɛntɪsʃɪp]

必
同 traineeship

After completing his **apprenticeship**, the welder found a job working at an auto assembly plant.

(n.) 見習期,學徒身分
完成學徒見習之後,焊接工找到在汽車裝配廠的工作。

0090

approach
[ə`protʃ]

必
同 near
形 approachable
　　同 accessible, reachable
　　反 inaccessible, unreachable
形 approaching

The tour bus slowed down as it **approached** the rest stop on the highway.

(v.) 接近,即將到達
遊覽車快要到達高速公路休息站時,減速前進。

0091

approachable
[ə`protʃəbl]

必
同 affable, friendly
反 unapproachable, unfriendly

The human resources manager is a very **approachable** guy; in fact, I go to him whenever I have problems at work.

(a.) 容易讓人親近的,可接近的
人力資源經理是很容易讓人親近的人;事實上,我工作上遇到問題都會去找他。

0092

approval
[ə`pruvl]

聽
同 consent, agreement
反 disapproval
動 approve 同 sanction
　　　　　　反 disapprove

In order to receive government **approval** to go into business, the company had to first go through a lengthy application process.

(n.) 核准,贊同
為了取得政府核准開業,這家公司得先經過冗長的申請過程。

0093

arbitration
[ˌɑrbəˋtreʃən]
- 同 **arbitrament, mediation**
- 名 **arbitrator**
  - 同 mediator
- 動 **arbitrate**
  - 同 intermediate, mediate

If **arbitration** with the company management fails, the union plans to go on strike.

(n.) 仲裁，調停
若和公司管理階層的調停失敗，工會計畫要罷工。

0094

argument
[ˋɑrgjəmənt]
- 同 **debate, dispute**
- 動 **argue**
  - 同 debate
- 形 **arguable**
  - 同 debatable, disputable
- 形 **argumentative**
  - 同 contentious, quarrelsome
- 副 **arguably**

An **argument** ensued between the two coworkers as it became evident that only one would receive the promotion.

(n.) 爭論
顯然只有一人會被升職，這兩名同事的爭論隨之而起。

0095

arrangement
[əˋrendʒmənt]
- 必
- 同 **agreement**
- 動 **arrange** 同 set up
- 形 **arranged** 同 organized

I'm sure we can come to some kind of **arrangement** on how to handle the matter of timely payment for services rendered.

(n.) 安排
我確定對於如何給付服務費用這件事，我們能夠達成某種安排。

0096

arrive
[əˋraɪv]
- 必
- 同 **reach**
- 反 **depart**
- 名 **arrival** 同 advent
- 片 **arrive at**

The director's plane will **arrive** at noon, and he will then have four short meetings in the afternoon.

(v.) 抵達，（時間）到來
那位主管的班機將在中午抵達，然後他在下午將有四場簡短的會議。

0097

as needed
[æz `nidɪd]
必

Employees will be required to work overtime on weekends and holidays **as needed**.

依需要
員工將依需要於週末和假日加班。

0098

as soon as
[æz `sun æz]

We'll let you know if you have been chosen for the position **as soon as** we reach a decision.

一…就…
一等我們做成決定，馬上會通知你是否錄取這職位。

0099

ascertain
[ˌæsɚ`ten]
必
同 determine, find out
形 ascertainable

It took several days to **ascertain** the cause of the product defect.

(v.) 查明
花了幾天才查明這產品瑕疵的肇因。

0100

aside from
[ə`saɪd frɑm]

Aside from a few minor tasks, my schedule is open for most of the afternoon.

撇開…不論
撇開幾項小工作不說，我下午的行程多半都是空檔。

0101

aspect
[ˈæspɛkt]

 必
同 facet, regard

In some **aspects**, the director of sales did not agree with the methods used by his direct superior.

(n.) 方面

在某些方面，銷售主管不認同直屬上司所採用的方法。

0102

assemble
[əˈsɛmbl]

 必　聽
同 gather, congregate
反 disperse
名 assembly
　同 gathering, convention, conference

Please be sure to **assemble** in front of the building at five pm to catch the company bus to the evening's event.

(v.) 集合，組裝

請務必於下午五點在大樓前面集合，以搭乘公司巴士前往晚會。

0103

assembly
[əˈsɛmblɪ]

 讀
同 gathering

There was an **assembly** of workers at the manufacturing facility to discuss recent work conditions.

(n.) 集會人群，集會

廠房集結了一群工人，討論最近的工作環境。

0104

assess
[əˈsɛs]

 必
同 appraise, evaluate
名 assessment
　同 appraisal, evaluation, estimation, rating

In order to **assess** the situation clearly, we will need you to provide us with all available information.

(v.) 評估，估價

為了清楚評估情況，我們將需要你提供所有可得的資料。

0105

assessment
[əˈsɛsmənt]

必
同 appraisal, evaluation, estimation, rating

The annual job performance **assessment** was held last week, and this week three people have been fired.

(n.) 評估，估價
年度工作考績評量在上週舉行，本週就有三個人被解雇。

0106

asset
[ˈæsɛt]

必
同 advantage, benefit
片 an asset to...

Anne is a terrific **asset** to the team; her extensive sales and marketing experience has helped us greatly improve our sales figures.

(n.) 資產
安是這個團隊珍貴的資產；她廣泛的業務與行銷經驗協助我們大大增進了銷售數字。

0107

assign
[əˈsaɪn]

聽
同 delegate, designate
形 assigned
名 assignment 同 task, duty

Our boss will **assign** you some specific tasks this afternoon, but for now why don't you just get settled in at your desk.

(v.) 分派（任務）
我們老闆今天下午會分派一些特定的工作給你，不過現在你何不先適應一下你的辦公桌。

0108

assignment
[əˈsaɪnmənt]

必 聽

Last week's **assignment** took me three days to finish, and this week my superior gave me two more to complete by the week's end.

(n.) 職務，任務
上週的任務花了我三天才完成，本週我的上司又給了我兩項任務要在週末前做完。

0109

assist

[ə`sɪst]

必
同 help, aid
反 hinder , thwart
名 assistance 同 help, aid
　　　　　　　反 hindrance
名 assistant

Please stay on the line, and a customer service representative will **assist** you shortly.

(v.) 協助

請排隊，客服代表將會立即協助您。

0110

assistance

[ə`sɪstəns]

必

As your manager, I would like to thank you for your invaluable **assistance** on the business planning project.

(n.) 協助

身為你的經理，我想要感謝你對於這項商業計畫方案所提供的珍貴協助。

0111

associate

[ə`soʃɪ,et]

同 colleague, coworker
動 associate 同 link
形 associate 同 related

My **associate** will be out to discuss your purchase with you in just a moment; would you like a cup of coffee while you wait?

(n.) 伙伴，同僚

我的同事一會兒將出來和你討論購買事宜，你想邊喝咖啡邊等嗎？

0112

association

[ə,sosɪ`eʃən]

必
同 affiliation, alliance, coalition, organization, society

The community **association** held a bake sale to raise funds for the upcoming celebration.

(n.) 協會

這個社區協會舉辦了糕餅義賣，替接下來的慶祝活動募款。

0113

assortment
[əˋsɔrtmənt]
同 variety, mixture
動 assort
　　同 categorize, classify
形 assorted
　　同 miscellaneous, mixed

Our company provides customers with a wide **assortment** of useful goods and services.

(n.) 形形色色
我們公司提供顧客各式各樣好用商品與服務。

0114

assume
[əˋsjum]
必
同 presume, suppose

If we lower our prices, it is safe to **assume** that our competitors will do likewise.

(v.) 以為，假定
若我們降低售價，可以想見對手將會比照辦理。

0115

assume responsibility
[əˋsjum rɪ͵spɑnsəˋbɪlətɪ]

I would like one team member to **assume responsibility** for this project, and if it is handled well, you will receive a bonus upon completion.

承擔責任
我希望有一名組員擔下這企畫的責任，如果處理得當，完成後將會獲得獎金。

0116

assumed
[əˋsjumd]
必
同 pretended, feigned
動 assume

Despite his **assumed** air of innocence, everyone knew that he was guilty of stealing the office supplies.

(a.) 假冒的，假定的
儘管他狀似一派無辜，大家都知道是他偷了辦公室用品。

0117

assurance
[əˋʃʊrəns]

必
同 affirmation, guarantee
動 assure　同 pursuade
形 assured　同 certain

You have our **assurances** that everything will go smoothly at this weekend's product launch.

(n.) 保證，有把握
我們向你保證，週末的產品發表會將會一切順利。

0118

attach
[əˋtætʃ]

同 affix, adhere
反 detach
形 attached
　　同 affixed, connected
　　反 detached, unattached
名 attachment
片 be attached to something

Please **attach** a recent two-inch photo to the job application form with a staple.

(v.) 附上
請用釘書機在應徵工作表格附上一張兩吋照片。

0119

attached document
[əˋtætʃt ˋdɑkjəmənt]

Please make sure to send this letter out to everyone in the office along with the **attached document**.

附加的文件
請務必連同附加的文件，把這封信寄給全公司的同事。

0120

attain
[əˋten]

必
同 achieve, accomplish
形 attainable 反 unattainable
名 attainability

As a result of his successful presentation last week, the young man **attained** a new level of respect from his coworkers.

(v.) 達到，獲得
由於上週的提案報告很成功，這個年輕人得到同事新一層的尊敬。

0121

attainment
[ə`tenmənt]
必

Attainment of all sales targets is our number one priority for this coming year.

(n.) 達到，獲得，造詣
達成所有銷售目標是我們來年的第一優先。

0122

attend
[ə`tɛnd]
必
同 go to

Please be sure to **attend** the company meeting this Thursday, as there will be a discussion about this year's company trip.

(v.) 出席
本週四請務必出席公司會議，因為將討論今年的員工旅遊。

0123

attendance
[ə`tɛndəns]
同 presence, participation
反 absence, nonattendance

Attendance at the sales workshop was not mandatory, but those who took part benefited greatly from it.

(n.) 出席，出席人數
這場銷售研討會並不是強制出席，但與會者都受益良多。

0124

attendee
[ə`tɛndi]
必
同 participant

One **attendee** of our Christmas Charity Bazaar made sure everyone knew who he was by handing out business cards all night.

(n.) 出席者
有個出席我們耶誕慈善義賣的人，整晚都在發名片，非要大家知道他是誰不可。

0125

attention

[əˈtɛnʃən]

同 **concentration, scrutiny**
反 **inattention, disregard**
形 **attentive**
　同 intent
　反 neglectful, heedless
副 **attentively**

Some **attention** must be given to the issue of after-sales service, because we have received many complaints from customers.

(n.) 注意力，專心
必須要注意售後服務的問題，因為我們接到許多客訴。

0126

attire

[əˈtaɪr]

聽
同 **garb, dress, clothing**
動 **attire**　　同 clothe

Formal **attire** is requested at the fundraising ball this spring, so be sure to make any necessary arrangements.

(n.) 服裝
今年春天的募款舞會要求穿著正式服裝，所以務必做好必要安排。

0127

attitude

[ˈætətjud]

必
同 **perspective, standpoint**

His **attitude** in the workplace left much to be desired, as he spent a great deal of time making annoying comments to coworkers.

(n.) 態度
他的職場態度有待加強，因為他動不動就跟同事說些討人厭的話。

0128

attn = for the attention of...

[fɔr ðə əˈtɛnʃən əv]

When you send that fax, mark it **attn** Carol Robbins to make sure she receives it.

…請查照
你傳真時要標明卡蘿羅賓斯請查照，以確保她會收到。

0129

attorney
[əˈtɝnɪ]

 聽
同 lawyer, counselor

An **attorney** from our legal department has been assigned to draw up the new contract with our supplier.

(n.) 律師
我們法務部門一位律師奉派要擬定和我們供應商的新合約。

0130

attract
[əˈtrækt]

 必
 同 entice, lure 反 repel, repulse
名 attraction
 形 attractive
　同 appealing, alluring
　反 unattractive, repulsive
副 attractively

The marketing department held a meeting to brainstorm about new ideas for **attracting** customers.

(v.) 吸引
行銷部門舉辦會議，腦力激盪吸引顧客的新點子。

0131

attraction
[əˈtrækʃən]

 必
同 appeal, charm, allure
反 repulsion, revulsion

The tour guide took us on a trip to visit local tourist **attractions**.

(n.) 景點，吸引力
導遊帶我們去遊覽當地的觀光景點。

0132

attribute
[əˈtrɪbjʊt]

 讀
 同 ascribe
名 attribute 同 characteristic
片 attribute... to,
　be attributed to...,
　be attributable to...

Our poor sales can be **attributed** to the store our competitor recently opened across the street from us.

(v.) 把…歸咎於
我們銷售欠佳可以歸咎於對手最近在我們對街開店。

0133

attrition
[əˋtrɪʃən]
同 decrease
動 attrite

The large company waged a war of **attrition** against the small family-run business until they agreed to be bought out.

(n.) 損耗，消耗
這大公司對那間家族經營的小公司祭出消耗戰，直到他們同意被收購為止。

0134

audience
[ˋɔdɪəns]
必
同 assembly, crowd

At the end of the ballet, the **audience** gave the dancers a standing ovation.

(n.) 觀眾，聽眾，讀者群
芭蕾舞表演結束時，觀眾對舞者起立鼓掌致敬。

0135

audit
[ˋɔdɪt]
必
同 examination, inspection

In order for the accounting firm to perform a full **audit**, we had to give them complete access to company accounts.

(n.) 查帳
為了讓會計事務所能進行完整查帳，我們得讓他們全權審視公司帳戶。

0136

auditor
[ˋɔdɪtə]
讀
同 accountant, bookkeeper

An **auditor** requested that we organize our tax receipts and have them ready for inspection by Wednesday afternoon.

(n.) 稽核員，查帳員
一名稽核員要求我們整理好稅單，並在週三中午前備妥以供查核。

0137

authority
[əˈθɔrətɪ]

聽
同 arbiter, power
名 authoritarian
　同 dictator
形 authoritarian
　同 tyrannic, tyrannical, autocratic, dictatorial
名 authoritarianism
　同 dictatorship, monocracy, totalitarianism, tyranny

Business license applications must be filed with the proper government **authority**.

(n.) 職權，權威
營業執照的申請，必須向適當的政府管理機關提出。

0138

authorization
[ˌɔθərəˈzeʃən]

必
同 permission, mandate, empowerment

Government **authorization** is required for foreign investment in certain sectors of the economy.

(n.) 授權，批准
外資需要政府批准才能投資某些經濟產業。

0139

authorize
[ˈɔθəˌraɪz]

讀
同 empower, commission, allow
形 authorized
　反 unauthorized
名 authorization

Our sales staff is not **authorized** to provide discounts of greater than ten percent to customers.

(v.) 授權，批准
我們的業務人員沒有權力，提供顧客低於九折的優惠。

0140

automatic
[ˌɔtəˈmætɪk]

必
同 automated
反 manual
副 automatically
名 automation
　同 mechanization

For a small fee, our bank offers an **automatic** bill payment service.

(a.) 自動的，自動裝置的
若是小額費用，我們銀行提供自動給付帳單服務。

0141

automation
[ˌɔtəˈmeʃən]
必

After some level of production **automation** is achieved, company profits should increase rapidly.

(n.) 自動化
生產自動化達到某個程度後，公司獲利應該會快速增加。

0142

available
[əˈvɛləbl]
必
同 accessible
反 unavailable
名 availability 同 accessibility

I am afraid I am not **available** this weekend, but perhaps we can have lunch with the director of the branch office sometime next week.

(a.) 有空的，能夠取得的
恐怕我這個週末沒空，但或許我們下週能找個時間和分公司的負責人吃午飯。

0143

avoid
[əˈvɔɪd]
必
同 bypass, eschew, escape, shun
反 face, confront
名 avoidance

If you have a tight budget, it's best to **avoid** traveling to Europe during the peak summer months.

(v.) 避免
若你預算有限，最好避免在夏天旺季去歐洲旅遊。

0144

award
[əˈwɔrd]
聽
同 prize, reward
動 award

Don Biggins received an **award** for being the top regional sales representative of the year.

(n.) 獎賞
唐比金斯獲頒年度最佳區域業務代表。

0145

aware

[ə`wɛr]

必
同 conscious
反 unaware, unconscious
片 be aware of/that

The chief financial officer was **aware** that something was amiss with the company finances, but he was unable to locate the source of the problem.

(a.) 有察覺到的

財務長察覺到公司的財務不對頭，但他找不出問題的根源。

New
TOEIC
新多益高分關鍵字彙
990

B
Group

0001

back taxes
[bæk `tæksɪz]

After missing the tax deadline last year, Maria now owes over two thousand dollars in **back taxes** and penalties.

欠稅
去年錯過報稅期限後，瑪麗亞現在欠稅加罰款超過兩千美元。

0002

background
[`bæk͵graʊnd]

必
同 experience

Adrienne had a **background** in international trade, which made it very easy for her to find work at a trading company.

(n.) 背景
愛君有國貿背景，這讓她很容易就能在貿易公司找到工作。

0003

balance
[`bæləns]

必
動 balance
片 balance of payments
　 收支平衡表

Trying to find a **balance** between work and relaxation has always been a little difficult for Cassandra, as she's a workaholic by nature.

(n.) 平衡
在工作和放鬆之間找到平衡，對卡珊卓來說始終有點困難，因為她天生就是工作狂。

0004

bankruptcy
[`bæŋkrəptsɪ]

讀
動 bankrupt
形 bankrupt
片 go bankrupt

The restaurant filed for **bankruptcy** after a month of floods and roadwork kept customers away.

(n.) 倒閉，破產
這家餐廳在經過一個月的洪水和道路施工而流失顧客後，申請倒閉。

0005

bargain
[ˈbɑrgɪn]
必
名 bargain

Smart consumers know that you should always **bargain** when purchasing a new car.

(v.) 講價
聰明的消費者知道買新車時一定要殺價。

0006

basis
[ˈbesɪs]
必
動 base
形 basic　圓 fundamental
副 basically　圓 essentially
片 the basis of...

On the **basis** of an extensive customer survey, the department store decided to extend its business hours.

(n.) 基礎，根據
根據大規模的消費者調查，這家百貨公司決定延長營業時間。

0007

bear
[bɛr]
必
同 stand, endure
動詞四態 bore, born, born, bearing

Most observers agree that small businesses will **bear** the brunt of the recent economic downturn.

(v.) 承擔，忍受
多數觀察家都同意小公司將會承受最近經濟衰退的衝擊。

0008

beforehand
[bɪˈforˌhænd]
必
反 afterward
形 beforehand

That Broadway show is very popular, so it's best to buy tickets **beforehand**.

(adv.) 事先地
那齣百老匯秀很受歡迎，所以最好事先買票。

0009

behalf

[bɪ`hæf]

讀片 on behalf of...

On **behalf** of my department, I'd like to apologize for losing such an important client to the competition.

(n.) 代表某人

我謹代表我的部門致歉，如此重要的客戶轉投競爭對手。

0010

behavior

[bɪ`hevjə]

 manner
動 behave

Her **behavior** on the phone with clients was deemed unprofessional, and as a result she was fired from her position.

(n.) 行為

她在電話中應對客戶的行為被認定為不專業，所以她丟了那個職位。

0011

bend over backwards

[bɛnd ovə `bækwədz]

Believe me, if you tell me what you need, I will **bend over backwards** to make sure you get it.

極盡所能去取悅

相信我，若你跟我說你需要什麼，我定將全力以赴好讓你如願。

0012

benefit

[`bɛnəfɪt]

 benefit 同 profit, gain

Many government jobs offer low salaries but excellent **benefits**.

(n.) 利益，好處

許多公職的薪水低，但福利很好。

0013

benefit
[ˈbɛnəfɪt]
必 聽 讀
片 **benefit from**

Hotels and restaurants will **benefit** from the government plan to increase tourism.

(v.) 有益於
旅館和餐廳將受惠於政府提振觀光業的計畫。

0014

beverage
[ˈbɛvərɪdʒ]
必
同 **drink**

Can I bring you some **beverages** while you're deciding on your main course?

(n.) 飲料
你在決定主餐時，要我先拿些飲料過來嗎？

0015

beyond control
[bɪˈjɑnd kənˈtrol]
讀

The tour itinerary may change due to circumstances **beyond** our **control**, such as bad weather or poor road conditions.

無法控制的，不可抗力的
旅遊路線可能會因我們無法控制的情況而改變，好比天氣不好或是路況差。

0016

bid
[bɪd]
聽
名 **bid**
片 **bid for**

A number of contractors have been invited to **bid** for the construction project.

(v.) 出價競標
許多包商受邀競標這個建案。

0017

bigamy
[ˈbɪgəmɪ]

Bigamy is a crime that is not taken lightly in many countries around the world.

(n.) 重婚
重婚罪在世界上許多國家都不是小事。

0018

bill
[bɪl]

聽
同 invoice, statement
動 bill

Electricity **bills** are highest during the summer months due to increased use of air conditioners.

(n.) 帳單
電費帳單在夏天月分最高，因為冷氣使用增加。

0019

blanket
[ˈblæŋkɪt]

必
同 cover
動 blanket
片 be blanked with
形 blanket

Blankets are provided to all airplane passengers, and earphones are available upon request.

(n.) 毯子
毯子會提供給所有飛機乘客，而耳機則是索取就有。

0020

board
[bord]

必 聽
同 get on
名 board

First-class passengers are allowed to **board** and exit the airplane before economy passengers.

(v.) 登機（車船）
頭等艙乘客能比經濟艙乘客先行上下飛機。

0021

board meeting
[bord `mitɪŋ]

The minutes from the **board meeting** showed that, as usual, it had lasted a lot longer than scheduled.

董事會

董事會的會議紀錄顯示，會議時間照例大大超出排程。

0022

board member
[bord `mɛmbə]

In looking over the recent company figures, the **board member** picked out one or two disturbing discrepancies.

董事會成員

在檢查公司最近的報表時，董事會成員挑出了一、兩處惱人的不一致。

0023

board of directors
[bord əv də`rɛktəz]
讀

A meeting of the **board of directors** was called to address the issue of salary caps.

董事會

董事會召開一項會議來處理薪資不限的問題。

0024

bond
[bɑnd]
動 **bond**　　同 connect, attach

Because **bonds** are low in risk, they usually offer a lower rate of return than stocks.

(n.) 債券

因為債券風險低，報酬率通常也低於股票。

0025

boost
[bust]
同 lift, increase, promote
名 boost

In order to **boost** sagging sales, the sales team sought advice from an outside consultant.

(v.) 提振，激勵

為了提振低迷的銷售，業務團隊尋求外部顧問的忠告。

0026

bore
[bor]
反 interest
名 bore

Bored with poring over facts and figures, the young attorney decided to hit the town for a night of dancing.

(v.) 使厭煩

厭煩於鑽研事實和數據，這年輕律師決定去城裡跳舞一夜。

0027

borrow
[ˋbɑro]
必
反 lend, loan

In the current economic environment, it is increasingly difficult for companies to **borrow** money.

(v.) 借入

在目前的經濟環境下，公司借錢越來越困難。

0028

bottleneck
[ˋbɑtḷˏnɛk]
同 obstruction

Due to a production **bottleneck**, the launch of our new product has been delayed by two months.

(n.) 瓶頸

由於生產遇到瓶頸，我們的新產品上市已經拖延了兩個月。

0029

brainstorm
[ˈbrenˌstɔrm]

The advertising team stayed late at the office **brainstorming** new ideas for the upcoming advertising campaign.

(v.) 腦力激盪
廣告團隊在辦公室加班，替即將到來的廣告宣傳腦力激盪新點子。

0030

branch office
[bræntʃ ˈɔfɪs]
聽

Last year our company opened twelve new **branch offices**, expanding our territory into the Asia-Pacific region and Latin America.

分公司
去年我們公司開設了十二個分公司，將版圖擴展至亞太區和拉丁美洲。

0031

brand
[brænd]
必
同 mark, label
動 brand

Creating a successful **brand** requires not only high-quality products, but also effective sales and marketing strategies.

(n.) 品牌
創立成功的品牌不只要有高品質的產品，也需要有效的銷售與市場策略。

0032

break even
[brek ˈivən]
名 breakeven

The venture capital firm estimates that it will take two years for the new technology company to **break even**.

打平收支
這家創投公司估計這家新的科技公司要兩年才能損益兩平。

0033

break-in
[ˈbrekˌɪn]

After a two months **break-in** period, new employees are given their first performance evaluation.

(a.) 試用期的
兩個月的試用期後，新進員工要接受初次考績評量。

0034

bring in
[brɪŋ ɪn]
必

We **brought in** an outside consultant last week to evaluate our employee training program and make recommendations for improvement.

增聘人員
我們上週外聘了一位顧問來評估我們的員工訓練計畫，並提出改進建議。

0035

bring together
[brɪŋ təˈgɛðə]
必

The management conference **brought together** business leaders, industry experts and scholars from around the world.

齊集，結合以共事或成就某事
來自世界各地的企業負責人、產業專家和學者於這場管理會議中齊聚一堂。

0036

bring up
[brɪŋ ʌp]
必

If you want to discuss an increase in salary with your boss, you need to **bring up** the subject at the proper time.

提起（話題）
若你想跟老闆討論加薪，必須在恰當的時間提起這件事。

0037

broad

[brɔd]

必
同 wide
名 broad
副 broad

This product appeals to a **broad** spectrum of consumers because of its reasonable price and excellent functionality.

(a.) 寬廣的，遼闊的

這產品吸引到廣大的客層，因其價格合理，功能又優異。

0038

brochure

[bro`ʃʊr]

聽
同 pamphlet, leaflet

Please make sure all visitors to the exhibition receive the **brochure** detailing our company's product line and shipping policy.

(n.) 小冊子

請確保來看展的來賓，都有拿到詳細介紹我們公司產品系列和貨運政策的小冊子。

0039

budget

[`bʌdʒɪt]

必 聽
動 形 budget

This year's **budget** calls for a reduction in non-essential expenses such as air travel and long-distance phone calls.

(n.) 預算

今年的預算需要減少非必要支出，好比搭機和長途電話等。

0040

bug

[bʌg]

動 bug

It will take us a few months to get all the **bugs** out of our new software, but I think that once we are finished, it will become one of our top sellers.

(n.)（軟體程式的）錯誤

清除我們新軟體的所有程式錯誤將費時數月，但我認為一旦完成，這將會成為我們最熱銷的商品之一。

0041

build up
[bɪld ʌp]
必

The company spent two years **building up** its customer base over the Internet before opening a real storefront.

累積起來

這家公司先花了兩年在網際網路上累積客層,才開設實體店面。

0042

burdensome
[ˈbɝdṇsəm]
必
同 **oppressive, arduous, onerous**

The **burdensome** task of informing employees that their contracts would not be renewed fell to the head of the human resources department.

(a.) 使人壓力沈重的

通知員工將不被續約這沈重任務,落在人力資源部門的主管頭上。

0043

burn rate
[bɝn ret]

With this sort of **burn rate**, we will need to find a new source for capital in two months' time.

燒錢的速度

依照這種燒錢的速度,我們必須在兩個月內找到新的資金來源。

0044

business capital
[ˈbɪznɪs ˈkæpətḷ]

The success of any new business depends on sufficient **business capital** and a talented management team.

商業資本

任何新公司的成功,都在於足夠的商業資本以及有才能的經營團隊。

New
TOEIC

新多益高分關鍵字彙

990

C
Group

0001

c/o (care of)
[kɛr əv]

This package was delivered to you **c/o** the San Francisco office, which explains the lengthy delay.

由⋯轉交
這包裹是先寄給舊金山辦公室再轉交給你,所以才拖了那麼久。

0002

calculate
[ˋkælkjəˌlet]

 compute, fingure

If you need to **calculate** your taxes, just figure that they will about be equal to the amount of two monthly salaries.

(v.) 計算
若你需要計算要繳多少稅,只要算算差不多等於兩個月薪水就是了。

0003

calculation
[ˌkælkjəˋleʃən]

 computation, figuring

There are tax tables on the back of the tax form to assist with **calculation** of the amount of income tax you owe to the government.

(n.) 計算
報稅表格背後有稅級表,協助你計算你欠政府多少所得稅。

0004

call in
[kɔl ɪn]

Please be sure to **call in** if you are unable to make it to work, as not calling in could result in the docking of your pay.

打電話去公司
若你無法來上班,請務必打電話來公司,否則可能會造成你被扣薪。

0005

cancel
[ˋkænsḷ]
必
 scrub, call off

We had to **cancel** our trip to the Bahamas last fall when Tom was called away on a business trip at the last minute.

(v.) 取消
我們去年秋天不得不取消巴哈馬之旅，因為那時湯姆在最後一刻被叫去出差。

0006

cancellation
[ˌkænsəˋleʃən]
 annulment

Please make a note that a **cancellation** fee of one-tenth of the total cost will be levied should you decide not to participate in the tour.

(n.) 取消
萬一你決定不參加旅行，請注意我們會收取總價十分之一的取消費用。

0007

candidate
[ˋkændədet]
必
 applicant

Candidates for the sales position will be required to take an aptitude test and complete a job interview.

(n.) 候選人
業務職位的候選人必須進行性向測驗，並完成工作面試。

0008

capacity
[kəˋpæsətɪ]
必
同 content

The event facility has a 12,000-person **capacity**, so it should be a suitable place to hold the electronics show next year.

(n.) 容納量，能力
這會場能容納一萬兩千人，所以應該很適合舉辦明年的電子展。

0009

capital
[ˋkæpət!]
聽
同 fund

Our company is going public next year in order to raise **capital** for expansion into new markets.

(n.) 資本，資金
我們公司明年將要上市，以募集資金來擴展進入新市場。

0010

capitalize
[ˋkæpətə͵laɪz]
同 take advantage

Our company plans to **capitalize** on the strong economy by introducing a new line of luxury products.

(v.) 利用…以獲利
我們公司計畫推出新的高檔產品線，從這波經濟走強中獲利。

0011

carrier
[ˋkærɪɚ]
必
同 courier, transporter

The main **carrier** for our company charges us for all pickups and deliveries on a monthly basis.

(n.) 運輸公司
我們公司主要的貨運公司，按月結算取貨與運送的費用。

0012

cash flow
[kæʃ flo]

Atlantis Ltd. has never had **cash flow** problems, so if you are looking for a good company to work for, I think it is an excellent choice.

現金流量
亞特藍提斯公司從來沒有現金周轉問題，所以若你想要找個好東家，我認為這是絕佳的選擇。

0013

casual
[ˈkæʒʊəl]

必

同 nonchalant, unceremonious

反 formal, serious

副 casually　**同** nonchalantly

名 casualness　**同** familiarity

The **casual** manner in which the boss announced that there would be no year-end bonus left the employees feeling very dissatisfied.

(a.) 隨意的

老闆用隨意的方式宣布沒有年終獎金，讓員工覺得很不滿意。

0014

catalog
[ˈkætələg]

必

同 list

This year we will send out a **catalog** of all our product lines to our best customers as well as key potential customers.

(n.) 型錄

今年我們將把列有所有產品的型錄，寄給最好的顧客以及重要的潛在客戶。

0015

catch up
[kætʃ ʌp]

必

反 lag behind, delay, linger, detain

After a faltering during the first two quarters, the sales department spent the second half of the year trying to **catch up**.

趕上

經過頭兩季的停滯不前之後，業務部門在下半年盡力要趕上。

0016

categorize
[ˈkætəgəˌraɪz]

必

同 assort, classify

Would you **categorize** yourself as a go-getter or more as someone who works better under the supervision of others?

(v.) 分類，歸類

你會把自己歸類為幹勁十足，或比較像是有人監督才會表現更好的人？

0017

category

[ˈkætəˌɡorɪ]

必

同 class, family

The director's latest movie was nominated for an award in the Best Picture **category** at the film festival.

(n.) 類型

這位導演的最新電影，在這影展中獲得最佳影片獎項提名。

0018

cautious

[ˈkɔʃəs]

必

反 incautious, careless

名 caution
　　反 incaution, carelessness

動 caution

副 cautiously

During economic downturns, banks become extremely **cautious** and conservative in lending money for business ventures.

(a.) 謹慎的

在經濟衰退期間，銀行對於借錢給創業公司變得十分謹慎和保守。

0019

chain

[tʃen]

必

The tycoon opened up a **chain** of coffee shops around the nation that only served to increase his wealth even more.

(n.) 連鎖店，鎖鍊

這個大亨在全國各地開了連鎖咖啡店，徒讓他財富更增。

0020

chance

[tʃæns]

同 opportunity, possibility, probability

動 chance 同 happen

形 chance 同 casual

片 chances are..., by chance

Chances are that if you can sell one of these machines in Vietnam this year, you will be able to sell another three or four in the next couple of years.

(n.) 可能性，機會

可能的情況是若你今年能在越南賣出一台這種機器，接下來幾年就能再賣掉三或四台。

0021

characteristic

[ˌkærəktəˋrɪstɪk]

必

同 trait, feature, attribute

形 characteristic

    同 typical

    反 uncharacteristic

One **characteristic** of a booming market is that consumers will continue to buy even when prices increase.

(n.) 特色，特徵

市場繁榮的特徵之一是，就算漲價，消費者也將繼續購買。

0022

charge

[tʃɑrdʒ]

必

同 attack

反 retreat

Instead of just **charging** into this new market, we should plan carefully and conduct marketing research.

(v.) 往…衝，攻擊

不要一頭衝進這個新市場，我們反倒應該悉心計畫並進行市場研究。

0023

charge

[tʃɑrdʒ]

同 mission, commission

片 in charge of,
    in someone's charge

Kellis is in **charge** of all of the financial matters regarding this event, so if you have any related questions, you should talk to her.

(n.) 掌管，照顧

凱莉絲負責這件事所有相關的財務問題，所以若你有任何相關問題，應該去問她。

0024

charisma

[kəˋrɪzmə]

同 allure, appeal, charm

形 charismatic

    同 magnetic

The young woman was able to secure a position in the advertising agency with sheer **charisma**.

(n.) 群眾魅力

這年輕女子全憑群眾魅力，穩坐廣告公司的職位。

0025

check in
[tʃɛk ɪn]
必
同 **sign in**
反 **check out**

We will need to **check in** at the main table of the electronics exhibition to find out where to set up our booth.

報到登記
我們必須到電子展的主桌登記，看是要在哪兒設置攤位。

0026

checkout
[ˈtʃɛkˌaʊt]
必

Ten people were already in the **checkout** line, so the computer technician decided to buy the accessories he needed another day.

(n.)（超市）結帳台，退房
已經有十個人在排隊結帳，所以這電腦技師決定改天再買他需要的配件。

0027

choice
[tʃɔɪs]
必
動 **choose**
 select, pick out
形 **chosen**
副 **choicely**

The **choice** to evolve from a small company to a large one is often a very difficult one to make.

(n.) 選擇
從小公司進化到大公司常是難以做出的選擇。

0028

choose
[tʃuz]
必

If you **choose** to stay with the company after the buyout, you may face a salary cut and the cancellation of some of your current benefits.

(v.) 選擇
若你選擇在公司被買下後繼續留下來，你可能會面臨薪水被 ，一些現有福利也會被取消。

0029

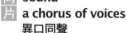

chorus

[ˈkorəs]

同 sound
片 **a chorus of voices**
異口同聲

A **chorus** of voices spoke out to deny the charges that the department head had misused funds allocated for year-end bonuses.

(n.) 合唱團

大家口徑一致，否認部門主管濫用分配給年終獎金的資金。

0030

circuit

[ˈsɝkɪt]

形 circuitous

Most computer chips nowadays contain tens of millions of miniature **circuits**.

(n.) 電路

今日大多數的電腦晶片，都包含有數以千萬的積體電路。

0031

circulation

[ˌsɝkjəˈleʃən]

同 distribution
動 circulate 同 spread
形 circulatory, circulative

The company newsletter, which is edited by our department, has now been in **circulation** for well over a decade.

(n.) 流通，發行量

由我們部門所編輯的公司電子報，如今已發行了十多年。

0032

circumstance

[ˈsɝkəmˌstæns]

必
同 situation, condition
片 **under no circumstances**

Under the **circumstances**, I would be really surprised if Mr. Collins allowed a New Year's party to be held in the main office area.

(n.) 情況

在這樣的情況下，如果柯林斯先生允許新年派對在主辦公區舉行，那我一定會很意外。

MP3
030

0033

cite

[saɪt]

讀
同 **mention, refer**
名 **citation**
　同 reference, quotation

During his management presentation, the speaker **cited** a number of well-known experts in the management field.

(v.) 引用，表揚

這位演講者在管理簡報當中，引述了許多管理領域知名專家的話。

0034

claim

[klem]

必 聽
同 **assert, demand, require**
反 **disclaim, give up**
名 **claim**
　同 declaration
　反 denial

When the manager was called before the board of directors, he **claimed** that he had never misused company funds.

(v.) 宣稱，要求（權利），請領（保險金）

經理被叫來董事會現場，他宣稱自己從未濫用公司的資金。

0035

clarity

[ˈklærətɪ]

讀
同 **clearness**
反 **obscurity**
動 **clarify**　同 clear up

I always have Carol look over everything I write, as her sense of what **clarity** is in a piece of writing is impeccable.

(n.)（思路）清晰，明瞭

我寫的東西總是會請卡蘿看過，因為她對於何謂文章的清晰具有無懈可擊的辨別力。

0036

clerical

[ˈklɛrɪkl]

聽
同 **secretarial**
名 **clerk**

After being with the company for several years, Flora was disappointed that she seemed doomed to be forever relegated to **clerical** duties.

(a.) 文書行政作業的

在這家公司任職幾年後，佛蘿拉很失望自己似乎注定永遠只能受困文書工作。

0037

client

[ˋklaɪənt]

必

同 **customer, buyer**

The unprepared sales engineer was left with nothing to say after the difficult **client** asked many difficult technical questions that he had no answers for.

(n.) 客戶

在被難纏的客戶問了許多他不知道答案的技術難題之後，這個沒準備的業務工程師是無話可說。

0038

code

[kod]

必

動 **code**　　同 cipher

Employees are strictly forbidden to give the office alarm **code** to anybody who does not work for the company.

(n.) 密碼，編碼

員工被嚴格禁止將辦公室的保全密碼，洩漏給不在公司工作的人。

0039

coincide

[ˏkoɪnˋsaɪd]

必

同 **concur**

形 **coincidental**

同 co-occurrent, simultaneous

Alex's birthday **coincided** with the launching of the product he had been working on for the last month, so he asked his family to postpone any party plans.

(v.) 同時發生，與⋯一致

艾利斯的生日和他上個月一直在忙的產品上市正好落在同一天，所以他請家人延後慶生計畫。

0040

coincidence

[koˋɪnsɪdəns]

必

同 **concurrence,**
　　happenstance

It was an interesting **coincidence** when Alex's former employer came into his office to apply for a job working under Alex.

(n.) 巧合

這是很有意思的巧合，艾利斯的前老闆來到他的辦公室應徵在他底下做事。

0041

collaborate
[kəˈlæbəˌret]
 必 讀
同 cooperate

If the design team and the advertising team can **collaborate** effectively on this project, I have every confidence that the new product line will succeed.

(v.) 合作，勾結

如果設計團隊和廣告團隊能有效地合作這個企畫，我完全有信心新產品一定會成功。

0042

collaboration
[kəˌlæbəˈreʃən]
 必 讀
同 teamwork
片 in collaboration with...

The great success of the new product launch is the result of close **collaboration** among the PR, marketing, and sales departments.

(n.) 合作，勾結

新產品發表能夠大獲成功，歸功於公關、行銷與業務部門之間的緊密合作。

0043

colleague
[ˈkɑlig]
 讀
同 associate, coworker

In order to become a productive member of the department, it is necessary to establish good relations with one's **colleagues**.

(n.) 同事

為了成為有生產力的部門成員，必須與同事建立良好的關係。

0044

collect
[kəˈlɛkt]
 必
同 gather
名 collector

Please fill out the questionnaire that is being handed out, and I will **collect** them at the end of the meeting.

(v.) 收集，蒐集

請填寫問卷調查表，我將於會議結束後統一收齊，請務必繳交！

0045

collection

[kəˋlɛkʃən]

必
同 compendium

All of the major fashion designers showed off their new fall **collections** at the prestigious fashion show in Milan.

(n.)（產品）系列，收藏

所有主要的時尚設計師，都會在知名的米蘭時裝秀展示自己的新系列秋裝。

0046

combine

[kəmˋbaɪn]

必
同 compound
名 combination

Our company's new business plan **combines** cutting edge technology with the latest in viral marketing techniques.

(v.) 結合

我們公司新的營運計畫，結合了最頂尖的科技以及最新的病毒式行銷技巧。

0047

come close to

[kʌm kloz tə]

同 approximate

With all of the extra hours our production team has been putting in over the last few months, I think our delivery times are **coming close to** being on schedule again.

接近

我們的製作團隊過去幾個月來投入額外的時間，我認為我們的交貨時間就快回到預定的時間了。

0048

come up with

[kʌm ʌp wɪð]

必
同 discover

When Jerry **came up with** a new way to manufacture running shoes, he presented the idea to his boss, who decided to use it and give him a percentage of the resulting profits.

想出（方法）

傑瑞想出製造慢跑鞋的新方法，把這點子跟老闆說，老闆決定採用並讓他分紅。

0049

comfort
[ˋkʌmfət]

必
反 discomfort
動 comfort
　同 ease
形 comfortable
　反 uncomfortable
副 comfortably

The high-end office chairs manufactured by that company are famous for their **comfort** and durability.

(n.) 舒適性，安慰
那家公司製造的高檔辦公椅以舒適和耐用聞名。

0050

comfortable
[ˋkʌmfətəbl]

必
同 comfy, cozy
反 uncomfortable

Comfortable in his current job, Bill decided not to apply for the management position that was posted on the office bulletin board.

(a.) 使人舒適的，感到舒適的
比爾安於目前的工作，決定不去應徵張貼在辦公室布告欄的管理職位。

0051

commensurate
[kəˋmɛnʃərɪt]

必
同 equal, equivalent
反 incommensurate
名 commensuration
副 commensurately

Please look over the benefits package we are offering you for this position; we hope you will find it **commensurate** with your experience in the field.

(a.) 相稱的，等量的
請看一下我們提供給你的福利配套；希望你會覺得這和你在業界的經驗相稱。

0052

commiserate
[kəˋmɪzəˏret]

同 sympathize
名 commiseration
　同 pity
形 commiserative
　同 compassionate

While I **commiserate** with Henry over the loss of his job, I feel that in light of his poor performance, management had no choice but to let him go.

(v.) 同情，悲憫
儘管我同情亨利丟了工作，但我也感覺依他糟糕的表現，管理部門別無選擇，只能叫他走。

0053

commit

[kə`mɪt]

必 聽
同 execute
片 be committed to...

In order for us to offer you this position as an overseas branch manager, and provided that you meet all of the required conditions, we will need you to **commit** to a three-year contract.

(v.) 做出保證，指定…用於

為了讓我們提供你這項海外分公司經理的職位，再加上你符合所有必要條件，我們必須請你簽下三年合約。

0054

commitment

[kə`mɪtmənt]

必
同 dedication, loyalty, devotion

The field technician showed his **commitment** to his job by making sure every customer he worked with was satisfied with the service he provided.

(n.) 承諾，付出

這位實地技師確保每個和他共事的客戶都滿意他所提供的服務，展現了他對工作的投入。

0055

common

[`kɑmən]

必
同 usual
反 uncommon
名 commoner
副 commonly

The most **common** complaint raised by our customers is the difficulty of finding replacement parts for older products when a new line comes out.

(a.) 普遍的，共同的

我們最常見的客訴就是，當新產品線推出時，比較舊的產品就很難找到替換零件。

0056

commute

[kə`mjut]

聽
同 travel
名 commute, commuter

Alexander had to **commute** 45 minutes to work six days a week, but after a while it became second nature to him.

(v.) 通勤

亞歷山大每週六天都得通勤四十五分鐘上班，但一陣子後他也就習慣成自然了。

0057

commuter train
[kə`mjutɚ tren]

One of the biggest struggles Kathy faced was in making it to work on time every day, as she had to take a **commuter train** that often ran behind schedule.

通勤列車
凱希所面對最大的掙扎之一，就是每天準時上班，因為她得搭乘常會誤點的通勤列車。

0058

compare
[kəm`pɛr]
必
形 **comparable, comparative**
副 **comparatively**
名 **comparison**

When you place these two products side by side and **compare** their strengths and weaknesses, I believe it is easy to see which is the better of the two.

(v.) 比較，比作
把這兩項產品並列來比較優缺點，我相信很容易就看得出這兩個孰優孰劣。

0059

comparison
[kəm`pærəsn̩]
必
同 **contrast**

Many people say that these two laser printers are similar in quality and durability, but in my opinion, there is no **comparison**.

(n.) 比較，比喻
很多人都說這兩部雷射印表機在品質和耐用度上很類似，但在我看來，兩者根本沒得比較。

0060

compatible
[kəm`pætəbl̩]
必
同 **consistent**
反 **incompatible**
名 **compatibility**

Brian says that his poor sales performance is due to lack of support from the sales manager, but his claim is not **compatible** with the facts.

(a.) 相容的
布萊恩說他業績欠佳是因為缺乏業務經理的支援，但他的說法與事實並不相符。

0061

compensate
[ˈkɑmpənˌset]

必
 make up, recompense,
remunerate, pay off

We know working overtime every day for the next four months will be very tough on you, but please be aware that we will **compensate** you generously for your efforts.

(v.) 補償

我們知道未來四個月每天加班對你將會很難熬,但是請你了解我們絕不會虧待你的努力。

0062

compensation
[ˌkɑmpənˈseʃən]

必
 recompense

After Zachary fell from a ladder in the company warehouse and broke his right leg, he received two months' pay in **compensation**.

(n.) 補償

薩查利在公司倉庫從梯子跌落而摔斷腿之後,獲得兩個月薪水的補償。

0063

compete
[kəmˈpit]

必
 vie, contend
形 competitive
副 competitively
名 competition, competitor

To be able to **compete** in the high stress world of advertising and marketing, it was necessary for Kris to frequently update her professional skills.

(v.) 競爭

為了在廣告行銷這個高度壓力世界中競爭,克里斯必須頻繁更新自己的專業技術。

0064

compile
[kəmˈpaɪl]

必
 accumulate, collect
名 compilation, compiler

Alice **compiled** a list of complaints filed by the workers in the factory and presented them to the factory manager the next time she saw him.

(v.) 彙整

愛麗絲彙整出工廠工人投訴的清單,並在下次見到面時呈交給工廠經理。

0065

complain
[kəm`plen]

讀
名 complaint
形 complaining
副 complainingly

I don't like to **complain**, but I was wondering if it would be possible to turn up the air conditioner in our office; it is very hot in here.

(v.) 抱怨，投訴
我不喜歡抱怨，但我在想是不是可以把辦公室裡的冷氣調冷一點；這裡頭很熱。

0066

complaint
[kəm`plent]

讀
同 accusation, protest, grumble

I'm afraid we've had many **complaints** about your work attitude from our customers and even though we've warned you on several occasions, you have not improved, so we will have to let you go.

(n.) 申訴，不滿
我恐怕我們接到了許多顧客投訴你的工作態度，儘管我們已在幾次場合中警告過你，你還是沒有改善，所以我們得解雇你。

0067

complete
[kəm`plit]

必
同 entire, all, full, whole
反 incomplete
名 completion
　　反 incompletion
動 complete
　　同 finish, accomplish, achieve, fulfill, realize, wrap up
副 completely 反 incompletely

Part of the job application for the government position was a **complete** physical to be done no more than one month prior to the time of application.

(a.) 完整的
這個政府職位的應徵要求，包括要在應徵時間前一個月內做完整的體檢。

0068

completion
[kəm`pliʃən]

必
同 closing

Upon **completion** of the acquisition, Costcom will own an 80% equity share in Qualcost, and a high-level executive from Costcom will be appointed CEO of Qualcost.

(n.) 完成
收購完成時，Costcom 將擁有 Qualcost 八成的股票，而且 Costcom 一位高階主管將被任命為 Qualcost 的執行長。

0069

compliant

[kəm`plaɪənt]

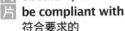 obedient, docile
片 be compliant with
符合要求的

Our customers have stated that they are very satisfied with our company offerings, as all of our products are **compliant** with international quality standards.

(a.) 順從的

我們的顧客指出，他們很滿意我們公司出售的東西，因為我們的產品都符合國際品質標準。

0070

complicated

[`kɑmplə,ketɪd]

必
同 difficult, complex
反 understandable, simple

The company decided to hire a patent lawyer to handle the **complicated** legal procedures involved in protecting its patents from competitors.

(a.) 複雜的

這家公司決定雇用專利律師來處理複雜的法律程序，避免自己的專利遭到競爭對手侵害。

0071

complication

[,kɑmplə`keʃən]

必
同 difficulty, obstacle

There was a minor **complication** during the current production run, so I am afraid your purchase will be shipped two weeks later than was originally agreed.

(n.) 新增的困難，併發症

目前的生產流程有些微的狀況，所以我恐怕你所購買的東西，將比原訂時間晚兩週才能出貨。

0072

component

[kəm`ponənt]

聽
同 element, factor, constituent
形 component

All of the **components** for this cell phone are manufactured overseas and shipped to our production facility for final assembly.

(n.) 組件，構成要素

這支行動電話所有零組件都是在海外製造，然後運送至我們的生產線進行最後組裝。

0073

comprehensive

[ˌkɑmprɪˈhɛnsɪv]

必 讀
同 **broad, full, complete, all-inclusive**
反 **incomprehensive, limited**
動 **comprehend**
　同 include, contain, cover
形 **comprehensively**

Our company offers all of our employees a **comprehensive** healthcare package, which our personnel manager will discuss with you shortly.

(a.) 廣泛的，全面包括的
我們公司提供所有員工全面的健保配套，我們的人事經理稍後會與你討論。

0074

comprehensive warranty

[ˌkɑmprɪˈhɛnsɪv ˈwɔrəntɪ]

Please rest assured that all of our products come with a **comprehensive warranty**, so should anything go wrong, your product will be repaired or replaced.

全面保固
請你放一百二十個心，我們所有產品都附有全面保固，所以若有任何差錯，你買的產品都會獲得修復或換貨。

0075

comprehensiveness

[ˌkɑmprɪˈhɛnsɪvnɪs]

必

I must say that I am very impressed with the **comprehensiveness** of your sales team's presentation; you have done a very good job indeed.

(n.) 面面俱到
我必須說我對你們銷售團隊提案的面面俱到大感驚豔；你們真的做得很棒。

0076

compromise

[ˈkɑmprəˌmaɪz]

必 聽
反 **disagreement**
動 **compromise**
形 **compromising**

After two months of intense negotiations, a **compromise** was reached between the trade union and the factory management, and the strike came to an end.

(n.) 妥協，和解
經過兩個月的密集協商後，工會和工廠管理部門達成妥協，罷工也告一段落。

0077

compromise
[ˈkɑmprəˌmaɪz]
同 **concede, meet halfway**

I can **compromise** only a little on the price, as I have already given you an excellent deal, but I may be able to extend the warranty for an additional six months.

(v.) 妥協，讓步
我在價格上只能稍做讓步，因為我已經給你很優惠的價格了，不過我也許能把保固延長六個月。

0078

concede
[kənˈsid]
同 **admit, confess**
反 **deny**

After hard evidence was presented by a government auditor, the company CEO finally **conceded** that accounting irregularities had taken place.

(v.) 勉強承認，讓與
在政府審計員提出如山鐵證後，這家公司的執行長終於勉強承認帳目不一致的情事。

0079

concentrate
[ˈkɑnsɛnˌtret]
必
同 **focus**

Noise from the construction site next door makes it very difficult to **concentrate**, so everyone in our office is falling behind in his/her work.

(v.) 全神貫注，集中
隔壁工地傳來的噪音讓人很難集中注意力，所以辦公室所有人的工作進度全都落後。

0080

concentrate on
[ˈkɑnsɛnˌtret ɑn]

Our project manager told each of us to **concentrate** solely **on** the tasks he has assigned us, and should we complete them, he will assign additional duties.

全神貫注於…
我們的專案經理要我們每個人只專注於他所指派的任務，待我們完成後，他將再指派額外的工作。

0081

concerned
[kən`sɜnd]

同 worried, troubled
反 unconcerned
名 concern

We are very **concerned** about your inability to conform to our company code of conduct; if you fail to heed this warning, we will be forced to dismiss you.

(a.) 感到憂心的

我們很擔心你沒辦法遵守公司的行為規範；若你在這次警告後再犯，我們就不得不解雇你。

0082

conclude
[kən`klud]

必
同 reason
名 conclusion
形 conclusive

Unless there are any questions, I would like to **conclude** this meeting now, and we will pick up again tomorrow afternoon at two o'clock.

(v.) 結束，下結論

除非還有任何問題，否則我想會議就到此為止，我們明天下午兩點鐘再繼續。

0083

conclusion
[kən`kluʒən]

必
同 decision, determination

After several years in sales, I came to the **conclusion** that I was not suited for this profession, and decided to try my hand at something else.

(n.) 結論

從事業務幾年後，我做出了自己不適合這一行的結論，也決定轉行試試看。

0084

condition
[kən`dɪʃən]

必
同 circumstances, status
形 conditional
片 on condition that...

Given the current **condition** of the market, the retail chain decided to put its plans for expansion on hold.

(n.) 狀態，環境條件

有鑑於市場目前的狀況，這家零售連鎖決定暫緩展店計畫。

0085

conditional

[kən`dɪʃənl]

必
反 **unconditional**

Sandy was hired on a **conditional** basis, and after successfully completing her three-month probation period, she was offered a permanent position.

(a.) 有條件的
珊蒂是有條件受雇，在成功完成三個月的試用期後，她獲得了永久正職。

0086

conducive

[kən`djusɪv]

必
同 **contributing, contributive, contributory**
動 **conduce** 同 contribute

As department manager, I must say that the constant bickering between you two is not **conducive** to creating a pleasant work environment.

(a.) 有助於促成…的
我身為部門經理，必須說你們兩個動不動就吵架，無助於創造愉快的工作環境。

0087

conduct

[kən`dʌkt]

必
同 **behave**
名 **conduct**
同 behavior, doings

As a customer service representative, you are the public face of our company, and are therefore expected to **conduct** yourselves professionally at all times.

(v.) 舉止，引導，處理
身為客服代表，你是我們公司的門面，所以也該時時保持專業舉止。

0088

conduct a survey

[kən`dʌkt ə sə`ve]

讀

Our research organization is **conducting a survey** on local white collar workers, and we were wondering if you would be willing to participate.

進行意見調查
我們的研究機構正在進行當地白領工人的調查，不知道你是否願意參與。

0089

conference
[ˋkɑnfərəns]
同 meeting, convention, forum

To improve the breadth of knowledge of the company's workforce, employees were encouraged to participate in two to three industry **conferences** annually.

(n.) 大會
為了增進公司全體人員的知識廣度，他們鼓勵員工每年參與二至三次的產業大會。

0090

confident
[ˋkɑnfədənt]
同 convinced, positive
反 diffident, unsure
名 confidence
　同 assurance
　反 diffidence, self-doubt

Sales representatives achieve the best performance when they are **confident** in the quality of the products they sell.

(a.) 有信心的
業務代表對自己販售的產品品質有信心時，就能達成最佳的表現。

0091

confidential
[͵kɑnfəˋdɛnʃəl]
同 secret

All information to be discussed during this meeting is strictly **confidential**; please do not reveal anything discussed here to unauthorized personnel.

(a.) 機密的
在這場會議期間討論到的所有資訊全屬機密；請勿將任何討論內容外洩給未獲授權的人員。

0092

confirm
[kənˋfɝm]
必 聽
同 affirm
名 confirmation
形 confirmed 反 unconfirmed

If your company is planning on sending a representative to the National Conference on Industrial Lighting, please **confirm** at your earliest convenience.

(v.) 確認
如果貴公司計畫派代表參加全國工業照明大會，請依貴公司方便，儘早確認。

0093

confirmation

[ˌkɑnfəˈmeʃən]

必
同 verification

I received **confirmation** yesterday that your purchase shipped out on the tenth, so you should be receiving it within six business days.

(n.) 確認

我昨天接獲確認，你購買的東西已於十日出貨，所以你在六個工作天內應該就會收到貨品。

0094

conflict of interest

[ˈkɑnflɪkt əv ˈɪntərɪst]

Two members of the board of directors were forced to resign due to **conflict of interest** when it was found that they also served on the board of a competing firm.

利益衝突

兩名董事會成員由於利益衝突而被迫辭職，因為他們被發現同時也擔任敵對公司的董事。

0095

conform

[kənˈfɔrm]

必
同 follow, comply
反 deviate
形 conformable

In response to your inquiry, I am pleased to inform you that Product No. 4329 **conforms** to all relevant international safety standards.

(v.) 符合，遵照

回覆你的詢問，我很高興通知你 4329 號產品符合所有相關的國際安全標準。

0096

confusingly

[kənˈfjuzɪŋlɪ]

動 confuse
　同 bewilder
形 confusing
　同 bewildering, perplexing
形 confused
　同 bewildered, perplexed

As our company's logo was found to be **confusingly** similar to that of another company, we were forced to design a new one.

(adv.) 令人混淆地

我們公司的商標被發現與另一家公司的商標雷同，造成混淆，所以我們被迫要設計新商標。

0097

confusion
[kən`fjuʒən]

必
同 mix-up
反 order, clarity

We are sorry for any **confusion** this situation may have caused, but just to be clear, we will be unable to ship this product until we receive an L/C for the amount previously agreed to.

(n.) 混淆，迷惑
我們遺憾此一情況所造成的任何混淆，但謹此聲明，在我們收到先前雙方所同意數量的信用狀之前，此產品將無法出貨。

0098

connected
[kə`nɛktɪd]

反 disconnected
名 connection
　　反 disconnection
動 connect 反 disconnect
副 connectedly
　　反 disconnectedly

With a cell phone, a computer with Internet access, a fax machine, and a land line, Josie felt very well **connected** to the outside world.

(a.) 有關連的，有聯絡的
靠著手機、能上網的電腦、傳真機和室內電話，喬希覺得自己與外界的聯繫非常良好。

0099

conscious
[`kanʃəs]

同 sensible, witting
反 unconscious
名 consciousness

In an effort to be more productive at work, Erika made a **conscious** decision to get more sleep, eat healthier and exercise regularly.

(a.) 神智清醒的
為了努力在工作上更有生產力，愛莉卡做出了明智的決定，要睡得更飽、吃得更健康，還要規律運動。

0100

conscious
[`kanʃəs]

同 awake
反 unconscious
名 consciousness

As an environmentally friendly corporation, we try hard to be **conscious** of the environmental impact of all the materials used in our products.

(a.) 有意識到的
我們做為一家重視環保的公司，會努力注意我們產品所使用的所有材料對環境的衝擊。

0101

consecutive
[kən`sɛkjʊtɪv]

 successive, continuous
 consecutively
consecutiveness

As you may well know, our firm has won the Best Product Award for seven **consecutive** years.

(a.) 連續不斷的
你或許已經知道，敝公司連續七年贏得最佳產品獎。

0102

consent
[kən`sɛnt]

 permission, agreement
consent
 go for, accept

Prior to raising a credit card limit, the bank must first obtain written **consent** from the cardholder.

(n.) 同意，答應
在提高信用卡額度之前，銀行必須先取得持卡人的書面同意。

0103

consequence
[`kɑnsə͵kwɛns]

effect, result, upshot
inconsequence
consequent
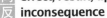 accompanying
consequently
as a consequence...

One **consequence** of the subprime mortgage crisis is that mortgage lenders have made it much more difficult for potential homeowners to obtain a home loan.

(n.) 後果
次級房貸危機的後果之一，就是想購屋的人更難向房貸提供者貸到房貸。

0104

conservative
[kən`sɝvətɪv]

progressive
conservation
conserve
conservatively

If you were to make a **conservative** guess about what our annual turnover will be, what would it be?

(a.) 保守的
若要你保守猜測我們一年的營業額，你會猜多少？

0105

conserve

[kən`sɝv]

讀
同 **preserve, economize**
反 **waste**

Our office tries to **conserve** energy by not overheating or overcooling, which is good for the environment and keeps office overhead low.

(v.) 節省，保護

我們辦公室設法節約能源，方法是冷暖氣不要開得太強，這對環境有好處，也有助於降低辦公室的經常開支。

0106

consider

[kən`sɪdɚ]

必
同 **contemplate**　反 disregard
形 **considerate**
　同 thoughtful
　反 inconsiderate
名 **consideration**
　同 thoughtfulness
　反 inconsideration

I hope that you will **consider** me for this position, as I am interested in furthering my understanding of product marketing and feel that I would be a good addition to your team.

(v.) 考量，考慮

我希望你考慮讓我擔任這職位，因為我有興趣增進我對產品行銷的瞭解，也感覺自己能替你的團隊加分。

0107

considerable

[kən`sɪdərəbl]

聽
同 **large, substantial**
反 **inconsiderable**
副 **considerably**

This weekend's bazaar brought in a **considerable** amount of cash; our accountants are still working to tally everything up.

(a.) 相當多的

週末的義賣帶進了相當多的現金，我們的會計還在結算。

0108

considerate

[kən`sɪdərɪt]

讀
同 **thoughtful**
反 **inconsiderate**

Dean is a very **considerate** man; each year, he gives flowers and a small gift to his secretary on secretary's day.

(a.) 體諒的，考慮周到的

迪恩是個很體貼的人，每年祕書節都會送花和小禮物給他的祕書。

0109

consideration

[kənsɪdəˋreʃən]

必
同 **thoughtfulness**
反 **inconsideration**

The director has given a lot of **consideration** to your proposal, and while he has his doubts about its potential for success, he is willing to let you put together a team and give it a go.

(n.) 考慮，體貼
主管認真考慮過你的提議，儘管他對於成功的可能性有所疑慮，但他願意讓你組成團隊去試一試。

0110

consistent

[kənˋsɪstənt]

同 **coherent**
反 **inconsistent**
名 **consistency**

Japan's GDP for the first quarter of this year is **consistent** with the projections of most government economists.

(a.) 前後一致的
日本今年第一季的國內生產毛額，與政府多數經濟學家的預估一致。

0111

constant

[ˋkɑnstənt]

必
同 **ceaseless, incessant**
反 **inconstant**
副 **constantly** 同 always
名 **constancy**

The **constant** stress of working overtime every day during the last two months has really taken a toll on my health, so I am afraid I need to take a few days off to recuperate.

(a.) 持續的，不變的
兩個月來每天加班所帶來的持續壓力，已經對我的健康造成損害，所以我恐怕需要休假幾天來休養生息。

0112

constantly

[ˋkɑnstəntlɪ]

必
同 **always**

Being **constantly** on the go can be quite exhausting, but most young salespeople know that legwork is the only way for them to learn the ropes quickly.

(adv.) 持續地，不變地
隨時持續不懈是相當累人的，但大多年輕的業務員都知道，唯有勤跑才能快速學會箇中技巧。

0113

constitute
[ˋkɑnstəˌtjut]

必
同 make up, comprise
名 constitution
形 constitutional

The fact that Mr. Roberts left the company and immediately went to work for the competition in violation of his contract **constitutes** good grounds for a lawsuit.

(v.) 組成，制定（法律）
羅伯茲先生一離開公司就去敵對公司上班，此一違反合約的事實構成了提告的有利證據。

0114

constrain
[kənˋstren]

讀

The reduced spending power of low-income shoppers has **constrained** sales growth at many discount retail chains.

(v.) 抑制，強迫
低收入消費者的消費能力降低，已經限制了許多折扣零售連鎖店的銷售成長。

0115

consult
[kənˋsʌlt]

必 聽
同 confer
名 consultant 　　同 advisor
名 consultation

After **consulting** with his secretary about his schedule for the coming month, Mr. Hirt decided to take a short vacation to recharge his batteries.

(v.) 諮詢
諮詢過祕書他下個月的行程之後，賀特先生決定度個短假來充電。

0116

consultation
[ˌkɑnsəˋteʃən]

必

In order for us to get a better understanding of your company's goals for the advertising campaign, we would like to schedule a series of initial **consultations** with our various departments.

(n.) 諮詢
為了讓我們更加瞭解貴公司的廣告宣傳目標，我們想要安排和我們各個部門進行一連串的初步諮詢。

0117

consume
[kən`sjum]

  consume 同 deplete
反 accumulate
名 consumer, consumption

While setting up a cost control system has **consumed** considerable time and resources, this system should enable the company to save approximately 2 million dollars every year.

(v.) 消耗

儘管設置成本控制系統已經消耗大量的時間與資源，但此系統應該能讓公司每年省下約兩百萬美元。

0118

consumer
[kən`sjumɚ]

必 聽
反 producer
動 consume
同 exhaust, use up, eat up
反 collect
形 consumable

Across the country, there are growing signs that **consumers** are worried about the weakening economy, which could slip into recession.

(n.) 消費者

全國各地都益加顯示，消費者擔心走弱的經濟會陷入經濟大衰退。

0119

consumption
[kən`sʌmpʃən]

聽

The majority of climate scientists believe that the **consumption** of fossil fuels is the primary cause of global warming.

(n.) 消耗量

絕大多數的氣象科學家都認為，化石燃料的消耗是全球暖化的主要肇因。

0120

contact
[`kɑntækt]

必
動 contact

Attending trade shows is an excellent way to make business **contacts** and promote the products sold by your company.

(n.) 聯絡人，人脈

參加商展是絕佳的方式，可以建立商業人脈，也能推銷自己公司販售的產品。

0121

contaminate
[kənˋtæməˌnet]

同 pollute, foul
反 decontaminate
形 contaminated
　同 polluted
名 contamination
　同 pollution
名 contaminant

When government inspectors discovered that the line of toys was **contaminated** with lead, the manufacturer was ordered to implement a full product recall.

(v.) 弄髒，使不純淨
當政府檢查員發現這系列玩具遭到鉛污染，製造商被下令要進行全面產品回收。

0122

continuation
[kənˌtɪnjuˋeʃən]

必
同 continuance
反 discontinuation

The opening of two new stores in Guangzhou marks a **continuation** of the retailer's expansion in Southern China.

(n.) 繼續，連續
廣州兩家新店開幕，顯示該零售商持續在中國南部展店。

0123

continue
[kənˋtɪnju]

必
同 proceed, keep, go on
反 discontinue
名 continuity
形 continual, continuous, continuative
副 continually, continuously

We are confident that our established customers will **continue** to do business with us as we offer quality products at reasonable prices.

(v.) 繼續，連續
我們有信心既有的顧客會繼續和我們做生意，因為我們以合理價格提供優質產品。

0124

contribute
[kənˋtrɪbjut]

必 聽
同 bring, add
形 contributive
名 contribution, contributor

A good manager understands all employees have unique knowledge and skills to **contribute** to the organization, and motivates them to perform at the best of their abilities.

(v.) 捐獻，提供，投稿
一個好的經理瞭解所有員工都具備獨有的知識和技巧可以貢獻給組織，也會激勵他們展現出最佳能力。

0125

contribution

[ˌkɑntrəˈbjuʃən]

必
同 donation, share

Your **contribution** to the discussion is appreciated, so please feel free to speak up if you have any ideas you would like to share.

(n.) 貢獻

我們很感謝你對這項討論所做的貢獻，所以若有任何想法要分享，請盡量開口。

0126

control

[kənˈtrol]

必
同 power
動 control
　同 command
形 controllable
　同 governable

The accounting department has **control** over all purchasing decisions, so if you need a new computer monitor, you need to take it up with them.

(n.) 控制

會計部門掌控所有採購決定，所以若你需要新的電腦螢幕，你得要去問他們。

0127

controversial

[ˌkɑntrəˈvɝʃəl]

同 debatable, contended,
　arguable, disputable
反 noncontroversial

The **controversial** new office dress code, which required women to wear skirts and high heels, was rescinded after many female employees complained about sexual discrimination.

(a.) 有爭議性的

這頗具爭議的辦公室服裝新規定，規定女性要穿著裙子和高跟鞋，因為許多女性抱怨這是性別歧視而被廢止。

0128

convenience

[kənˈvinjəns]

必
同 usefulness
形 convenient
　同 handy
　反 inconvenient

For the **convenience** of our employees, we deposit monthly pay directly into their bank accounts, rather than issuing paper checks.

(n.) 方便，便利

為了員工方便，我們直接把月薪存入他們的銀行帳戶，而非發放支票。

0129

at someone's earliest convenience
[æt `sʌmˌwʌnz `ɝlɪəst kən`vinjəns]

Please look over this noncompetition agreement, sign it and return it to us **at your earliest convenience**.

依某人方便儘早…
請看過這分競業禁止協議，簽名後依你方便儘早送回。

0130

convenient
[kən`vinjənt]

必
同 **handy**
反 **inconvenient**

Renting an apartment in a **convenient** location near the office may be a little more expensive, but in the long run you will save money on transportation.

(a.) 方便的，便利的
在靠近辦公室的便利地點租公寓或許比較貴一些，但長期來看你會省下交通費。

0131

convince
[kən`vɪns]

必
同 **win over**
形 **convincing**
　　同 persuasive
形 **convinced**

To **convince** her boss of her determination to be a great sales rep, Helen worked longer hours than her coworkers and consistently brought in the biggest orders.

(v.) 使信服
為了讓老闆相信她決心成為一流的業務代表，海倫的工作時數比同事長，也一直替公司帶進最大的訂單。

0132

coordinate
[ko`ɔrdn̩et]

必
同 **organize**
名 **coordinator**
名 **coordination**

As project manager, it is your responsibility to **coordinate** the efforts of your team members and make sure that all project goals are met.

(v.) 協調
身為專案經理，你要負責協調旗下組員的工作成效，也要確保達成所有專案目標。

0133

corner the market
[ˋkɔrnɚ ðə ˋmɑrkɪt]

The computer manufacturer tried to **corner the market** on tablet PCs, but encountered unexpected competition from their largest competitor.

獨占市場
這家電腦製造商想要獨占平板個人電腦的市場，未料遭遇最大對手的競爭。

0134

corporate buyer
[ˋkɔrpərɪt ˋbaɪɚ]

Our company always looks for **corporate buyers**, because while the profit margin is lower, payments are usually made in a very timely manner.

公司的採購人員
我們公司總是會找公司的採購人員，因為儘管利潤比較低，但付款通常都很準時。

0135

corporate ladder
[ˋkɔrpərɪt ˋlædɚ]

Making your way up the **corporate ladder** is never easy, but getting to the top is definitely something to be proud of.

公司的職位層級
在公司裡層層晉升絕對不容易，但是爬到最高階層肯定是值得驕傲的事。

0136

courier
[ˋkurɪɚ]
必 聽

The **courier** comes every day at 9:00 am and 2:00 pm to drop off and pick up express packages.

(n.) 快遞
快遞每天早上九點和下午兩點會過來收送件。

0137

cover
[ˈkʌvə]
必
同 report
名 coverage

The financial press **covered** the merger between the two large investment banks in great detail.

(v.) 採訪，報導
財經媒體詳細報導這兩家大型投資銀行的合併案。

0138

cover letter
[ˈkʌvə ˈlɛtə]

Should you be interested in applying for this job, please respond by sending in a résumé and a **cover letter**.

應職信
若你有興趣應徵這份工作，請寄履歷和應職信。

0139

coverage
[ˈkʌvərɪdʒ]
讀

The company provided basic insurance **coverage** to protect all employees in case of accident.

(n.)（保險）範圍
這家公司提供基本的保險項目，以在意外發生時保護所有員工。

0140

create
[krɪˈet]
必
反 destroy, smash
名 creation
形 creative　反 uncreative
副 creatively

Should you **create** a product that the board of directors likes, you will receive a bonus and possibly a promotion, so be sure to work hard on this project.

(v.) 創造
若你能創造出董事會喜歡的產品，你就會獲得獎金，可能還會升職，所以務必努力進行這個企畫。

creation

[krɪ`eʃən]

必

同 **founding, introduction**

The **creation** of an outdoor smoking area made it much more convenient for employees that smoke to take cigarette breaks.

(n.) 創設，創作
室外吸菸區的設立，更加方便抽菸的員工忙裡偷閒。

critical

[`krɪtɪk!]

讀

同 **crucial, decisive**
反 **unimportant**
名 **critic, criticism**
動 **criticize**

The computer technician alerted his supervisor when he discovered a potentially **critical** flaw in the recently developed software.

(a.) 關鍵的，批判的
這個電腦技師發現最近開發的軟體可能有重大瑕疵，並提醒上司。

criticism

[`krɪtə,sɪzəm]

必

同 **disapproval, critique**

Constructive **criticism** is encouraged in this office, but negative **criticism** will not be tolerated.

(n.) 批評
這個辦公室歡迎有建設性的批評，但不會容忍負面批評。

criticize

[`krɪtɪ,saɪz]

必

同 **condemn**
反 **praise**

When my boss **criticized** my work, I chose to not back down; I stood up for myself, and I proved in the long run that I was right.

(v.) 批評
老闆批評我的工作時，我選擇不退讓；我挺身捍衛自己，最後也證明了我是對的。

0145

crucial
[ˈkruʃəl]
必
同 important, essential

In today's global business environment, the ability to adapt quickly to new markets is **crucial** to the success of any business organization.

(n.) 決定性的，重要的
在今日全球化商業環境中，快速適應新市場的能力，是所有商業組織能否成功的關鍵。

0146

culinary
[ˈkjulɪˌnɛrɪ]
必

After graduating from the **culinary** school, Jane worked as a chef at a French café, and eventually opened her own restaurant.

(a.) 烹飪的
自烹飪學校畢業後，珍在一家法國餐館當主廚，最後開了自己的餐廳。

0147

currency
[ˈkɜənsɪ]
聽

The **currency** market is in turmoil at the moment, with the Dollar at its weakest levels in a decade.

(n.) 貨幣
貨幣市場目前一片混亂，美元處於十年來最低點。

0148

current
[ˈkɜənt]
必
同 present, up-to-date
副 currently

Current information on industry trends tells us that we are performing in the top ten percent, and may reach the top five percent in two years' time.

(a.) 現時的，（貨幣）流通的
產業趨勢目前的資訊告訴我們，我們正處於前百分之十，兩年內或許能到達前百分之五。

0149

customer
[ˈkʌstəmɚ]

必

同 client, consumer

At our company, we take **customer** complaints very seriously, because satisfied customers are the cornerstone of our success.

(n.) 顧客
我們公司對客訴看得很重,因為滿意的顧客是我們成功的基石。

0150

cut corners
[kʌt ˈkɔrnəz]

I hate to say that we are going to have to **cut corners**, but realistically, given the recent economic slowdown, there is just no way around it.

取巧,簡便行事
我很不想說我們得取巧,但實際上,有鑑於最近經濟遲緩,實在沒有別條路可走。

0151

cut down
[kʌt daʊn]

In order to **cut down** on the amount of paper used by workers in the office, the manager required everyone to rely solely on e-mail for communication.

削減,減低
為了削減辦公室人員的用紙量,經理要求每個人只能用電郵來溝通。

0152

cut a deal
[kʌt ə dil]

Last week, our San Francisco office **cut a deal** with a large corporate customer, so our company will be starting the new year on a strong footing.

(在生意或政治上)談定交易
上週我們的舊金山辦公室和一個大公司客戶談定交易,所以我們公司將以穩健步伐展開新的一年。

New TOEIC 990 新多益 高分關鍵字彙

New
TOEIC
990

新多益高分關鍵字彙

D

Group

0001

daring
[ˈdɛrɪŋ]

必
同 **bold, adventurous**
反 **timid**
名 **daring**
副 **daringly**

At the press conference, the CEO of the troubled company announced a **daring** new plan to cut costs and bring the company out of debt.

(a.) 大膽的

在記者招待會當中，這家落難公司的執行長宣布一項大膽的新計畫，要刪減成本讓公司擺脫負債。

0002

deadline
[ˈdɛdˌlaɪn]

必

If you fail to file your income tax return, or an extension request, before the **deadline**, you will be charged a 5% penalty.

(n.) 最後期限

若你沒有在期限內報稅或是申請延期，將會被處以百分之五的罰金。

0003

deal
[dil]

聽
同 **trade**
動 **deal**　同 handle, manage

After several weeks of intensive negotiation, the two companies reached a **deal**, and a new partnership was formed.

(n.) 交易

經過幾週的密集協商，這兩家公司達成交易，一段新的合夥關係就此形成。

0004

deal with
[dil wɪð]

必
同 **cope with**

I enjoy **dealing with** all kinds of people on a daily basis, so I think I would be very well suited to a front desk position.

處理，對付

我很喜歡每天應對各式各樣的人，所以我自認很適合櫃臺的職位。

0005

debt

[dɛt]

必 讀
同 liabilities
名 debtor
片 in debt

After a while, the **debt** our boss had taken on to start the company began to weigh him down, and after careful consideration, he decided to sell the business.

(n.) 債務

我們老闆開公司所背負的債務沒多久便開始壓得他喘不過氣來,在深思熟慮過後,他決定賣掉公司。

0006

decade

[ˈdɛked]

必
同 decennium

Our company has been in business for over five **decades**, and has a proven record of providing customers with excellent products and service.

(n.) 十年

我們公司開業已經超過五十年,已經證明能提供顧客優異的產品與服務。

0007

deceased

[dɪˈsist]

同 dead
反 alive
名 deceased
動 decease

Our company was started in 1943 by Paul Jones, who is now **deceased**, and it has remained a family-run business up to the present day.

(a.) 已歿的

我們公司由已過世的保羅瓊斯於 1943 年創立,時至今日依然是家族事業。

0008

decisive

[dɪˈsaɪsɪv]

必
同 resolute, crucial
反 indecisive
名 decision
動 decide

Our marketing director is known not only for his creative abilities and knowledge of the marketplace, but also for his **decisive** manner and ability to work under pressure.

(a.) 有決斷力的,決定性的

我們的行銷主管出名的不只是他的創意能力以及市場知識,還有他的當機立斷,以及在壓力下工作的能力。

0009

declare
[dɪ`klɛr]

聽
同 **announce, assert, state**
名 **declaration**
　同 announcement

If you have nothing to **declare** to Customs, or if you have not exceeded your duty free allowance, you may immediately collect your bags from the baggage carousel.

(v.) 申報（納稅品等），宣告，宣稱
若你沒有東西要向海關申報，或是沒有超過免稅商品的限額，便可逕行前往旋轉台提領行李。

0010

decline
[dɪ`klaɪn]

讀
同 **worsen, slump**
名 **decline**
　同 fall

After spiking in the first quarter, crude oil prices have been steadily **declining** over the second and third quarters.

(v.) 下跌，衰退
原油價格經過第一季的飆升之後，在第二季和第三季已不斷下滑。

0011

decrease
[dɪ`kris]

同 **reduction, decline**
反 **increase**
動 **decrease** 同 shrink, diminish
形 **decreasing**
副 **decreasingly**

The removal of WTO quotas has caused a sharp **decrease** in the production of textiles and footwear in the U.S.

(n.) 減低，減少
世貿組織解除限額，已造成美國境內紡織品與鞋品的生產銳減。

0012

dedicate
[`dɛdə,ket]

同 **devote, commit**
形 **dedicated**
　同 devoted
名 **dedication**
　同 devotion, commitment

After **dedicating** ten years pursuing a career in accounting, Lisa decided to switch gears and try her hand at being a personal financial advisor.

(v.) 奉獻，致力於
奉獻十年追求會計事業之後，莉莎決定轉換跑道，嘗試擔任私人財務顧問。

0013

dedication
[ˌdɛdəˈkeʃən]
必
同 devotion, commitment

Your **dedication** to this project has earned you the chance to serve as project leader when we begin our new marketing project next month.

(n.) 奉獻，投入
你對於這企畫的投入已經替你贏得了機會，下個月我們新的行銷企畫開跑時，將由你擔任領導人。

0014

deduct
[dɪˈdʌkt]
必
同 subtract, take off
名 deduction

Any transportation costs and business expenses can be **deducted** from your taxable income, so be sure to keep all of your receipts.

(v.) 扣除，減除
凡交通費與營業支出均可自應納稅的所得收入中扣除，所以務必保留所有收據。

0015

deduction
[dɪˈdʌkʃən]
必
副 deductive

If you need to have the accountant make any additional **deductions**, please make note of them and communicate them to her before the fifteenth.

(n.) 扣除
若你需要會計做額外的扣除額，請記錄下來，並在十五號之前傳達給她知道。

0016

defect
[dɪˈfɛkt]
必 聽 讀
同 fault, flaw
名 defection
形 defective

A product **defect** discovered during the initial production run caused a delay that resulted in several orders leaving the factory behind schedule.

(n.) 缺陷，不良
在最初的試量產期間發現一項產品瑕疵，造成幾張訂單延後出廠。

0017

deficit

[`dɛfɪsɪt]

讀
同 shortfall
形 deficient

Our business has been operating at a **deficit** for the past two quarters, but we are confident that a turnaround is under way.

(n.) 虧損，赤字

我們的生意過去兩季都呈現虧損，但我們有信心翻盤在即。

0018

deformed

[dɪ`fɔrmd]

同 ill-shapen, malformed
名 deformation, deformity
動 deform

Interestingly, although Jessica's left hand was **deformed**, she had no problem handling all of her office duties, including typing and filing.

(a.) 變形的，畸形的

有趣的是雖然潔希卡的左手畸形，卻完全無礙她處理所有辦公室庶務，包括打字和建檔。

0019

delay

[dɪ`le]

必
同 postponement, time lag
動 delay　　同 detain
　　　　　　反 hurry
形 delayed

While shipping **delays** are difficult to avoid during the holiday season, we must still do our utmost to keep delays to a minimum.

(n.) 延遲

儘管在連假期間很難避免運貨延遲，但我們依然得盡量將延遲減至最低。

0020

delete

[dɪ`lit]

必
同 cancel, erase
名 deletion

After spending two hours writing an angry complaint letter to her supervisor, Angie decided not to send it, and **deleted** it from her computer.

(v.) 刪除

花兩小時寫了一封氣憤的抱怨信給上司後，安姬決定不寄，還把信從電腦裡刪除了。

0021

delicate
[ˋdɛləkət]

必
同 **ticklish, difficult**
副 **delicately**
名 **delicacy**

Determining the salary to be received by each employee is a **delicate** matter, and to avoid jealousy, all employees are advised not to discuss their pay with others.

(a.) 需要小心處理的，嬌貴的
決定每名員工的薪水是動輒得咎的事，而且為了避免吃味，建議所有員工不要與別人討論自己的薪水。

0022

deliver
[dɪˋlɪvɚ]

聽 讀
同 **distribute, bring, carry**
名 **delivery**
片 **deliver to...**

We plan to **deliver** this system to you before the end of the year, and at the time of delivery, we will send a technician over to help you with installation.

(v.) 配送，陳述見解
我們計畫在年底前將此系統配送給你，而在配送時，我們將派遣技師過去協助你安裝。

0023

delivery
[dɪˋlɪvərɪ]

必

Delivery time for items that we have in stock is usually three to five weeks; for made-to-order items, the delivery time is significantly longer.

(n.) 配送，分娩
庫存貨的配送時間通常是三到五週，訂製品的配送時間則會增加許多。

0024

deluxe
[dɪˋlʌks]

必
同 **sumptuous, opulent**

In response to customer feedback, we have decided to develop a **deluxe** version of our most popular desktop computer.

(a.) 豪華高級的
為了回應顧客的意見，我們已決定開發我們最受歡迎的桌上電腦的豪華版本。

0025

demand
[dɪˋmænd]

讀 同 **request**
動 **demand** 同 ask (for)
形 **demanding** 同 difficult
片 **in demand, on demand, demand for...**

When it came time to renegotiate his contract, Joe's **demands** were so outrageous that instead of getting everything he wanted, he was fired.

(n.) 要求，需求
重新協商合約的時間到，而喬的要求太豈有此理，非但沒有得償所願，反而被解雇。

0026

demanding
[dɪˋmændɪŋ]

必
同 **difficult**
反 **undemanding**

After a very **demanding** initial year on the job, Amanda realized she had finally learned the ropes one evening when she found she did not need her supervisor's assistance in negotiating a contract.

(a.) 要求高的，令人吃力的
度過這份工作非常吃力的第一年之後，愛曼達有天晚上體會到她終於學會了箇中訣竅，因為她發現不需要上司協助就能協商合約。

0027

demonstrate
[ˋdɛmənˏstret]

必
同 **exhibit, show**
名 **demonstration** 同 presentation
名 **demonstrator**
形 **demonstrative**

My boss always tells me that I **demonstrate** all the qualities he admires in a good employee, and yet I have been passed over for promotion six times in the last five years.

(v.) 展現出，示範
老闆總是告訴我，我展現了所有他欣賞的好員工特質，然而五年來六次升遷機會都沒我的份。

0028

demonstration
[ˏdɛmənˋstreʃən]

必
同 **presentation**

Because of his excellent communication skills and good looks, Robert has been chosen to perform product **demonstrations** at the upcoming trade show.

(n.) 展現，示範
由於擁有優異的溝通技巧與帥氣外貌，羅伯獲選在即將來臨的商展中，負責產品展示。

0029

denote
[dɪˋnot]

同 refer, indicate
名 denotation　　同 indication

I would have to say that the bickering in upper management **denotes** an upcoming period of upheaval for our company.

(v.) 預示，表示
我得說上層管理階層的爭吵，預示著我們公司即將有一段動盪。

0030

denounce
[dɪˋnaʊns]

同 criticize, condemn
名 denouncement

Kevin was mortified when the department head **denounced** his performance in front of all of his coworkers, and he quit the following week.

(v.) 指責，告發
凱文大感屈辱，因為部門主管當著他所有同事的面，指責他的表現，他在隔週就辭職。

0031

dependent
[dɪˋpɛndənt]

形 dependent
　　反 independent

To keep pace with inflation, the top amount a family with several **dependents** can receive in Social Security payments has been raised from $200 to $240.

(n.) 撫養親屬
為了趕上通貨膨脹，擁有數名撫養親屬的家庭，領取社會年金的最高額度從兩百美元增加至二百四十美元。

0032

describe
[dɪˋskraɪb]

必
同 portray
名 description
　　同 portrayal, depiction
形 descriptive
副 descriptively

When Pauline went to the medical clinic, the doctor asked her to **describe** in detail the symptoms she had been experiencing.

(v.) 描述
寶琳去診所的時候，醫生要她詳細描述她體驗到的症狀。

0033

description

[dɪˋskrɪpʃən]

必
同 portrayal, depiction

The **description** you gave of your most recent project idea sounds fascinating; I can't wait to see you bring it to fruition.

(n.) 描述
你對最近企畫構想的描述很引人入勝，我等不及要看你付諸實現。

0034

deserve

[dɪˋzɝv]

聽
同 merit
形 deserving

You **deserve** a vacation after winning such a large account, so I have decided to reward you with an all-expenses-paid two-week trip to Hawaii.

(v.) 應該得到
你爭取到這麼大一個客戶，應該獲得休假，所以我決定獎賞你全額補助的夏威夷兩週之旅。

0035

designate

[ˋdɛzɪɡˌnet]

必 讀
同 assign, delegate
形 designated   同 assigned
名 designation
　　同 assignment

A General Power of Attorney is a legal document whereby you **designate** someone to take care of any financial and general decisions on your behalf should you become mentally or physically unable to do so.

(v.) 指派，標明
委任狀是法律文件，以此指定某人在你生理或心理無行為能力之時，代你行使所有財務或一般決定。

0036

designated

[ˋdɛzɪɡˌnetɪd]

同 assigned

Before our team went to the bar to celebrate completing our most recent project, we drew straws to decide who would be the **designated** driver.

(a.) 指定的
我們小組去酒吧慶祝最近這個企畫完成之前，我們先抽籤決定是誰要當指定駕駛。

0037

designation

[ˌdɛzɪɡˋneʃən]

必
同 **assignment, appointment**

Mr. Johnson's **designation** as company treasurer was confirmed at the last meeting of the insurance company's board of directors.

(n.) 任命，指定，稱號

強森先生被任命為公司財務主管，已在上次保險公司的董事會中獲得證實。

0038

desire

[dɪˋzaɪr]

必
同 **want, longing**
動 **desire**　　同 want
形 **desired**　　同 coveted
形 **desirable**　同 wanted
　　　　　　　反 undesirable

Erica's desire to succeed surpassed her **desire** to make friends in the office, so while she became very powerful, she was not well liked.

(n.) 慾望

艾莉卡想要成功的慾望，凌駕了她想在辦公室交朋友的慾望，所以儘管她大權在握，卻不是很得人緣。

0039

desired

[dɪˋzaɪrd]

必
同 **coveted**

In order to achieve their **desired** effect, company policies must be implemented at all levels and enforced rigorously.

(a.) 被渴望的，屬意的

為了達成想要的效果，公司政策必須落實於各個層級，並且嚴格執行。

0040

desolate

[ˋdɛsəlɪt]

同 **deserted, uninhabited**
動 **desolate**
　　同 forsake, abandon

In contrast to the hustle and bustle of weekdays, the downtown business district is **desolate** and quiet on weekends and holidays.

(a.) 荒蕪的，無人煙的

對比於週一到週五的熙來攘往，市中心商業區在週末和假日人煙稀少靜悄悄。

0041

destination
[ˌdɛstə`neʃən]
必 聽
反 beginning, start

The final **destination** of this flight is San Francisco International Airport; passengers continuing on to New York should proceed to Gate 25 after passing through customs and immigration.

(n.) 目的地
這班飛機的終點是舊金山國際機場，要繼續往紐約的旅客請直接穿過海關和入境櫃臺前往 25 號門。

0042

detach
[dɪ`tætʃ]
同 disconnect
反 attach
形 detached, detachable
名 detachment

Please **detach** the bottom part of this form and send it along with your check or money order to the address indicated below.

(v.) 使分開
請撕下這張表格的下半部，連同支票或匯票寄至下列地址。

0043

detail
[`ditel]
必
片 in detail

After agreeing on the major points of the cooperation agreement, the CEOs of the two companies brought in their legal teams to work out the contract **details**.

(n.) 細節
同意合作協議的重點之後，這兩家公司的執行長帶來自己的法務小組，制訂合約細節。

0044

detect
[dɪ`tɛkt]
必
同 discover
名 detection, detector, detective

The new test instruments we have installed on the production line can **detect** product imperfections that are invisible to the naked eye.

(v.) 偵測，察覺
我們安裝在生產線上的新測試儀器，可以偵測肉眼看不到的產品瑕疵。

0045

detection
[dɪ`tɛkʃən]
必
同 discovery

After **detection** of a slight design flaw in the latest version of the product, production was halted and several design modifications were made.

(n.) 偵測，察覺
在偵測出最新版本的產品稍有設計瑕疵後，生產線暫停，並做了幾項設計上的修改。

0046

determination
[dɪ,tɜmə`neʃən]
同 resolution
動 determine
　同 decide
形 determined
　同 resolute, single-minded
　反 undetermined

His **determination** to develop into an exceptional speaker was demonstrated when he gave a presentation at the annual board meeting.

(n.) 決心，果斷
他想成為傑出演講者的決心，在他於年度委員會的提案報告時展露無遺。

0047

determine
[dɪ`tɜmɪn]
必
同 decide

Please give me a minute while I check our order tracking system to **determine** precisely why you have not yet received your shipment.

(v.) 確定，使下定決心
請給我一點時間查詢訂單追蹤系統，以詳細確定你為何還沒有收到貨。

0048

detract
[dɪ`trækt]
同 take away

When showing up for a job interview, you should dress appropriately, and not wear any jewelry or accessories that may **detract** from your professional image.

(v.) 減損
求職面試時，應該要穿著合宜，不要穿戴可能減損專業形象的珠寶或飾品。

0049

develop
[dɪˋvɛləp]

必
同 evolve, work out
形 developed, developing
　反 underdeveloped
名 development

In order for a company to survive in today's competitive marketplace, it must continue to devote resources to **developing** new products and services.

(v.) 發展，開發
為了在今日競爭激烈的市場上存活，公司必須持續投入資源來開發新產品與服務。

0050

development
[dɪˋvɛləpmənt]

必

Providing on-the-job training and career **development** opportunities is a good way for businesses to attract and retain top-quality employees.

(n.) 發展
提供在職訓練以及生涯發展機會，是公司吸引並留住優質員工的好方法。

0051

devote
[dɪˋvot]

同 dedicate, commit
形 devoted 同 dedicated
名 devotion, devotee

After **devoting** 35 years of her life to working as secretary to the CEO, Gladys decided she was ready to retire and spend her golden years in the Bahamas.

(v.) 奉獻，致力於
奉獻三十五年的青春擔任執行長祕書之後，葛拉迪絲決定準備退休，去巴哈馬群島度過養老的黃金歲月。

0052

diagnose
[ˋdaɪəgnoz]

必
名 diagnosis
形 diagnostic, diagnosable

In order to **diagnose** the cause of the computer malfunction, the technician requested that the machine be brought to the IT Department.

(v.) 診斷
為了診斷出電腦故障的肇因，技師要求把機器送至資訊技術部門。

0053

diagnosis

[ˌdaɪəɡˋnosɪs]

必

Your concise **diagnosis** of the network problem proved to be very helpful to us when we submitted a trouble ticket to our Internet service provider.

(n.) 診斷
你對於網路問題精確的診斷，在我們向網路服務供應商提出報修單時，證明是很有幫助的。

0054

dialogue

[ˋdaɪəˌlɔɡ]

必

同 conversation

By maintaining an ongoing **dialogue** with employees and including them in the decision-making process, management can ensure that employees feel valued and respected.

(n.) 對話
維持與員工的持續對話，並讓他們參與決策過程，能讓管理階層確保員工感到被珍視與對重。

0055

dignitary

[ˋdɪɡnəˌtɛrɪ]

同 notable

Our former CEO devoted more time playing golf and hobnobbing with stars and **dignitaries** than he did to actually running the company.

(n.) 顯貴，要人
我們的前執行長投注於打高爾夫球、和明星要人密切往來的時間，還多過他真正經營公司。

0056

dimension

[dɪˋmɛnʃən]

必

同 measure, size

形 dimensional

The **dimensions** of the machine had to be modified so that it could be shipped in a standard-sized shipping container.

(n.) 尺寸
這機器的尺寸得要修改，才能用標準尺寸的貨櫃船運。

0057

directory

[dəˋrɛktərɪ]

必

The **directory** on the wall of the ground-floor lobby lists the floor and office numbers of all the businesses in the building.

(n.) 樓層介紹，分機表
一樓大廳牆上的樓層介紹，列出大樓所有公司行號的樓層和號碼。

0058

disappoint

[ˌdɪsəˋpɔɪnt]

必
同 let down
形 disappointing,
　 disappointed
名 disappointment

Deborah was extremely **disappointed** that she did not receive a raise, and while her first impulse was to quit immediately, she later decided to stay on until she found a better position at another company.

(v.) 使失望
黛博拉沒獲得加薪，十分失望，儘管她當下的衝動是想立刻辭職，但後來她決定先留下，直到在另一家公司找到更好的職位為止。

0059

disappointing

[ˌdɪsəˋpɔɪntɪŋ]

聽 讀
同 discouraging,
　 dissatisfactory,
　 unsatisfying

While Ben's sales figures for the first quarter were rather **disappointing**, his performance improved considerably over the following months.

(a.) 使人失望的
儘管班恩第一季的銷售業績很讓人失望，但他在接下來幾個月的業績有大幅改善。

0060

discard

[dɪsˋkɑrd]

同 throw away
反 keep
形 discarded
　 同 thrown-away

Before packing your belongings for the move to our new office facility, please **discard** any unwanted items in the bin at the end of the hall.

(v.) 丟棄，摒棄
在你打包個人物品搬去我們新的辦公室設施前，請把任何不要的東西丟進走廊盡頭的箱子裡。

0061

discount

[ˋdɪskaʊnt]

必
同 reduction, deduction
動 discount

A **discount** of ten percent brought the customer around, and the deal was signed that afternoon.

(n.) 折扣，打折

打九折讓顧客回心轉意，當天下午便成交。

0062

discouraging

[dɪsˋkɜɪdʒɪŋ]

讀
同 dispiriting
反 encouraging
形 discouraged 反 encouraged
動 discourage 反 encourage
名 discouragement
　　反 encouragement

His **discouraging** sales performance led to his being removed from the sales team and assigned to perform routine office work.

(a.) 令人洩氣的

他令人洩氣的銷售業績讓他自業務小組除名，轉任例行的辦公室作業。

0063

discrepancy

[dɪˋskrɛpənsɪ]

必
同 disagreement
形 discrepant 同 incompatible

We must go over company accounts very carefully to ensure that no **discrepancies** are found when our auditor comes next week.

(n.) 不一致，不符

我們必須仔細檢查公司帳目，確保下週審計員來時不會發現不一致之處。

0064

discrimination

[dɪˏskrɪməˋneʃən]

同 favoritism, bias, prejudice
動 discriminate
形 discriminating

Although gender **discrimination** in the sales department is something that is not discussed openly, it is a fact that there are very few women on the sales staff.

(n.) 歧視，辨別力

雖然業務部門的性別歧視不是會被公開討論的事，但女性業務員很少是個事實。

0065

disk

[dɪsk]

必

At the end of each business day, all files on the company computer system are saved to a **disk** and filed away.

(n.) 碟片，圓盤
每天營業結束時，公司電腦系統內所有資料都會存進光碟裡建檔。

0066

dismiss

[dɪsˋmɪs]

聽

同 fire, discharge, sack, give the axe, give the sack

名 dismissal

John was **dismissed** by his boss after it was discovered that his drinking problem made it difficult for him to perform his duties.

(v.) 解雇，解除職務
約翰被發現酗酒問題嚴重影響他的工作表現後，遭老闆辭退。

0067

disparate

[ˋdɪspərɪt]

必

同 different

名 disparity 同 difference

While the CEO and the board of directors had **disparate** views on how the company should be run, they did agree that poorly performing divisions should be sold off.

(a.) 大相逕庭的
儘管執行長和董事會對於應該如何經營公司，看法大相逕庭，但雙方都同意表現欠佳的部門應該賣掉。

0068

disperse

[dɪˋspɝs]

必

同 sprinkle, scatter

名 dispersal

The new management team believes that knowledge of company finances should be **dispersed** among all departments, thus enabling department heads to make better budgeting decisions.

(v.) 散播，驅散
新的經營團隊認為，公司的財務知識應該傳播給所有部門知道，進而使部門主管做出更明智的預算決策。

0069

display

[dɪˋsple]

必
同 presentation,
   demonstration, exhibition
動 display

A new designer has been hired to create window **displays** for the upcoming holiday season, as last year's displays were less than satisfactory.

(n.) 展示，陳列

一名新設計師受雇替即將到來的連續假期創作櫥窗展示，因為去年的展示讓人不甚滿意。

0070

display

[dɪˋsple]

必
同 present, exhibit
反 conceal

Those of you in the training program who **display** leadership qualities and strong communication skills will be considered for a management position.

(v.) 展示，陳列

你們參與訓練計畫的人若是展現出領袖特質以及優異的溝通技巧，將被考慮派任管理職。

0071

disposable

[dɪˋspozəbl]

名 disposable
形 disposable
   反 nondisposable
動 dispose
   同 arrange
名 disposal
片 at one's disposal

As the poor economy has left consumers with less **disposable** income, we have decided to devote more resources to the promotion of our low-price product line.

(a.) 可支配的，用過即丟的

經濟不振讓消費者的可支配所得減少，我們決定投入更多資源來推銷我們的低價產品線。

0072

dispose (of)

[dɪˋspoz (əv)]

讀
同 discard, throw away
片 dispose of

An office cleaning lady was hired to dust and clean all the desks, vacuum or mop the floors and **dispose of** all waste.

(v.) 處理，扔掉

一名清潔辦公室的女士被雇用來打掃清理所有辦公桌、吸塵拖地，處理掉所有垃圾。

0073

dispute
[dɪ`spjut]

聽
同 difference, conflict
動 dispute　同 quarrel
形 disputable　同 debatable

If we are unable to resolve the **dispute** with our supplier soon, we may have no choice but to take them to court.

(n.) 爭論，糾紛

若我們無法快點解決和供應商的糾紛，可能就別無選擇，只能對簿公堂。

0074

disrupt
[dɪs`rʌpt]

必
同 interrupt, cut off
名 disruption
　　同 interruption, break
形 disruptive
　　同 disturbing

The meeting was **disrupted** when the power suddenly went out, throwing the conference room into darkness.

(v.) 使分裂，使中斷

突然停電造成會議中斷，會議室陷入一片黑暗。

0075

disruption
[dɪs`rʌpʃən]

必
同 interruption, break

The firing of the new secretary caused little **disruption** in the office, as the boss waited until after hours to call her into his office.

(n.) 分裂，中斷

解雇新祕書沒有在辦公室造成多少激盪，因為老闆等到下班後才打電話叫她進他的辦公室。

0076

disseminate
[dɪ`sɛmə͵net]

必
同 distribute, pass around, circulate
名 dissemination

We need to **disseminate** this information throughout the office so that anyone with questions will be sure to bring them up at the lunch discussion tomorrow.

(v.) 散播消息

我們需要將這消息傳遞給全辦公室知道，好讓有疑問的人可以在明天午餐討論時提出來。

0077

distinct

[dɪˋstɪŋkt]

聽
同 **distinguishable**
反 **indistinct**
形 **distinctive**
　同 **characteristic**
副 **distinctively**

We are confident that the cutting-edge technology featured in our new product will give us a **distinct** advantage over our competitors.

(a.) 有區別的，明顯的
我們有信心新產品的頂尖技術將帶給我們明顯勝過競爭對手的優勢。

0078

distinguish

[dɪˋstɪŋgwɪʃ]

必
同 **differentiate, tell**
形 **distinguished**
　同 **celebrated, imposing**
　反 **common, unknown**

As counterfeiters become increasingly sophisticated, it is more and more difficult to **distinguish** between knock-offs and genuine products.

(v.) 區別，辨別
由於仿冒者的技術越來越老練，越來越難以辨別贗品與真品。

0079

distinguished

[dɪˋstɪŋgwɪʃt]

聽 讀
同 **celebrated, imposing**
反 **common, unknown**

Many **distinguished** guests have been invited to attend the product launch, which should guarantee extensive media coverage.

(a.) 聲譽卓越的，高級的
許多顯赫的客人都受邀參加這場產品發表會，這應該能保證會有媒體大幅報導。

0080

distract

[dɪˋstrækt]

必 讀
同 **deflect**
形 **distracting, distracted**
名 **distraction**
　同 **interference**

An efficiency expert was called in to advise the company on how to eliminate all the factors in the workplace that **distract** employees from their work.

(v.) 使分心
一名效率方面的專家被請來給公司建議，傳授如何消除職場中讓雇員在工作時分心的因素。

0081

distraction

[dɪ`strækʃən]

必

同 interference

When brainstorming new ideas, our manager likes to shut out all **distractions** by closing his office door and telling his secretary to hold all calls.

(n.) 分心，讓人分心的人事物

我們的經理在腦力激盪新點子時，喜歡杜絕所有讓人分心的東西，不但關起辦公室門，還要祕書幫他擋電話。

0082

distribute

[dɪ`strɪbjut]

聽 讀
同 pass out, hand out
名 distribution
名 distributor

In an effort to attract customers, the new restaurant hired students to **distribute** flyers advertising their lunch special around the neighborhood.

(v.) 分配，發送

為了吸引顧客，這家新餐廳雇用學生在附近發送廣告他們中午特餐的傳單。

0083

distribution

[ˌdɪstrə`bjuʃən]

聽

The **distribution** of free samples proved to be an effective promotional strategy, as sales of the product rose dramatically during the following months.

(n.) 分配，通路

發送免費試用品證明是有效的促銷策略，因為產品在接下來的幾個月銷售激增。

0084

distributor

[dɪ`strɪbjətə]

同 allocator

Several firms are vying to become the sole **distributor** of our beauty products in North America, but we have yet to make a final decision.

(n.) 經銷商

有幾家公司要角逐成為我們美容產品在北美的獨家經銷商，但我們還沒做出最後決定。

0085

district

[ˋdɪstrɪkt]

聽 讀
同 **area, region**

The main offices of the corporation are housed in the downtown business **district**, but their production facilities are located in outlying areas.

(n.) 地區，區域

這家公司主要的辦公室設在市中心的商業區，但他們的生產設施則位於外圍區域。

0086

disturb

[dɪsˋtɝb]

必
同 **interrupt**
名 **disturbance**
　　同 perturbation
形 **disturbed, disturbing**

I'm sorry to **disturb** you during your lunch hour, but there is a call for you from Mr. Henderson on line two.

(v.) 打擾，使心神不寧

抱歉打擾你的午餐時間，但二線有韓德森先生來電找你。

0087

disturbance

[dɪsˋtɝbəns]

必
同 **perturbation**

A disgruntled former employee caused a **disturbance** at the office when he entered the building and demanded to talk to the president.

(n.) 打擾，騷亂

一名挾怨的離職員工在辦公室造成騷動，因為他進入大樓要求和總裁說話。

0088

disused

[dɪsˋjuzd]

同 **obsolete**
名 **disuse**　　同 neglect

The **disused** warehouse was eventually torn down to make way for more parking spaces for the new office complex.

(a.) 廢棄不用的

廢棄不用的倉庫最後被拆除，好讓新的辦公大樓有更多停車位可用。

0089

diverse

[daɪˋvɝs]

必 讀
同 various
反 alike, similar

That software company creates software products and solutions for a **diverse** range of corporate and government clients.

(a.) 多樣化的，不同的

那家軟體公司創造軟體產品與解決方案，服務各式各樣的公司與政府機關客戶。

0090

diversify

[daɪˋvɝsəˌfaɪ]

必
名 diversity
形 diverse 　同 various
　　　　　　反 alike, similar
副 diversely

In an attempt to **diversify** their product line, the company hired two top-notch designers known for their creativity and knowledge of market trends.

(v.) 多樣化

為了讓產品線多樣化，這家公司雇用了兩位以創意和嫻熟市場趨勢出名的頂尖設計師。

0091

divide

[dəˋvaɪd]

必
同 split
反 unite, unify
形 divisible, divisional
名 division

The workload for this project should be **divided** equally among team members, and tasks should be assigned in accordance with members' skill sets.

(v.) 劃分

這企畫案的工作量應該均分給組員，並根據每人的專長來分派任務。

0092

dividend

[ˋdɪvəˌdɛnd]

必

Many investment experts recommend buying stocks that pay dividends, as they tend to exhibit less price volatility than stocks that don't pay **dividends**.

(n.) 股息，被除數

許多投資專家推薦購買會配發股息的股票，因其價格的波動小於不配發股息的股票。

0093

donate
[`donet]
同 give
名 donation 同 contribution
名 donor

When asked if he would be willing to **donate** to the charity, the president very generously signed a check for a large sum of money.

(v.) 捐贈

被問到是否願意捐錢給慈善機構時，總裁大方簽下一張高額支票。

0094

down payment
[daʊn `pemənt]
必

To get rid of overstock, the auto dealership decided to offer full financing with no **down payment** on last year's models.

頭期款

為了消化庫存，這家車商決定對去年的車款提供免頭款的全額貸款。

0095

draw
[drɔ]
必
同 pull, attract
名 draw
　 同 attraction, attractor

The exhibition of paintings by Renaissance masters **drew** large crowds to the museum throughout its two-month run.

(v.) 吸引，引來

為期兩個月的文藝復興大師畫展，從頭到尾都吸引大批群眾前來美術館。

0096

dress code
[drɛs kod]

Our **dress code** is extremely clear, and we expect you to follow it consistently or consider looking for a new job elsewhere.

服裝規定

我們的服裝規定十分明確，我們希望大家一貫遵守，否則可以考慮另謀高就。

0097

dry run
[draɪ rʌn]

Everyone needs to clear their schedule tomorrow, as we will be performing a final **dry run** in preparation for the product launch on Monday.

排練，演習
明天每個人都必須挪出時間來，因為我們為了準備週一的產品上市，將進行最後的排練。

0098

due
[dju]
同 scheduled, expected
反 undue

The final payment on this machine was **due** last month, but as of now, we have heard nothing from our customer regarding the payment.

(a.) 到期的，預定應到的
這部機器的尾款上個月到期，但到現在客戶對這筆款項還是不吭一聲。

0099

due(largely) to…
[dju(ˋlɑrdʒlɪ) tə]
必

Our increase in prices this year is **due largely to** the fact that the raw materials used to produce our products have become significantly more expensive.

由於…
我們今年漲價多半是由於用於製造產品的原物料變貴很多。

0100

duplicate
[ˋdjupləkɪt]
必
同 duplication
動 duplicate　同 reproduce
形 duplicate　同 identical

Mr. Jacobs asked his secretary to make **duplicates** of the files and have them on his desk by 10 o'clock the following morning.

(n.) 副本，完全一樣的東西
雅各斯先生要他祕書把這資料複製一份，隔天早上十點之前放在他的辦公桌上。

0101

durable
[ˋdjʊrəbl]
必
同 long-wearing
名 durability

A key selling point of our new line of kitchen knives is that they are more **durable** than those sold by our competitors.

(a.) 耐用的
我們新系列廚房刀具的關鍵賣點，就是比我們對手販售的產品更耐用。

0102

duration
[djʊˋreʃən]
必 讀

The meeting was slated to last for two hours, but the total **duration** from start to finish turned out to be considerably longer.

(n.) 持續時間
這場會議預定進行兩小時，但最後從頭到尾持續的時間卻長很多。

0103

duty
[ˋdjʊtɪ]
聽
同 task, work
片 on duty, off duty

Catherine's **duties** as administrative assistant include answering phones, setting up appointments and performing general clerical work.

(n.) 職務，關稅
凱薩琳擔任行政助理的職務包括接電話、敲定約會以及執行一般文書工作。

0104

dynamic
[daɪˋnæmɪk]
同 active, vital

Our firm is seeking **dynamic**, goal-oriented management professionals who are skilled at motivating employees to perform at their best.

(a.) 有活力的，動能的
敝公司正在尋找有活力而且目標導向、精於激勵員工達成最佳表現的管理專才。

New TOEIC990 新多益 高分關鍵字彙

New
TOEIC
990
新多益高分關鍵字彙

E

Group

0001

earnings
[`ɜnɪŋz]

聽 讀
同 income, revenue
動 earn

Earnings have grown steadily since the company went public in 1998, increasing at a compound annual rate of 12%.

(n.) 收入，收益

這家公司自 1998 年股票上市後的盈餘便穩定成長，以 12% 的年複利持續增加。

0002

economical
[ˌikə`nɑmɪkl]

必
同 frugal, sparing
副 economically
名 economy 同 thriftness, saving
　　　　 反 squandering
名 economics
動 economize

Employees who commute by car to work every day are advised to purchase an **economical** model that gets good gas mileage.

(a.) 節約的，經濟的

每天開車通勤上班的雇員，被建議購買油耗表現佳的經濟車款。

0003

economy
[ɪ`kɑnəmɪ]

必
同 financial system

The government recently introduced a financial stimulus package in an attempt to bolster the weakening **economy**.

(n.) 節約，經濟

政府最近祭出刺激金融的方案，試圖提振疲弱的經濟。

0004

effective
[ɪ`fɛktɪv]

必 讀
反 ineffective
名 effect, effectiveness
動 effect
副 effectively

Many businesses find participating in job fairs to be a highly **effective** and cost-efficient means of recruiting new employees.

(a.) 有效的，生效的

許多公司行號發現參加就業博覽會，是招募新員工一個非常有效又划算的方法。

0005

efficient

[ɪˋfɪʃənt]

必 聽
同 **effective**
反 **inefficient**
名 **efficiency** 同 effectiveness
　　　　　　　　反 inefficiency
副 **efficiently**

Because Andrew was a very **efficient** worker, he always finished projects on time and never had to put in overtime.

(a.) 有效率的

因為安德魯是很有效率的員工，所以他總是準時完成企畫，從來不用加班。

0006

electrician

[ˌilɛkˋtrɪʃən]

聽
同 **lineman**

An **electrician** was called in to inspect the building's electrical system and replace any damaged wiring.

(n.) 電工

一名電工被找來檢查大樓的電路系統，並且更換受損的線路。

0007

elegance

[ˋɛləgəns]

必
同 **grace**
反 **inelegance**
形 **elegant** 同 graceful, refined

Elaine wore a stunning dress, and she was the picture of **elegance** that night at the Christmas Ball.

(n.) 優雅，典雅

依蓮那身洋裝令人驚豔，她也是耶誕舞會那晚優雅的寫照。

0008

elegant

[ˋɛləgənt]

必
同 **graceful, refined**

Our hotel's luxury business suites, which boast **elegant** furnishings and wireless Internet access, are popular with executive travelers.

(a.) 優雅的，典雅的

我們飯店的豪華商務套房有典雅家具及無線上網，頗受高階主管旅客的歡迎。

0009

element
[ˈɛləmənt]

必
同 component, factor, ingredient, constituent
形 elementary
片 in one's element

The key **elements** of a good business plan include an executive summary, company analysis, industry analysis, marketing plan, and financial plan.

(n.) 要素，元素
一個優良商業計畫的關鍵要素包括執行大綱、公司分析、產業分析、行銷計畫與財務計畫。

0010

eligible
[ˈɛlɪdʒəbl]

必

Part-time employees are **eligible** for the same benefits available to full-time employees, with the exception of long-term disability coverage and participation in the company retirement plan.

(a.) 法律上合格的，婚姻上合適的
兼職雇員可以享有和正職雇員相同的福利，只是沒有長期的失能保險，也不能參加公司的勞保退休計畫。

0011

eliminate
[ɪˈlɪməˌnet]

同 get rid of, remove
名 elimination

As part of the restructuring process, the corporation will be reducing or **eliminating** all unnecessary employee and infrastructure costs.

(v.) 排除，淘汰
這家公司將減少或清除所有不必要的員工和基礎建設的成本，做為重整過程的一部分。

0012

embark
[ɪmˈbɑrk]

必
反 disembark
名 embarkation

After working as a chemical engineer for eight years, Howard decided to join a chemical supply firm and **embark** on a new career in sales.

(v.) 從事，著手
擔任化學工程師八年之後，華決定加入化學用品公司，在業務方面展開新職涯。

0013

embassy

[ˈɛmbəsɪ]

聽

相關字彙 **ambassador** 大使
consulate 領事館
consul 領事

After receiving a threatening letter, the **embassy** decided to shut its doors for three days as it assessed the viability of the threat.

(n.) 大使館

收到一封威脅信後，大使館決定閉館三日，評估此威脅的真假。

0014

emphasis

[ˈɛmfəsɪs]

必

動 **emphasize**   同 stress
形 **emphatic**
副 **emphatically**

The department head has decided that in the coming year, more **emphasis** will be placed on maintaining relationships with established customers than on developing new customers.

(n.) 強調

部門主管決定在來年要把更多重心放在維持與既有客戶的關係，而非開發新顧客。

0015

emphasize

[ˈɛmfəˌsaɪz]

必

同 stress

During the meeting, the vice president of sales **emphasized** the need to devote more company resources to the development of new sales channels.

(v.) 強調

業務副總在開會期間，強調公司需要投入更多資源於開發新的銷售管道。

0016

enclose

[ɪnˈkloz]

讀

同 **enfold, wrap, envelop**
名 **enclosure**

When sending in your completed job application form, please **enclose** a cover letter, résumé and any other relevant documentation.

(v.) 隨信附寄，圍住

交寄完整的應徵表格時，請附上應職信、履歷及其他相關文件。

0017

encounter
[ɪnˈkaʊntɚ]

讀
名 encounter

I'm confident that your first sales presentation will go smoothly, but should you **encounter** any difficulties, please don't hesitate to call me.

(v.) 遭遇（困難），偶遇

我有信心你第一次業務報告一定會很順利，但若是遇到任何困難，儘管打電話給我。

0018

encourage
[ɪnˈkɜɪdʒ]

同 inspire, cheer
反 discourage
名 encouragement
　　反 discouragement
形 encouraging
　　反 discouraging
副 encouragingly
片 be encouraged to...

To **encourage** our sales staff to shine, in addition to regular sales commissions, we are also offering generous bonuses to sales reps who meet monthly sales targets.

(v.) 鼓勵，激勵

為了激勵我們的業務人員發光發亮，除了固定的業務佣金外，我們也將大方分紅給達成月銷售目標的業務代表。

0019

encouragement
[ɪnˈkɜɪdʒmənt]

必
反 discouragement

Managers at our firm are taught to use **encouragement** rather than criticism to motivate employees who are not performing up to their potential.

(n.) 鼓勵，激勵

我們公司的經理被教導要用鼓勵而非批評，來激發未發揮潛力的員工。

0020

engage
[ɪnˈgedʒ]

必
同 hire, employ
名 engagement
　　同 employment
形 engaging
形 engaged
　　同 committed

Karen's boss instructed her to **engage** the services of a rental agency to find a new office space before the lease on the current office expires.

(v.) 聘僱，使從事

凱倫的老闆指示她聘僱一家租屋公司，在辦公室租約到期前，找到新的辦公室地點。

0021

engagement

[ɪnˋgedʒmənt]

同 appointment

Ms. Connelly's personal assistant left her a note on her desk to remind her about her business **engagement** that afternoon.

(n.) 約定會面

康紮利女士的私人助理在她桌上留了張紙條，提醒她那天下午約了要談生意。

0022

enhance

[ɪnˋhæns]

必
同 reinforce
名 enhancement

The company president would like to **enhance** our production capabilities, but he realizes that the process will be an arduous one.

(v.) 加強，增加

這公司的董事長想要增加我們的產能，但他明白這過程將會很艱鉅。

0023

enroll

[ɪnˋrol]

同 recruit, inscribe
名 enrollment
　同 registration

In order to fine-tune my writing skills, I decided to **enroll** in a business writing class through the local university extension program in the fall.

(v.) 登記註冊，加入

為了琢磨我的寫作技巧，我決定參加當地大學推廣部在秋天開設的商業寫作班。

0024

enrollment

[ɪnˋrolmənt]

讀

Summer **enrollment** slipped last year after many people decided not to travel because of the weak dollar.

(n.) 登記人數，入伍

許多人因為美元貶值而決定不去旅遊，造成去年夏天的登記人數下滑。

0025

ensure

[ɪnˋʃʊr]

聽 讀
同 **assure, guarantee**

We can **ensure** you that there is nothing we won't do to make sure you are satisfied with our product and with the post-sales service we provide.

(v.) 確保

我們可以跟您確保，務必讓您滿意我們的產品以及我們提供的售後服務。

0026

enterprise

[ˋɛntɚˌpraɪz]

必
同 **company, business**
形 **enterprising**  同 ambitious, venturesome, vigorous
名 **enterpriser**

At the present time, small business **enterprises** account for nearly half of the nation's employment and over one-third of the Gross Domestic Product.

(n.) 企業

目前小型企業佔國內近一半的就業人口，以及超過 1/3 的國內生產毛額。

0027

entertain

[ˌɛntɚˋten]

同 **amuse, please**
形 **entertaining**
　　同 enjoyable, diverting
副 **entertainingly**
名 **entertainment, entertainer**

In order to be reimbursed for funds spent on travel and **entertaining** clients, sales representatives are required to fill out an expense account form.

(v.) 款待，娛樂

為了核銷出差及招待客戶的花費，業務代表必須填寫費用報支單。

0028

enthusiastic

[ɪnˌθjuzɪˋæstɪk]

讀
同 **passionate, earnest**
反 **unenthusiastic**
副 **enthusiastically**
名 **enthusiasm, enthusiast**

Our marketing and promotion firm is currently seeking **enthusiastic**, experienced individuals to work as Account Executives within the client services group at our Los Angeles office.

(a.) 熱切的

我們的行銷推廣公司目前正在徵求有熱誠的老手，在我們洛杉磯分公司的客服部門擔任客戶專員。

0029

entitle
[ɪn`taɪtl]

必
同 **enable, permit**
形 **entitled** 同 eligible
名 **entitlement**

This coupon **entitles** you to a free coffee when you order a business lunch special at any of our coffee shops throughout the city.

(v.) 給予⋯權利，給予⋯資格
你在本市任何一家我們的咖啡店點用中午商業特餐，就能以這張兌換券免費享用一杯咖啡。

0030

entitled
[ɪn`taɪtld]
同 **eligible**

After completing their probation period, full-time members of our staff are **entitled** to a full range of benefits, including pension, paid holidays, and maternity/paternity pay.

(a.) 有權利去⋯的，有資格享有⋯的
在完成試用期後，正職員工有權享有一切福利，包括退休金、有給假以及產假（陪產假）薪水。

0031

entrepreneur
[ˌɑntrəprə`nɜ]
同 **enterpriser**
形 **entrepreneurial**
名 **entrepreneurship**

In five short years, the young **entrepreneur** successfully started a business from scratch and built it into a successful company with offices in five major cities.

(n.) 企業家，創業家
這年輕的創業家在短短五年內，成功從無到有建立起事業，打造出成功的公司，並在五個主要城市設有辦公室。

0032

entry-level
[`ɛntrɪ`lɛvl]

As this is an **entry-level** position, you will need to spend some time proving yourself before you can advance to a higher position within the company.

(a.) 入門級的
因為這是入門的職位，你將需要花點時間證明自己，才能在公司晉升到更高的職位。

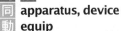
0033

equipment
[ɪˋkwɪpmənt]
聽 讀
同 **apparatus, device**
動 **equip**

Our office **equipment** service technicians are skilled at installing, repairing and maintaining all kinds of office equipment, including computers, monitors, printers, scanners, photocopiers, and fax machines.

(n.) 器材，裝備
我們的辦公室器材服務技師，精於安裝、修理與保養各種辦公室器材，包括電腦、顯示器、印表機、掃描器、影印機和傳真機。

0034

equivalent
[ɪˋkwɪvələnt]
必
同 **equal, even**
名 **equivalent, equivalence**

My current salary is approximately **equivalent** to the salary I was making in my previous job.

(a.) 相等的，同等的
我目前的薪水和我先前那分工作的薪水差不多。

0035

escort
[ˋɛskɔrt]
必
同 **guard, accompany**
名 **escort**　　同 bodyguard

When traveling on business, both locally and abroad, the CEO is always **escorted** by his personal bodyguard.

(v.) 護送
執行長不管是在國內還是國外出差，總是有私人保鏢護送。

0036

essential
[ɪˋsɛnʃəl]
必 讀
同 **indispensable**
名 **essence**
副 **essentially**　　近 basically

Andy always found that the most **essential** piece of equipment he had besides his cell phone was his PDA.

(a.) 必須的，極為重要的
安迪始終認為他最必要的裝備除了手機外，就是個人數位助理。

0037

establish

[ə`stæblɪʃ]

必 聽 讀

同 found, set up

反 abolish

形 established

　同 accomplished

名 establishment

　同 institution, organization

名 establisher

Since **establishing** his first computer company a decade ago, Gavin has become a serial entrepreneur, starting a dozen companies in the computer and communications industries.

(v.) 設立

自從在十年前設立了第一家電腦公司後，蓋文已成為連環創業家，開設了十幾家電腦通訊公司。

0038

estate

[ɪs`tet]

聽

同 property, asset

片 real estate

In the United States, the **estate** tax, otherwise known as the "death tax," is a tax levied on the transfer of the "taxable **estate**" of a deceased person.

(n.) 財產，地產

在美國，也稱為「死亡稅」的遺產稅，是針對死者轉移「可稅財產」所課徵的稅。

0039

estimate

[`ɛstə͵met]

必 讀

同 guess, judge

名 estimate

　同 estimation

名 estimation

　同 appraisal, estimate

形 estimated

The financial analyst's forecast of 13 billion for this year's revenue turned out very near the mark; he **estimated** 13 billion, and our actual revenue was 13.2 billion.

(v.) 預測，估計

這位金融分析師預估今年營收是一百三十億美元，非常接近；他預估一百三十億美元，而我們實際的營收是一百三十二億美元。

0040

estimation

[͵ɛstə`meʃən]

必

同 appraisal, estimate

Please make an **estimation** of your expenditures this month and submit it to the accounting department for reimbursement.

(n.) 預測，估計

請預估一下你這個月的開銷，然後報請會計部門核銷。

0041

evaluate

[ɪˋvæljʊˏet]

必 聽
同 appraise, assess, value
名 evaluation
　同 rating, valuation

In the interests of **evaluating** employee performance and providing relevant feedback, our Human Resources Department holds quarterly employee performance reviews.

(v.) 評量，評價
以評量員工表現並提供相關的回應為著眼點，我們的人力資源部每季都會舉行員工績效檢討。

0042

evaluation

[ɪˏvæljʊˋeʃən]

必
同 rating, valuation

Employees who change position due to promotion or transfer are required to complete an additional three-month **evaluation** period on top of the evaluation period completed when first joining the company.

(n.) 評量，評價
因為升職或轉調而有職位變動的員工，必須在初次加入公司所完成的評量期之餘，額外完成三個月的評量期。

0043

evidence

[ˋɛvədəns]

必
同 proof
動 evidence 同 certify

Any **evidence** of misconduct by other employees should be brought to the attention of your supervisor immediately.

(n.) 證據
凡有其他員工行為不端的證據，均應立即向上司報告。

0044

evident

[ˋɛvədənt]

必
同 plain, apparent, obvious
副 evidently

From continuing weak sales of our core product lines, it is **evident** that the recent marketing plan has been a complete failure.

(a.) 顯而易見的
從我們核心產品線持續銷售低迷看來，顯然最近的行銷計畫完全失敗。

0045

exact

[ɪgˋzækt]

必
同 **accurate, precise**
反 **inexact**
名 **exactness**
動 **exact**　同 demand
形 **exacting**　同 demanding
副 **exactly**　同 precisely

It would be very difficult for me to give you an **exact** arrival date for your shipment, but we will do our very best to make sure you receive it within two weeks.

(a.) 確切的
我很難給你到貨的確切日期，但我們將盡力確保你在兩週內收到。

0046

examine

[ɪgˋzæmɪn]

必
同 **inspect, check**
名 **examination**　同 scrutiny

To determine what went wrong in the negotiation process, the manager **examined** recent correspondence for any evidence of miscommunication.

(v.) 檢查，詳查
為了確定協商過程是哪裡出了錯，經理詳查了最近的通訊，尋找有無溝通不良的證據。

0047

exceed

[ɪkˋsid]

聽
同 **transcend, surpass**
形 **exceeding**
　同 exceptional, surpassing
副 **exceedingly**

Your performance has **exceeded** our expectations once again, and in recognition of your contributions we have decided to give you a 10% raise.

(v.) 勝過，超出
你的表現再次超越我們的預期，為了表彰你的貢獻，我們決定給你加薪 10%。

0048

exception

[ɪkˋsɛpʃən]

同 **exclusion**
反 **inclusion**
動 **except**　同 exclude
形 **exceptional**　同 special
副 **exceptionally**

Almost without **exception**, those who complete our management training program are placed in management positions within the company.

(n.) 例外
幾乎沒有例外，完成我們管理訓練計畫的人，在公司都位居管理職。

0049

exchange

[ɪks`tʃendʒ]

同 change, interchange

Our design team holds weekly meetings so that team members can **exchange** ideas and update each other on their progress.

(v.) 交換，兌換

我們的設計團隊每週開會，好讓組員交換點子，並且告知彼此的進度。

0050

exchange

[ɪks`tʃendʒ]

同 interchange

In **exchange** for giving Brian a promotion and pay raise, his supervisor required him to take charge of establishing and running a new human resources department.

(n.) 交換，交易所

做為讓布萊恩升職與加薪的交換條件，他的上司要求他負責成立並運作新的人力資源部門。

0051

exchange rate

[ɪks`tʃendʒ ret]

聽 讀

Exchange rate fluctuations can have a significant impact on the profit margins of multinational corporations.

匯率

匯率波動足以嚴重衝擊到跨國公司的獲利率。

0052

excitement

[ɪk`saɪtmənt]

必

同 excitation, exhilaration

形 exciting 同 thrilling, stimulating

形 excited 反 unexcited

動 excite 同 stir, stimulate

Richard could hardly contain his **excitement** when he received the news that he was being sent to work at the company's Paris office.

(n.) 興奮

理查獲知他將被派往公司在巴黎的辦公室，幾乎按捺不住興奮之情。

0053

exciting

[ɪkˋsaɪtɪŋ]

必
同 exhilarating, thrilling, stimulating
反 unexciting
副 excitingly

For qualified applicants, our company offers **exciting** opportunities in the areas of account management, Internet marketing and customer service.

(a.) 令人感到興奮的

對於符合資格的應徵者，我們公司在客戶管理、網路行銷與客戶服務方面，提供令人感到興奮的機會。

0054

exclusive

[ɪkˋsklusɪv]

讀
反 inclusive
副 exclusively
名 exclusive 同 scoop
名 exclusion 同 exception
動 exclude 同 leave out, omit
　　反 include

Patent law grants **exclusive** rights to produce, utilize and sell technological inventions for no more than twenty years.

(a.) 獨占的，除外的

專利法准予在二十年之內有製造、使用及販售技術發明的獨家權利。

0055

excursion

[ɪkˋskɝʒən]

必
同 outing

The weekend company **excursion** to a mountain resort gave employees the opportunity to become better acquainted by spending time together outside of the work environment.

(n.) 遠足

公司週末去山區度假村遠足，讓員工有機會在工作環境之外，透過共同相處而變得更熟。

0056

executive

[ɪgˋzɛkjʊtɪv]

同 administrator,
形 executive
　　同 administrative, controlling
動 execute
　　同 carry out
名 execution

The government is currently debating a plan to mandate shareholder approval of **executive** pay packages at publicly traded companies.

(n.) 高階主管，高級官員

政府目前正在爭論一項計畫，授權股東可以核准上市公司高階主管的薪資配套。

0057

exhausted
[ɪɡˋzɔstɪd]

聽
同 fatigued, tired
動 exhaust　　同 tucker
名 exhaustion　同 fatigue

The extensive overtime that our company's accountants and bookkeepers must put in during tax season leaves them **exhausted**.

(a.) 感到筋疲力竭的
我們公司的會計和簿記員在報稅季節得要長時間加班，讓他們感到筋疲力竭。

0058

exhibit
[ɪɡˋzɪbɪt]

聽 讀
同 display, demonstrate
名 exhibit
　同 exhibition
名 exhibition
　同 display, exposition

Managers should be taught to identify and provide appropriate assistance to employees who **exhibit** signs of stress, abnormal behavior or work performance problems.

(v.) 展示
經理應該要被教導去找出及提供適當協助給出現壓力跡象、行為異常或是工作表現有問題的員工。

0059

expand
[ɪkˋspænd]

必 讀
同 extend, increase, develop
反 shrink
名 expansion 同 enlargement
名 expanse　　同 sweep

Our plan is to **expand** our markets in Eastern Europe and Mexico over the next two years and then gain a foothold in the East Asian marketplace.

(v.) 擴展
我們的計畫是在接下來兩年將市場擴展至東歐和墨西哥，然後在東亞市場打下穩固的基礎。

0060

expansion
[ɪkˋspænʃən]

必
同 enlargement

An aggressive $2 billion, five-year **expansion** plan was announced yesterday by Preston Corp., the nation's third largest retailer, with 1,462 stores in 48 states.

(n.) 擴展
在四十八州擁有一千四百六十二家店、位居全國第三大零售商的佩斯頓公司，在昨天宣布了一樁積極、為期五年的二十億美元擴展計畫。

0061

expect
[ɪkˋspɛkt]

必
同 **anticipate, hope**
名 **expectation**
形 **expecting**
形 **expected** 反 unexpected
形 **expectant** 同 anticipant

The corporation **expects** rising taxes to take a bite out of annual revenues, but it is hoping that the impact will not be too severe.

(v.) 預料，期待
這家公司預料加稅會啃掉年度營收，但是希望這衝擊不會太嚴重。

0062

expectation
[ˌɛkspɛkˋteʃən]

必 聽
同 **prospect, anticipation**

Our sales department strives to manage customer **expectations** and improve customer satisfaction by learning from customer feedback, service requests and complaints.

(n.) 期待，可能性
我們的業務部門努力因應顧客的期待，並改善顧客滿意度，方式是得知顧客的反應、服務要求與客訴。

0063

expense
[ɪkˋspɛns]

必 聽 讀
同 **spending**

Business **expenses** such as legal and accounting fees, employee pay, business-related rent and interest on money borrowed for business activities are all tax deductible.

(n.) 花費
法務和會計費用、員工薪水、與營業相關的租金，以及生意借款的利息等等業務開銷，均可以抵稅。

0064

expensive
[ɪkˋpɛnsɪv]

必
同 **overpriced, uneconomical**
反 **inexpensive, low-priced**

Due to **expensive** housing and a high cost of living, wages in this area are much higher than the national average.

(a.) 昂貴的
由於昂貴的房價，以及高昂的生活成本，這區域的薪資高於全國平均很多。

0065

experience
[ɪkˋspɪrɪəns]

必
反 inexperience
動 experience
形 experienced

While no formal work **experience** is required for this position, candidates should have a strong academic background in accounting and financial analysis.

(n.) 經驗
儘管這職位不需要正式的工作經驗，但應試者應該要在會計與財務分析擁有堅強的學術背景。

0066

experienced
[ɪkˋspɪrɪənst]

必
反 inexperienced

Our software company only hires **experienced** project managers with proven track records of successfully managing major software development projects.

(a.) 有經驗的
我們的軟體公司只雇用有經驗、並已實際成功管理過軟體研發案的專案經理。

0067

experiment
[ɪkˋspɛrəmənt]

必
同 trial, test
動 experiment
　同 try out
名 experimentation

Several **experiments** were developed to test the durability of the product and ensure that it meets all international standards.

(n.) 實驗
開發了好幾項實驗來測試這產品的耐用度，並且確保其符合所有國際標準。

0068

experimentation
[ɪkˌspɛrəmɛnˋteʃən]

必
同 experiment
動 experimentalize
形 experimental
名 experimentalism,
　experimentalist

After several years of **experimentation**, a commercial application was finally found for the new remote sensing technology.

(n.) 實驗（法、過程）
經過多年的實驗過程，這項新的遠距感應技術終於找到了商業應用。

0069

expert

[ˈɛkspɚt]

必
同 **master, specialist**
反 **amateur, inexpert**
形 **expert**
　　同 proficient, skillful

The manufacturer hired a factory automation **expert** to assess the feasibility of automating heir production and assembly lines.

(n.) 專家

這廠商雇用一名工廠自動化專家，評估生產與組裝線自動化的可行性。

0070

expertise

[ˌɛkspɚˈtiz]

必 讀
同 **know-how, skill**

Crystal's **expertise** in international corporate law allowed her to become a freelance legal consultant and travel the world working for different companies.

(n.) 專才，專精

克莉絲朵在國際公司法方面的專才，讓她成為自由工作的法律顧問，到世界各地替不同公司工作。

0071

expiration

[ˌɛkspəˈreʃən]

動 **expire**　　同 run out
名 **expiry**

Our supermarket has a strict policy of never selling any product that has exceeded its **expiration** date.

(n.) 期滿，死亡

我們的超市有嚴格政策，絕不販售已超過保存期限的產品。

0072

expire

[ɪkˈspaɪr]

同 **run out**

Tenants who decide to terminate their rental contract before it **expires** must give one month's notice, otherwise their security deposit will not be returned.

(v.) 到期

決定在租約到期前終止契約的房客，必須提前一個月通知，否則將不退還押金。

0073

exploration
[ˌɛkspləˈreʃən]

必
同 **investigation**
名 **explorer**
　同 adventurer
動 **explore**
　同 research, search
形 **exploratory**

As oil prices continue to rise, oil **exploration** firms are devoting greater resources to the search for new oilfields.

(n.) 探勘，探索
油價繼續上漲，石油探勘公司正投注更多資源，尋找新油田。

0074

explore
[ɪkˈsplor]

同 **research, search**

Corporate headquarters has put together a team to **explore** the possibility of outsourcing customer service and technical support operations.

(v.) 探勘，探索
公司總部已組成一個小組，探索將客服及技術支援部門外包的可能性。

0075

export
[ɪksˈport]

反 **import**
名 **export, exportation**
　反 import, importation

Due to the rise of the Euro against the dollar, **export** sales of German automobiles to the U.S. have steadily declined over the past two years.

(n., a.) 出口（的）
由於歐元對美元升值，德國車出口到美國的銷售在過去兩年來持續下滑。

0076

expose
[ɪkˈspoz]

反 **protect, shield**
名 **exposure**

The relaxation of import quotas, while providing consumers with cheaper products, has also **exposed** many local companies to fierce competition from foreign manufacturers.

(v.) 暴露
放寬進口限額，雖然提供了消費者更便宜的產品，但也讓許多本土公司暴露在外國廠商的激烈競爭之下。

0077

exposure
[ɪkˋspoʒɚ]

同 promotion, publicity

Setting up a company website has proved to be an inexpensive and flexible way to increase product **exposure**.

(n.) 暴露，曝光
架設公司網站已證明是增加產品曝光一個便宜又有彈性的方法。

0078

express
[ɪkˋsprɛs]

必
同 verbalize, utter, convey
名 expression
形 express
形 expressive　　同 vivid
反 impassive
副 expressively

The department manager always encourages his subordinates to **express** their opinions at department meetings, as he finds that they often have useful ideas and insights.

(v.) 表達
這個部門的經理總是鼓勵部屬要在部門會議中表達自己的意見，因為他發現他們常有好用的點子和精闢見解。

0079

express mail
[ɪkˋsprɛs mel]

While **express mail** is usually delivered overnight, it may take two days to arrive in some locations.

限時郵件，快捷郵件
儘管限時郵件通常隔天就會寄到，但寄達某些地點或許需要兩天。

0080

extend
[ɪkˋstɛnd]

必 讀
同 reach out, stretch out
反 shrink, contract
名 extension
形 extensive　　反 intensive
副 extensively

For the low price of $100, you can **extend** the warranty on your laptop computer from one year to three years.

(v.) 延展，延長
只要區區一百元，你就能把你的筆電保固，從一年延長至三年。

0081

extension
[ɪkˋstɛnʃən]

We are willing to grant you a one-month **extension**, but if we do not receive your payment by that time, we will be forced to turn your account over to a collection agency.

(n.) 延展，延長
我們願意准予你寬限一個月，但若屆時我們還是沒收到你的付款，我們就不得不把你的帳戶轉交給催收公司。

0082

extracurricular
[ˌɛkstrəkəˋrɪkjələ]

Any **extracurricular** activities you choose to participate in should not interfere with your ability to perform your office duties.

(a.) 課外的，工作外的
凡你選擇參與的餘興活動，都不該妨礙你履行公務責任的能力。

0083

eye-catching
[ˋaɪˌkætʃɪŋ]
同 **attention-getting, noticeable**

Our **eye-catching** advertisements in local newspapers have increased sales by 20% over the past two months.

(a.) 引人注目的
我們在當地報紙刊登引人注目的廣告，兩個月來已讓銷售增加了 20%。

New
T
O
E
I
C

新多益高分關鍵字彙

990

F

Group

0001

faced with

[fest wɪð]

Faced with the difficult decision of whether to lay off employees or cut payroll costs, the company decided to offer all employees continued employment at a lower salary.

面對到

面對該裁員或降低薪水成本的困難抉擇，這家公司決定以較低的新水，繼續雇用所有員工。

0002

facilitate

[fə`sɪlə,tet]

同 ease, help
名 facilitation
名 facility　**同** installation

To **facilitate** the processing of orders, I have hired a student intern to come in and help you fifteen hours a week.

(v.) 促進，使便利

為了加速訂購程序，我請了一名工讀生每週來幫你十五小時。

0003

facility

[fə`sɪlətɪ]

同 installation

The installation of new assembly equipment at the production **facility** will increase the production rate of 2,000 units a day to a maximum rate of 5000 units per day.

(n.) 設施，設備

這製造設施安裝了新的組裝配備，將能讓每日兩千台的產能，提升至每天最高五千台。

0004

factor

[`fæktə]

同 element

Rising oil prices and a decrease in consumer spending are two **factors** contributing to the likelihood of an economic downturn.

(n.) 因素，要素

油價攀升和消費降低，是造成經濟可能下滑的兩個因素。

0005

fad
[fæd]
必
同 **craze, furor**
形 **faddish**

Women wearing pinstripe suits and cutting their hair in masculine styles to defocus the attention on their gender in the workplace seems to be a **fad** that has run its course.

(n.)（一時的）潮流
女性身穿細條紋套裝，留著男性幹練的短髮，以便在職場模糊他人對其性別的注意力，似乎是一時的潮流，自然會過去。

0006

fail
[fel]
必
同 **neglect**
反 **succeed**
名 **failure**　　反 success
形 **failed**　　反 successful

He **failed** to meet any of the deadlines set down by his superiors, so it was no surprise that he received a poor performance review.

(v.) 失敗，辜負
他完全沒在上司設下的最後期限內完成，所以考績不佳也不令人意外。

0007

failure
[ˈfeljɚ]
必

The head of the Public Relations Department took full responsibility for the **failure** of the PR campaign, and promised that he would devote his full efforts to rectifying the situation.

(n.) 失敗，故障
公關部門的主管承擔起公關活動失敗的完全責任，並保證他會投注全力來導正這個情況。

0008

fall to
[fɔl tə]
必

Drew **fell to** work as soon as he received his new graphic design assignment, drawing rough drafts and working out a color scheme.

開始做
德魯一接到新的平面設計任務，便馬上開始畫草圖並研究色彩主軸。

0009

familiar
[fə`mɪljə]

必
反 unfamiliar
名 familiarity
　同 acquaintance
　反 strangeness
動 familiarize

Your face looks very **familiar** to me; did you work for Norman and Associates a few years ago?

(a.) 讓人熟悉的，感到熟悉的
你看起來很面熟，你幾年前在諾曼聯合公司做過事嗎？

0010

fare
[fɛr]

必 聽
同 price, charge, cost

Discussion about increasing the public bus **fare** came to a standstill after so many people protested against the idea.

(n.)（交通工具）票價
在這麼多人抗議這想法後，調漲公車票價的討論陷入了僵局。

0011

fatal
[`fetl̩]

讀
同 lethal, deadly
反 harmless
副 fatally
名 fatality　同 death

Even though the vice president warned the president not to go through with the deal, the president chose not to listen, and the deal proved to be a **fatal** one for the company.

(a.) 關係重大的，致命的
儘管副總裁警告總裁不要同意這交易，但總裁選擇不聽，最後證明這交易對公司很致命。

0012

faulty
[`fɔltɪ]

同 defective
名 fault
片 at fault, find fault, to a fault

Faulty plumbing on the sixth floor caused the leak that damaged all of the copy machines on the fifth floor.

(a.) 有缺點的
六樓的水管有問題而造成漏水，殃及五樓所有的影印機。

0013

favorable

[ˋfevərəbl̩]

必
反 **unfavorable**
名 **favor**

A **favorable** company image is necessary for a company to be able to do business with a government organization.

(a.) 討喜的，贊同的，對…有利的
要和政府機構做生意，公司形象良好是必要條件。

0014

feature

[ˋfitʃɚ]

聽
同 **characteristic**
動 **feature**
形 **featured** 反 featureless

One **feature** of this PDA that I am sure you will be impressed with is that it also serves as a cell phone, allowing you to carry less devices with you when you're on the go.

(n.) 特徵，容貌
我確定這台個人數位助理有個功能一定會讓你驚豔，就是它也能當手機用，讓你外出不用帶那麼多東西。

0015

fee

[fi]

聽
同 **charge**

The total **fee** for studio rental will be determined after your recording work is complete and we know how much studio time was actually necessary.

(n.) 服務費，費用
等你們錄音完成後，我們知道實際需要多少錄音室的時間，才能確定總共的租用費。

0016

figure

[ˋfɪgjɚ]

聽
同 **digit**
動 **figure** 片 figure out

As sales **figures** for January were far below expectations, a meeting was held to discuss possible adjustments to sales and marketing strategies.

(n.) 數字
由於一月的銷售數字遠低於預期，所以舉行了一場會議來討論對於業務和行銷策略的可能調整。

0017

figure out
[ˈfɪgjɚ aut]
必

I can't **figure out** why my computer keeps crashing; I guess I'll have to call in someone from the IT department to take a look at it.

釐清，理出頭緒
我搞不懂電腦怎麼老是當機；我想我得找資訊部的人來看一看了。

0018

file
[faɪl]
必 聽 讀
同 register
名 file　　　同 folder
片 file for

When all of the tax withholding statements are prepared, please hand them out to all employees so that they can **file** whenever it is convenient for them.

(v.) 報稅，提出申訴
所得稅扣繳憑單均備妥時，請發給所有員工，好讓他們依自己方便擇時申報。

0019

finance
[faɪˈnæns]
聽 讀
同 commerce, money
動 finance　同 fund
形 financial　同 fiscal

After obtaining an MBA degree with a specialization in banking and **finance**, Martin found a position as an investment banker at a large Manhattan investment bank.

(n.) 金融，財務
在取得了專攻金融和財務的企業管理碩士學位後，馬丁在曼哈頓一家大型投資銀行找到了投資銀行員的職位。

0020

financial
[faɪˈnænʃəl]
同 fiscal

Please tell me what that means in **financial** terms; am I still going to own a majority in my business?

(a.) 財務的，金融的
請告訴我那在財務用語中是什麼意思，我仍然擁有公司過半的股權嗎？

0021

fine
[faɪn]
聽
同 **penalty, punishment**

Those convicted of copyright infringement may be punished with a one-year prison sentence and a **fine** of up to $50,000.

(n.) 罰金

違反著作權而被定罪的人，可能會被處以一年徒刑，併科最高五萬元罰金。

0022

fiscal year
[ˈfɪskḷ jɪr]
讀

If employment terminates prior to the end of the **fiscal year**, employees will be paid for unused vacation to which they are entitled.

會計年度

如果在會計年度結束前終止受雇，員工未休完的假將可折算成薪資給付。

0023

flexible
[ˈflɛksəbḷ]
必
同 **pliable**
反 **inflexible**
副 **flexibly**
名 **flexibility**
  同 elasticity, adaptability

In instituting a **flexible** work schedule, each department in the firm should be sensitive to the impact one employee's flexible schedule may have on work distribution for other employees in the same department.

(a.) 有彈性的，可變通的

制定彈性上班制度時，公司各部門應該要隨時注意某個員工的彈性工時，或許會衝擊到同部門其他員工的工作。

0024

fluctuate
[ˈflʌktʃʊˌet]
必 讀
同 **waver**
名 **fluctuation**
  同 wavering, instability
形 **fluctuant**

While business trends can cause the sales figures to **fluctuate** in the short term, they have shown a steady rise over the past decade.

(v.) 變動，波動

儘管商業趨勢會造成短期銷售數字波動，但十年來的銷售呈現穩定成長。

0025

fluctuation

[ˌflʌktʃʊˋeʃən]

必
同 **wavering, variation**

Fluctuations in commodity prices are the primary cause for short-term changes in company cash flow from operating activities.

(n.) 變動，波動

公司營運的現金流量出現短期變化，主要肇因是原物料的價格波動。

0026

fluency

[ˋfluənsɪ]

名 **fluency**　　同 eloquence
形 **fluent**
副 **fluently**

The **fluency** with which he could discuss trade law made him the perfect candidate to testify for the corporation in court.

(n.) 流暢，流利

他能流暢討論交易法，使得他成為出庭替公司作證的完美人選。

0027

focus on

[ˋfokəs ɑn]

We plan to **focus on** increasing production speed in the coming years, as this will allow us to lower inventory costs and still deliver products to customers in a timely manner.

專注在…

我們計畫在未來幾年專注於增加量產速度，因為這將讓我們降低庫存成本，同時也能及時出貨給顧客。

0028

fold

[fold]

必
同 **shut down**
名 **fold**

In spite of the tireless efforts of management and employees, the company finally **folded** after 40 years in business.

(v.) 關店，折疊

儘管管理部門和員工不懈的努力，這家公司最後還是在經營四十年後結束營業。

0029

follow up
[ˈfɑlo ʌp]
必

By **following up** on sales leads generated at the recent trade show, our sales staff has been successful in bringing in a number of valuable new clients.

後續追蹤
透過後續追蹤在最近商展所得的業務線索，我們的業務人員成功帶入許多寶貴的新客戶。

0030

forecast
[ˈfɔrˌkæst]
必 聽 讀
同 prognosis, prediction, expectation
動 forecast 同 foresee
名 forecaster

At the press conference, the CEO announced that the company would be unable to meet its previous **forecast** of a 15% annual rise in sales.

(n.) 預測
在記者招待會上，執行長宣布公司將無法達到先前預測的 15% 銷售年成長。

0031

forecast
[ˈfɔrˌkæst]
同 foresee

The General Manager **forecas** to a difficult fourth quarter for the company, as there was very little promise of new sales and the several members of the production crew had recently quit.

(v.) 預測
總經理預測公司在第四季會很艱困，因為沒有什麼新銷售，而且幾名生產人員又在最近辭職。

0032

foremost
[ˈfɔrˌmost]

Of the **foremost** importance for discussion at this meeting should be the distribution of brochures in preparation for this weekend's conference.

(a.) 最先的，第一流的
這場會議中最重要的討論，應該是為了準備本週末的大會而發送的手冊。

0033

foresee

[for`si]

聽 讀
同 **anticipate, envision**
名 **foresight**

Luckily, because our company was able to **foresee** the rapid increase in commercial rents, we were able to negotiate a ten-year office lease at a reasonable rate before rents began to rise.

(v.) 預見
幸好我們公司預見辦公室租金會急速升高，我們才得以在租金上漲前，以合理價格談定了十年的辦公室租約。

0034

forgetful

[fɚˋgɛtfəl]

必
反 **mindful**
名 **forgetfulness**
動 **forget** 同 **bury**
　　　　　　反 **remember**
副 **forgetfully**
動詞三態
forget, forgot, forgotten

Alexandra is very **forgetful**, which cost her her job after she forgot to lock up the office when she left on Friday evening.

(a.) 健忘的
亞歷珊卓很健忘，她週五晚上下班忘記鎖辦公室，害她丟了工作。

0035

free delivery

[fri dɪˋlɪvərɪ]

Everyone in our office likes to order lunch from the Chinese takeout restaurant down the street because the food is tasty and they offer free delivery for orders over $20.

免費運送
我們辦公室的人都喜歡跟街上那家中國外賣餐廳訂午餐，因為東西好吃，而且訂購二十美元以上還有免費外送。

0036

freelancer

[ˋfriˌlænsɚ]

名 **freelancer**
動 **freelance**

Fred worked as a freelancer for years, but finally took a job at a large company so that he could enjoy the benefits of health insurance and a pension plan.

(n.) 自由工作者
福瑞德先生做過多年自由工作者，但最後在一家大公司工作，以便能享受健保和退休金這些福利。

0037

freight

[fret]

讀

Luckily, the **freight** shipping cost was not determined by weight but instead by size, so the final price was very reasonable.

(n.) 貨運（非快遞），貨物

幸好貨運費用不是以重量計算，而是以尺寸計，所以最後的價格很合理。

0038

frequently

[ˈfrikwəntlɪ]

必

同 often

形 frequent 反 infrequent

動 frequent 同 patronize

名 frequenter

Employees who are **frequently** late to work or leave before the scheduled time, and fail to make improvements after receiving a warning, may be terminated.

(adv.) 頻繁地

動不動就遲到早退的員工，在接受警告後又未見改進，可能會被解雇。

0039

fulfill

[fuˈfɪl]

必

同 accomplish

名 fulfillment

Employees who **fulfill** all the terms of their employment agreement will be eligible to receive a year-end bonus and stock options.

(v.) 實現，履行

完全履行雇用合約條款的員工，將能獲得年終獎金以及認股權。

0040

fulfillment

[fuˈfɪlmənt]

必

同 accomplishment

The turnaround time for **fulfillment** of orders at our firm is currently five working days; it is our goal to reduce this time to three days.

(n.) 實現，履行

目前我們公司完成訂單所需的時間是五個工作天，我們的目標是減至三天。

0041

function

[ˈfʌŋkʃən]

必
同 **purpose**
動 **function**
　反 operate, work
形 **functional**

The **function** of a human resources department is to ensure that a company has a talented, highly motivated employee base and that suitable candidates are selected for each position.

(n.) 功能

人力資源部門的功能是要確保公司擁有才華洋溢且高度積極的員工群，也要確保每個職位都由合適人選來擔任。

0042

fund

[fʌnd]

必

Five percent of each employee's monthly salary will be automatically placed in the company retirement **fund**.

(n.) 基金，資金

每名員工月薪的 5% 將自動被放進公司的退休基金。

0043

fund

[fʌnd]

必

As our company does not have sufficient capital to **fund** further growth, the CEO plans to take the company public early next year.

(v.) 提供資金

因為我們公司沒有足夠資本來挹注進一步的成長，執行長計畫在明年提早讓公司上市。

0044

furthermore

[ˈfɝðəˌmor]

同 **moreover**

We believe that you have not yet been with the company long enough to be considered for a management position, and **furthermore**, we don't have any management openings at this time.

(adv.) 再者，而且

我們認為你在公司服務的時間不夠久，不足以被考慮擔任管理職，再者，目前的管理職位沒有空缺。

New

T
O
E
I
C

新多益高分關鍵字彙

990

G

Group

0001

garment
[ˈgɑrmənt]

必
同 clothes, wear
動 garment 同 clothe

The market for domestically produced **garments** has really been booming since people started becoming more leery about buying goods made in China.

(n.) 服裝，衣著
自從人們對於購買中國製造的貨品開始變得更加猜疑，國產服裝的市場已是一片繁榮。

0002

gather
[ˈgæðə]

必
同 put together, collect
反 spread, distribute
名 gather, gathering

The company will be conducting an internal survey to **gather** information on areas of company operations that are in need of improvement.

(v.) 蒐集
這家公司將進行內部調查，針對公司運作需要改善的方面，加以蒐集資訊。

0003

general
[ˈdʒɛnərəl]

必
同 broad, universal
反 particular, specific
副 generally
動 generalize 反 specify
形 generalized
名 generalization

The **general** consensus among employees is that the new computer operating system is much more user-friendly than the previous one.

(a.) 普遍的，全體的，籠統的
雇員之間普遍的共識是，新的電腦作業系統比先前的更易於使用。

0004

generalize
[ˈdʒɛnərəˌlaɪz]

必
反 specify

I hate to **generalize**, but I have always felt that people who work in upper management are out of touch with the needs of rank-and-file employees.

(v.) 泛指，泛稱
我不想要一竿子打翻一船人，但我總覺得上層管理階層的人，完全不懂得一般員工的需要。

0005

generate
[ˋdʒɛnəˌret]
必
同 bring forth, produce, create
名 generation, generator

Our goal for this year's charity bazaar is to **generate** enough funds to be able to open a small facility for the homeless.

(v.) 產生
我們今年慈善義賣的目標是帶來足夠的資金，開設小型的遊民之家。

0006

get back to
[gɛt bæk tə]

I'm sorry to say that I'm not authorized to give discounts; I'll have to ask my supervisor and **get back to** you later.

回覆
抱歉我無權提供折扣；我得先去請示上司，再向你回覆。

0007

get in touch
[gɛt ɪn tʌtʃ]
必

None of our office equipment needs servicing at this time, but we will be sure to **get in touch** with you if the need arises.

聯絡
我們的辦公室設備目前均無須保養，但若有需要，我們一定會跟你聯絡。

0008

get out of
[gɛt aʊt əv]
必

There is no way I can **get out of** this meeting today, so I'm afraid we'll have to reschedule our appointment.

抽身，離開
今天這會議我絕對無法抽身，所以我恐怕我們得要重新約時間見面。

0009

give and take
[gɪv ænd tek]

A willingness to **give and take** on the part of both parties ensured that an agreement was reached quickly.

互相讓步
雙方願意互相讓步，確保了協議得以快速達成。

0010

give up
[gɪv ʌp]
必
同 surrender

Although this last year has been frustrating because of the economic slump, I advise you not to **give up**; you have natural talent for sales.

放棄，死心
儘管過去這一年因為經濟上振而讓人洩氣，但我建議你別放棄，你有銷售的天份。

0011

glimpse
[glɪmps]
必
同 **sighting, sight, glance, peep, peek**
動 **glimpse** 同 spot, sight

The automaker's concept car on display at the auto show provided attendees with a **glimpse** at the firm's future design direction.

(n.) 瞥見
這家車廠在車展中展出的概念車，讓參觀者一窺這家公司未來的設計走向。

0012

go ahead
[go əˋhɛd]
必

The home appliance company decided to **go ahead** with plans to build a new production facility to meet growing demand for their products.

取得進展，繼續做
這個家電公司決定按照計畫興建新的量產設施，以滿足其產品日益增加的需求。

0013

go by the book
[go baɪ ðə bʊk]

Be sure to **go by the book** when you conduct your investigation into this information leak, because what you turn up will probably result in a lawsuit.

照章辦事

當你調查這起資料外洩案時，務必照章辦事，因為你的發現八成將以對簿公堂作結。

0014

go on
[go ɑn]

It is the responsibility of department managers to know what is **going on** in their departments at all times.

發生

部門經理的責任是時時知悉部門內的狀況。

0015

go public
[go ˋpʌblɪk]

Although the company had done very well for years as a privately-owned business, they decided to **go public** in the fall.

股票上市，公開

儘管這家公司多年來是績效非常好的未上市公司，他們依然決定在秋天公開上市。

0016

go through a difficult time
[go θru ə ˋdɪfəˌkəlt taɪm]

The company is **going though a difficult time**, and I regret to inform you all that we will be forced to make layoffs in the coming months if business does not improve.

歷經千辛萬苦

公司正處於難關，我很遺憾要通知大家，若是未來幾個月生意沒有起色，我們將被迫裁員。

0017

goal

[gol]

必
同 **target, aim, end**

The basic **goals** of most businesses are to sell products or services, increase revenues, decrease expenses, and expand their market share.

(n.) 目標
大部分公司行號的基本目標都是販售產品或服務、增加營收、減低開支與拓展市占率。

0018

groundwork

[ˋgraʊndˌwɝk]

同 **foundation, base, cornerstone**

During a series of initial meetings, representatives from both companies laid the **groundwork** for merger negotiations.

(n.) 根基，底子
在一系列初步會議上，兩家公司的代表替合併案的協商奠定了根基。

0019

guarantee

[ˌgærənˋti]

同 **warranty**
動 **guarantee**
　　同 assure

We offer a standard 30-day money-back **guarantee** on all of our products, but in special circumstances, we may extend that to a 60-day guarantee.

(n.) 保證
我們對所有產品均提供標準三十天無條件退費的滿意保證，但在特殊情況下，或許會延長至六十天滿意保證。

0020

guidance

[ˋgaɪdn̩s]

必
同 **counsel, direction**
名 **guide** 　同 leader
動 **guide** 　同 lead

Hughes Brothers is a full-service investment firm that specializes in providing financial **guidance** to high net worth investors.

(n.) 指導，輔導
休斯兄弟是一家全方位服務的投資公司，專門提供高淨值投資人財務指導。

0021

guide
[gaɪd]
必
同 lead

The president did an excellent job of **guiding** his company through the recession, and was therefore given a generous bonus by the board of directors.

(v.) 帶領，指導
這位總裁成功帶領公司度過經濟蕭條，因而獲得董事會發給豐厚的紅利。

0022

guideline
[ˋgaɪd͵laɪn]
同 road map

The company has clear **guidelines** for the investigation of alleged code of conduct violations, which include a safe, confidential process for interviewing employees without penalizing them or jeopardizing their jobs.

(n.) 指導方針
這家公司對於涉嫌違反行為規範的調查，明訂出指導方針，其中包括以安全且機密的過程來訪談員工，不會造成其損害或危害其工作。

New
TOEIC 990 新多益 高分關鍵字彙

New

新多益高分關鍵字彙

T
O
E
I
C

990

H

Group

0001

habit
[ˈhæbɪt]
必
同 wont
形 habitual
同 accustomed, customary

Employees are encouraged to develop good work **habits**, including arriving to work on time, maintaining a good attendance record, dressing appropriately, and following instructions.

(n.) 習慣
員工被鼓勵去發展良好的工作習慣,包括準時上班、維持高出席率、穿著合宜以及遵守指示。

0002

habitual
[həˈbɪtʃuəl]
同 accustomed, customary

While Doug was competent in his work and well-liked by his coworkers, he was eventually fired because of his **habitual** tardiness.

(a.) 習慣的,慣常的
雖然道格對他的工作勝任愉快,也很受到同事喜愛,但由於他習慣性拖拖拉拉,最後還是被解雇。

0003

hamper
[ˈhæmpɚ]
必
同 halter, cramp
名 hamper
同 shackle

I wouldn't discuss your fear of talking in front of audiences with anyone, as it could **hamper** your chances of getting a promotion.

(v.) 妨礙
我不會跟別人討論你害怕在觀眾面前說話,因為這可能會妨礙你升遷的機會。

0004

hand in
[hænd ɪn]
聽
同 submit

After completing the job application form, please review the information you have provided for completeness and accuracy and **hand** it **in** at the front desk.

繳交,提出
填寫完應徵工作表格後,請檢查你提供的資訊是否完整無誤,並繳交至櫃臺。

0005

hang up
[hæŋ ʌp]
聽

We're sorry, but the number you are trying to reach is currently busy; please **hang up** and try your call again later.

掛斷電話
很抱歉，您撥打的電話號碼目前忙線中；請掛斷稍後再撥。

0006

have yet to
[hæv jɛt tə]

I **have yet to** discuss your concerns with the sales director, but trust me, I will talk to him as soon as I get the chance.

尚待
我還沒和業務主管討論你的疑慮，但是相信我，我一有機會就會跟他說。

0007

hedge fund
[hɛdʒ fʌnd]

A small portion of the business profits were invested into a **hedge fund** each year, but not enough that it would effect business operations if the fund performed poorly.

對沖基金
這家公司每年將小部分的獲利投資於對沖基金，但就算基金表現不佳，也不至於影響公司的運作。

0008

hesitate
[ˈhɛzəˌtet]

必
同 waver
名 hesitation, hesitance, hesitancy
 vacillation, wavering
形 hesitant, hesitating
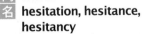 vacillating, wavering, uncertain

If you have any questions regarding your new checking account, or any banking questions in general, please do not **hesitate** to call our toll-free customer service number.

(v.)猶豫
若你對你新的支票帳戶或其他銀行業務有任何問題，請勿猶豫，直接撥打我們的免費客服號碼。

0009

high-ranking
[ˋhaɪˏræŋkɪŋ]

The **high-ranking** official was ushered into his waiting limo and whisked away to his hotel suite.

(a.) 高階的
這位高官被引領到等候他的禮車，立即開往他的飯店套房。

0010

hire
[haɪr]
必
同 employ

I believe our company is **hiring** part-time secretaries and base-level technicians at the moment if you know anyone who might be interested.

(v.) 雇用
若你知道誰或許有興趣，我想我們公司正在招聘兼職祕書以及基層技師。

0011

hit the streets
[hɪt ðə strits]

After a series of production delays and delivery problems, the new product line finally **hit the streets** in late October last year.

上市
經過連串的量產延遲與運送問題，新的產品線終於在去年十月底上市。

0012

hold
[hold]
必 聽
名 holder   同 possessor

The president will be **holding** a press conference this afternoon to field questions from the media in regard to the closure of several production facilities.

(v.) 舉辦，持有
總裁將在今天下午舉行記者招待會，回答媒體關於幾處生產設施關門的問題。

0013

hold
[hold]
同 **hang on**

Please **hold** the line and someone will be with you momentarily; your call is important to us.

(v.) 不掛斷電話
請勿掛斷電話，稍後將有專人接聽；我們很重視您的來電。

0014

hospitality
[ˌhɑspɪˋtælətɪ]
同 **reception, affability, cordiality**
反 **inhospitality**
形 **hospitable**
　　同 cordial, congenial
形 **hostile**
　　反 friendly, amiable
副 **hostilely**

After studying **hospitality** and food service management in college, Katherine found a position in the catering department of a four-star hotel.

(n.) 好客
在大學攻讀旅館與餐飲管理後，凱薩琳在一家四星級飯店的外燴部門找到工作。

0015

housekeeper
[ˋhaʊsˌkipɚ]
必
同 **housemaid**
動 **housekeep**
形 **housekeeping**

Our hotel is currently seeking an experienced **housekeeper** to supervise our housekeeping team and check all rooms for cleanliness on a daily basis.

(n.) 佣人領班，管家
我們飯店正在徵求有經驗的領班，每日監督打掃小組以及檢查所有客房的整潔。

0016

human resources
[ˋhjumən rɪˋsorsɪz]

The goal of the **Human Resources** Department is to continually assess the organization's human resource needs in light of organizational goals and implement policies to insure that a stable, competent workforce is employed.

人力資源
人力資源部門的目標是按照組織的目標來持續評估組織的人力資源需求，並且執行政策以確保雇用了穩定、有能力的人力。

New TOEIC990 新多益 高分關鍵字彙

New

TOEIC

新多益高分關鍵字彙

990

IJK

Group

0001

ideal
[aɪˋdiəl]

必
同 perfect
名 ideal　　同 model
動 idealize　同 glorify
形 idealist, idealistic
副 ideally, idealistically

The **ideal** candidate for the accounting director position will be someone with a bachelor's degree in accounting, a CPA license and at least 5 years of supervisory experience.

(a.) 理想的，空想的
會計主任這職位的理想人選將是擁有會計學士文憑、會計師執照，以及至少五年的管理經驗。

0002

idealize
[aɪˋdiəl͵aɪz]

必
同 glorify

While many businesspeople **idealize** free market capitalism, a certain level of government intervention is necessary to prevent monopolies and ensure that competition occurs on a level playing field.

(v.) 理想化
儘管許多生意人理想化了資本主義的自由市場，但某種程度的政府干預實屬必要，以避免壟斷，並確保彼此在公平的立足點上競爭。

0003

identifiable
[aɪˋdɛntə͵faɪəbl]

必
同 recognizable
動 identify　同 recognize, name
名 identity, identification

A product differentiation strategy for mass market goods is most likely to be effective when consumers care about the product and there are **identifiable** differences between brands.

(a.) 可認明的，可識別的
產品區隔的策略要在大眾市場商品中奏效，多半得靠消費者在意產品，而品牌之間又具有可識別的差異性。

0004

identify
[aɪˋdɛntə͵faɪ]

必 聽 讀
同 recognize, name

The first step in targeting markets is to **identify** market segments by dividing general markets into smaller groupings based on selected characteristics or variables shared by those in the group.

(v.) 確認，識別
確定目標市場的第一步是要確認市場區隔，方法是按照所選的特色或是變數，將一般市場區分成較小的群組。

0005

ignore
[ɪgˋnor]

必
同 **neglect, disregard**
反 **note, notice**
形 **ignorant**
　　同 illiterate, uneducated
名 **ignorance**
　　同 stupidity 反 knowledge

Increasing numbers of women are now playing video games, and if our game developers continue to **ignore** this trend, we will miss out on an important market opportunity.

(v.) 忽視，不理會
現在有越來越多的女性打電動，若是我們電玩研發者繼續忽視此一趨勢，將會錯失一個重要商機。

0006

illuminate
[ɪˋluməˏnet]

必
同 **brighten, enlighten**
反 **darken, obscure**
名 **illumination**
　　同 clarification, light
形 **illuminating**
　　同 enlightening
形 **illuminated**

I would like you to **illuminate** the inventory problem for us, as I understand that you have firsthand knowledge of this issue.

(v.) 闡明，照亮
我想請你替我們闡述存貨問題，因為我知道你對此議題有第一手的知識。

0007

immediate supervisor
[ɪˋmidɪɪt ˏsupɚˋvaɪzɚ]

Employee grievances about working conditions should be brought to the attention of their **immediate supervisor** within ten days of the date of the circumstances giving rise to the complaint.

直屬上司
員工對於工作環境的抱怨，應在此情況開始造成抱怨當天的十天內，呈報給直屬長官知悉。

0008

impact
[ˋɪmpækt]

必
同 **influence, consequences**
動 **impact**

When news of the company's pending sale was leaked, the **impact** was felt throughout the organization, from upper management to entry-level employees.

(n.) 衝擊
當公司轉賣在即的消息走漏後，從上層管理單位到基層員工，組織上下都感受到衝擊。

0009

impact on…

[`ɪmpækt ɑn]

I'm afraid last quarter's dip in sales will have a serious **impact on** this year's figures if we can't find some way to boost sales this quarter.

對…造成衝擊
若我們找不出方法提振這一季的銷售，恐怕上一季的銷售下滑會對今年的數字造成嚴重的衝擊。

0010

implement

[`ɪmplə,mɛnt]

聽
同 enforce, carry out
名 implement
名 implementation

Soon after joining the firm, the new CFO **implemented** an aggressive restructuring plan in an attempt to quickly improve the firm's financial performance and thus increase its value as an acquisition target.

(v.) 執行
新任財務長加入公司後不久，便執行積極的重整計畫，以求快速改善公司的財務表現，進而提高公司的收購價。

0011

imply

[ɪm`plaɪ]

必
同 connote, hint
名 implication

While I am no big fan of Jessica's work style, please don't think that what I said about her at last week's meeting was meant to **imply** that she has been lax in her duties.

(v.) 暗示
雖然我不很欣賞潔西卡的工作風格，但請別認為我在上週開會時說到她，就是在暗示她怠忽職守。

0012

import

[ɪm`port]

反 export
名 import, importation
　　反 export, exportation
名 importer

We will soon be closing down our domestic production facilities, as we have found that it will be cheaper to have our products produced by an overseas OEM manufacturer and then **import** and distribute them locally.

(v.) 進口
我們即將關閉我們的國內生產設施，因為我們發現，請海外代工廠製造我們的產品，然後再進口至本地分銷，成本將會比較低。

0013

impose

[ɪm`poz]

必
同 **enforce, inflict**
名 **imposition**
　同 inflection

I don't mean to **impose**, but if you have a moment, I would like to tell you about our company's new line of high-quality, low-priced office supplies.

(v.) 打擾，強加

我無意打擾，但若你有空，我想跟你說說敝公司高品質低價的新系列辦公室用品。

0014

imposition

[ˌɪmpə`zɪʃən]

必
同 **inflection**

While it is natural to think of sales calls as an **imposition** on others, if you're offering your customer something they truly need or want, you're actually doing them a service.

(n.) 強加，強迫接受

儘管推銷電話很自然會被看做是強迫他人接受，但若你提供的是客戶真正需要或想要的東西，那麼你其實是在服務他們。

0015

impress

[ɪm`prɛs]

必
同 **strike, affect**
名 **impression**
　同 notion, feeling, opinion
形 **impressive**
　同 moving, telling
　反 unimpressive

In a bid to **impress** the prospective client, Bill wore his best suit on the sales visit, and brought free samples of a number of his company's best-selling products.

(v.) 使印象深刻

為了打動潛在的客戶，比爾穿上他最好的西裝去業務拜訪，還帶了公司許多熱銷產品的免費樣本。

0016

impression

[ɪm`prɛʃən]

必
同 **notion, feeling, opinion**

While Michael felt he had left a good **impression** on the interview committee, he received a call the following week informing him that the position had been given to another applicant.

(n.) 印象

儘管麥可覺得他給面試委員會留下了好印象，但他隔週接到電話，通知他說那個職位已經給了別位應徵者。

0017

impressive
[ɪm`prɛsɪv]

聽 讀
同 moving, telling
反 unimpressive

In spite of his **impressive** sales record, Robert was passed over for promotion to Sales Manager in favor of a coworker with better teamwork and communication skills.

(a.) 令人印象深刻的

儘管羅伯的銷售紀錄令人驚豔，但他未獲拔擢升任業務經理，而是給了在團隊合作與溝通技巧上表現更佳的同事。

0018

improvement
[ɪm`pruvmənt]

同 advance, betterment
反 decline
動 improve
　同 better, amend

We would really like to make some **improvements** to management procedures, because the current procedures have proved ineffective in coordinating the activities of the various departments.

(n.) 改善，進步

我們很想要改善管理流程，因為目前的流程證明了無法有效協調不同部門的活動。

0019

in case
[ɪn kes]

In case you haven't heard of George Hall yet, I assure you that he has an excellent reputation in the corporate training field.

免得，萬一

為免你沒聽說過喬治霍爾，我向你保證他在公司訓練領域大名鼎鼎。

0020

in common
[ɪn `kɑmən]

While the two employees had a lot **in common**, they still found it difficult to cooperate effectively on team projects.

有共通點

雖然這兩名員工有許多共通點，但他們依然認為很難在團隊企畫中有效合作。

0021

in depth
[ɪn dɛpθ]
必

I just want to touch on all the key topics right now, and then I'll go into each one **in depth** over the course of the next few hours.

深入地，全面地

現在我想先提一下所有關鍵主題，然後在接下來幾小時內逐一深入詳述。

0022

in the red
[ɪn ðə rɛd]

The mom-and-pop business has been operating **in the red** for the past five years, but they decided to stick with it because it was the family business.

呈現赤字，負債

這傳統小生意的運作在過去五年來都虧損，但他們決定撐下去，因為這是家族事業。

0023

incentive
[ɪnˋsɛntɪv]
同 inducement, motivator
反 deterrence, disincentive

One thing you want to make sure of when you're looking for a good sales job is that there are good sales **incentives** in place.

(n.) 激勵因素

尋找業務工作時，最好要確定公司有完善的業績獎勵政策。

0024

inclined
[ɪnˋklaɪnd]
同 liable, likely
反 disinclined
動 incline
　同 tend, lean
片 be inclined to 有⋯傾向

After looking at a number of economic indicators, I am **inclined** to believe that the current economic slump will continue for at least three more quarters.

(a.) 有⋯傾向的

在看過許多經濟指標後，我傾向相信目前的經濟衰退起碼還將持續三季。

0025

inconsiderate
[ˌɪnkənˈsɪdərɪt]

必
同 selfish, self-centered
反 considerate
副 inconsiderately
名 inconsideration,
   inconsiderateness
   同 thoughtlessness

John is such an **inconsiderate** person that none of his colleagues are willing to work with him on the same project team.

(a.) 不體貼的

約翰非常不體貼，沒有同事願意和他在同一個企畫小組共事。

0026

incorporate
[ɪnˈkɔrpəˌret]

必
同 integrate
形 incorporated
   同 integrated, merged
名 incorporation
   同 integration, unifying

In order to continue to develop and grow, a company must be able to **incorporate** the latest management practices and technological advances.

(v.) 納入

為了繼續成長發展，公司務必要納入最新的管理作為和科技革新。

0027

incorporation
[ɪnˌkɔrpəˈreʃən]

必
同 integration, unifying

With the assistance of an **incorporation** service agency, the entire incorporation process can be completed in only a few days for a reasonable fee.

(n.) 成立公司，納入

透過一家成立公司服務單位的協助，成立公司的整個過程只需幾天便可完成，而且費用很合理。

0028

increase
[ɪnˈkris]

同 gain, addition
反 decrease
動 increase
   同 extend, enhance
形 increasing   反 decreasing
副 increasingly
   同 progressively

The steady **increase** in sales over the last three years has provided us with the capital necessary to implement an aggressive growth plan for the coming year.

(n.) 增加

三年來銷售穩定增加，已提供我們在來年執行積極成長大計所需的資金。

0029

increasingly
[ɪnˋkrisɪŋlɪ]

The manager became **increasingly** disturbed by the reports he was receiving of office infighting.

(adv.) 漸增地
經理接獲辦公室內鬥的報告，變得更加煩惱。

0030

incur
[ɪnˋkɝ]
必
同 **provoke, induce, arouse**

In order to avoid **incurring** a late penalty, we must be sure to ship this product within the next three days.

(v.) 招致，惹來
為了避免招致延遲處罰，我們務必要在未來三天內將這產品送運。

0031

indicate
[ˋɪndəˏket]
必
同 **point, designate, show**
形 **indicative**
　　同 indicatory, suggestive
名 **indicator**
　　同 index, pointer, benchmark

A recent market survey **indicates** that there is a strong demand for renewable energy among both consumers and businesses.

(v.) 顯示，指示
最近一項市場調查顯示，消費者和商家都對可更生能源有強烈需求。

0032

indicative
[ɪnˋdɪkətɪv]
讀
同 **indicatory, suggestive**

I would definitely say that these figures are **indicative** of an economic slump, so we should take immediate measures to streamline our operations and reduce costs and expenses.

(a.) 表示的，暗示的
我可以肯定地說，這些數據就是經濟衰退的象徵，所以我們應該立即採取行動，精簡我們的運作並降低成本與開銷。

.0033

indicator
[ˋɪndə͵ketə]
必
同 index, pointer, benchmark

It is commonly believed that the stock market is a leading **indicator** of how the economy as a whole will perform six to nine months in the future.

(n.) 指標
一般認為，股市是整體經濟未來六到九個月表現的領先指標。

.0034

indirect
[͵ɪndəˋrɛkt]
同 secondary
反 direct
名 indirectness

Links to your website not only have the direct benefit of leading new visitors to your site, but also the **indirect** benefit of increasing your site's search engine ranking.

(a.) 間接的
網站連結不僅有帶領新訪客到你網站的直接好處，同時也有提高你的網站在搜尋引擎排名的間接好處。

.0035

individual
[͵ɪndəˋvɪdʒʊəl]
必
同 single
反 collective
名 individual　　反 group
副 individually
名 individuality, individualism
動 individualize
　　同 personalize

The decision by that frozen food company to package its food products in **individual** servings was ingenious; their sales have risen over 30% since they began selling this new line of products.

(a.) 個別的，個體的
那家冷凍食品公司決定單一分裝產品真是天大的好主意；自從他們開始販賣這新系列產品，他們的銷售已成長超過 30%。

.0036

induce
[ɪnˋdjus]
同 stimulate, cause
名 inducement
　　同 incentive, motivator
形 inducible

Cardholders sued the credit card company for using deceptive marketing practices to **induce** consumers to open credit card accounts.

(v.) 誘導
持卡人控告信用卡公司利用欺騙的行銷手法，誘導消費者開信用卡帳戶。

0037

industry

[ˋɪndəstrɪ]

同 **trade, business**
形 **industrial**
形 **industrialized**
名 **industrialization**

The Mexican auto parts **industry** has been strongly affected by the economic slowdown in the United States, which is the major market for its products.

(n.) 產業
墨西哥的汽車零件業已嚴重受到美國經濟遲緩的影響，美國是其產品主要的市場。

0038

infer

[ɪnˋfɝ]

聽 讀
同 **deduce, derive, deduct**
名 **inference** 同 deduction
形 **inferential** 同 illative

I suppose you could **infer** from her comments that the engineer was inept, but I must say that I question the value of her opinion.

(v.) 推論
我猜你能從她的評論中推論出那個工程師很無能，但我得要說，我質疑她所提意見的價值。

0039

influence

[ˋɪnflʊəns]

必
同 **affect**
名 **influence** 同 result, effect
形 **influential**
　　同 important, powerful
片 **under the influence**

To become an effective salesperson, you must understand the factors that **influence** customers to purchase products and services.

(v.) 影響
為了成為有戰鬥力的業務員，你必須瞭解影響消費者購買產品和服務的因素。

0040

influx

[ˋɪnflʌks]

必
同 **inflow**

An **influx** of orders left the main office pleasantly surprised, and before they knew it, it was necessary to increase production in order to meet demand.

(n.) 湧進，注入
訂單一波波湧進，使得總辦公室大感驚喜，轉眼之間，就已經需要增加產量來因應需求。

0041

inform

[ɪn`fɔrm]

聽
同 notify, tell
形 informed
　同 knowledgeable
　反 uninformed
形 informative
　同 instructive
　反 uninformative
名 information 同 facts, news

There are no vacancies in our telemarketing department at present, but we will **inform** you if any openings become available.

(v.) 通知
我們的電話行銷部門目前沒有空缺，但若有任何職缺，我們將會通知你。

0042

informative

[ɪn`fɔrmətɪv]

讀
同 instructive
反 uninformative

The speaker at the management seminar gave a highly **informative** presentation on retail management and strategic planning.

(a.) 提供有益資訊的
這位演講人在管理研討會上針對零售管理以及策略規畫，提出了資料豐富的報告。

0043

informed decision

[ɪn`fɔrmd dɪ`sɪʒən]

In order to ensure customer satisfaction, we always give them all the information necessary to make an **informed decision** prior to purchasing our products.

充分知情的決定
為了確保顧客滿意，我們都會先提供必要資訊，好讓他們在購買我們的產品前，做出充分知情的決定。

0044

ingredient

[ɪn`gridɪənt]
必

In the United States, food manufacturers are required by law to list all the **ingredients** in their products on the product packaging.

(n.) 成分
在美國，食品製造商依法規定要將產品中的所有成分，列在產品包裝上。

0045

inhalation
[ˌɪnhə`leʃən]

同 **intake**
反 **exhalation**
動 **inhale**　同 exhale

After the office was evacuated by firefighters, several employees were taken to the hospital and treated for smoke **inhalation**.

(n.) 吸入
消防隊員淨空辦公室後，幾名員工被送往醫院，治療濃煙吸入嗆傷。

0046

initiate
[ɪ`nɪʃɪˌet]

必
同 **originate, start**
名 **initiation**
　同 installation, founding
名 **initiative**
　同 ambition, drive

In addition to voluntary bankruptcy filed by a debtor, a creditor can also **initiate** bankruptcy proceedings against a debtor.

(v.) 起始
除了債務人自願申請破產外，債權人也可主動對債務人提出破產訴訟。

0047

initiative
[ɪ`nɪʃətɪv]

必
同 **ambition, drive**

Employees are encouraged to take the **initiative** in identifying problems and proposing solutions, instead of waiting passively for instructions from their superiors.

(n.) 主動權，倡議
員工被鼓勵去主動找出問題並提出解決方案，而非被動等待上司的指示。

0048

inquire
[ɪn`kwaɪr]

聽 讀
同 **ask, enquire**
名 **inquiry**
　同 enquiry, investigation

If you plan on holding a convention at our hotel's convention center, please call at least one month in advance to **inquire** about the availability of meeting rooms.

(v.) 詢問，調查
若你打算在敝飯店的會議中心舉行會議，請至少提前一個月來電詢問會議室有無空檔。

0049

inquiry
[ɪnˋkwaɪrɪ]
 聽 讀

The members of our customer service team are trained to handle all product **inquiries** and technical support questions promptly and efficiently.

(n.) 詢問，調查
我們的客服小組成員都受過訓練，可以立即處理所有關於產品的詢問以及技術支援的問題。

0050

insight
[ˋɪn͵saɪt]
 perceptiveness, discernment
形 insightful
　同 perceptive

Our company recently conducted a market survey to gain **insight** into the minds of consumers across various age groups, income levels and gender.

(n.) 洞見
我們公司最近進行了市場調查，以深刻瞭解各個年齡層、收入及性別的消費者心理。

0051

insightful
[ˋɪn͵saɪtfəl]
 perceptive

The recently hired consultant has provided our marketing department with **insightful** advice on how to increase the effectiveness of marketing campaigns.

(a.) 有洞見的
最近受雇的顧問提供我們行銷部門精闢見解，建議我們要如何增加行銷宣傳的效力。

0052

inspect
[ɪnˋspɛkt]
必
 examine
名 inspection
　 investigation, scrutiny

All products are carefully **inspected** for flaws prior to shipping to insure that customers receive only the highest quality merchandise.

(v.) 檢查，審查
所有產品在運送前均經悉心檢查有無瑕疵，以確保顧客只會收到最高品質的商品。

0053

inspection
[ɪn`spɛkʃən]
必
同 investigation, scrutiny

An **inspection** of the manufacturing plant is scheduled for early next week, but the inspectors did not give a specific time, so we should have everything ready by Monday at the latest.

(n.) 檢查，審查
生產工廠的檢查訂在下週初開始，但是檢查員並未指明時間，所以我們最遲要在週一前將一切就緒。

0054

inspiration
[ˌɪnspə`reʃən]
同 idea, thought
動 inspire 同 stimulate, spur
形 inspiring 同 uplifting
　　　　　　 反 uninspiring
形 inspired 同 stimulated
　　　　　　 反 uninspired

The **inspiration** for the new line of tropical floral print bathing suits came to the designer while she was on vacation in Hawaii.

(n.) 靈感
這新系列熱帶印花泳裝的靈感，來自這位女設計師去夏威夷度假時。

0055

inspire
[ɪn`spaɪr]
必
同 stimulate, spur

Carol's positive attitude and dedication to her work has **inspired** everyone on her team to set higher goals for themselves and devote their full efforts to achieving them.

(v.) 啟發
卡蘿積極的態度以及對工作的投入，啟發了小組中的每一個人，為自己設下更高的目標，並投注全力來達成。

0056

install
[ɪn`stɔl]
同 set up
名 installation
　　同 instalment, facility
名 instalment

The company has decided to **install** a new customer relationship management software package in order to gather, store, and access customer information more efficiently.

(v.) 安裝
這家公司決定安裝一套新的顧客關係管理軟體，以便更有效率地蒐集、儲存、取用顧客資訊。

0057

instigate

[ˈɪnstəˌget]

同 incite, set off

名 instigation
　同 abetment

名 instigator

When a group of dissatisfied customers hired a lawyer to **instigate** a lawsuit, the company decided that it would be in their best interests to settle out of court.

(v.) 煽動，唆使

當一群不滿意的顧客雇用律師來興訟，這家公司決定庭外和解最符合公司的利益。

0058

instinct

[ˈɪnstɪŋkt]

必
同 impulse, intuition
形 instinct
形 instinctive
副 instinctively

The CEO's keen business **instinct**, honed through long years of experience, enabled him to spot and take advantage of market opportunities before his competitors became aware of them.

(n.) 直覺，本能

這位執行長多年經驗所磨練出的敏銳生意直覺，讓他得以在對手察覺之前，就發現商機並加以利用。

0059

instruction sheet

[ɪnˈstrʌkʃən ʃit]

All new employees were provided with an **instruction sheet** to familiarize them with company policies, guidelines, and procedures.

說明書

所有新員工都會拿到說明書，以便熟悉公司政策、準則與流程。

0060

instrument

[ˈɪnstrəmənt]

必

Our company manufactures and distributes precision surgical **instruments** for all operating procedures in primary and secondary healthcare.

(n.) 儀器

我們公司製造、經銷精準的外科儀器，提供一級和二級醫療機構所有的手術程序來使用。

insufficient

[ˌɪnsəˈfɪʃənt]

讀
同 **deficient**
反 **sufficient**
副 **insufficiently**
名 **insufficiency**

The company's limited financial resources and **insufficient** warehouse space prevented it from keeping sufficient supplies in stock or retaining, on a permanent basis, an adequate, knowledgeable sales staff.

(a.) 不足的，不適任的

這家公司有限的財務資源以及倉庫空間不足，使其無法維持充足的庫存，長期來看，也無法留住適任、有見地的業務人員。

insulate

[ˈɪnsəˌlet]

同 **isolate**
名 **insulation, insulator**
形 **insulated**

Every box needs to be **insulated** from heat and cold in order to ensure that the perishable fruits and vegetables will still be fresh upon arrival.

(v.) 使絕緣

每個箱子都必須與冷熱隔絕，以確保易腐爛的蔬果在送達時依然新鮮。

insurance carrier

[ɪnˈʃurəns ˈkærɪə]

聽
同 **insurance company**
相關字彙
　　insurance policy 保單
　　premium 保險金

The **insurance carrier** sent a representative to the company to see if any of the employees had questions about recent changes to their policies.

保險公司

這家保險公司派了一名代表來公司，瞭解員工是否對最近保單的變更有疑問。

integral

[ˈɪntəgrəl]

必
同 **built-in, constitutional**
反 **inessential**
形 **integrable**
名 **integrality**

The Internet has become an **integral** business tool for many companies, enabling them to communicate with potential customers around the world and open new distribution channels for their products.

(a.) 不可或缺的，整體的

網路已經成為許多公司不可或缺的生意工具，使他們得以和世界各地的潛在客戶聯絡，並且替產品開闢出新的經銷管道。

0065

intend
[ɪn`tɛnd]

必
同 mean
形 intent 同 earnest, absorbed
名 intent 同 aim, purpose
名 intention
　　同 aim, intent, purpose
形 intentional 同 knowing
　　　　　　　反 unintentional
副 intentionally 同 deliberately

We **intend** to launch our new line of luxury cell phones this fall, and have already made distribution arrangements with a number of high-end department stores.

(v.) 意欲，打算
我們打算在今秋推出新系列的豪華手機，並已和一些高檔百貨公司談定了經銷協議。

0066

intent
[ɪn`tɛnt]

必
同 aim, purpose

The **intent** of this meeting is to review the progress each department has made in implementing the new quality management system.

(n.) 意圖
這次會議的用意是檢討每個部門執行新品管系統的進展。

0067

intention
[ɪn`tɛnʃən]

必
同 aim, purpose

Laura went to her boss with the **intention** of submitting her resignation, but her boss convinced her to stay by giving her a large raise.

(n.) 用意
蘿拉去找老闆的用意是遞辭呈，但她老闆用大幅加薪，說服她留了下來。

0068

interaction
[ˌɪntə`ækʃən]

必
動 interact
形 interactive 同 interactional

Please remember to be very careful in any **interaction** you have with the press, because they will try their best to get you to reveal company secrets.

(n.) 互動
請記住，和媒體的任何互動一定要非常小心，因為他們會盡其所能讓你洩漏公司的機密。

0069

internship

[ˋɪntɜn͵ʃɪp]
動 名 **intern**

Alice's **internship** would be ending in a few months, but she didn't think the company would invite her to stay on afterwards.

(n.) 見習，實習

愛麗絲的見習在幾個月後就會結束，但她不認為公司之後會邀她留下。

0070

intervene

[͵ɪntəˋvin]
聽
同 **interfere, interpose**
名 **intervention**
　　同 intercession, interposition
　　反 noninterference
形 **intervening**

When negotiations between the two parties dissolved into argument, the designated mediator **intervened** and got the discussion back on track.

(v.) 干涉，介入

當雙方的協商化為爭執，指定調停人介入，讓討論重回正軌。

0071

inventory

[ˋɪnvən͵torɪ]
必 聽
同 **stock**

An **inventory** revealed that the company was turning over merchandise at a rapid rate, but strangely, this was not reflected in the sales figures.

(n.) 存貨

存貨顯示這家公司的商品周轉得很快，但奇怪的是這並未反映在銷售數字上。

0072

invest

[ɪnˋvɛst]
必
同 **commit, put, place**
名 **investment**
　　同 investing, funding
名 **investor**
　　同 shareholder, capitalist

In order to continue coming up with useful new products, our company plans to **invest** 10% of revenues in research and development over the next five years.

(v.) 投資

為了繼續想出有用的新產品，我們公司計畫在未來五年投資 10% 的營收來進行研發。

0073

investigation
[ɪnˌvɛstəˈgeʃən]

必
同 **probe**
名 **investigator**
　　同 inspector, detective
動 **investigate**
　　同 scrutinize, look into
形 **investigatory**

An **investigation** uncovered the source of the information leak, and the guilty party was promptly fired for breach of contract.

(n.) 調查
一項調查找出了資訊外洩的源頭，而罪方立即因毀約而被解雇。

 0074

investigator
[ɪnˈvɛstəˌgetə]

同 **inspector, detective**

A police **investigator** visited our office last week to ask questions about a coworker in our department who has been reported missing.

(n.) 調查員
警方一名調查員上週來我們辦公室問案，事關我們部門一位被報案失蹤的同事。

 0075

investment
[ɪnˈvɛstmənt]

必
同 **investing, funding**

Mutual funds are always considered to be a sound **investment**, but I believe that we should diversify our portfolio with bonds and other fixed income securities.

(n.) 投資
共同基金始終被認為是穩當的投資，但我認為我們應該讓投資組合更多樣化，納入債券和其他固定收益證券。

0076

invoice
[ˈɪnvɔɪs]

聽 讀
同 **bill, account**
動 **invoice**

Please retain the **invoice** included with your shipment as proof of purchase, as it will be required if you decide to return or exchange your purchase.

(n.) 發票
請保留隨貨附上的發票做為購買證明，因為若你決定退換貨將需要發票。

0077

irrelevant to

[ɪˋrɛləvənt tə]

形 **irrelevant**
　同 unconnected
反 **relevant**
名 **irrelevance**

While it may seem **irrelevant to** the matter at hand, the employees are very concerned about the delay in receiving last month's salary.

與…無涉、無關

儘管這似乎和手邊的問題無關，但員工都很關心上個月薪水遲發的事。

0078

irritate

[ˋɪrəˌtet]

必
同 **annoy, vex**
名 **irritation**
　同 annoyance, botheration, vexation
形 **irritable**
　同 peevish, petulant
形 **irritating** 同 nettlesome

Poorly targeted and **irrelevant** business e-mails are likely to irritate customers and end up unread in their trash folders.

(v.) 激怒

亂槍打鳥又不相關的商業電子郵件，可能會激怒顧客，落得連看都不看就被丟進垃圾信件匣。

0079

irritation

[ˌɪrəˋteʃən]

必
同 **annoyance, botheration, vexation**

The company's new hand lotion was taken off the market after many customers complained that it caused skin **irritation**.

(n.) 發炎反應，激怒

這家公司新的護手乳液被許多顧客抱怨會造成皮膚發炎，因而下架。

0080

isolate

[ˋaɪsəˌlet]

同 **insulate, keep apart**
名 **isolation**
　同 separation, closing off
形 **isolated**
　同 detached, separated

After using a diagnostic program to **isolate** the source of the network problem, the IT technician resolved the issue by installing a new router.

(v.) 使孤立

利用診斷程式將網路問題的源頭分離出來之後，這位資訊部技師安裝新的路由器，解決了問題。

0081

item

[ˈaɪtəm]

同 object, article

When all **item**s on the invoice have been received, please send the signed pink copy of the purchase order to our accounting department.

(n.) 物件，品項

發票上所列的物品都收到後，請在購物訂單的粉紅色那張簽名，並寄至我們的會計部門。

0082

itinerary

[aɪˈtɪnəˌrɛrɪ]

同 route, path

Please take a look at our **itinerary** for the upcoming business trip; should you have any questions, please feel free to ask me.

(n.) 行程路線

請參看即將來臨的出差行程；若有任何問題，儘管問我。

0083

joint venture

[dʒɔɪnt ˈvɛntʃə]

The **joint venture** between the two businesses was a great success, so the two parties considered cooperating again at a later date.

合資企業

這兩家公司的合資企業大獲成功，所以雙方考慮以後再次合作。

0084

judgment

[ˈdʒʌdʒmənt]

同 assessment

名 judge
　同 judiciary, evaluator

動 judge　　同 evaluate

形 judgmental
　同 critical
　反 nonjudgmental

While our company code of conduct provides general guidelines for employee conduct, it is up to each individual to use good **judgment** in dealing with fellow employees, customers, and suppliers.

(n.) 判斷

儘管我們公司的行為規範替員工的行為提供了通則，但如何和同事、客戶和供應商往來，還是要靠個人運用良好的判斷。

0085

justify
[ˈdʒʌstəˌfaɪ]
聽 讀
同 **warrant**
名 **justification**
形 **justifiable**
反 **indefensible**

Please don't try to **justify** your performance on this project, because I am sure that if you had wanted to, you could have done a better job.

(v.) 正當化，辯解
請不要嘗試辯解你在這個企畫案的表現，因為我確定若你想要做，你可以做得更好。

0086

keep up with
[kip ʌp wɪð]
必

Our computer engineers are encouraged to attend IT conferences and read trade journals in order to **keep up** with new developments in the field.

趕上（趨勢）
我們的電腦工程師被鼓勵參與資訊技術研討會，並閱讀業內的雜誌，以便趕上業界的新發展。

0087

key
[ki]
同 **solution, answer**
形 **key**　　同 crucial, principal

We believe that the **key** to our company's success is our ability to keep in touch with our customers' needs and provide them with products and services that fulfill these needs.

(n.) 關鍵
我們相信公司成功的關鍵在於，我們有能力切中顧客的需要，並且提供產品與服務來滿足這些需求。

0088

kickback
[ˈkɪkˌbæk]
同 **bribe, payoff**

Government investigators are probing allegations that the medical equipment manufacturer made illegal **kickbacks** to hospitals that purchase its products.

(n.) 回扣
政府調查人員正在探究一些指控：醫療器材商給予購買其產品的醫院非法回扣。

New
TOEIC 990 新多益 高分關鍵字彙

New
TOEIC
新多益高分關鍵字彙
990

L
Group

0001

layout
[ˈleˌaʊt]
必
同 formation, design

The **layout** of our product catalog has been simplified to make it easier for customers to quickly find the items they are looking for.

(n.) 版面編排

我們產品型錄的排版已經簡化，方便顧客更快找到他們要的產品。

0002

lead time
[lid taɪm]
必

Our goal for the coming year is to enhance competitiveness by reducing the **lead time** between order and delivery of our products.

前置時間

我們來年的目標是增加競爭力，方法是縮短從訂單到送貨間的前置時間。

0003

lean
[lin]
聽
同 thin
動 lean　　反 tilt
片 lean against...

After several **lean** years, the auto manufacturer was on the verge of bankruptcy and accepted a buyout offer from one of its rivals.

(a.) 收益差的，貧乏的

在幾年的慘淡經營後，這家車廠瀕臨破產，並接受其中一家對手的收購提議。

0004

lease
[lis]
必
同 letting, rental
動 lease　　反 rent

The building **lease** has a 10-year term, and grants to the tenant an option to purchase the building at any time during said term at a price not to exceed $2,250,000, plus increases based on a multiple of the consumer price index.

(n.) 租約

這棟建築打了十年的租約，並准予承租人在此期間內可選擇購買此建築，價格保證不超過二百二十五萬，外加基於消費者物價指數的倍數增加。

0005

legislation

[ˌlɛdʒɪsˈleʃən]

聽 讀
同 **law, lawmaking**
名 **legislator**
動 **legislate** 同 pass
形 **legislative**

We have hired a tax consultant to advise our accounting department on how to comply with the new tax **legislation**.

(n.) 立法，法規
我們雇用了稅務顧問來建議我們的會計部門如何遵守新的稅務法規。

0006

leisure

[ˈliʒɚ]

必
同 **spare time, recreation**
形 副 **leisurely**
　　同 easygoing, at leisure
　　反 hurried

Our company has added a new line of outdoor **leisure** products, including garden furniture, patio umbrellas, beach umbrellas, beach chairs, and camping equipment.

(n.) 休閒，閒暇
我們公司增加了新系列的戶外休閒產品，包括花園家具、露台大陽傘、海灘陽傘、海灘椅和露營裝備。

0007

lengthy

[ˈlɛŋθɪ]

必
同 **extended, prolonged, protracted**
反 **brief**
名 **lengthiness**

It was a **lengthy** process to convince the media to cover the product launch party, but the free exposure we gained made our efforts worthwhile.

(a.) 冗長的
說服媒體報導產品上市派對，是一個冗長的過程，但這免費曝光讓我們的辛苦很值得。

0008

level

[ˈlɛvl]

必
同 **degree, grade**
形 **level** 同 flat
動 **level** 同 dismantle

Peter's high **level** of fluency in both Mandarin and English, as well as his many years of overseas experience, made him a valuable asset to the international law firm.

(n.) 程度，等級
彼得的中英文高度流利，再加上他在海外的多年經驗，使他成為這家國際法律事務所的珍貴資產。

0009

liability
[ˌlaɪəˈbɪlətɪ]
 必讀
同 **indebtedness**
形 **liable**
　　同 answerable, obligated

The CEO instructed the accounting department to compile a complete list of company assets and **liabilities** for the upcoming meeting with the auditor.

(n.) 債務，責任
執行長指示會計部彙整完整的公司資產負債表單，以供即將與審計員會面之用。

0010

liable
[ˈlaɪəbḷ]
同 **answerable, obligated**

The tenant is **liable** for all replacements and repairs that are outside what is considered normal wear and tear, as defined in this lease.

(a.) 具法律責任的，有義務的
承租人於法有義務更換、修復租約中被定義為自然損耗之外的所有東西。

0011

license
[ˈlaɪsṇs]
必
同 **permit**
動 **license**
　　同 permit

Merchants who knowingly sell cigarettes or alcohol to minors may have their business **license** suspended or revoked, and will be subject to a heavy fine.

(n.) 執照
故意販售菸酒給未成年人的商家，營業執照可能會遭吊扣或吊銷，還可能被處以高額罰金。

0012

limit
[ˈlɪmɪt]
必
同 **restriction, limitation**
動 **limit**　　同 restrict, confine
名 **limitation**
形 **limited**　　同 restricted
　　　　　　反 unlimited
形 **limitless**　同 infinite, endless

If I remember correctly, there is a **limit** to how many items you can purchase at an employee discount price in the course of a year.

(n.) 限制
若我沒記錯的話，你在一年之間能用員工價購買的東西有數目限制。

0013

link

[lɪŋk]

必

Many retail chains are using supply chain management to forge stronger **links** with their suppliers and reduce costs.

(n.) 連結

許多零售連鎖店正運用供應鏈管理,來增強與供應商的連結並降低成本。

0014

list

[lɪst]

必

The **list** of candidates for the promotion was submitted to upper management for review, and then a final series of interviews was conducted to determine who would receive the promotion.

(n.) 表單

升職候選人的名單被送交管理高層審核,然後要進行一系列的最後訪談,以決定誰將獲得升職。

0015

load

[lod]

聽

同 **loading, burden**

動 **load** 　 同 **load up, lade**
　　　　　 反 **unload**

形 **loaded**

相關字彙 **workload** 工作量

Our cargo ships are capable of carrying **loads** of up to 100 metric tons to any major port around the world.

(n.) 載貨,承載

我們的貨船有高達一百立方噸的載貨量,運往全球任何主要港口。

0016

lobby

[ˈlɑbɪ]

必

同 **hall**

動 **lobby** 　 同 **campaign**

名 **lobbyist**

When you arrive at the convention center, simply stop by the registration table in the **lobby** to pick up your registration packet, which will include your program booklet, name tag, meal ickets, and registration receipt.

(n.) 大廳;遊說團

你抵達會議中心時,直接去大廳的報到桌領取你的報到資料袋,裡頭將包括節目手冊、名牌、餐券和報名收據。

0017

locate
[lo`ket]
聽
同 **place, situate**
名 **location**　同 place

We will have to **locate** an appropriate building site for a new, larger production facility, as the current facility is incapable of meeting the increased demand for our products.

(v.) 找出所在位置
我們必須找出建造更大新生產設施的適合地點，因為目前的設施已無法滿足我們產品日益增加的需求。

0018

location
[lo`keʃən]
必
同 **place**

The new shopping mall downtown would be an excellent **location** to open a new store, but with rents being so high, it would be difficult to turn a profit.

(n.) 地點
市中心新的購物中心將是開設新店面的絕佳地點，但是房租這麼高，很難獲利。

0019

lock in
[lɑk ɪn]
必

We wanted to switch to a cheaper supplier, but were unable to because we were **locked into** a 3-year contract with our original supplier.

鎖住，使受限
我們想要換用更便宜的供應商，但是沒辦法，因為我們受限於和原本的供應商簽下的三年契約。

0020

logical
[`lɑdʒɪkl]
必
同 **rational**
反 **illogical**
副 **logically**
名 **logic**　同 reason

The corporation was so far in debt that the only **logical** choice was to declare bankruptcy and sell off all their assets to repay creditors.

(a.) 合邏輯的，合理的
這家公司深陷債務中，唯一合理的選擇就是宣告破產，並賣掉所有資產來償還債權人。

0021

long-term
[`lɔŋ,tɝm]
必

We are slowly developing a **long-term** relationship with many of our clientele, and our revenues are growing steadily as a result.

(a.) 長期的
我們正慢慢發展與許多客戶的長期關係,我們的營收也因而持續成長。

0022

look forward to
[luk `fɔrwəd tə]
必

I am thrilled to be offered a position at your law office, and I eagerly **look forward to** working with all of the fine lawyers at your firm.

期待
我很興奮能在貴律師事務所獲得一份職位,我也熱切期待和貴事務所所有優秀律師共事。

0023

look out
[luk aut]

When company management looks out for the interests of employees, employees are more likely to **look out** for the company's interests.

小心注意
公司管理階層顧及員工的利益,員工也比較可能會顧及公司的利益。

0024

look over
[luk `ovə]

We've **looked over** your résumé and feel that you're well qualified for our sales opening; would it be possible for you to come in for an interview next Monday?

詳查,瀏覽
我們看過了你的履歷,也感覺你很有資格填補我們的業務職缺,你下週一方便過來面試嗎?

0025

look up to
[luk ʌp tə]
必

Jeff really **looks up to** his older brother who is a corporate lawyer in a big firm in Chicago, and has decided to attend law school after graduating from university.

尊敬

傑夫很尊重他在芝加哥一家大律師事務所當公司法律師的哥哥，也已經決定大學畢業後要去唸法學院。

0026

loyal
[ˈlɔɪəl]
必
同 **faithful**
反 **disloyal**
名 **loyalty**
　 同 **faithfulness, trueness**

The low-cost airline launched a new frequent flyer program to reward **loyal** customers and raise its competitive edge in the industry.

(a.) 忠實的，忠誠的

這家低價航空公司推出了新的酬賓計畫，用以回饋忠實的顧客，並提升其於業界的競爭優勢。

0027

luggage
[ˈlʌgɪdʒ]
聽
同 **baggage**

For short business trips, we advise our employees to take only carry-on luggage, as carry-on **luggage** is less likely to get lost or stolen than check-in luggage.

(n.) 行李

以短程出差而言，我們建議員工只攜帶手提行李，因為手提行李比起托運的行李，較不容易弄丟或被偷。

New
TOEIC
990

新多益高分關鍵字彙

M
Group

0001

machinery
[mə`ʃinərɪ]

讀
同 equipment

With proper maintenance, most of the **machinery** at our factory can be used for many years without need for replacement.

(n.) 機械設備
靠著妥善的保養，我們工廠的機械設備大多能使用多年而無須更換。

0002

made of
[med əv]

必

I'm not really sure what this is **made of**; why don't you take it over to the R&D Department and have them take a look at it.

以⋯製成
我不確定這是用什麼做的；不如你把東西拿去研發部門，讓他們看一看。

0003

mailer
[`melə]

We sent out a new promotional **mailer** last month to all the customers on our mailing list, and the response has been excellent.

(n.) 郵寄的廣告
我們上個月寄了新的促銷廣告給郵寄清單上的所有客戶，反應很熱烈。

0004

maintain
[men`ten]

必
同 hold, keep
名 maintenance
  同 care
  反 desertion, forsaking

Please try your best to **maintain** a professional tone in any correspondence you send out to your customers.

(v.) 維持
在寄給客戶的所有信件中，請盡力維持專業的口吻。

0005

maintenance
[ˈmentənəns]
同 care
反 desertion, forsaking

The best way to keep your computer running smoothly is to spend a few minutes each month performing routine **maintenance**.

(n.) 維持，保養
保持電腦運作順利最好的方法，就是每個月花幾分鐘做例行的保養。

0006

majority
[məˈdʒɔrətɪ]

The **majority** of board members believe the current president has done a very poor job while in office, and have decided to demand his resignation.

(n.) 絕大多數，過半數
董事會大多數的成員都認為現任董事長在職務上的表現很差，並已決定要求他辭職。

0007

manage
[ˈmænɪdʒ]
必

David did an excellent job of **managing** the sales staff and coordinating marketing activities, and as a result was promoted to VP of Sales.

(v.) 管理
大衛在管理業務人員與協調行銷活動方面，表現優異，因而被晉升為業務副總。

0008

mandatory
[ˈmændəˌtorɪ]
必

Attendance at the meeting this afternoon is **mandatory** for all IT Department employees, so please clear your schedule from 2 to 4 pm.

(a.) 強制的，義務性的
資訊部員工都要強制出席今天下午的會議，所以請空出下午兩點到四點的時間。

0009

manufacture

[ˌmænjəˈfæktʃə]

同 **produce, construct**
名 **manufacture**
　同 producer, maker
名 **manufacturer**
形 **manufacturing**

If you agree to **manufacture** this product for us, we are willing to offer you sole manufacturing rights.

(v.) 製造
若你同意替我們製造這個產品，我們願意提供你獨家製造權。

0010

manufacturer

[ˌmænjəˈfæktʃərə]

讀
同 **producer, maker**

The **manufacturer** had some questions about potential design flaws in the new product, so they got in contact with the R&D department at the contracting company.

(n.) 製造業者，廠商
這家製造商對於新產品可能的設計瑕疵有些疑問，所以他們聯繫承包公司的研發部門。

0011

manuscript

[ˈmænjəˌskrɪpt]

聽 讀
相關字彙 **transcript** 副本
　　　　 script 底稿、筆跡

After reading the young author's **manuscript**, the editor at the large publishing house decided to publish his work.

(n.) 原稿，手稿
讀過這位年輕作家的手稿後，這位任職大型出版公司的編輯決定出版他的作品。

0012

market

[ˈmɑrkɪt]

必
同 **marketplace**
動 **market**
　同 sell, promote, retail
名 **marketing**
　同 merchandising, selling
形 **marketable**

As the domestic **market** for plumbing supplies is completely saturated, we are considering expanding into overseas markets.

(n.) 市場
因為水電管用品的國內市場已經完全飽和，我們正考慮擴展至海外市場。

0013

marketing

[ˈmɑrkɪtɪŋ]

必
同 **merchandising, selling**

As an intern in our **Marketing** Department, you will work closely with members of our marketing staff to develop and execute marketing strategy.

(n.) 行銷
身為我們行銷部的見習生，你將和行銷人員緊密共事，開發並執行行銷策略。

0014

match

[mætʃ]

必
同 **fit, correspond**
名 **match**
　　同 equal, peer
形 **matching**
　　同 paired
形 **matchless**
　　同 unmatched, peerless

My job as a corporate recruiter is to **match** employee skills and experience to the specific positions that my corporate clients are looking to fill.

(v.) 使搭配，比對
我身為企業人才招募者的工作是替我的公司客戶想填補的特定職缺，找到適合的員工技術與經驗。

0015

material

[məˈtɪrɪəl]

聽

It doesn't really matter what kind of **material** you choose to use as long as it has been approved by the international standards agency.

(n.) 資料，原料
你決定使用哪種原料其實不很重要，只要通過國際標準局批准即可。

0016

matter

[ˈmætə]

必 聽 讀
同 **count, weigh**
名 **matter** 　同 affair, thing
片 **no matter** 無論

We must figure out what **matters** most to our customers and do our best to deliver it to them on a consistent basis.

(v.) 要緊
我們必須釐清什麼對我們的顧客最要緊，並盡力持續達成。

0017

matter

[ˈmætɚ]

同 affair, thing

Martin asked his supervisor if he could take the afternoon off so that he could take care of a personal **matter**.

(n.) 問題，事項
馬丁問上司下午能否請假，好處理一件私事。

0018

means

[minz]

聽 讀
同 method, way
片 by all means... 當然地
　 by no means 不可能
　 by means of... 靠…方法

Internet access is becoming increasingly important to businesses because it gives them the **means** to more effectively communicate with business partners, conduct research, and gather information.

(n.) 手段，方法
網路使用對公司行號正益加變得重要，因為這給他們一個管道去更有效地和生意伙伴溝通、進行研究與蒐集資訊。

0019

measure

[ˈmɛʒɚ]

聽
同 assess
名 measure 同 size
名 measurement
片 take measures 採取手段

By using standard metrics to **measure** our business performance against that of comparable organizations, we have been able to pinpoint areas where improvement is needed.

(v.) 測量
使用標準的衡量指標來測量我們相對於同類組織的生意表現，我們得以精確點出需要改進的方面。

0020

mechanic

[məˈkænɪk]

聽
形 mechanical
名 mechanics
動 mechanize

The company has a full-time team of experienced **mechanics** to repair and service its large fleet of delivery trucks.

(n.) 技工，修理工
這家公司擁有經驗老到的全職技工團隊，負責貨車大隊的保修。

0021

mention
[ˋmɛnʃən]

必
同 **point out, note**
名 **mention** 同 reference
形 **mentionable**
片 **not to mention**

Please don't **mention** this to our manager, but I will be giving my two-weeks notice in a day or two.

(v.) 提及
請別跟經理提到這件事，但我一、兩天後會提出兩週前預告的辭職通知。

0022

mentor
[ˋmɛntɚ]

必
同 **counsellor, adviser**

When starting a new job, it is best to find a **mentor** to show you the ropes and help you adapt to your new work environment.

(n.) 良師
開始新工作時，最好找一個良師帶著你進入狀況，並協助你適應新的工作環境。

0023

merchandise
[ˋmɝtʃənˏdaɪz]

必 聽
同 **product, ware, goods**
動 **merchandise** 同 trade
名 **merchandiser** 同 merchant
形 **merchandising**
　　同 marketing, selling

In order to obtain a full refund, all **merchandise** ordered from our company must be returned within 14 days in its original packaging.

(n.) 商品，製品
要獲得全額退費，從我們公司訂貨的商品需在十四天內以原包裝退回。

0024

merchant
[ˋmɝtʃənt]

聽

Merchants who sell goods and services on the Internet are taxed at a different rate than those who sell their wares in brick-and-mortar stores.

(n.) 商人，零售商
在網路上販售商品與服務的商家被課徵的稅率，不同於在實體店面賣東西的人。

0025

merge
[mɜdʒ]

讀
同 unify, unite
形 merging 同 confluent
名 mergence
名 merger 同 amalgamation
相關字彙 merge and
acquisition 併購

The two businesses discussed **merging**, but the proposed deal was scrapped due to strong opposition from a number of key shareholders on both sides.

(v.) 合併

這兩家公司討論要合併，但因為雙方都有一些關鍵股東強力反對，所提的交易便作廢。

0026

merger
[ˈmɜdʒə]

讀
同 amalgamation

The CEOs of the two companies held a joint press conference to announce the upcoming **merger** of their companies and answer questions from the media.

(n.)（公司）合併

這兩家公司的執行長召開了聯合記者會，宣布他們公司即將合併，並回答媒體的問題。

0027

merit
[ˈmɛrɪt]

必
同 virtue
反 demerit
形 meritorious

While both proposals have their **merits**, I think it will be easier to make modifications to our existing product rather than developing an entirely new product.

(n.) 優點，記功

儘管兩個提議都有優點，但我認為修改我們現有的產品，將比開發全新產品來得容易。

0028

method
[ˈmɛθəd]

必
同 approach
形 methodical
同 ordered, structured
名 methodology

Our company has invented a new and more effective **method** of converting analog signals into digital signals, and we are currently applying for a patent.

(n.) 方法，條理

我們公司已經發明出更有效的新方法，可以把類比訊號轉為數位訊號，我們目前正在申請專利。

0029

methodology

[ˌmɛθəˋdɑlədʒɪ]

必

That investment firm uses a proprietary **methodology** to measure the relative risks of different investment vehicles.

(n.) 方法論，教學法

那家投資公司使用獨有的方法來測量不同投資工具的相對風險。

0030

microscope

[ˋmaɪkrəˌskop]

聽

Ivan eventually quit his job because the work environment left him feeling like his every move was being scrutinized under a **microscope**.

(n.) 顯微鏡

艾文最後辭掉了工作，因為這工作環境讓他感覺自己的一舉一動都在顯微鏡底下被仔細檢查。

0031

mind

[maɪnd]

同 care

Jerry didn't **mind** working long hours of overtime at the accounting firm, because he knew this would increase his chances of becoming a partner.

(v.) 介意

傑瑞不介意在會計事務所長時間加班，因為他知道這將增加他成為合夥人的機會。

0032

minimal

[ˋmɪnəməl]

必

同 minimum

反 maximum

This week's remodeling will have to take place during normal work hours, but we will try to ensure that there is **minimal** disturbance to employees.

(a.) 最小的，極微的

本週的重新裝潢得在正常的上班時間進行，但我們將設法確保員工受到最少的打擾。

0033

minimize

[ˈmɪnəˌmaɪz]

必

同 shrink, diminish

In order to **minimize** the time necessary to process these documents, please make sure that all of your paperwork is in order.

(v.) 將…減到最小

為了將處理這些文件所需的時間減至最少，請確認所有文書資料都有按順序排好。

0034

minutes

[ˈmɪnɪts]

同 transactions

After reviewing the **minutes** of last Tuesday's meeting, I believe we'll need to hold another meeting this Thursday to touch on everything that wasn't covered.

(n.) 會議紀錄

審視過上週二的會議紀錄後，我認為我們週四必須再開一次會，處理上次沒有討論到的。

0035

missing

[ˈmɪsɪŋ]

必

同 absent

The **missing** project folder turned up on another employee's desk in a completely different department.

(a.) 失蹤的，缺少的

那個不見的企畫案資料夾後來出現在完全不同部門另一個員工的辦公桌上。

0036

mistake

[mɪˈstek]

必

同 error, fault

動 mistake　同 misidentify

形 mistaken

　同 misguided, wrong

副 mistakenly

Please accept my apologies for our **mistake**; we are making every effort to correct the situation, and will be happy to provide you with a full refund if you desire.

(n.) 錯誤

請接受我為我們的錯誤致歉；我們正盡全力修正這個情況，若你希望的話，我們也樂意提供你全額退費。

0037

mistaken

[mɪˋstekən]

必
同 **misguided, wrong**

If I am not **mistaken**, hard copies were made of all the important documentation related to the copyright infringement case.

(a.)（人）弄錯的，（事）被誤解的

若我沒弄錯的話，紙張複本都是與侵害版權案有關的重要文件。

0038

mix

[mɪks]

必
同 **blend, fusion**
動 **mix** 同 blend, merge

Due to changes in the marketplace, we are making adjustments to our products **mix**, adding a number of new items and discontinuing several less profitable products.

(n.) 混合，混合物

由於市場的變化，我們正在調整我們的產品組合，增加一些新的品項，並中斷幾樣獲利較低的產品。

0039

mixture

[ˋmɪkstʃɚ]

必
同 **mix**

Our employee training program consists of a **mixture** of workshops, lectures, group discussions and on-the-job training.

(n.) 混合，混合物

我們的員工訓練計畫由混合了研討會、授課、團體討論與在職訓練所構成。

0040

mix-up

[ˋmɪks͵ʌp]

必

After the reservation **mix-up** last year, we have decided to hold this year's corporate retreat at a different resort.

(n.) 搞混

在去年預約混亂之後，我們決定在另一個度假村舉辦今年的公司靜修營。

0041

modest
[ˋmɑdɪst]

聽
同 **moderate**
反 **immodest**
副 **modestly**
名 **modesty**

While Jennifer is **modest** about her abilities, everyone in the Sales Department knows she has the best performance record of all the sales reps.

(a.) 謙虛的，適度的
雖然珍妮佛對自己的能力很謙虛，但業務部的人都知道她是所有業務代表中業績最棒的。

0042

modification
[͵mɑdəfəˋkeʃən]

同 **adjustment, alteration**
動 **modify** 同 alter, change

With a few slight **modifications** to the user interface, I think this software package will have broad mass market appeal.

(n.) 修改
稍加修改使用介面，我認為這個套裝軟體對大眾市場將有廣泛的吸引力。

0043

modify
[ˋmɑdəͺfaɪ]

讀
同 **alter, change, revise**

I'm afraid that I'm not authorized to **modify** the terms of your sales contract; I'll have to check with my manager and get back to you later.

(v.) 修改
恐怕我無權修改你的銷售合約條款，我得和經理確定再回覆你。

0044

monitor
[ˋmɑnətə]

必
同 **supervise**
名 **monitor**

After **monitoring** the production facility for several days, the efficiency expert wrote a report detailing his recommendations for improvement and submitted it to company management.

(v.) 監測，監控
監控生產設施幾天後，效率專家寫了報告，詳述他的改善建議，並呈交給公司的管理部門。

0045

monogamy

[mə`nɑgəmɪ]

反 polygamy
形 monogamous
　反 polygamous

Among higher management, **monogamy** seems to be the rule, as a stable family life helps executives deal with the intense pressure they face in their work.

(n.) 一夫一妻制

在較高階的管理職中，一夫一妻似乎是通則，因為穩定的家庭生活有助於主管處理工作上面臨的密集壓力。

0046

monopoly

[mə`nɑplɪ]

動 monopoly
名 monopolist

The government tobacco company held a **monopoly** on tobacco imports that was only lifted a few years ago.

(n.) 壟斷，獨佔

政府的菸草公司壟斷菸草進口，在幾年前才解禁。

0047

monotony

[mə`nɑtənɪ]

同 humdrum, sameness
形 monotonous

The increasing use of industrial robots in manufacturing plants is helping to free human workers from the **monotony** of assembly line work.

(n.) 單調，千篇一律

製造工廠越來越大量使用工業機器人，協助工人免除單調的組裝線作業。

0048

mortgage

[`mɔrgɪdʒ]

必

The man's **mortgage** payments on his house were quite costly, and as a result, he decided to search for a higher paying job.

(n.) 房貸

這位男士的房屋貸款金額相當高，因此他決定去找薪水較高的工作。

0049

motivational

[ˌmotəˈveʃənəl]

名 motivation　同 motive
動 motivate　同 incite, prompt
形 motivating
形 motivated

We have hired a well-known **motivational** speaker to deliver the keynote speech at our annual sales conference next month.

(a.) 激發動機的

我們聘請一位知名的激勵演說家，來替我們下個月的年度業務大會發表主題演說。

0050

move up

[muv ʌp]

必

In the interests of **moving up** the corporate ladder, Joel took advanced classes in macroeconomics and international trade

提升

為了要在公司內層層高昇，喬爾去上總體經濟學和國際貿易的進階課。

0051

movement

[ˈmuvmənt]

同 motion, move
動 move

An upward **movement** in the price of pork bellies has forced us to adjust the pricing of our entire line of pork breakfast sausages.

(n.) 移動

豬肚的價格上揚，逼使我們調整全系列豬肉早餐香腸的訂價。

0052

multiple

[ˈmʌltəpl]

必
同 various, numerous
反 single
動 multiply

Although Joe received **multiple** requests for price quotes on products from potential clients, none of these requests resulted in sales.

(a.) 多重的

儘管喬接到來自潛在客戶多筆詢價，但全都沒有成交。

0053

mutual

[ˈmjutʃuəl]

相關字彙

mutual trust 相互信任
mutual understanding 相互理解
mutual interests 互利

After long months of negotiation, management and labor were finally able to reach an agreement based on the **mutual** interests of both parties.

(a.) 相互的，雙方的

經過漫長數月的協商後，管理階層與勞方終於在雙方互惠的基礎下，達成協議。

0054

mutual fund

[ˈmjutʃuəl fʌnd]

Funds in the company retirement plan are invested in a portfolio that includes stocks, treasury bonds, and **mutual funds**.

共同基金

公司退休計畫的基金是投資於包括有股票、長期公債和共同基金的投資組合。

New
TOEIC 990 新多益 高分關鍵字彙

New TOEIC

新多益高分關鍵字彙

990

N

Group

0001

narrow down
[ˈnæro daʊn]
必

We have **narrowed down** the list of long-distance service providers, and will be making a final decision on which company to go with next week.

縮減
我們縮減了長途（電話）服務供應商的清單，會在下週做出最後決定要採用哪家公司。

0002

negligence
[ˈnɛglɪdʒəns]
聽 讀
同 carelessness, neglect
動 neglect
形 negligent
副 negligently

Due to gross **negligence** on the part of the head office, none of the orders were delivered on time, and many did not meet client specifications.

(n.) 疏忽，過失
由於總公司的嚴重疏失，這些訂單全都沒有準時交貨，而且有許多都未達客戶指定的規格。

0003

negotiate
[nɪˈgoʃɪˌet]
必
同 bargain, talk terms
形 negotiable
名 negotiation
　同 talks
名 negotiator

When the contract with our key supplier comes up for renewal in two months, we will try to **negotiate** better payment and discount terms.

(v.) 協商，談判
兩個月後我們和主要供應商的契約要換新時，我們將設法協商出更好的付款與折扣條款。

0004

negotiation
[nɪˌgoʃɪˈeʃən]
必
同 talks

While it is widely believed that good **negotiation** skills are something people are born with, the truth is that you can learn to become a skilled negotiator through hard work and practice.

(n.) 協商，談判
儘管普遍認為好的談判技巧是天生的，但其實你可以透過努力和練習來學習成為有技巧的談判者。

0005

nervous

[ˋnɝvəs]

必
同 uneasy, anxious
副 nervously
名 nerve
名 nervousness

While it is natural to be **nervous** during a job interview, the more time you take to prepare for the interview, the less nervous you will be.

(a.) 感到緊張的

儘管在應徵工作面試時會緊張是很自然的,但你花越多時間準備面試,你就越不會緊張。

0006

network

[ˋnɛt͵wɝk]

必
名 network 同 web

Because the best jobs are rarely advertised, learning how to **network** is one of the most critical skills young professionals need to learn in order to advance their careers.

(v.) 維持人脈

因為最好的工作很少會登廣告,所以學習如何廣結人脈,是年輕專業人士必須學習的最關鍵技能之一,才能在事業上更上一層樓。

0007

no longer

[noˋlɔŋɚ]

反 still

Jane **no longer** kept up with all the latest technical specifications, so she knew her technical knowledge was becoming outdated.

不再

珍不再趕得上所有最新的技術規格,所以她知道自己的技術知識越來越過時了。

0008

no sooner...

[no ˋsunɚ]

No sooner had the consumer electronics company released its latest MP3 player than its competitors started producing cheap copies.

才一…就…

這家消費電子公司才一推出最新的 MP3 播放器,對手就開始製造便宜的複製品。

0009

not yet
[nɑt jɛt]

Although we have **not yet** started the advertising campaign for our new flat screen TV, news of the product has already been leaked to the media.

尚未

儘管我們尚未開始替我們新的平面電視做廣告宣傳，但這產品的消息已經被披露給媒體。

0010

notarize
[ˈnotəˌraɪz]
同 **certify**
名 **notarization**

All Chinese-language legal documents relating to the joint venture will need to be translated into English and **notarized** by a notary public.

(v.) 對⋯公證

所有關於此合資企業的中文法律文件，都必須翻譯成英文，並經公證人公證。

0011

notice
[ˈnotɪs]
 讀
同 **warning**
名 **notification**
　　同 notice
動 **notify**　同 inform
形 **noticeable**　同 evident, distinct
片 **take notice of...** 注意⋯
相關字彙 **without notice** 不另通知
　　　　one month notice
　　　　到期前一個月通知

If you do not remit payment by the due date printed on this invoice, you will receive a **notice** from us, and then a second reminder if payment is overdue by more than one month.

(n.) 通知

如果你在發貨單所載之到期日前未寄款，你將收到我們的一封通知，若付款延遲超過一個月，將會有第二封通知。

0012

notify
[ˈnotəˌfaɪ]
 必 聽 讀
同 **inform**

If we are unable to supply a particular item that you've ordered, we will **notify** you as soon as possible so that you can cancel your order or change to another available product.

(v.) 通知

若我們無法提供你所訂購的特定品項，我們將盡快通知你，好讓你能取消訂單或是換成其他可得的產品。

New

ToEIC

新多益高分關鍵字彙

990

O

Group

0001

obligate
[ˈɑbləˌget]
必
同 **oblige**
名 **obligation**
　　同 duty, responsibility
形 **obligatory**
　　同 necessary 反 optional
形 **obliged**　同 forced, required,
　　　　　　　　duty-bound

Customers are **obligated** to strictly limit the usage of products and/or information obtained from our firm in compliance with state and federal laws.

(v.) 使有義務
依照州及聯邦法律，顧客有義務嚴格限制自本公司取得的產品及資訊之使用。

0002

obligation
[ˌɑbləˈgeʃən]
必
同 **duty, responsibility**

We would like to offer you a free three-month trial subscription to our magazine; after the three month trial, you will have the option of continuing your subscription, but are under no **obligation** to do so.

(n.) 義務
我們願意提供你免費試閱三個月我們的雜誌；三個月試閱期後，你將可選擇續訂，但並無義務非這樣做不可。

0003

observe
[əbˈzɝv]
同 **detect, discover**
名 **observance**　同 survey
名 **observer**
名 **observant**
　　同 observing
形 **observatory**

During the on-the-job training program, instructors will be closely **observing** each intern's performance and providing them with needed instruction and guidance.

(v.) 觀察
在職訓練計畫期間，講師會仔細觀察每名實習生的表現，並提供他們必要的指導與諮詢。

0004

obsolete
[ˈɑbsəˌlit]
同 **passé, outdated**

The IT budget at our firm is spent mostly on maintaining existing IT equipment and replacing old equipment when it becomes **obsolete**.

(a.) 過時的，淘汰的
我們公司的資訊科技預算，大多花在維護現有的資訊科技設備，以及替換過時的舊設備。

0005

obstacle

[ˈɑbstəkl]

同 obstruction

One **obstacle** to implementing a global brand strategy is that it is extremely difficult to impose identical brand attributes in all markets.

(n.) 障礙

執行全球品牌策略的一個障礙是，很難用同一個品牌特質打遍所有市場。

0006

obstruct

[əbˈstrʌkt]

讀
同 block
名 obstruction
　　同 impediment
形 obstructive

Further expansion of the company's business has been **obstructed** by such factors as market saturation, a poor economy, and increased competition from new market entrants.

(v.) 堵塞，阻撓

這家公司生意進一步的擴展，受到市場飽和、經濟衰退以及市場新進對手增加等因素阻撓。

0007

obtain

[əbˈten]

必
同 gain, acquire
形 obtainable
　　同 procurable
　　反 unobtainable

The purpose of our feedback form is to **obtain** additional information from our clients that can be used to improve our products and services in the future.

(v.) 取得

我們意見回函的用意是要取得客戶的額外資訊，未來可以用於改善我們的產品與服務。

0008

obvious

[ˈɑbvɪəs]

必
同 apparent, visible
副 obviously　同 evidently

One **obvious** business advantage of setting up an office in Sydney is its proximity to Asian markets.

(a.) 明顯的

在雪梨設立辦公室的一個明顯生意優勢是，那兒鄰近亞洲市場。

0009

occupancy
[ˋɑkjəpənsɪ]

必
同 tenancy, occupation
名 occupation
動 occupy 同 inhabit
名 occupant
名 occupier

Due to recent bad weather and increased fears of terrorism, **occupancy** rates at local hotels have reached a record low of 30%.

(n.) 居住，佔有
由於最近氣候不佳，以及對恐怖主義的恐懼日增，本地飯店的住房率來到 30% 的歷史新低。

0010

occupy
[ˋɑkjəˏpaɪ]

同 inhabit

The technology start-up, which has a staff of 25 employees, **occupies** a 550 square meter office on the second floor of an office building in downtown San Jose.

(v.) 占地，佔領
這家擁有二十五名員工的新興科技公司，在聖荷西市中心一棟辦公大樓的二樓，佔據五百五十平方公尺的辦公室面積。

0011

occur
[əˋkɝ]

必
同 happen, take place
名 occurrence
同 happening
片 occur to someone
憶起，想起

If a toxic chemical spill were to **occur** at the plant, all personnel are expected to follow the emergency evacuation procedures.

(v.) 發生
萬一工廠發生有毒化學物質外洩，所有人員都應該遵照緊急疏散程序。

0012

offer
[ˋɔfɚ]

必
同 offering, proposal, suggestion
動 offer

Plateau Oil Co., the nation's largest oil company, has made an **offer** for rival Stillwell Oil, and has said that it plans to make a number of additional acquisitions over the coming year.

(n.) 提議
高原石油公司這國內最大的油公司，已向對手史提威油業開出提議，並表示計畫在來年進行另外數起的收購案。

0013

offset

[ˈɔfˌsɛt]

必

同 **cancel, set off**

名 **offset**

Key person life insurance can provide a "cash cushion" to help **offset** loss of profits if a key company executive dies, suffers a major illness or becomes disabled.

(v.) 抵銷

重要幹部壽險能提供「現金緩衝」，在公司重要主管死亡、罹患重病或殘障時，協助抵銷掉公司的利潤損失。

0014

on hand

[ɑn hænd]

必

Would you happen to have a copy of last year's turnover figures **on hand** so that we can compare them with this quarter's results and get an idea of our relative performance so far this year?

在手邊的

你手邊是否正好有去年營業額的數據，好讓我們用來比對這一季的結果，進而瞭解今年到目前為止的相對表現？

0015

on track

[ɑn træk]

必

The department head said he was quite pleased with our performance, as we seem to be **on track** to meet and exceed annual sales and profit targets.

朝著達成某事邁進

看來我們即將達到並超越年度銷售與獲利的目標，部門主管表示對我們的表現相當滿意。

0016

onboard

[ɑnˋbord]

必

Options on our new line of midsize sedans include leather seats, air conditioning, cruise control, 16-inch alloy rims and an **onboard** computer.

(a.) 車、船和飛機上的

我們新中型轎車系列的選配包括皮椅、冷暖空調、定速巡航、十六吋鋁圈和行車電腦。

0017

open to
[ˈopən tə]
必

While the Board of Directors is **open to** new perspectives that will help us enhance shareholder value, we do not believe that takeover by a larger firm would be in the company's best interests.

願意接受…，易招致…
雖然董事會願意接受任何有助於提高股東價值的新看法，但我們不認為接受大型企業併購會是對公司最有利的作法。

0018

operate
[ˈapəˌret]
必
同 run
名 operation
　　同 running, functioning, performance
名 operator
形 operational　　同 working

The mining company currently **operates** three open-pit gold mines, and is in the process of developing two underground silver mines.

(v.) 經營，管理
那間採礦公司目前經營三座露天開採的金礦礦坑，並正著手開發兩座地下銀礦礦坑。

0019

operation
[ˌapəˈreʃən]
必
同 running, functioning, performance

An **operation** of this size requires an extensive management team to guarantee that everything runs smoothly and efficiently.

(n.) 營運，運作
這種規模的營運需要龐大的經營團隊，以確保一切得以順利且有效率地進行。

0020

opportunity
[ˌapəˈtjunətɪ]
同 chance
名 opportunist 同 self-seeker

Because every kind of company, from small local businesses to large international corporations, requires the services of accounting professionals, graduates of accounting programs can look forward to excellent career **opportunities**.

(n.) 機會
因為從小型的本地公司到大型的國際企業，每一種公司都需要會計專業人才的服務，因此會計學術背景的畢業生可以期待有很好的工作機會。

0021

opt
[ɑpt]
必
同 choose,
名 option
　同 alternative, choice
形 optional
　同 elective
反 obligatory

The normal retirement age at our firm is 65; those over the age of 60 who **opt** for early retirement will have their annual benefits reduced by 10% for every full year remaining prior to normal retirement age.

(v.) 選擇
我們公司正常的退休年齡是六十五歲；超過六十歲而選擇提早退休的人，每提早退休年齡一年退休，年度分紅將扣掉百分之十。

0022

option
[ˈɑpʃən]
必
同 alternative, choice

For the convenience of our customers, we provide a variety of payment **options**, including online payment by credit card, personal checks, and money orders.

(n.) 選項，選擇
為了顧客的方便，我們提供多種付款方式的選擇，包括線上信用卡付款、私人支票以及匯票。

0023

optional
[ˈɑpʃənl̩]
必
同 elective
反 obligatory

For $50, we offer an **optional** two-year extended factory parts and labor warranty on all of our home appliances.

(a.) 可自由選擇的，非強制的
我們所有的家電用品皆可選購延長兩年原廠零件及人工保固期，費用五十元。

0024

orchestra
[ˈɔrkɪstrə]
形 orchestral

Prizes for this year's charity raffle include a luxury cruise, a 50-inch flat screen TV, a digital camera, a case of wine, and a pair of **orchestra** tickets.

(n.) 交響樂團，管弦樂團
今年慈善彩券的獎項包括豪華郵輪之旅、一台五十吋平面電視、一台數位相機、一箱葡萄酒，以及兩張交響樂音樂會門票。

0025

out of order
[aut əf `ɔrdə]
聽

Both of our copy machines are **out of order**, so you'll have to wait until after the repairman comes on Monday to make copies of that report.

故障
我們的兩台影印機都故障了，因此你必須等到維修人員週一過來後，才能影印那份報告。

0026

out of stock
[aut əf stɑk]
聽

That product and all the others in the same series are currently **out of stock**, but if you leave a contact number, I'll let you know when we get some in.

無庫存的
該產品以及其他同系列產品目前都沒有庫存，不過如果你留下連絡電話，貨到時會通知你。

0027

outdated
[ˌaut`detɪd]
必

Although great advances in computer technology have been made in the past few years, many organizations are still using **outdated** computer systems due to the high cost of switching to a new system.

(a.) 過時的，舊的
雖然在過去幾年電腦科技有顯著的進展，許多機構仍使用過時的電腦系統，因為改用新系統的花費很高。

0028

outgrow
[aut`gro]

Our company is beginning to **outgrow** our present office space, so we are beginning to draw up plans for the design and construction of a new facility.

(v.) 長大而上適用於
我們公司逐漸擴大而導致現有辦公空間不敷使用，所以我們要開始制定新辦公室設計與興建的計畫。

0029

outlet
[ˈaʊtˌlɛt]
必

In addition to designing and producing several lines of clothing for sale in department stores, we also sell our clothes directly at our two factory **outlets**.

(n.) 暢貨中心
除了設計和生產幾種服裝系列在百貨公司販賣，我們也在兩間工廠暢貨中心直接販賣我們的服裝。

0030

outline
[ˈaʊtˌlaɪn]

At the meeting, the head of the R&D department presented an **outline** of current and future product design projects.

(n.) 概要，要點
會議中，研發部門的主管提出目前和將來產品設計計畫的概要。

0031

output
[ˈaʊtˌpʊt]
聽
同 **production, turnout**

About 80% of the company's **output** is exported to North America, with the remainder being sold in Japan, Korea, and the PRC.

(n.) 產量
公司大約百分之八十的產量出口至北美，其餘則在日本、韓國以及中國銷售。

0032

outstanding
[aʊtˈstændɪŋ]
必 聽
同 **owing, undischarged**

The goal of our collection agency is to assist clients in the recovery of **outstanding** payments as quickly, effectively, and cost effectively as possible.

(a.) 懸而未決的
我們催收公司的目標是要協助客戶盡可能迅速、有效並節省成本地追討回未付款項。

0033

overall
[ˋovɚˏɔl]
必
同 in general
名 overall

Overall, I have been very pleased with our sales performance this quarter, but we do need to focus more on encouraging repeat business from existing customers and less on attracting new customers.

(adv.) 總的來說，大體上
整體而言，我對於我們這一季的銷售表現非常滿意，但是我們必須更把注意力放在鼓勵現有顧客重複消費，而非著重在吸引新顧客。

0034

overcrowded
[ˏovɚˋkraʊdɪd]
必
名 overcrowding

The laptop manufacturer's greatest challenge was how to make its products stand out in an increasingly competitive and **overcrowded** market.

(a.) 過度擁擠的
那家筆記型電腦製造商最大的挑戰在於，如何讓它們的產品在日益競爭且過度擁擠的市場中脫穎而出。

0035

overdue
[ˏovɚˋdju]
聽
同 delinquent

I sent a notice of **overdue** account to that client two weeks ago, but I haven't received a response from him yet.

(a.) 過期的，未兌現的
我兩週前寄了一封催繳通知給那位客戶，但尚未收到他的回覆。

0036

overlook
[ˏovɚˋlʊk]
聽
同 neglect, omit
反 notice

The supervisor **overlooked** the young employee's forgetfulness because he saw real talent and promise in the man.

(v.) 不介意，忽略
上司不介意那名年輕員工的健忘，因為他在此人身上見到真正的天分與潛力。

0037

overnight

[ˈovɚˌnaɪt]

聽
副 overnight

In regard to sales trips, you can expect at least one **overnight** stay per month, with the average being closer to two.

(a.) 過夜的

關於商務旅行，你可以預計每個月至少會有一次要停留過夜，平均可能接近兩次。

0038

oversight

[ˈovɚˌsaɪt]

同 lapse

An **oversight** by the planning committee caused several hundreds of thousands of dollars to be lost when the completion date for building had to be pushed back.

(n.) 疏忽出錯，失察

籌備委員會的疏忽導致了數十萬美元的損失，因為建築完工日被迫延期。

0039

overtime

[ˈovɚˌtaɪm]

聽
形 副 overtime

I put in 25 hours of **overtime** last month, and while I received time-and-a-half for it, it was really exhausting.

(n.) 加班，加班時間

我上個月申請二十五小時的加班，雖然得到一點五時薪的津貼，但那真的很累人。

0040

overview

[ˈovɚˌvju]

必 聽
同 summary, outline

Here is an **overview** of our company's current financial status; look it over first, and then I'll go into detail about each point in a few minutes.

(n.) 概況，總覽

這是我們公司目前財務狀況的概要，請先看過一遍，幾分鐘後我會逐一詳細說明。

0041

overwhelm

[ˌovɚˋhwɛlm]

同 **overcome**

形 **overwhelming**
　同 overpowering

副 **overwhelmingly**

Although Derek was **overwhelmed** by the increase in his workload, he tried to keep up to prove to upper management that they had promoted the right employee.

(v.) 壓倒

雖然戴瑞克被增加的工作量給壓得喘不過氣來，不過他努力堅持下去，好向上級主管證明拔擢他是正確的選擇。

0042

owe

[o]

必

片 **owing to...** 由於…

I believe you **owe** me an explanation for your behavior at the meeting yesterday; why did you just leave like that with no notice?

(v.) 應給予

我想你應該向我解釋昨天你在會議中的舉動；為什麼你沒有知會一聲就那樣離開了？

0043

owner

[ˋonɚ]

必

同 **holder, keeper**

The **owner** of the brown Opel returned to find that his car had been towed away after he parked in the CEO's space.

(n.) 所有人

那輛棕色歐寶的車主把車停在執行長的專用車位，回來後發現他的車已經被拖走了。

New
TOEIC
新多益高分關鍵字彙
990

P
Group

0001

palatable
[ˈpælətəbl]
同 **acceptable, satisfactory**
反 **unpalatable**
名 **palatability**

Special deductions for small businesses should make the new business tax more **palatable** to small business owners.

(a.) 可接受的，承受得住的
小型企業的特殊減免，應該會讓業者較能接受新制營業稅。

0002

parcel
[ˈpɑrsl]

When we opened the **parcel** from the software company, we discovered that they had sent the wrong software package, and had to return it to them for exchange.

(n.) 包裹
當我們打開軟體公司寄來的包裹，發現他們寄錯了軟體套件，所以必須退還給他們作更換。

0003

partially
[ˈpɑrʃəlɪ]
同 **partly**
形 **partial** 同 biased
反 **impartial**
名 **partiality** 同 fondness, fancy
反 **impartiality, nonpartisanship**

I am **partially** to blame for the recent increase in everyone's workload, as I was the one who suggested to the boss that we raise our sales targets and expand our customer service offerings.

(adv.) 部分地
最近大家工作量的增加，我要負部分責任，因為是我建議老闆提高銷售目標以及提供更廣泛的客戶服務。

0004

party
[ˈpɑrtɪ]
必
同 **side**

The **parties** involved in the business dispute decided to settle out of court in order to save on legal fees and reach a quick settlement.

(n.)（合約等的）一方
那起商業糾紛中的雙方決定庭外和解，以節省法律費用並盡快達成決議。

passenger

[ˈpæsn̩dʒə]

同 **commuter, traveler**

A **passenger** in the business class section suddenly became very ill, and the plane had to make an emergency stop so he could be taken to a hospital for treatment.

(n.) 乘客

商務艙一名乘客突然感到非常不適,班機必須緊急降落,好讓他能送去醫院接受治療。

patron

[ˈpetrən]

必

同 **frequenter**

名 **patronage** 同 sponsorship

動 **patronize**
　　同 **sponsor, frequent**

形 **patronizing**
　　同 **condescending, superior**

副 **patronizingly**

In the interests of increasing repeat business, the hotel implemented a loyalty program to identify and reward its best **patrons**.

(n.) 主顧,老顧客

為有利於增加顧客回流,這家飯店實行忠誠方案,找出最捧場的顧客,並給予回饋。

pay off

[pe ɔf]

If we work hard and save every penny, we should be able to **pay off** our mortgage in five or six years.

償還

如果我們努力工作並省下每一毛錢,應該可以在五到六年後還清房貸。

paycheck

[ˈpe,tʃɛk]

Chris used to make a trip to the bank every month to deposit his **paycheck**, but now his employer deposits his pay directly into his bank account.

(n.) 薪水支票

克里斯以前每個月都要到銀行去存薪水支票,但現在他老闆直接把薪資存到他的銀行戶頭中。

0009

payment
[ˈpemənt]

The customer's final **payment** for the order delivered last week will be remitted into our bank account this afternoon.

(n.) 付款
上周完成交貨的訂單尾款，客戶今天下午會匯入我們的帳戶。

0010

payroll
[ˈpeˌrol]
聽

After being put on the **payroll**, Greg felt assured that his savings would begin growing in no time.

(n.) 發薪名單
被列入發薪名單之後，葛瑞格確信他的存款會馬上開始增加。

0011

pedestrian
[pəˈdɛstrɪən]
聽
同 **stroller, walker**
形 **pedestrian**
相關字彙 **sidewalk** 人行道

The shop owner decided to enlarge the sign on his shop and design a new window display to attract **pedestrians** and increase sales.

(n.) 行人
店老闆決定加大店外的招牌，並設計新的櫥窗擺設，以吸引行人及提升銷售。

0012

penalize
[ˈpinəˌlaɪz]
必
同 **punish**
名 **penalty** 同 **punishment**
反 **reward**

Businesses that are late in paying their taxes will be **penalized** for each month the payment is late in an amount that equals 1% of the unpaid tax, not to exceed 25% of the unpaid tax.

(v.) 處罰
逾期繳稅的公司在延遲期間會被按月處以罰款，金額為未納稅額的百分之一，而上限為百分之二十五。

0013

penalty

[ˈpɛn̩tɪ]

必
同 **punishment**
反 **reward**

Employees who are caught surfing the Web during office hours will be given a warning the first time; the **penalty** for being caught a second time is suspension or dismissal.

(n.) 罰則，處罰

被抓到在辦公時間上網的員工，第一次會予以警告，被抓到第二次就會停職或解雇。

0014

penetration

[ˌpɛnəˈtreʃən]

聽 讀
同 **invasion, perforation**
動 **penetrate** 同 probe
形 **penetrating**
　　同 penetrative, harsh, piercing

While a company that uses low prices to promote its products can achieve high market **penetration** rates quickly, it may develop a reputation as a low-price provider and have difficulty making a profit.

(n.) 穿入，貫穿

雖然用低價促銷商品的公司很快就能有高市佔率，但也可能會發展出低價供應商的名號，而很難獲利。

0015

perceive

[pɚˈsiv]

必
同 **sense, identify**
名 **perception**
　　同 awareness, discernment
形 **perceptive**

Our company conducted an extensive market survey to gain a better understanding of how our brand is **perceived** by consumers.

(v.) 觀感，認知

我們公司進行一項廣泛的市場調查，以更加了解消費者對我們品牌的看法。

0016

perception

[pɚˈsɛpʃən]

必
同 **awareness, discernment**

Even if a company has high quality products and services, it only takes one bad experience to ruin a customer's **perception** of the company.

(n.) 觀感，認知

即使公司有優質的商品以及服務，但只要有一次糟糕的消費經驗就足以毀掉消費者對該公司的觀感。

0017

perform

[pəˋfɔrm]

必
同 **act, stage**
名 **performance**
　　同 presentation
名 **performer**

In order to **perform** to the best of her abilities, Natalie made sure to eat a balanced diet and get plenty of rest and exercise.

(v.) 表現，演出

為了展現出最好的能力，娜塔莉確實攝取均衡飲食並充分地休息及運動。

0018

performance

[pəˋfɔrməns]

必 讀
同 **presentation**

While our overall sales **performance** this year is in line with our expectations, not all of our sales teams met their sales targets, and will be expected to do better in the coming year.

(n.) 表現，演出

雖然我們今年整體的銷售表現已符合預期，但並非所有的銷售團隊都達到銷售目標，希望來年會更好。

0019

period

[ˋpɪrɪəd]

必
同 **term, phase**
形 **periodic, periodical**
副 **periodically**
　　同 sporadically, intermittently
名 **periodical**

At the annual general meeting, Mr. Phillips was re-elected to the board of directors for a **period** of four years.

(n.) 期間，週期

在年度大會中，菲利浦先生再度獲選為董事會成員，任期四年。

0020

periodically

[pɪrɪˋɑdɪkəlɪ]

必 讀
同 **sporadically, intermittently**

The IT department **periodically** shuts down the office network to perform maintenance, make needed rapairs, and ensure that everything is functioning smoothly.

(adv.) 定期地

資訊技術部門定期關閉公司網路來進行維修、執行必要的修復，並確保一切功能運作順利。

0021

permissible
[pɚˋmɪsəbl]

必
同 **admissible, allowable**
反 **prohibited**
動 **permit** 同 allow, let
　　　　反 interdict, disallow
名 **permit** 同 permission, license
形 **permissive** 反 preventative

Our company code of ethics clearly specifies what types of behavior are **permissible** and what types of behavior are prohibited.

(a.) 可允許的，可容許的
我們公司的倫理規範清楚地載明哪些舉動是被允許的，而哪些又是被禁止的。

0022

permit
[pɚˋmɪt]

必 聽
同 **allow, let, authorize**
反 **interdict, disallow**

Supervisors should not **permit** employees to perform work past their regular schedule without specific approval, and overtime may be authorized only if appropriate budget arrangements have been made.

(v.) 准許，許可
主管不應准許員工未經特定許可而超時工作，也只有在已編列適當預算時，才可核准加班。

0023

personnel
[ˌpɝsn̩ˋɛl]

必
同 **employee**

All company **personnel** are required to protect the company's intellectual property and confidential information as stipulated in the company's Disclosure Policy.

(n.) 員工
公司訊息披露政策中明定，所有公司員工皆被要求必須保護公司的智慧財產以及機密資料。

0024

perspective
[pɚˋspɛktɪv]

必
同 **view, position**

From the **perspective** of company management, it is always best to ensure that employees are treated with dignity and respect by the company and by fellow employees.

(n.) 觀點，看法
從公司管理階層的觀點來看，最好要確保員工都有受到公司和同仁有尊嚴及尊重的對待。

0025

persuade

[pəˋswed]

必
同 carry, sway
反 dissuade
名 persuasion 同 inducement
反 dissuasion
形 persuasive

Although we tried to **persuade** Joseph to stay on, he was convinced that it was time for him to move to another company where his prospects for promotion would be better.

(v.) 說服
雖然我們試圖說服喬瑟夫留任,但他相信該是他轉任另一公司的時候了,因為在那裡他升職的前景會更好。

0026

persuasion

[pəˋsweʒən]

同 inducement
反 dissuasion

The gentle **persuasion** used by the sales manager to convince the customer of the benefits of the company's products greatly impressed the young sales representative.

(n.) 說服,勸說
業務經理用溫和勸說的方式讓顧客相信公司產品的優點,這讓年輕的業務代表大感佩服。

0027

pertinent data

[ˋpɝtɪnənt ˋdetə]

Please provide us with all of your **pertinent data** within the next few days so that we can start the process of putting you on the payroll.

相關資料
請在接下來幾天提供我們所有你的相關資料,好讓我們可以開始進行將你列入薪資名單的程序。

0028

petition

[pəˋtɪʃən]

必
同 request, postulation
動 petition 同 plead, request
名 petitioner
形 petitionary

The long distance service provider filed a **petition** with the National Communication Authority requesting permission to raise its domestic long distance rates.

(n.) 申請,請願
這長途電話服務業者向國家通訊管理局提出申請,要求核准提高其國內長途電話的費率。

0029

pharmaceutical

[ˌfɑrməˈsjutɪk]]

聽
同 pharmaceutic
名 pharmaceutics

At the present time, growth in the **pharmaceutical** industry is being driven by innovation in the biotechnology field, increasingly aging populations worldwide, and emerging geographical markets such as India and China.

(a.) 製藥的，藥學的
目前，製藥業的成長動力是來自生物科技領域的創新、全世界老年人口越來越多、印度和中國等新崛起的地理市場。

0030

pharmacy

[ˈfɑrməsɪ]

聽
同 pharmaceutics
相關字彙 pharmacist 藥劑師

The **pharmacy** said they were out of the particular medicine I needed, but that they would be getting some in next week.

(n.) 藥局，藥學
那間藥局說我需要的那種藥賣完了，但下周會進貨。

0031

philharmonic

[ˌfɪləˈmɑnɪk]

名 philharmonic

The **philharmonic** orchestra will be performing at the downtown concert hall tonight, and my coworker and I have front-row seats.

(a.) 愛好音樂的
愛樂交響樂團今晚將在市中心的音樂廳演出，我和同事有前排座位的票。

0032

physical

[ˈfɪzɪk]]

必
同 corporal, carnal
反 mental
副 physically
名 physical

The delivery driver position involves intermittent **physical** exertion, including walking, stooping and lifting of packages and equipment, some of which may be heavy.

(a.) 身體的
貨運司機的職務需要間歇性的體力消耗，包括走路、彎腰抬起可能很重的包裹和器材。

0033

physical
[ˈfɪzɪkl]

After being hired, new employees must undergo a **physical** by a licensed physician and successfully pass a drug screening test before they can begin work.

(n.) 健康檢查

受雇後，新進員工必須接受合格的醫師來進行健康檢查，並順利通過藥物篩檢，才能正式上任。

0034

pick up
[pɪk ʌp]
必

The CEO's secretary had a car sent to the airport to **pick** him **up** after he arrived from his business trip to Hong Kong and Japan.

以汽車搭載某人

執行長從香港和日本出差回來之後，他的祕書派了一輛車到機場去接他。

0035

pile
[paɪl]
聽
同 stack

After coming back from his two-week vacation, the file clerk had a huge **pile** of files on his desk waiting to be filed.

(n.) 疊

休假兩週回來之後，那位檔案管理人員的桌上有一大疊檔案等著歸檔。

0036

plan
[plæn]
必
同 design, program

The company **plan** is to hire an auditor to go over their books and make sure they are filing their taxes correctly.

(n.) 規畫，計畫

公司的規畫是雇用一名查帳人員，檢視帳冊並確認他們報稅無誤。

0037

plant
[plænt]
聽
同 **factory**

The plastics plant was located in an industrial zone far away from residential areas to protect residents from possible health risks caused by **plant** emissions.

(n.) 工廠
塑膠工廠位於離住宅區很遠的工業區當中，以保護居民不受工廠排放物可能帶來的健康危害。

0038

plug and play
[plʌg ænd ple]

I don't believe you need to install a driver for **plug and play** peripherals; usually the computer will recognize them automatically.

隨插即用
我不認為你需要為隨插即用的週邊裝置安裝驅動程式，通常電腦可以自動辨識出這些裝置。

0039

plumber
[plʌmɚ]
名 **plumbing**

The city **plumber** spent the entire day making emergency repairs after some pipes burst at a large office building downtown.

(n.) 配管工
市區一棟大型辦公大樓的水管爆裂之後，市府的配管工人花了一整天緊急搶修。

0040

policy
[pɑləsɪ]
必
同 **scheme**

Company **policy** states that purchasing personnel may not accept gifts from suppliers, either current or prospective, unless such gifts are nominal in value and bear the supplier's name.

(n.) 政策
公司政策明定，採購人員不得收受現有或未來可能的供應商致贈之禮品，除非是非常便宜且標明供應商名稱。

0041

poll
[pol]

聽
同 survey, canvass

The employee satisfaction **poll** has been analyzed, and it was determined that while some are satisfied with their working conditions, many are not.

(n.) 意見調查
員工滿意度調查已經分析完成，結果顯示儘管部分員工滿意工作環境，但有許多員工並不滿意。

0042

popularity
[ˌpɑpjəˋlærətɪ]

必
形 popular
動 popularize
   同 generalize

The **popularity** of the carpool plan was so great that additional carpool incentives, including free coffee and lunch coupons for carpoolers, were introduced.

(n.) 受歡迎，普及
共乘計畫非常受歡迎，所以開始出現附加的誘因，包括免費咖啡和午餐折價券。

0043

popularize
[ˋpɑpjələˌraɪz]

必

In an attempt to **popularize** their new soft drink, the beverage company ran a series of TV commercials and print ads, and hired several celebrities to endorse the product.

(v.) 使流行，使普及
為了讓公司新的非酒精飲料廣為流行，那間飲料公司推出一系列的電視廣告、平面廣告，並請來多位名人代言他們的新產品。

0044

portable
[ˋportəbl]

同 handy, lightweight, compact

Our company manufactures, distributes, and sells **portable** toilets, showers, offices, and kiosks for use at construction sites and outdoor entertainment events.

(a.) 攜帶式的
我們公司製造、配銷並販賣流動式洗手間、淋浴間、辦公室以及小亭，可供工地或戶外娛樂活動使用。

0045

portfolio
[portˋfolɪˏo]
必

Applicants for the graphic artist position who are invited for an interview should be prepared to present a personal **portfolio** of their work for review.

(n.) 作品集，投資組合
獲邀參加面試的美工設計人員應徵者，應呈交個人作品集備審。

0046

portion
[ˋporʃən]
必
同 **component, constituent**
動 **portion**
　同 **allot, assign**

A **portion** of the proceeds from today's charity auction will be donated to hurricane disaster victims, and the rest will go to a scholarship fund for disadvantaged children in the local community.

(n.)（一）部分
今日慈善拍賣的部分所得將捐贈給颶風受災戶，其餘將作為本地社區弱勢兒童的獎學金基金。

0047

position
[pəˋzɪʃən]
必
同 **place**
名 **position**
　同 **location**

As consumers become more health-conscious, many food companies are trying to **position** their products as being healthy and natural.

(v.) 定位
由於消費者越來越重視健康，許多食品公司正試著將他們的產品定位為健康及天然食品。

0048

positive
[ˋpazətɪv]
反 **disconfirming, negative, harmful**
副 **positively**

People who maintain a **positive** attitude at work are much more likely to have successful and rewarding careers.

(a.) 正面的
工作上保持正面態度的人，大有機會獲得成功且有回報的事業。

0049

possess
[pəˋzɛs]

同 own, have
名 possession
　同 ownership
名 possessor
　同 owner
形 possessive
　同 controlling, dominating

Companies value employees who **possess** the ability to work with diverse groups of people and cooperate with others in achieving common goals.

(v.) 具有，持有
有能力與各種不同團隊的人員共事、與他人合作達成共同目標的員工，非常受到公司企業的重視。

0050

possession
[pəˋzɛʃən]

讀
同 ownership
相關字彙 possessions 財產

For those wishing to apply for the truck driver's position, **possession** of a valid driver's license, a good driving record, and the willingness to work flexible hours are required.

(n.) 持有，擁有
有意應徵卡車司機職務的人，須擁有效期內之駕照、良好的駕駛紀錄，並願意配合彈性工作時間。

0051

post
[post]

同 place, office, position

John was transferred from company headquarters to a **post** in Hong Kong, where he was responsible for handling trade issues for sales and marketing in the Asia-Pacific region.

(n.) 分部，支處
約翰從總公司被調派到香港分公司，負責掌管亞太區業務與行銷的貿易事務。

0052

postage
[ˋpostɪdʒ]

讀

Postage rates for first-class mail are calculated in one-ounce increments, whereas the per-piece rate for standard mail letters is the same for pieces weighing up to 3 ounces.

(n.) 郵資
優先投遞的郵件郵資費率計算是以一盎司為單位向上遞增，而一般郵件凡三盎司以下，每件費率皆相同。

0053

potential
[pəˋtɛnʃəl]

必
同 likely, possible
名 potential 同 possibilities
副 potentially

I have a lead on a **potential** customer who is in the process of setting up a new factory and is interested in making several large purchases.

(a.) 潛在的，有可能的
我得到消息，一名潛在客戶正在設立新工廠，並有興趣大量採購。

0054

potential
[pəˋtɛnʃəl]

必

In view of Jason's excellent management and communication skills, I believe he has the **potential** to become a regional manager in a few years' time.

(n.) 可能性，潛力
有鑑於傑森優異的管理及溝通技巧，我相信他有潛力在幾年內成為區經理。

0055

power outage
[ˋpauɚ ˋautɪdʒ]

The **power outage** knocked out the office's air conditioning, lighting and computer system, so the boss declared the day a holiday and sent everyone home.

停電
停電使得辦公室的空調、照明以及電腦系統停擺，因此老闆宣布放假一天，讓大家回家。

0056

practice
[ˋpræktɪs]

必

After obtaining his law degree and passing the bar, Barry decided to teach law at a local college rather than set up a law **practice**.

(n.)（醫生、律師等）營業，業務
取得法律學位並通過律師考試之後，巴瑞決定在當地一所大學教授法律，而非開設律師事務所。

0057

precision
[prɪˋsɪʒən]
同 **preciseness, accuracy, exactness**
形 **precise** 同 accurate, exact
反 **imprecise**
副 **precisely** 同 exactly, just

Great **precision** is required in crafting the lenses and mirrors used in our company's telescopes, binoculars, and spotting scopes.

(n.) 精密（度）
我們公司的單筒望遠鏡、雙筒望遠鏡和可攜式望遠鏡所使用的鏡片與鏡子，製作時都需要非常精密。

0058

preclude
[prɪˋklud]
必
同 **obviate**
形 **preclusive**
副 **preclusively**
名 **preclusion**

A general meeting at the beginning of the new year was **precluded** because the CEO and several other high-level executives were away at the time.

(v.) 排除
新年度一開始的大會被排除，因為執行長和幾位高階主管當時都不在。

0059

predict
[prɪˋdɪkt]
必 讀
同 **forecast, foresee, presage**
名 **prediction**
　同 prevision, forecasting, foretelling
形 **predictable**
　同 foreseeable, likely
反 **unpredictable**
副 **predictably**
相關字彙 **predictability** 可預測性
　　　　 predictor 預言者

Mismatches often occur between consumer demand and product supply because producers cannot accurately **predict** future market conditions.

(v.) 預測
消費者需求和產品供應之間常會出現不相符的情況，因為生產者無法精確預測未來的市場態勢。

0060

prediction
[prɪˋdɪkʃən]
必

The general manager's **prediction** that we would gross 2.3 million dollars last year turned out to be extremely close to the actual figure.

(n.) 預測
總經理預測我們去年的毛利會是兩百三十萬美元，結果極為接近實際數字。

0061

prefer

[prɪˋfɝ]

必 聽
同 favor
名 preference
　同 leaning, orientation
形 preferred
形 preferable
副 preferably

Our supervisor **prefers** to discuss any matter that may be embarrassing to the responsible party in private.

(v.) 偏好

我們主管傾向於私下討論任何可能令當事人尷尬的議題。

0062

preference

[ˋprɛfərəns]

必
同 leaning, orientation

Julie's **preference** is to find employment with a large firm, because she feels that this would provide her with more opportunities to learn new skills and advance her career.

(n.) 優先選擇，優先權

茱莉的優先選擇是找大公司的工作，因為她覺得那能提供她更多機會去學習新技能並在事業上更進一步。

0063

premium

[ˋprimɪəm]

聽
同 fee, charge, payment

The annual **premium** that a health insurer charges an employer for each employee enrolled in a company health plan has risen steadily over the last decade.

(n.) 保費，津貼

過去十年來，健保單位針對每一名登錄在公司投保計畫名單上的員工，向雇主索取的年保費逐年增加。

0064

preparation

[ˌprɛpəˋreʃən]

必
同 readiness
動 prepare
形 preparatory
形 prepared

In **preparation** for the office Christmas party, the general manager asked all employees to pitch in and help decorate the office space, set up tables and chairs, or prepare snacks.

(n.) 準備，準備工作

為準備公司的耶誕派對，總經理要求所有員工都要出力，幫忙布置辦公室環境、擺設桌椅或準備點心。

0065

prepare
[prɪˋpɛr]
必

Prior to the department meeting, Karl **prepared** a brief PowerPoint presentation and went over his figures to make sure they were up to date.

(v.) 準備
在部門會議之前，卡爾用 PowerPoint 準備了簡報，並且再把他的數據看過一遍，確定這些數據是最新的。

0066

prerequisite
[ˌpriˋrɛkwəzɪt]
必
 requirement
形 prerequisite
同 obligatory, required

A broad understanding of the international market and thorough familiarity with all of the company's product lines are **prerequisites** for transfer to an overseas branch office.

(n.) 必要條件，前提
廣泛了解國際市場以及完全熟悉公司所有的產品線，是轉派到海外分公司的必要條件。

0067

prescribe
[prɪˋskraɪb]
名 prescription

The doctor **prescribed** a two-week course of antibiotics for Tom's infection, and reminded him to be sure and take all of his medicine, even if he felt better before the two weeks were up.

(v.) 為…開藥
醫生開了兩星期療程的抗生素治療湯姆的感染，並提醒他，即使他在兩週結束前就已經覺得好轉，也務必把藥都吃完。

0068

prescription
[prɪˋskrɪpʃən]
讀
同 formula
形 prescription
反 nonprescription, over-the-counter

In accordance with hospital rules, the hospital pharmacy only fills **prescriptions** written by physicians who work at this hospital.

(n.) 處方箋
依照醫院規定，醫院藥局配藥只限於院內醫師開立的處方箋。

0069

present

[ˈprɛznt]

必
同 **existing, current**
反 **future, past**
名 **present** 同 nowadays
片 **at present** 當下

(a.) 目前的，現在的

As the **present** CEO will be retiring in six months, a search is underway to find a suitable candidate to take over for him.

現任執行長將在六個月後退休，已開始尋找接替他的合適人選。

0070

presentation

[ˌprizɛnˈteʃən]

必
同 **demonstration**
形 **presentational**

In light of the increasing importance of the Internet as a marketing tool, the marketing department hired an e-marketing expert to give a **presentation** on Internet marketing to the marketing staff.

(n.) 描述，呈現

有鑑於網路是越來越重要的行銷工具，行銷部請來一名網路行銷專家，針對網路行銷向行銷人員進行報告。

0071

prestigious

[prɛsˈtɪdʒɪəs]

讀
同 **esteemed**
反 **unknown**
名 **prestige**

After bringing in a **prestigious** Fortune 500 client, Steven was rewarded with a pay raise and promotion to the position of Account Executive.

(a.) 聲譽卓著的，一流的

在爭取到一流的《財星》五百大客戶之後，史蒂芬得到加薪以及升職為客戶主任做為獎勵。

0072

presumably

[prɪˈzuməblɪ]

同 **probably, seemingly**
形 **presumable** 同 supposable
動 **presume** 同 assume
名 **presumption** 同 assumption

As Andrew has had the best sales record in the department over the past several years, he will **presumably** be promoted to sales manager when the current manager leaves at the end of next month.

(adv.) 想必，據推測

由於安德魯幾年來都保有部門內最佳的業務紀錄，現任的經理下個月底離開時，他想必將會被升為業務經理。

0073

prevent

[prɪˋvɛnt]

必 讀
同 **impede, hinder**
名 **prevention** 同 precaution
形 **preventive** 同 precautionary

All employees at our firm are required to sign a nondisclosure agreement to **prevent** them from disclosing proprietary information.

(v.) 預防，防止

我們公司所有的員工都被要求簽署保密條款，以防他們洩露專利資料。

0074

prevention

[prɪˋvɛnʃən]

必
同 **precaution**

The purpose of our factory safety rules is the **prevention** of workplace injuries and accidents, so all employees are requested to follow these rules at all times.

(n.) 預防

我們工廠安全規則的目的是在預防職場傷害及意外，因此所有員工都被要求隨時遵守這些規定。

0075

previously

[ˋprivɪəslɪ]

同 **antecedently, formerly**
形 **previous**
　　同 former, preceding
　　反 later

I **previously** worked for a small investment company, but I left in search of more challenging work, and ended up starting my own company.

(adv.) 以前

我以前在一間小型的投資公司工作，但我離職尋找更具挑戰性的工作，最後自己開公司。

0076

primary

[ˋpraɪˏmɛrɪ]

必
同 **chief**
反 **secondary, subordinate**
副 **primarily** 同 mainly
形 **primal**
　　同 primary, first, initial
名 **primacy**

Advertising is the **primary** source of income for newspapers and other print media, and the advent of online media has made the competition for advertising dollars increasingly intense.

(a.) 主要的

廣告是報紙和其他平面媒體主要的收入來源，而網路媒體的出現已讓廣告收入的競爭越來越激烈。

0077

prior to
[ˈpraɪɚ tə]
讀

Prior to working for my present employer, I headed up an office in Borneo for two years; and before that I worked as an assistant manager in Singapore.

在…之前

在為我目前的雇主工作之前,我擔任婆羅洲分公司主管有兩年的時間;在那之前我在新加坡擔任副理。

0078

prioritize
[praɪˈɔrəˌtaɪz]
必
名 priority   同 prime concern

As the father of two children, I know now how difficult it is to **prioritize** work and family life issues.

(v.) 按優先順序處理

身為兩個孩子的父親,我現在知道排出工作與家庭生活的優先順序有多困難。

0079

priority
[praɪˈɔrətɪ]
必
同 prime concern

Our highest **priority** at this time is to hire a training consultant and get the new sales training program up and running.

(n.) 優先考慮的事,重點

我們目前的第一優先是聘請一位訓練顧問,並開始進行新的業務訓練課程。

0080

procedure
[prəˈsidʒɚ]
必 聽 讀
同 process
動 proceed
名 proceeding
形 procedural

If your computer becomes infected with a Trojan horse virus, please follow the **procedures** listed below to isolate and remove the virus.

(n.) 手續,既定的作法步驟

如果你的電腦受到木馬病毒感染,請依循下列步驟隔離並移除病毒。

0081

proceed
[prə`sid]

必 讀
同 **carry on**　　反 discontinue
名 **proceeding**　同 move, act

Now that we have received an OK from the vice president of marketing, we can **proceed** with the new viral marketing campaign.

(v.) 著手，進行

既然我們已經得到行銷副總的同意，就可以著手進行新的病毒性行銷活動。

0082

process
[`prɑsɛs]

必
同 **procedure**
動 **process**　同 transform, treat

Drawing on advances in cell biology, the scientists in our R&D department have invented a new **process** to isolate and purify the cells that produce insulin from donated pancreases.

(n.) 程序，步驟

利用細胞生物學的進展，我們研發部門的科學家已經發明一個新步驟，可將捐贈胰臟中製造胰島素的細胞隔離、淨化。

0083

procrastinate
[pro`kræstə‚net]

同 **put off, defer, postpone**
名 **procrastination**

It is not wise to **procrastinate** in filing your tax return, because if you file late you will be subject to penalties and interest assessed on the amount of taxes you owe.

(v.) 延遲，耽擱

延遲報稅是很不智的行為，因為如果晚申報，將被處以罰款並按欠稅金額繳交利息。

0084

procure
[pro`kjʊr]

讀
同 **obtain**
名 **procurement**

The corporation decided to go public in order to **procure** the capital needed to pay off their debt, expand their manufacturing facilities, and develop new products.

(v.) 取得，採買到，實現

為取得償還債務、擴充生產設施以及開發新產品所需的資本，該公司決定股票上市。

0085

production
[prə`dʌkʃən]

同 **manufacture**
名 **product**
  同 merchandise, ware, goods
形 **productive**   同 prolific
反 **fruitless, unproductive**
名 **productivity**   同 efficiency

Production costs have increased ten percent over the past year, and if they continue to rise, we may be forced to raise our prices and pass these costs on to our customers.

(n.) 生產
過去一年生產成本已經增加百分之十,如果再繼續上漲,我們可能被迫要提高售價,將成本轉嫁到消費者身上。

0086

productive
[prə`dʌktɪv]

必 聽
同 **prolific**
反 **fruitless, unproductive**

The key to holding a **productive** meeting is to draft a clear agenda and hand it out to attendees several days in advance so that they have time to prepare.

(a.) 有建設性的,有成效的
要舉辦一場有成效的會議,關鍵在於擬定一份清楚的議程,並提前幾天分發給與會者,好讓他們有時間做準備。

0087

productivity
[ˌprodʌk`tɪvətɪ]

讀
同 **efficiency**

Advances in automation technology in recent years have enabled many manufacturers to increase **productivity** and reduce costs.

(n.) 生產力,豐饒
近年來自動化科技的進步,已使許多製造商得以增加生產力並降低成本。

0088

profession
[prə`fɛʃən]

必
同 **occupation**
形 **professional**   同 competent
反 **nonprofessional, unprofessional**
名 **professional**   反 amateur
副 **professionally**
名 **professionalism**

Modeling is an extremely competitive **profession** and requires a lot of dedication, hard work, and ambition in order to succeed.

(n.) 行業
模特兒是一個極度競爭的行業,需要許多的投入、努力工作以及野心,才能成功。

0089

professional
[prə`fɛʃən!]
必

A **professional** photographer came to the office to do a photo shoot for the upcoming issue of City Business.

(a.) 專業的
一位專業攝影師來到辦公室,為新一期的《城市商業》拍照。

0090

profile
[`profaɪl]
必
同 outline

After glancing over the company **profile**, Keira knew that it would be the perfect place for her to pursue her career.

(n.) 簡介
大致看過公司簡介後,綺拉知道那會是她追求事業最理想的地方。

0091

profit
[`prɑfɪt]
必
同 earnings, gain
反 loss
動 profit 　　同 benefit, gain
形 profitable
　　同 lucrative, rewarding
反 unprofitable
名 profitability

The **profit** we have made over the past decade has made it possible for us to expand our business and tap into new markets.

(n.) 盈利,獲利,利潤
我們十年來的獲利,使我們得以擴展生意並打入新市場。

0092

profit
[`prɑfɪt]
必
同 benefit, gain

If the deal is structured properly, both companies stand to **profit** handsomely from the upcoming merger.

(v.) 獲益
如果這交易的結構完善,雙方公司都能從即將進行的合併案中獲得可觀的利益。

0093

profitable
[ˋprɑfɪtəbḷ]
必
同 **lucrative, rewarding**
反 **unprofitable**

Instead of developing new products, the company decided to focus its efforts on selling more of its most **profitable** products and phasing out products with low profit margins.

(a.) 獲利的，營利的
這間公司決定不開發新產品，而是把主力放在販售該公司利潤最高的產品，並逐步淘汰利潤微薄的產品。

0094

profusely
[prəˋfjuslɪ]
同 **abundantly, copiously, extravagantly**
形 **profuse**
　　同 plentiful, ample, prolific
　　反 lacking, sparse
名 **profusion**
　　同 overflow, plenitude, surplus

The customer service representative apologized **profusely** to the customer for the delay and promised that the order would be sent out immediately.

(adv.) 大量地，毫不吝惜地
客服代表因作業延誤而頻頻向客戶致歉，並承諾這筆訂單會立即出貨。

0095

program
[ˋproɡræm]
同 **scheme, plan**
動 **program**
名 **programming**
名 **programmer**

Our company's internship **program** is intended to provide university students from diverse backgrounds with the opportunity to practice the business skills learned in school while gaining valuable work experience.

(n.) 計畫，方案
我們公司的實習計畫意在提供機會給各種背景的大學生，讓他們實際演練在學校所學的商業技能，並獲得寶貴的工作經驗。

0096

programming
[ˋproɡræmɪŋ]

Michael studied computer **programming** in university, and after working as a programmer for several years, he decided to open his own software company.

(n.) 程式設計
麥可大學時攻讀電腦程式設計，擔任程式設計師幾年之後，他決定開設自己的軟體公司。

0097

progress
[ˋprɑgrɛs]

必
同 **advancement, improvement**
反 deterioration, retrogression
動 **progress** 同 proceed, improve
名 **progression** 同 advancement,
amelioration, progress
形 **progressive** 同 reformist
副 **progressively**
片 **in progress** 進行中的

I am pleased to say that we have made great **progress** this year in establishing better relations with our suppliers and improving our distribution channels.

(n.) 進步
我很高興地說，我們今年在與供應廠商建立更好關係，以及改善經銷通路方面已大有進步。

0098

prohibit
[prəˋhɪbɪt]

必
同 **proscribe, interdict**
反 **allow**
名 **prohibition**
同 ban, proscription
形 **prohibitive** 同 restrictive
形 **prohibited**
同 forbidden, banned

Employees are **prohibited** from using their cell phones in the workplace because they tend to have a negative impact on productivity.

(v.) 禁止
員工在工作場所禁止使用手機，因為手機容易對生產力帶來負面影響。

0099

project
[ˋprɑdʒɛkt]

必
同 **undertaking**
動 **project**

The high speed railway **project** cost billions of dollars and took nearly a decade to complete and get up and running.

(n.)企畫，專案
高速鐵路案斥資數十億美元，花了近十年始完工並通車營運。

0100

promise
[ˋprɑmɪs]

必
同 **guarantee, pledge**
動 **promise** 同 assure
形 **promising**

Managers must be careful to keep all of the **promises** they make; otherwise, they will lose credibility in the eyes of their subordinates.

(n.) 承諾
經理人必須謹慎信守他們許下的所有承諾，否則他們在下屬眼中將失去公信力。

0101

promote

[prə`mot]

必
同 **advertise, boost**
名 **promotion** 同 publicity
反 **demotion**

We're planning on **promoting** our new fashion line with a big party and a series of fashion shows over the next few months.

(v.) 宣傳

我們打算接下來幾個月舉辦一場大型派對及一連串的時尚秀來宣傳新時裝系列。

0102

promotion

[prə`moʃən]

必
同 **publicity**
反 **demotion**

If you want to be considered for a **promotion**, you must display leadership skills and be willing to put in long hours of overtime.

(n.) 晉升，升職

如果想成為升官的考慮人選之一，就必須展現領導才能，並願意長時間加班。

0103

prompt

[prɑmpt]

必 讀
同 **immediate, quick, rapid**
動 **prompt**
　　同 inspire, stimulate
副 **promptly**
　　同 quickly, pronto, readily
名 **promptness**
　　同 promptitude

His **prompt** response pleased the customer, as it showed the company's commitment to keeping customers happy.

(a.) 迅速的，即時付款的

他迅速的回覆讓顧客滿意，因為這展現出這間公司保證讓顧客滿意的承諾。

0104

promptness

[`prɑmptnɪs]

必
同 **promptitude**

The **promptness** with which this package arrived was amazing given the fact that it only was sent out yesterday.

(n.) 迅速

此包裹到貨的速度之快令人驚奇，因為昨天才剛寄出。

0105

proof
[pruf]
必
同 evidence

The employee demanded **proof** of her poor work habits from her supervisor when he tried to use it as grounds for dismissing her.

(n.) 證據

這位員工要求她的上司拿出她工作習慣不良的證據，因為上司試圖以此為理由來解雇她。

0106

proofreader
[ˋprufˏridə]
必
動 proofread

After editing the work for several hours, the **proofreader** began to wonder if it wouldn't make more sense for him to write it from scratch.

(n.) 校對人員

校訂這份作品數小時後，校對人員開始懷疑他是不是重寫一份會比較有意義。

0107

property
[ˋprɑpətɪ]
讀
同 belongings, possessions

Company assets include not only tangible assets like land and equipment, but also intangible assets such as brand names and intellectual **property**.

(n.) 資產，財產

公司資產不只包括土地與設備等有形資產，還有好比品牌名稱和智慧財產等無形資產。

0108

proposition
[ˏprɑpəˋzɪʃən]
同 plan, suggestion
動 propose suggest, advise
名 proposal
　　 proposition, suggestion
形 propositional

Vivian had a **proposition** for her coworker Glenda; if Glenda would cover the late shift tonight, she would work the late shift for the next two days.

(n.) 提議，建議

薇薇安向她的同事葛蘭達提了一個建議；如果葛蘭達今晚幫她上晚班的話，她明後兩天就都上晚班。

0109

prospect
[`prɑspɛkt]

聽
同 **expectation, outlook**
形 **prospective**
　同 upcoming, potential
　反 retrospective

In view of the excellent market **prospects** for organic products, many cosmetics firms are developing new lines of organic makeup.

(n.) 前景，預期會發生的事
考慮到有機產品的市場前景大好，許多化妝品公司正在開發新的有機化妝品系列。

0110

prospective
[prə`spɛktɪv]

必
同 **upcoming, potential**
反 **retrospective**

All **prospective** employees are given a tour of the company facilities, which include a gym, swimming pool, and cafeteria.

(a.) 未來的，預期的
所有可能被錄取的員工被帶去參觀公司設施，其中包括健身房、游泳池和員工餐廳。

0111

prosperity
[prɑs`pɛrətɪ]

聽
同 **successfulness**
動 **prosper**
形 **prosperous**
　同 affluent, booming, thriving

The firm's recent **prosperity** was evident at the end of the year, when every employee received a generous Christmas bonus and a pay raise.

(n.) 繁榮
這間公司最近的榮景在年終時顯而易見，因每位員工都獲得豐厚的耶誕獎金與加薪。

0112

protect
[prə`tɛkt]

必
同 **defend, safeguard, shield**
名 **protection**
　同 safety, security
名 **protector**
　同 guardian, champion
形 **protective**　同 sheltering
　　　　　　　　反 unprotective

In order to **protect** our company secrets from being leaked, all employees must sign a confidentiality agreement, and will face a lawsuit should they violate the contract.

(v.) 保護，防護
為防止我們公司的機密外洩，全體員工都必須簽署保密協議，萬一違約將吃上官司。

0113

protection

[prə`tɛkʃən]

必

同 safety, security

The main duty of our legal department is the **protection** of company trademarks and copyrights, as the survival of our business depends on intellectual property.

(n.) 保護，防護

我們的法務部門主要職責在於保護公司商標與著作權，因為我們業務的存續端繫於智慧財產。

0114

prototype

[`protə,taɪp]

同 epitome, paradigm, model

形 prototypical 同 archetypal

The engineers in the R&D department are working overtime to have a **prototype** of the new digital camera ready to demonstrate at the meeting next week.

(n.) 原型

研發部門的工程師正在加班準備新數位相機的原型，以便在下週的會議上展示。

0115

proven record

[`pruvn̩ `rɛkəd]

Our company has a **proven record** when it comes to meeting all our business commitments and providing outstanding service to our customers.

有紀錄為證

一說到達成所有商業承諾與提供顧客優良服務，我們公司有良好紀錄為證。

0116

provide

[prə`vaɪd]

同 furnish, supply

名 provider

In a bid to **provide** the lowest possible price to an important customer, the sales manager practically begged his boss to approve a steep discount.

(v.) 提供

業務經理為了提供一位重要客戶可能的最低價格，簡直是求老闆同意這超高的折扣。

0117

provider
[prə`vaɪdə]
必
同 **supplier**

The Internet connection at our office has been unstable for weeks, and we are now considering switching to a different **provider**.

(n.) 供應商，提供者
我們公司的網路連線幾個星期以來都不穩，我們正在考慮換一家網路服務供應商。

0118

provided that
[prə`vaɪdɪd ðæt]

I am giving you permission to go ahead with this project **provided that** you take all of the responsibility should something go wrong.

倘若，以…為條件
我會允許你繼續進行這個企畫案，前提是如果出錯你要負全責。

0119

provision
[prə`vɪʒən]
必
 condition, agreement, requirement, demand
形 **provisional**
同 transitional, temporary
反 permanent

There is a **provision** in this contract stipulating what will happen if payments are not made in a timely manner, so please look it over closely.

(n.) 條款
這份合約上有個條款明訂若未及時付款的後果，所以請詳閱。

0120

proximity
[prɑk`sɪmətɪ]
必
 propinquity, vicinity, closeness
形 **proximate**
 near, close
 ultimate

The **proximity** of the club to the building makes it the perfect spot to hit for an after-work happy-hour drink.

(n.) 鄰近
這個俱樂部因為鄰近這座大樓，所以成了下班後喝一杯的不二選擇。

0121

punctual
[ˈpʌŋktʃʊəl]

必
同 on time
名 punctuality
　同 promptness
反 tardiness

Carl is usually very **punctual** to work, but for some reason, he didn't hear his alarm clock go off this morning and woke up late.

(a.) 準時的

卡爾上班通常都很準時，但他今天早上因故沒有聽到鬧鐘響而晚起了。

0122

punctuality
[ˌpʌŋktʃʊˈælətɪ]

必
同 promptness
反 tardiness

We demand **punctuality** of all our employees, and will take disciplinary action against those who arrive late on a regular basis.

(n.) 準時

我們要求所有員工準時，常遲到的人將會受到紀律處分。

0123

purchase
[ˈpɝtʃəs]

聽
同 buy
名 purchase

The client will **purchase** two large systems consisting of three of our machines each this year, and may consider purchasing two more systems next year.

(v.) 採購

這位客戶今年將採購各由我們三台機器所組成的兩個大型系統，明年可能會考慮再買兩個系統。

New
TOEIC
新多益高分關鍵字彙
990

Q
Group

0001

qualification

[ˌkwɑləfəˈkeʃən]

 必 讀
同 eligibility
形 qualified 同 fit, equipped
反 unqualified
動 qualify 同 measure up
反 disqualify

We are very impressed by your professional **qualifications** and extensive management experience, and would like to offer you a management position at our company.

(n.) 資格，條件限制
我們對你的專業資格與豐富的管理經驗印象很深刻，想請你在我們公司擔任管理職。

0002

qualified

[ˈkwɑləˌfaɪd]

 聽 讀
同 fit, equipped
反 unqualified

While Richard holds a law degree and passed the bar in Maryland, he must pass the California bar exam in order to be **qualified** to practice law in California.

(a.) 具備應有條件的，適任的
理察擁有法律學位並通過了馬里蘭州的律師考試，但為了有資格在加州執業，他還必須通過加州的律師考試。

0003

qualify

[ˈkwɑləˌfaɪ]

 必
同 measure up
反 disqualify

Lenders use specific criteria, including income and credit history, to determine if potential borrowers **qualify** for a loan.

(v.) 使有資格，使合格
貸方用包括收入、信用紀錄等特定標準，來決定可能的借方是否有資格貸款。

0004

quotation

[kwoˈteʃən]

 必
名 動 quote

For a sales **quotation**, please contact our sales rep with the specific model number and information on any options you may need.

(n.) 報價單
欲取得銷售報價，請跟我們的業務代表聯絡，告訴他您可能需要的型號及資料。

0005

quote
[kwot]
必

The **quote** was prepared by the American office overnight and delivered to the client via e-mail so that he received it first thing in the morning.

(n.) 報價

這份報價是由美國辦公室花了一整晚準備好後，以電子郵件寄給客戶，好讓他明天一早就能收到。

New
TOEIC
990

新多益高分關鍵字彙

R
Group

0001

raise
[rez]

必
同 **wage increase**
動 **raise** 同 lift, elevate

The offer of a **raise** has made me reconsider leaving my position, since it would be difficult for me to get a better offer from another firm.

(n.) 加薪
公司提出加薪已讓我重新考慮離職一事，因為我很難在其他公司獲得更好的待遇。

0002

random
[ˈrændəm]

必
副 **randomly**
名 **randomness**
片 **at random** 隨意地

The factory inspector tested **random** samples from the production line to insure that products were in compliance with government regulations.

(a.) 隨機的
工廠品管人員從產品線隨機抽樣來測試，確保產品都合乎政府法規。

0003

range
[rendʒ]

必
同 **scope**
動 **range**

Our company offers a full product **range** of office supplies, equipment and furniture, so just let me know if you would like me to send you a catalog.

(n.) 類別，範圍
我們公司提供各類辦公用品、設備與家具，若需要我寄目錄給您，請告訴我。

0004

rapid
[ˈræpɪd]

讀
同 **speedy, prompt**
副 **rapidly**
名 **rapidness, rapidity**

China's **rapid** economic growth in recent years has been driven by high rates of investment, gains in productivity, and liberalized foreign trade and investment.

(a.) 迅速的
中國近年來經濟快速成長的動力，來自於高投資率、生產力的提升以及外貿與外資的自由化。

0005

rate

[ret]

必
同 pace, frequency
動 rate　　　同 evaluate
名 rating　　同 evaluation

The unemployment **rate** in Japan has increased steadily over the past 10 years, and is likely to rise further as deflation continues.

(n.) 率，比率

十年來日本的失業率不斷升高，還可能隨著通貨緊縮持續而進一步攀升。

0006

real estate

[ˋriəl ɪsˋtet]

聽 讀

Carrie worked at a **real estate** agency for several years before deciding to open her own office to handle mainly luxury apartments.

房地產，不動產

凱莉在一家房屋仲介公司工作數年後，決定自己開一家主要經手豪華公寓的公司。

0007

realistic

[rɪəˋlɪstɪk]

必
同 pragmatic, pratical
反 unrealistic
副 realistically
名 realist

If you take the time now to define **realistic** career goals and learn as much as you can about the career or job you wish to pursue, all the decisions ahead of you will be easier.

(a.) 實際可行的

若你現在花時間來確定實際可行的事業目標，並盡量去學習你想從事的事業或工作，往後的決定都將變得比較容易。

0008

reality

[rɪˋælətɪ]

必
同 truth, fact, actuality
片 in reality 事實上

After struggling to retain all of its employees for several years, the company was finally forced to face **reality** and recognized that layoffs had to be made.

(n.) 現實

數年來勉強留住所有員工之後，這間公司終於被迫面對現實，承認必須裁員。

0009

reason

[ˈrizn̩]

必

形 reasonable

The **reason** I would like to work for your company is that I feel I can be a valuable asset to your sales team, and I am very interested in growing and developing with your company.

(n.) 理由

我想為貴公司工作的原因是，我認為我能成為貴業務團隊的珍貴資產，而且我很有興趣跟貴公司一起發展成長。

0010

recede

[rɪˈsid]

反 advance

形 receding

As the founder aged, he was forced to **recede** from active involvement in company business due to his failing health.

(v.) 退出，後退

創辦人年事已高，由於健康狀況走下坡，不得不退出公司的主動經營。

0011

recognition

[ˌrɛkəgˈnɪʃən]

必

同 acknowledgement

動 recognize

同 accredit, acknowledge

形 recognizable

The best way to improve employee performance is to ensure that they always receive **recognition** for their accomplishments.

(n.) 認可

改善員工表現的最好方法，就是確保他們的成就都能獲得賞識。

0012

recognize

[ˈrɛkəgˌnaɪz]

聽

同 accredit, acknowledge

I'm afraid our computer does not **recognize** this account number; please check your passbook and enter the account number again.

(v.) 辨認

我們的電腦恐怕無法識別這個帳號，請檢查您的存摺並再次輸入帳號。

0013

recommend

[ˌrɛkəˈmɛnd]

必
同 **advocate, urge, commend**
名 **recommendation**
 **testimonial, commendation**

I just started working here today, and I'm not very familiar with this area; could you **recommend** a good restaurant around here for lunch?

(v.) 推薦，介紹

我今天剛開始在這裡工作，對這一區還不是很熟，能請你推薦這附近可以吃午餐的好餐廳嗎？

0014

recommendation

[ˌrɛkəmɛnˈdeʃən]

必
同 **testimonial, commendation**

Because William left the company on good terms, he received a **recommendation** from his former boss that was very helpful to him in obtaining his current position.

(n.) 推薦信

威廉離開公司時是好聚好散，因此獲得前老闆寫推薦信，對於得到他目前的工作很有幫助。

0015

reconcile

[ˈrɛkənˌsaɪl]

必
同 **settle**
名 **reconciliation**
 rapprochement

With the help of an outside mediator, the two firms were able to **reconcile** their difference and continue with their partnership.

(v.) 調解，使一致

在外部調停人的協助之下，這兩家公司得以消弭歧見，繼續合夥關係。

0016

record

[rɪˈkɔrd]

必
同 **document, file**
名 **record** **file, document**
名 **recorder**
形 **recording**

The secretary **recorded** the minutes of the meeting in shorthand, and then typed them up and made copies to pass out at the next meeting.

(v.) 記錄

這位祕書以速記方式記下會議紀錄，然後打好字並影印副本於下次會議中分發。

0017

recourse
[rɪˋkors]

同 refuge, resort

Going directly to the boss and presenting her idea of developing a creative design team was her last **recourse** after her department head chose not to listen to her.

(n.) 辦法，手段

在她的部門主管選擇不聽她的意見之後，她最後的手段就是直接去找老闆並提出她開發創意設計團隊的點子。

0018

recovery
[rɪˋkʌvərɪ]

同 recuperation
動 recover　同 regain, retrieve

The **recovery** of the important missing documents made the vice president breathe a sigh of relief.

(n.) 復得

這些重要文件失而復得，使副總鬆了一口氣。

0019

recrimination
[rɪ͵krɪməˋneʃən]

同 retaliation, counterattack
動 recriminate

When Melanie accused a coworker of falsifying her time sheet, the coworker responded with **recriminations**.

(n.) 反控

梅蘭妮指控一名同事竄改她的工作時間紀錄卡時，該同事也回以反控。

0020

recruit
[rɪˋkrut]

必
同 enlistee
動 recruit　同 enroll
名 recruiter
名 recruitment
　　同 enlisting

Many companies are now striving to implement personnel policies that not only attract the best **recruits**, but also keep them happy in order to minimize employee turnover.

(n.) 新成員

許多公司現在努力實施的人事政策不僅要吸引最佳新進人員，還要讓員工開心，將員工流動率減到最低。

0021

recruiter
[rɪˋkrutɚ]

Each year, hundreds of corporate **recruiters** from the nation's top firms visit the campuses of ivy-league universities to recruit promising graduates.

(n.) 招募人員
每年，來自全國頂尖公司數以百計的招募人員，會造訪長春藤盟校校園，招募有前途的畢業生。

0022

recruitment
[rɪˋkrutmənt]

必
同 enlisting

After several months trying to find a job on her own with little luck, Leslie decided to contact a **recruitment** agency.

(n.) 招募
試圖碰碰運氣自己找工作幾個月後，萊斯利決定跟職業介紹所聯絡。

0023

rectify
[ˋrɛktə͵faɪ]

必
同 reform, correct
名 rectification
形 rectifiable

The boss spent two weeks and a great deal of money **rectifying** the mistake made by an inexperienced employee who no longer works for the company.

(v.) 改正
老闆花了兩週時間與一大筆金錢，修正一名已離職菜鳥員工所犯下的錯誤。

0024

recur
[rɪˋkɝ]

必
同 repeat
名 recurrence
　同 return, reappearance
形 recurrent
形 recurring

Investors who learn to spot and take advantage of **recurring** market patterns can both increase their profits and reduce investment risk.

(v.) 循環；再發生
投資人如果能自己學會找出、善用股市再出現的走勢，就可以同時增加獲利並減少投資風險。

0025

recurrence
[rɪˋkɜəns]

必
同 return, reappearance

After two **recurrences** of unusual and undocumented expenditures, Mr. Jensen decided to hire an auditor to look into the matter.

(n.) 復發，再發生

重複發生兩次不尋常且沒有記錄的花費後，簡森先生決定雇用一名查帳員來調查此問題。

0026

reduce
[rɪˋdjus]

必
同 lessen, cut down
名 reduction
　　同 decrease
形 reducible

In an effort to make our work environment more environmentally friendly, we are going to try to **reduce** paper use by handling the bulk of our transactions by e-mail.

(v.) 減少

為了努力使工作環境更為環保，我們將以電子郵件處理我們的大部分交易，試著減少紙張的使用。

0027

reduction
[rɪˋdʌkʃən]

必
同 decrease

A **reduction** in work hours across the board made it difficult for part-time employees to make ends meet.

(n.) 減少，削減

全面縮短工時使得兼職員工很難收支平衡。

0028

refer
[rɪˋfɜ]

必 讀
同 mention, cite
名 referral
名 reference
　　同 recommendation, endorsement
片 refer to...

I would like to talk to you about the major makeup of our customer base, so please turn to page 23 and **refer** to the pie chart provided.

(v.) 參照，提及

我想跟你們談談我們客群的主要構成，所以請翻到第二十三頁，參照上面提供的圓餅圖。

0029

reference

[ˈrɛfərəns]

同 recommendation,
   endorsement

Theo asked me if he could use me as a **reference**, so I gave him my full contact information and thought about what I would say if I received a call from a prospective employer.

(n.) 推薦人／信

提歐問我他可不可以請我當推薦人，所以我給了他我完整的聯絡資料，也想了想要是接到他未來可能的雇主來電時，我要怎麼說。

0030

reflect

[rɪˈflɛkt]

必
同 meditate
名 reflection
   同 rumination, thoughtfulness,
      contemplation
形 reflective

The section chief loved the end of the year because it was the perfect time to **reflect** on the good and bad things that happened during the previous year.

(v.) 思考，反省

科長喜歡年底，因為此時最適合反省這一年所發生的好事和壞事。

0031

reflection

[rɪˈflɛkʃən]

必
同 slur, reproach

I'm sure that the poor performance this quarter is in no way a **reflection** on your managerial skills; I just think it takes time to get everyone on the same page.

(n.) 非議，有損的事

我確定這一季糟糕的表現絕對無損你的管理技能，我只是覺得要讓大家都有共識需要時間。

0032

refrain

[rɪˈfren]

聽 讀
同 forbear
名 refrain   同 chorus
片 refrain from 避免

Please **refrain** from bringing strong smelling foods into the office, as our office space is very small, and everyone is affected by these smells.

(v.) 克制，節制

請克制不要攜帶會散發強烈氣味的食物進公司，因為我們的辦公室空間很小，大家都會受到這些氣味影響。

0033

refund

[ˈrɪˌfʌnd]

必 聽
同 **repay, return, reimburse**
動 **refund**
　同 reimbursement
形 **refundable**

Clients who are not satisfied with our products in any way will receive a full **refund** within 30 days, minus shipping and handling fees.

(n.) 退費

凡因故不滿意我們產品的顧客，將可在三十天內獲得扣除運費與手續費之後的全額退費。

0034

refund

[rɪˈfʌnd]

必
同 **repay, return**

If it is necessary to cancel your flight, our airline will **refund** the value of tickets purchased by you from our offices or airport ticketing counters directly to you.

(v.) 退費

若是您的班機必須取消，我們航空公司將直接退還您向敝公司或機場售票櫃臺購買的機票費用。

0035

regardless

[rɪˈɡɑrdlɪs]

必
同 **no matter, nevertheless, nonetheless**

I know you feel it is of no importance to maintain a neat and organized office space, but as your supervisor, I say it needs to be straightened up **regardless**.

(adv.) 無論如何

我知道你覺得維持辦公室空間的整潔有序並不重要，但身為你的上司，我認為無論如何都需要整理。

0036

regardless

[rɪˈɡɑrdlɪs]

必 讀
用法為 **regardless of**

Regardless of how often you manage to secure a great sale, there will always be days when you feel like you can do nothing right.

(a.) 不論的

不論你多常能保住一筆大生意，總是會有覺得什麼事都做不好的時候。

0037

register
[ˈrɛdʒɪstə]

必
同 **sign up**
名 **register** 　同 registry
形 **registered** 　反 unregistered
名 **registration** 同 enrollment

If your business is organized as a corporation or limited partnership, in most states you automatically **register** your business name when you file your articles of incorporation with your state filing office.

(v.) 登記，註冊
如果你的公司被劃分為股份公司或有限合夥公司，當你在大多數州向州政府提出公司章程時，公司名稱就會自動註冊。

0038

registered
[ˈrɛdʒɪstəd]

必
反 **unregistered**

A **registered** letter came in the mail yesterday and was left on the director's desk first thing in the morning.

(a.) 掛號的
昨天寄來了一封掛號信，一早就被放在總監桌上。

0039

registration
[ˌrɛdʒɪˈstreʃən]

必
同 **enrollment**

New hires are requested to report to the Human Resources Department on Monday morning at 9 a.m. to complete the employee **registration** process.

(n.) 登記，掛號
新進員工星期一早上九點必須向人力資源部報到，以完成員工報到手續。

0040

regrettably
[rɪˈgrɛtəblɪ]

同 **unfortunately, unluckily**
形 **regrettable**
　　同 unfortunate, sad
形 **regretful**
名 **regret**

Regrettably, I will be unable to attend this evening's event, as some personal business has come up that requires my immediate attention.

(adv.) 抱歉地，遺憾地
由於臨時有些私事需要立即處理，我很遺憾將無法參加今晚的活動。

0041

regularly

[ˋrɛgjələlɪ]

必
反 **irregularly**
形 **regular** 反 irregular

Elaine went to the gym **regularly**, knowing that frequent exercise gave her the energy she needed to perform at the best of her abilities at the office.

(adv.) 定期地

伊蓮定期上健身房，因為她知道規律運動會供給她所需的活力，好在公司將能力發揮得淋漓盡致。

0042

regulate

[ˋrɛgjəˌlet]

必
同 **modulate, govern**
名 **regulation**
　同 regulating, rule
形 **regulatory**

As revenues are down by ten percent this quarter, we must carefully **regulate** company spending if we are to stay in the black.

(v.) 控制，管理

由於這一季的營收下滑了百分之十，我們若是要保持盈餘就必須謹慎控管公司開銷。

0043

regulation

[ˌrɛgjəˋleʃən]

必
同 **regulating, rule**

Company **regulations** clearly stipulate that employees who are absent from work due to illness may be required to present evidence of illness for each leave of more than three consecutive work days.

(n.) 規定，規章

公司明文規定，因病缺勤的員工連續請假超過三天就須出示醫生診斷證明。

0044

rehearsal

[rɪˋhɜsl]

必
動 **rehearse**

Internships can provide college students with a valuable **rehearsal** for their future role in their chosen career field.

(n.) 排練

實習可以提供大學生寶貴的練習機會，以利他們在未來所選擇的職場之用。

0045

rehearse

[rɪˋhɜs]
必

Annie **rehearsed** for several hours to make sure that her sales pitch sounded convincing and confident, but not too pushy.

(v.) 排練，彩排
安妮排練了數小時，以確保其銷售辭令聽起來具說服力又有自信，但不會太咄咄逼人。

0046

reimburse

[ˌriɪmˋbɜs]
聽
同 repay, refund, recompense
名 reimbursement

After Martin fell from the ladder while doing inventory, the company made sure to **reimburse** him for all of his medical expenses.

(v.) 償還，補償
馬丁盤點時從梯子上摔落後，公司確定會賠償他全額醫療費用。

0047

reimbursement

[ˌriɪmˋbɜsmənt]
聽
同 refund

Employees who work overtime (more than eight hours per day or 40 hours per week) are eligible to receive **reimbursement** for overtime meals.

(n.) 退款，賠償
加班（一天超過八小時或一週超過四十小時）的員工有領取誤餐費的資格。

0048

reinforce

[ˌriɪmˋfɔrs]
必
同 strengthen, fortify
名 reinforcement
同 fortification

As this region is prone to severe earthquakes, the walls of all buildings here are **reinforced** with steel rebar.

(v.) 增援，加強
此地容易發生強烈地震，這裡所有建築物的牆壁均以鋼筋強化。

0049

reinforcement

[ˌriɪnˈforsmənt]

必
同 fortification

The **reinforcement** of the riverbanks, which was completed over a period of six months, drastically reduced the chances of another flood occurring.

(n.) 加強，強化
費時六個月完工的河岸強化工程，大幅減少再次發生水災的可能性。

0050

reject

[rɪˈdʒɛkt]

必
同 decline
反 accept
名 rejection 同 denial

Some real estate buyers may intentionally submit offers that expire before the designated time in an attempt to force the seller to accept or **reject** their offer before all offers are considered.

(v.) 拒絕
部分不動產買家也許會故意在指定時間到期前出價，試圖迫使賣家在考慮過全部報價之前就先接受或回絕其出價。

0051

rejection

[rɪˈdʒɛkʃən]

必
同 denial

When Melissa's dream company sent her a **rejection** letter, instead of accepting an offer from another firm, she decided to go back to school and get an MBA.

(n.) 拒絕
梅莉莎夢寐以求的公司寄了拒絕信給她時，她沒有接受另一家公司的工作機會，反倒決定返回校園攻讀企管碩士學位。

0052

relatively

[ˈrɛlətɪvlɪ]

必
同 comparatively
形 relative

Being **relatively** new at her position, Cathy was unsure whether she was handling her work correctly, so she looked for someone to give her advice.

(adv.) 相對地，比較不地
凱西在這個職位相對較資淺，她不確定自己的工作是否處理正確，所以找人給她建議。

0053

relax
[rɪˋlæks]

必
同 **loosen up**
名 **relaxation**

The store manager was on his feet all day, so after he got off work, all he wanted to do was go home, put his feet up, and **relax**.

(v.) 使放鬆

店長站了一整天，所以下班後只想回家，把腳抬高放鬆。

0054

relaxation
[ˌrilæksˋeʃən]

必

In order to cope with the stresses of the workplace, it is vital for employees to get ample rest and **relaxation**.

(n.) 放鬆

為了應付職場壓力，員工充分休息與放鬆至關重要。

0055

release
[rɪˋlis]

必
同 **handout**
名 **release**

The software firm issued a press **release** to announce the launch of the latest version of its popular anti-virus software.

(n.) 發表；釋放

這家軟體公司發表一則新聞稿，宣布最新版人氣防毒軟體上市。

0056

relevant
[ˋrɛləvənt]

反 **irrelevant**
名 **relevance**

Applicants for the senior brand manager's position are requested to send their résumés, cover letters, and all other **relevant** documentation to our office before September 30th.

(a.) 有關的

應徵資深品牌經理的求職者必須於九月三十日前，把他們的履歷表、應職信等相關文件寄到我們公司。

0057

reliability

[rɪˌlaɪəˈbɪlətɪ]

必
同 **dependability**
形 **reliable**　同 dependable
　　　　　　　　反 unreliable
名 **reliance**
動 **rely**

If product **reliability** is consistently falling short of customer expectations and warranty costs are abnormally high, then changes are needed to the reliability process.

(n.) 耐用度，可靠性

如果產品耐用度持續不符顧客期望，而保固的成本又異常昂貴，那麼耐用度檢測程序就需要改變。

0058

relinquish

[rɪˈlɪŋkwɪʃ]

必
同 **resign, abandon**
名 **relinquishment**

Market leaders are more likely to concede market share at the low end of technological production, where profit margins are sparse, than to **relinquish** market share on advanced products that generate higher returns.

(v.) 放棄

市場領導品牌較有可能棄守利潤少的低階科技產品市占率，而不是放棄可帶來較高利潤的高階產品市佔率。

0059

rely

[rɪˈlaɪ]

必
同 **trust**

I don't think you can **rely** on any of the data collected by Brian, because it turns out that he was actually spying for the competition.

(v.) 信賴，相信

我不認為你可以信賴布萊恩所蒐集的任何資料，因為結果證明他其實是對手公司的間諜。

0060

remainder

[rɪˈmendɚ]

必
同 **remnant**
動 **remain**

After completing initial design work on the new hybrid car, the R&D team spent the **remainder** of the year building and testing a working prototype.

(n.) 剩餘物

研發團隊完成新款油電混合車的初步設計之後，把這一年剩下的時間用來打造與測試一部可運作的原型。

0061

remind

[rɪ`maɪnd]

必 讀
名 reminder

I hope I don't need to **remind** you that I expect to receive your project analysis report by the end of the month.

(v.) 提醒

我希望毋須提醒你，我預計能在月底之前收到你的專案分析報告。

0062

remote

[rɪ`mot]

必
同 distant
副 remotely　同 distantly
名 remoteness　同 farness

If there is even a **remote** chance that the client will sign, let me know ASAP and I will hop a plane and be there right away to help you close the sale.

(a.) 微乎其微的；偏遠的

只要客戶有一絲絲的機會可能簽約，盡快通知我，我會馬上飛過去幫你談成生意。

0063

remoteness

[rɪ`motnɪs]

必
同 farness

The **remoteness** of rural areas, combined with poor communications networks, makes it difficult for rural entrepreneurs to keep up with changes in market conditions.

(n.) 偏僻，遙遠

鄉村地區地處偏僻，加上通訊網絡不良，讓鄉間創業者很難跟上市場狀況的改變。

0064

remove

[rɪ`muv]

聽 讀
同 withdraw, eliminate, displace
名 removal
形 removable
形 removed

Please **remove** your shoes before entering the yoga studio; you will find a rack to place your shoes on in the entryway.

(v.) 移除

進入瑜伽教室前請脫鞋，你會在入口處看到一個鞋架來放鞋。

0065

renew
[rɪ`nju]

讀

同 furbish, regenerate, continue, extend, update

名 renewal

形 renewable

相關字彙
　subscribe 定期訂閱
　subscription 訂閱（費）

If you would like to **renew** your subscription to our monthly newsletter, please let us know so that we can keep you on our mailing list.

(v.) 繼續（訂閱），更新
您若想要繼續訂閱我們每月發行的電子報，請通知我們，好讓我們將您保留在我們的郵件名單上。

0066

repel
[rɪ`pɛl]

必

同 repulse, ward off

名 repellent

As our first priority is to protect the interests of our shareholders, we will make every effort to **repel** the hostile takeover bid from our competitor.

(v.) 抵制，擊退
我們的當務之急是保障股東利益，所以我們會盡每一分力量來抵抗競爭對手的惡意併購。

0067

repellent
[rɪ`pɛlənt]

必

Our new spray-on insect **repellent** keeps away mosquitoes, ticks, fleas, and other biting insects for up to 24 hours after each application.

(n.) 驅蟲劑
每次使用我們新的噴霧驅蟲劑之後，即可防蚊、壁蝨、跳蚤等會叮人的昆蟲長達二十四小時。

0068

replace
[rɪ`ples]

必 **聽**

同 supersede, supplant

名 replacement
　　同 substitute

形 replaceable

片 replace... with...

The CEO will be retiring in December after 12 years of service, and the board of directors will meet in November to choose the best candidate to **replace** him.

(v.) 替換，取代
執行長任職十二年後將於十二月退休，董事會將於十一月開會選出接替他的最佳人選。

0069

replacement

[rɪˋplɛsmənt]

必 讀
同 substitute

Employees are required to give one month's notice before quitting so that the company has sufficient time to find a suitable **replacement**.

(n.) 代替者
員工必須於離職前一個月提出書面通知，好讓公司有充分時間找到合適的替代人選。

0070

replenish

[rɪˋplɛnɪʃ]

同 refill
名 replenishment

The company coffers were **replenished** after strong sales of the new toy line during the Christmas shopping season which sent revenues soaring.

(v.) 把……裝滿
新玩具產品線在耶誕購物季熱賣，大幅增加公司營收，公司資金因而滿滿。

0071

reply

[rɪˋplaɪ]

讀
同 answer, respond
名 reply, answer, response

If you plan on attending the product launch, please **reply** to this invitation by e-mail or phone by October 25 to reserve your space.

(v.) 答覆，回應
打算參加產品發表會的人，請於十月二十五日前以電郵或電話回覆此邀請函，以保留座位。

0072

represent

[ˌrɛprɪˋzɛnt]

必 聽 讀
同 personify, epitomize, exemplify
名 representative
  同 deputy, delegate
形 representative
  同 archetypal, exemplary
名 representation

In order for the board to better understand the needs of the various departments, it was **requested** that one person from each department be present at board meetings to represent their respective departments.

(v.) 代表
為了讓董事會更了解各部門的需要，每個部門均須派出一人代表其部門出席董事會議。

0073

representative
[ˌrɛprɪˈzɛntətɪv]

同 deputy, delegate
形 representative
　　同 archetypal, exemplary
相關字彙 sales representative
　　業務員

A **representative** from each branch office was present at the annual company gathering in Las Vegas.

(n.) 代表
每間分公司都有一位代表出席公司在拉斯維加斯的年度聚會。

0074

reputable
[ˈrɛpjətəbl]

必
同 respectable
反 disreputable
名 reputation
　　同 respectability, honor, fame
名 repute
　　同 reputation

Blackstone and Brothers is a very **reputable** law firm, so we hired them to handle any legal issues that may arise.

(a.) 聲譽良好的
黑石兄弟是一間聲譽良好的法律事務所，因此我們聘請該公司來處理任何可能出現的法律問題。

0075

reputation
[ˌrɛpjəˈteʃən]

必
同 respectability, honor, fame

The **reputation** of the company rests in your hands, so when dealing with customers, make sure to maintain a professional and courteous attitude at all times.

(n.) 名譽，名聲
公司名譽掌握在你的手中，所以面對顧客時，務必時時保持專業有禮的態度。

0076

require
[rɪˈkwaɪr]

必
同 postulate
名 requirement
　　同 demand, necessity

I think this project is going to **require** the help of one of our top number crunchers, so I'll assign him to your team for support over the next few weeks.

(v.) 需要
我認為這個企畫案需要我們一位頂尖統計師的協助，所以我接下來幾個星期會派他去你的團隊支援。

0077

requirement

[rɪˋkwaɪrmənt]

必
同 **demand, necessity**

Key **requirements** for the Financial Communications Associate position include extensive knowledge of financial markets, a minimum of 3 years of experience in media relations, and strong written and spoken communication skills in English and Mandarin Chinese.

(n.) 必要條件

財經傳播專員一職的主要條件包括：對金融市場有廣博知識、至少三年媒體公關經驗，以及優秀的中英文說寫溝通能力。

0078

research

[ˋrisɝtʃ]

必
同 **inquiry, enquiry, investigation**
動 **research** 同 explore, search
名 **researcher**

After years of **research** on a revolutionary new way to record sound, Mr. Alberts realized that his product was ready for the market.

(n.) 研究

艾伯茲先生研究革命性的新式錄音方法多年後，了解到他的產品已可準備上市。

0079

reservation

[͵rɛzɚˋveʃən]

必
同 **booking, retainment**

Your secretary has made a **reservation** for you at the Grand Hyatt in Hong Kong, and she has arranged for a limo to take you from destination to destination during your stay.

(n.) 預訂（的房間、座位等）

您的祕書已為您在香港君悅酒店訂房，她還在您住宿期間安排一輛豪華轎車接送您往來各地。

0080

reserve

[rɪˋzɝv]

必
同 **keep, hold, preserve**
名 **reserve**
名 **reservation**
　　同 booking, retainment
形 **reserved**

We **reserve** the right to deny any change request once the order is confirmed, and will not be responsible for any loss it might incur to the customer.

(v.) 保留

訂單一旦確定，我們即保留拒絕任何要求更改的權利，也不負責客戶可能蒙受的任何損失。

0081

resident

[ˈrɛzədənt]

讀
同 **inhabitant**
動 **reside**
名 **residence**
形 **residential**

All citizens and permanent **residents** have full work rights in this country; all non-citizens who are not permanent residents must possess a valid visa with work rights to work here legally.

(n.) 居民
這個國家所有的公民與永久居民都有完整的工作權；而所有非永久居民的非公民要在這裡合法工作，必須擁有有效的工作簽證。

0082

resign

[rɪˈzaɪn]

聽
同 **quit, leave**
名 **resignation**
形 **resigned**

Jackson **resigned** as chief engineer after repeated attempts to convince upper management to cancel the doomed project had failed.

(v.) 辭職
傑克森一再試圖說服上司取消注定失敗的企畫案未果後，辭去了總工程師一職。

0083

resolve

[rɪˈzɑlv]

必 聽
同 **decide, solve, settle**
名 **resolve** 同 **resolution**
　　　　　 反 **indecision**

It is our policy to provide front-line employees with the authority to **resolve** customer complaints whenever possible.

(v.) 解決；決心去做；決議通過；使分解
我們的政策是授權給第一線服務人員盡可能解決客訴。

0084

resource

[rɪˈsors]

必
同 **source, supply**
形 **resourceful**
名 **resourcefulness**

While our **resources** are somewhat limited, we like to pride ourselves in thinking that we can find creative ways to use what we have available to us effectively.

(n.) 資源
儘管我們的資源有點不足，但我們很驕傲我們找得到有創意的方法來有效運用我們現有的資源。

0085

respective

[rɪ`spɛktɪv]

讀
同 **individual, specific**
副 **respectively**

The HR staff met to discuss the **respective** merits of each candidate before making a final decision on who to hire for the managerial position.

(a.) 各自的
人事部門的職員開會討論每一位候選人各自的優點，然後才做出最後決定雇用誰來擔任這管理職。

0086

respond

[rɪ`spɑnd]

必
同 **reply, answer**
名 **response**
　同 answer, reaction
形 **responsive**
副 **responsively**
名 **responsibility**
　同 accountability

I'm sorry I haven't had a chance to **respond** to your e-mail; I will send you an answer by this afternoon at the latest.

(v.) 回答，回覆
很抱歉我還沒有機會回覆你的電子郵件，我最晚會在今天下午之前給你答案。

0087

response

[rɪ`spɑns]

必

I mailed my résumé to 30 different companies, but have only received a **response** from two of them, and have not yet been invited for an interview.

(n.) 回應
我寄了履歷表給三十家不同的公司，但只收到其中兩家的回應，而且還沒被邀請參加面試。

0088

responsibility

[rɪˌspɑnsə`bɪlətɪ]

必
同 **accountability**
反 **irresponsibility**
形 **responsible**
　同 accountable
　反 irresponsible

It is the **responsibility** of employers to ensure that the equipment used in the workplace is in compliance with all applicable safety regulations.

(n.) 責任
確保工作場所中使用的設備都符合所有相關的安全規範，是雇主的責任。

0089

responsible

[rɪˋspɑnsəbl]

必
同 accountable

While not **responsible** for the misspelling of the company's name, the secretary was given a talking to all the same, since she had not been careful enough to catch the mistake.

(a.) 負責任的

雖然不須為拼錯公司名稱負責任，那位祕書還是被訓了一頓，因為她不夠細心，沒有抓到這個錯誤。

0090

restore

[rɪˋstor]

必
同 repair
反 demolish
名 restoration

It is hoped that the current government investigation into banking irregularities will help **restore** order and stability to financial markets.

(v.) 恢復

希望目前政府針對銀行業不法情事的調查，將能幫助金融市場恢復秩序及穩定。

0091

restrict

[rɪˋstrɪkt]

必 聽 讀
同 curb, regulate
名 restriction
　同 confinement

All company employees are **restricted** from using and disclosing personal information collected by the company for any purpose that is not in accordance with this Privacy Statement.

(v.) 禁止，限制

公司員工皆禁止使用或洩露公司所蒐集的個人資料，做為任何違反隱私權條例之用途。

0092

restriction

[rɪˋstrɪkʃən]

必
同 confinement

We will be holding a meeting this Friday to discuss the possible impact of new import **restrictions** on cost-effective access to raw materials for our production facility.

(n.) 限制規定

我們將在本週五舉行一場會議，討論新的進口限制對我們生產線取得划算的原物料可能造成的衝擊。

0093

result

[rɪˋzʌlt]

必 讀
同 consequence, effect
動 result
形 resultant
片 result in 導致
　result from 起因於

The **results** of our latest customer survey indicate that while most customers are satisfied with the quality of our products, they feel that there is room for improvement in our customer service.

(n.) 結果，（計算的）答案
我們最新的顧客調查結果指出，儘管大多數顧客對我們的產品品質感到滿意，但覺得我們的顧客服務仍有進步空間。

0094

result in

[rɪˋzʌlt ɪn]

In the past, high oil prices have **resulted in** gradual declines in demand as more energy efficient equipment and other energy saving measures were put into place.

導致
過去這段期間，隨著越來越多節能設備的使用以及其他節能方法的實施，高油價已導致原油需求量逐漸下滑。

0095

résumé

[ˌrɛzjuˋme]

聽 讀

While your **résumé** is impressive, I'm sorry to say that your qualifications do not match our current needs; we will, however, keep your résumé on file and contact you if a suitable position arises.

(n.) 履歷表
雖然您的履歷表令人印象深刻，不過很抱歉您的資格不符合我們目前的需求，但是我們會將你的履歷表歸檔，有適合職位出現時會與您聯繫。

0096

retailer

[ˋritelɚ]

聽 讀
形 副 動 retail
　　　反 wholesale
參考字彙 wholesaler 批發商
　　　　distributor 經銷商

Now that suburban markets have become saturated, big-box **retailers** are shifting their focus to opening new stores in urban areas.

(n.) 零售業者
郊區的市場已經飽和，大賣場零售業者現在將重心轉往在市區開設新店面。

0097

retain
[rɪˋten]

讀
同 preserve, keep
反 let go

The woman, who slipped and fell in the restaurant bathroom, **retained** a lawyer to represent her in a personal injury suit against the restaurant.

(v.) 聘僱，保持
那位在餐廳洗手間內滑倒的婦人聘請了一名律師，代表她對餐廳提起個人傷害訴訟。

0098

retard
[rɪˋtɑrd]

同 detain, defer
形 retarded
名 retardation

Many investors fear that rising interest rates and high commodity prices will **retard** growth in the corporate sector.

(v.) 減緩
許多投資人擔心日漸上升的利率以及居高不下的原物料價格，將會減緩企業的成長。

0099

retire
[rɪˋtaɪr]

必
同 withdraw
名 retirement
  同 retreat, withdraw

I plan to **retire** from the company this spring, and I wanted to let you know that I have you in mind to replace me as President.

(v.) 退休
我計畫今年春天從公司退休，而且我要告訴你，我想讓你接替我的董事長職位。

0100

retirement
[rɪˋtaɪrmənt]

必
同 retreat, withdraw

An amendment to the company pension plan stipulates that those who opt for early **retirement** will receive significantly lower pensions.

(n.) 退休
公司退休金制度的修正案中明定，選擇提早退休的員工所領的退休金將會大幅減少。

0101

return
[rɪˋtɝn]
必
動 return

Our store **return** policy states that all items in our store may be exchanged or returned for a full refund within 30 days of the purchase date.

(n.) 退還
我們店內的退換貨政策中聲明，所有店內商品在購買後三十天內皆可換貨或全額退款。

0102

reveal
[rɪˋvil]
讀
同 uncover, unveil, disclose
形 revealing

While I'm not sure exactly when the event will take place, I've heard that the boss plans to **reveal** the latest product design sometime next week.

(v.) 展現，揭示
雖然我不很確定時間，但我聽說老闆計畫在下周某日公開最新的產品設計。

0103

review
[rɪˋvju]
必 聽
同 go over, critique, access
名 review
　同 commentary, evaluation

Our legal team will be coming in to **review** all of the legal documents to make sure everything is in order before we sign the contract.

(v.) 檢閱
我們的法律團隊將過來檢閱所有的法律文件，以確保在我們簽約前一切就緒。

0104

revise
[rɪˋvaɪz]
必 聽 讀
同 review, edit, modify
名 revision
　同 correction

As a result of increases in productivity, estimates for fourth-quarter GDP growth are likely to be **revised** upwards.

(v.) 修正，校訂
由於生產力上升，第四季國內生產毛額成長的估計數字可能會向上修正。

0105

revolution
[ˌrɛvəˋluʃən]

必
同 **revolt**
動 **revolutionize**
　　同 revamp, modernize
形 **revolutionary**

The invention of the Internet has created a **revolution** in the ways people search for information, shop, and interact with each other.

(n.) 革命，革新
網際網路的發明引起了一場人們在搜尋資料、購物以及人際互動方式上的大革命。

0106

revolutionize
[ˌrɛvəˋluʃəˌnaɪz]

必
同 **revamp, modernize**

New advances in biotechnology promise to **revolutionize** the health sciences and agriculture in coming decades.

(v.) 在…方面實現突破性大變革
生物科技的新進展在未來數十年中，可能會讓健康科學與農業產生突破性大變革。

0107

reward
[rɪˋwɔrd]

聽
反 **penalty**
動 **reward**　同 payoff
形 **rewarding**

One of the most important aspects of managing a retirement portfolio is balancing risk and **reward** through diversification and asset allocation.

(n.) 報酬
管理退休投資組合時，其中一個最重要的部分是透過投資多樣化以及資產分配來平衡風險與報酬。

0108

risk
[rɪsk]

必
同 **hazard, jeopardy**
形 **risky**
片 **at risk**

While emerging markets present great opportunities, companies must also consider the **risks** of doing business in countries with unstable governments and lack of legal protections.

(n.) 風險
雖然新興市場有大好機會，企業還是必須考量在這些政局不穩、缺乏法律保護的國家做生意的風險。

0109

▼

run

[rʌn]

必

同 operate

Cathy was confident that she could **run** an entire department herself, and hoped that she would be promoted to department manager so that she would have the chance to prove herself.

(v.) 管理

凱西有信心可獨力管理整個部門，並希望會被升到部門經理的職位，好讓她有機會證明自己的能力。

New TOEIC 990 新多益 高分關鍵字彙

New
TOEIC

新多益高分關鍵字彙

990

S

Group

0001

sacrifice
[ˋsækrəˌfaɪs]

同 forfeit
動 sacrifice 同 give
形 sacrificial
副 sacrificially

In order to start and run a successful business enterprise, it is necessary to work hard and make many **sacrifices**.

(n.) 犧牲

為了開創並經營一個成功的企業，努力工作以及做出許多犧牲是必然的。

0002

salary
[ˋsælərɪ]

同 payroll

In addition to base **salary**, new recruits receive a signing bonus of $5,000, and are eligible for performance-based bonuses and stock options after completing one year of service.

(n.) 薪資

除了底薪之外，新進員工還獲得一筆五千元的簽約金，並在服務滿一年後有資格獲得績效獎金以及認股權。

0003

sales quota
[selz ˋkwotə]

Sales representatives who fail to meet their monthly **sales quota** will be placed on probation; those who don't show improvement within three months will be terminated.

銷售額度

未達成每月銷售額度的業務代表將被列入觀察，若三個月內仍看不出有改善，將予以解雇。

0004

sales slip
[selz slɪp]

I'm sorry; without a **sales slip** or other proof of purchase it won't be possible for us to give you a refund on this item.

銷貨車，銷貨發票

很抱歉，沒有發票或其他購買證明，這項商品我們不可能讓你退款。

0005

sample
[ˋsæmpl]

同 **specimen, example, model**
動 **sample** 同 test
名 **sampling**

Product **samples** are available upon request, but only for certain products; please check our catalog for availability.

(n.) 樣品

產品樣品可供索取，但僅限特定商品；可索取商品細目請查閱我們的目錄。

0006

satisfy
[ˋsætɪsˌfaɪ]

同 **gratify, please, fulfill**
反 **dissatisfy**
形 **satisfactory**
　　反 unsatisfactory
形 **satisfied**
形 **satisfying** 同 hearty, cheering
名 **satisfaction**

I am confident that we can **satisfy** all of your office supply needs, so why not make us your sole supplier and simplify your ordering process.

(v.) 滿足

我有信心我們可以滿足你們辦公用品的所有需求，那麼何不讓我們成為你們的單一供應商，簡化訂貨程序。

0007

scan
[skæn]

必
同 **examination, scanning**
動 **scan** 同 skim, look over
名 **scanner**

A **scan** of the computer revealed that it was infected with a dangerous virus that would have to be removed before the secretary could use it again.

(n.) 掃描

掃描電腦後顯示它感染了一種危險病毒，必須先將病毒移除，那位祕書才能再次使用電腦。

0008

schedule
[ˋskɛdʒʊl]

必
同 **arrange, organize**
名 **schedule**
　　同 plan, agenda, timetable

I'd like to **schedule** a meeting with you sometime next week; please let me know when you're available so we can set up a specific time.

(v.) 安排

我想安排下周與你會面，請讓我知道你何時有空，好讓我們定下確切的時間。

0009

scrutinize

[ˈskrutəˌnaɪz]

必
同 study, inspect
名 scrutiny
　　同 surveillance, inspection

The CFO instructed the accounting department to **scrutinize** all company financial statements and make sure everything was in order in preparation for the upcoming 3rd party audit.

(v.) 詳細檢查，細看

財務長指示會計部門詳細檢查公司所有財務報表，確定一切在即將到來的第三方稽核之前準備就緒。

0010

scrutiny

[ˈskrutn̩ɪ]

必
同 surveillance, inspection

The report appeared to be well written and accurate, but under closer **scrutiny**, a number of mistakes and inconsistencies were discovered.

(n.) 詳細的檢查

這份報告看來好像寫得很好也很精確，但在進一步詳細檢查下，發現了一些錯誤以及前後不一致的地方。

0011

search

[sɜtʃ]

必
同 probe, forage
名 search　　同 pursuit, quest
形 searching
　　同 inquisitory, probing
副 searchingly
名 searcher

Successful managers are constantly **searching** for new tools that will motivate their employees to perform at the highest possible level.

(v.) 尋找

成功的經理人會持續不斷尋找新的方法，來激勵員工發揮最大能耐。

0012

secure

[sɪˈkjʊr]

讀
同 safe, protected, sheltered
反 insecure, unsafe
副 securely
動 secure
名 security
　　同 protection, surveillance
　　反 insecurity, vulnerability

When making financial transactions online, it is best to ensure that your connection to the Internet is **secure**.

(a.) 安全的

進行線上金融交易時，最好確定你的連線是安全的。

0013

select
[sə`lɛkt]

必
同 choose, pick
形 select
　同 choice, quality, prime
名 selection
　同 choice, option, pick
形 selective

We regret to inform you that the product you have **selected** is currently out of stock; if you would still like to order it, please allow an additional 10 days for delivery.

(v.) 選擇

很遺憾要通知您，您所選購的商品目前沒有存貨；如果仍欲下訂，請多給我們十天的出貨時間。

0014

selection
[sə`lɛkʃən]

必
同 choice, option, pick

The wide **selection** of accommodations in the beach town, from simple hostels to five-star hotels, made it an ideal destination for vacationers of all ages and budgets.

(n.) 選擇

那個海濱小鎮的住宿選擇很廣，從簡單的青年旅社到五星級大飯店都有，使該鎮成為各種年齡層與預算的度假者理想的去處。

0015

self-starter
[`sɛlf startɚ]

Our company is now hiring for store management/sales positions; we are looking for **self-starters** with a great attitude who have the desire to succeed and excel in a fast paced and exciting environment.

(n.) 工作積極的人

我們公司目前正在招募店面管理人員或銷售人員；我們想找態度良好、工作積極、想在快速刺激的環境中成功卓越的人。

0016

sense
[sɛns]

必
同 sensibility
動 sense　　同 perceive
形 sensible　同 prudent, shrewd
形 senseless
副 sensibly

It doesn't make **sense** to expend resources on developing new markets unless the current market for your products is extremely small or already saturated.

(n.) 道理，意義

除非你產品目前的市場極小或已達飽和，否則沒道理把資源用於開發新的市場。

0017

sensible

[ˈsɛnsəbl]

同 **prudent, shrewd**
名 **sensibility**

The **sensible** thing to do when saving money for a short-term objective is to invest in a certificate of deposit, short-term bond fund or money market fund.

(a.) 明智的
為了短期目標而儲蓄時，明智的作法是投資定存、短期債券基金或貨幣市場基金。

0018

separate

[ˈsɛpəˌret]

必
同 **divided, individual**
動 **separate** 同 divide
副 **separately**
名 **separation**
形 **separable** 反 inseparable
名 **separatist**

In order to simplify accounting procedures, when starting a business it is a good idea to open a **separate** banking account for business income and expenses.

(a.) 獨立的，單獨的
為簡化會計程序，成立公司時最好開立一個獨立銀行帳戶供公司收入和支出使用。

0019

serenity

[səˈrɛnətɪ]

同 **peace, tranquillity, composure,**
形 **serene**
　同 calm, tranquil, unagitated
副 **serenely**

Our jungle resort is an oasis of **serenity** and luxury set amidst the lush greenery of one of the world's largest remaining tropical rainforests.

(n.) 寧靜，平靜
我們的叢林度假村是寧靜奢華的綠洲，坐落於世界上現存最大熱帶雨林之一的蒼翠綠色植物之中。

0020

serious

[ˈsɪrɪəs]

必
同 **earnest, grave, stern**
反 **frivolous**
副 **seriously**
名 **seriousness**

I appreciate your interest in obtaining samples of several items in our product catalog, but please be aware that we are focusing our full attention on clients showing **serious** intent to purchase at the moment.

(a.) 認真的，認真對待的
很感謝您有興趣索取我們產品目錄中幾項商品的樣品，但也希望您了解，我們只會把全副精力放在當下認真想購買商品的客戶身上。

0021

service

[ˈsɝvɪs]

必
同 labor, facility
形 serviceable

In addition to high-quality products, good after-sales **service** is also of considerable importance in the establishment of long-term relationships with clients.

(n.) 服務

要與客戶建立長期合作關係，除了優質的產品之外，良好的售後服務也相當重要。

0022

session

[ˈsɛʃən]

必
同 term, period

The customer relations training course, which will be held every Tuesday from two to four p.m. in the main conference room, will consist of lectures, demonstrations, and practice **sessions**.

(n.) 一段時間

顧客關係訓練課程將於每周二下午兩點到四點舉行，上課地點在大會議室，課程將包括授課、示範以及練習時段。

0023

set aside

[sɛt əˈsaɪd]

聽

Young workers are advised to **set aside** at least ten percent of their monthly salaries in a tax-deferred retirement account, and twenty percent if possible.

撥出（一筆錢）

年輕的員工被建議撥出至少月薪百分之十的金額存入緩課稅的退休帳戶，如果可能的話，百分之二十更好。

0024

set up

[sɛt ʌp]

必

Our president intends to spend several months this year **setting up** new branch offices in countries across Eastern Europe.

建立，創建

我們總裁今年打算花幾個月的時間，在東歐各國成立新的辦事處。

0025

settle
[ˈsɛtl]
必
同 resolve
名 settler
名 settlement
片 settle down

Hopefully, you two will be able to **settle** your disagreement outside of court, because hiring a lawyer can be very expensive, and even if you win the case, your legal expenses may exceed the settlement you obtain.

(v.) 解決，結束

希望你們雙方能在法庭外解決你們的歧見，因為聘請律師可能會很貴，而且即使打贏了，你的法律費用可能會比得到的和解金還多。

0026

shareholder
[ˈʃɛrˌholdə]
同 stockholder

Several of the major **shareholders** were disappointed with the actions taken by the president in recent months, as they didn't feel that these actions were beneficial to the company.

(n.) 股東

幾個主要股東對於總裁近幾個月所採取的行動，感到失望，因為他們不覺得那些動作對公司有益。

0027

sharp
[ʃɑrp]
必
同 abrupt, sudden
反 gradual
副 sharply
名 sharpness

A combination of higher borrowing costs and a lack of affordability have caused a **sharp** drop in housing prices, a slowdown in home building, and consequently a large build-up in inventories of unsold new and existing homes.

(a.) 急遽的

越來越高的貸款成本加上負擔不起，已經造成房價急遽下滑、住宅建案減緩，結果新成屋與中古屋未售出的數量大加累積。

0028

shift
[ʃɪft]
同 alteration
動 shift

Employees who are assigned to work the graveyard **shift** will receive eight hours' pay for seven hours' work, as well as an hourly rate 15% over the base hourly rate.

(n.) 排班

被排到上大夜班的員工，上班七小時將領到八小時的工資，而且時薪也比基本時薪高出百分之十五。

0029

ship

[ʃɪp]

必

同 **embark, transport**

名 **ship** 同 **boat, vessel**

名 **shipping**

名 **shipment**

名 **shipper**

Please don't be nervous, as your order will **ship** tomorrow at the latest and should arrive within one to three business days, which means you should receive it no later than next Wednesday.

(v.) 上船，船運

請不要緊張，您訂的貨品最慢將在明天裝載上船，應該會在一至三個工作天內抵達，亦即您最晚在下星期三就應該會收到。

0030

shipment

[ˈʃɪpmənt]

聽 讀

If you give me your tracking number, I can tell you exactly when your **shipment** went out, and approximately what day it will arrive at your office.

(n.) 裝載運送的貨物

如果給我您的追蹤代碼，我可以明確告訴您運送貨物寄出的時間，以及大約會在哪一天送達您的公司。

0031

shipper

[ˈʃɪpɚ]

必

The **shipper** made a deal with the company that in exchange for the best prices on all shipments, the company had to agree to ship exclusively with them.

(n.) 運貨人

貨運業者和這家公司達成協議，所有貨運都以最低價格計算，交換條件是該公司必須同意獨家委託它們運送。

0032

shortage

[ˈʃɔrtɪdʒ]

讀

同 **deficit, shortfall, lack**

反 **abundance**

形 **short**

同 **meagre, sparse, deficient**

反 **plenty**

A **shortage** of qualified office temps made it difficult for the company to maintain normal operations during the six-month union strike.

(n.) 短缺

合格的辦公室臨時雇員短缺，使得該公司在六個月的工會罷工期間，難以維持正常運作。

0033

shut down
[ʃʌt daʊn]
必

The company was **shut down** by the government after an Immigration and Naturalization Service investigation revealed that large numbers of illegal workers were employed there and were being treated inhumanely.

停工
移民局的調查揭露，這家公司雇用大量非法勞工，並以不人道的方式對待，該公司因而被政府勒令停業。

0034

shuttle
[ˈʃʌtl]
同 go back and forth

Our hotel is located just 15 minutes from the Vancouver International Airport, and offers complementary 24-hour airport **shuttle** service, free high-speed Internet access, and unlimited local calls.

(n.) 接駁
我們飯店距離溫哥華國際機場僅十五分鐘車程，並提供免費的二十四小時機場接駁服務、高速無線上網，以及無限撥打市內電話。

0035

sign
[saɪn]
必
同 mark, symbol, emblem
動 sign　　反 autograph
名 signature

A **sign** on the president's door indicated that he was not to be disturbed, so naturally his secretary thought twice before knocking on his door.

(n.) 牌示，告示
總裁辦公室門口的牌子指出他不想被打擾，因此他的祕書敲門之前當然會再三考慮。

0036

signature
[ˈsɪgnətʃə]
必

For courier shipping, please note that a **signature** is required for the delivery to be completed; the package must be accepted and signed for at the delivery address specified on your order.

(n.) 簽名
請注意急件運送一定要有簽名，運送程序才算完成，必須要有人在訂單上指定的收件地址簽收包裹。

0037

significant
[sɪgˈnɪfəkənt]

必
同 important, substantial
反 insignificant, unimportant
副 significantly
名 significance

There really have been some **significant** changes for the better at this office in the eight years I have worked here.

(a.) 顯著的
我在這間辦公室工作的八年當中，這兒真的有一些顯著的改變。

0038

site
[saɪt]

必 聽
同 place, setting

The construction **site** was bustling with activities when the company president went to inspect the progress on the new company headquarters building.

(n.) 場地
當總裁到公司新的總部大廈視察進度時，工地正忙著進行工事。

0039

situation
[ˌsɪtʃuˈeʃən]

必
同 condition, circumstances
動 situate   同 locate

In view of the gravity of the current economic **situation**, the government has decided to enact a stimulus package to help forestall a major economic turndown.

(n.) 情況，局面
有鑑於經濟現況低迷，政府已經決定制定刺激經濟方案，以協助抑止重大的經濟衰退。

0040

skill
[skɪl]

必
同 proficiency, experience, art, technique
形 skilled
形 skillful
名 skillfulness

The young man's good phone **skills** and extensive sales experience made him an obvious choice for placement in the telemarketing department.

(n.) 技巧
這名年輕男士純熟的電話談話技巧，以及豐富的銷售經驗，使得他顯然適任於電話行銷部門。

MP3 146

0041

smooth
[smuð]

必
反 rough
副 smoothly
名 smoothness
動 smoothen

To ensure a **smooth** transition from a traditional marketing approach to a customer targeted approach, an organization must reflect carefully on the changes that need to be made and understand the ramifications of such a transition in the organization.

(a.) 進行順利的

為了確保能順利從傳統行銷方式轉變成顧客導向的方式，組織一定要悉心考慮必要的改變，並了解這樣的轉變會在組織內造成的複雜後果。

0042

smooth out
[smuð aut]

必

There are a few problems with the contract that need to be **smoothed out**, but after these issues are resolved, I am confident that we can come to an agreement that will be beneficial to both parties.

排除

合約中有幾個問題需要排除，但在這些議題解決後，我很有信心我們可以達成對雙方都有利的協議。

0043

software
[ˈsɔft͵wɛr]

必

Typically, after the first release of a **software** product, enhancements are made and new functions are added, and new releases of the product are made available at regular intervals.

(n.) 軟體

一般來說，軟體產品在初次推出後，會加以改良並增加新功能，然後會定期推出新版本。

0044

sell out
[sɛl aut]

必

With seats to the NFL playoff game being **sold out**, the sales manager decided to take his visiting client to a Broadway production instead.

賣光

由於國家美式足球聯盟的季後賽門票已銷售一空，業務經理轉而決定帶來訪的客戶去看百老匯表演。

0045

solve
[sɑlv]

必
同 **resolve**
形 **solvable** 同 resolvable

After studying the prototype and looking over the blueprints, I think we have finally figured out how to **solve** the heat dissipation problem in the new graphics card.

(v.) 解決
研究過原型並檢查藍圖之後，我想我們終於釐清要如何解決新型顯示卡的散熱問題了。

0046

sophisticated
[səˋfɪstɪˌketɪd]

聽 讀
同 **complicated, refined**
反 **simple**
動 **sophisticate**
名 **sophistication**

The company's new security system makes use of a variety of **sophisticated** technology, including biometric readers, infrared security cameras, and wireless motion detectors.

(a.) 精密的，複雜的
這間公司新的保全系統利用了各種精密複雜的科技，其中包括生物特徵測定裝置、紅外線監視攝影機，以及無線動態偵測器。

0047

source
[sors]

必
同 **origin, root**

Our trading company is constantly looking for new **sources** of low-cost, high-quality products to sell in the lucrative North American market.

(n.) 來源
我們的貿易公司持續尋找低成本、高品質的產品來源，以便在有利可圖的北美市場中銷售。

0048

specialist
[ˋspɛʃəlɪst]

必
同 **specializer, professional**
反 **generalist**
動 **specialize**
　 同 particularize, narrow down
形 **special**

Sales **specialists** at the retail store are responsible for processing over the counter sales transactions and providing customers with information on product availability and pricing.

(n.) 專家
零售商店的銷售專員負責處理櫃檯買賣交易，並將產品的供貨及價格資訊提供給顧客。

0049

specialize
[ˈspɛʃəˌlaɪz]

必
同 **particularize, narrow down**

After graduating from law school and passing the bar, Elizabeth decided to set up her own law practice and **specialize** in real estate and tax law.

(v.) 專門從事
從法學院畢業並通過律師考試之後，伊麗莎白決定自己開業，專攻房地產以及稅法。

0050

specifically
[spɪˈsɪfɪkḷɪ]

讀
反 **in general, generally**
名 **specification**
　同 stipulation, detail
動 **specify**
　同 designate, detail
形 **specific**

The software company's new accounting software package is the first product that they have designed **specifically** to meet the needs of small businesses and self-employed individuals.

(adv.) 具體地，明確地
那間軟體公司新推出的套裝會計軟體，是他們專為符合小型企業及獨立工作者需求所設計的第一項產品。

0051

specification
[ˌspɛsəfəˈkeʃən]

必 聽
同 **stipulation, detail**

If you send us **specifications** of the proposed product and an estimate of the quantity required, we can get back to you with a price quote within one week.

(n.) 規格明細，產品說明
如果您將所提商品的詳細規格以及預估需求量送過來，我們可以在一週內回覆報價給您。

0052

specify
[ˈspɛsəˌfaɪ]

必
同 **detail**

When ordering products from our company, please **specify** the quantity, size, color, and model number of each item, as well as the method of delivery.

(v.) 詳細說明
向我們公司訂購產品時，請詳述數量、尺寸、顏色、每一個產品的型號，連同運送方式。

0053

spectrum
[ˈspɛktrəm]
必

The human resources consulting firm provided a full **spectrum** of HR consulting services, including employee retention guidance, training and development, and compensation and benefits assessment.

(n.) 範圍，光譜
那間人力資源顧問公司提供全方位的人資諮詢服務，其中包括員工留任輔導、訓練和發展，還有津貼與福利評估。

0054

speculation
[ˌspɛkjəˈleʃən]
讀
同 **guess, supposition**
動 **speculate**
形 **speculative**

Speculation about a merger between the nation's two largest automakers began to spread after a newspaper reported that the chief financial officers of the two companies met last month to discuss an alliance.

(n.) 臆測，投機買賣
報紙報導國內兩家最大車廠的財務長，上個月會面討論結盟，然後這兩家公司將合併的臆測就開始散播開來。

0055

spoil
[spɔɪl]
同 **destroy, wreck, ruin**
名 **spoiler**
形 **spoiled**　同 spoilt

No matter how carefully you plan your vacation, there is always a chance that it will be **spoiled** by bad weather or cancelled flights.

(v.) 搞糟
不論你多謹慎地計畫你的假期，總還是有因惡劣天候或班機取消而泡湯的可能。

0056

sponsor
[ˈspɑnsə]
同 **fund, patronize**
名 **sponsor**
　同 supporter, patron
名 **sponsorship**

In order to enhance its corporate image, the company made every effort to establish good relations with the local community, and even going as far as **sponsoring** a junior high school soccer team.

(v.) 贊助
為了強化企業形象，那間公司用盡全力與當地社區建立良好關係，甚至贊助一所國中的足球校隊。

0057

spouse
[spauz]
必

Employees will be allowed to take their **spouses** along with them on the company trip to Japan; the company will cover their food, lodging, and sightseeing expenses, but they must pay for their air tickets.

(n.) 配偶
員工將可以帶配偶一同參加去日本的員工旅遊，公司會負責配偶的食宿和觀光費用，但是他們必須自己支付機票費用。

0058

stack
[stæk]
聽
同 **pile, heap**
名 **stack**　　同 **pile, heap**

The supermarket clerk **stacked** box after box of cereal into a pyramid display at the end of the cereal aisle.

(v.) 堆積
超市的店員將玉米片盒子一個接著一個堆疊成金字塔，展示在早餐玉米片走道區的盡頭。

0059

stage
[stedʒ]
必
動 **stage**　　同 **perform**

As the CEO walked onto the **stage** in the meeting hall to give his speech, the assembled employees broke into applause.

(n.) 舞台
執行長步上會議廳的舞台發表演講的時候，與會員工給予熱烈掌聲。

0060

startup
[ˈstɑrtˌʌp]

Most **startups** fail because they either run out of money before they can gain market share, or they make products that do not meet consumers' needs.

(n.) 新創公司
大部分新創公司失敗的原因，若非他們在取得市占率之前就把錢用光了，就是他們做的產品不符合消費者的需求。

0061

statement
[ˈstetmənt]
必
同 **report, argument**
動 **state** 同 report

Before investing in a company, it is wise to look over its financial statements including its balance sheet, income **statement**, statement of retained earnings, and statement of cash flows in order to determine its financial health.

(n.) 報告書
在投資一間公司之前，檢閱它的財務報表是很明智的──包括資產負債表、營收報表、保留盈餘表以及現金流量表──目的是為了判定其財務是否正健全。

0062

stationery
[ˈsteʃəˌnɛrɪ]
必 聽

In addition to greeting clients, answering phones, and handling incoming and outgoing mail, the receptionist is also responsible for ordering **stationery** and other office supplies as needed.

(n.) 文具，辦公事務用品
除了招呼顧客、接聽電話以及處理收發信件之外，接待人員也負責訂購所需的文具等辦公室用品。

0063

stay on top of
[ste ɑn tɑp əv]
必

Please be sure to **stay on top** of any last minute contract changes your client may require, and keep us informed so that we can draw up a new contract in time for the signing deadline.

掌握情況
請務必掌握住你的客戶對合約內容可能的臨時修改，並隨時告知我們，以利我們在簽約期限前，及時擬妥新合約。

0064

step up
[stɛp ʌp]

To meet growing market demand, domestic bottled water producers plan to **step up** production and improve their distribution networks.

加快，增快
為滿足逐漸成長的市場需求，國內的瓶裝水製造商計畫加快生產速度，並改善經銷網。

0065

stock
[stɑk]

必 聽
同 assets, share
動 形 stock
相關字彙 stock price 股價
　　　　stock marke t股市

The certified financial planner advised his client not to invest in the **stock** of the company he worked for, as this was tantamount to putting all of his eggs in one basket.

(n.) 股票

那名合格的理財規劃師建議他的客戶不要投資自己服務公司的股票，因為這等於是把雞蛋放在同一個籃子裡。

0066

stock options
[stɑk `ɑpʃən]

Part of the compensation package for all employees who had been with the company for at least five years was that a portion of their salary would be paid in the form of **stock options** every year.

認股權

津貼配套方案中有一部分是，在公司任職至少五年以上的員工，一部分薪資每年將會以認股權的方式支付。

0067

stock up on
[stɑk ʌp ɑn]

When we heard on the weather report that a hurricane was coming in a few days, we went to the supermarket to **stock up on** food, bottled water, flashlights, and candles.

儲備

當我們聽氣象報告說颶風會在幾天後登陸時，我們到超市去儲備食物、瓶裝水、手電筒和蠟燭。

0068

stockbroker
[`stɑk͵brokə]

While the **stockbroker** had a very dismal outlook on the market, he still recommended that clients hold on to their stocks and wait for the market to improve.

(n.) 股票經紀人

雖然那位股票經紀人對於股市的前景非常悲觀，他還是建議客戶持有股票等市場回溫。

0069

stocker
[ˋstɑkɚ]

The **stocker** at the company warehouse used a forklift to move the pallet of heavy machinery to the appropriate storage area.

(n.) 倉儲人員
公司倉庫的倉儲人員用堆高機把裝有重型機具的棧板，搬運到適當的存放區。

0070

stockholder
[ˋstɑkˌholdɚ]

At the annual **stockholders**' meeting, the company's stockholders approved the proposal to change the company's name from Alpha Beta Oil and Gas to Alpha Beta Energy Corporation.

(n.) 股東
在年度股東大會中，公司股東通過一項提案，把公司名稱由阿法貝塔石油天然氣改成阿法貝塔能源公司。

0071

stockroom
[ˋstɑkˌrum]

The man started out as a clerk in the **stockroom** was promoted to salesman after several months, and after three years became manager of the sales department.

(n.) 倉庫，貯藏室
那名一開始在倉庫擔任職員的男子，幾個月後被升為業務員，三年後成了業務部門的經理。

0072

storage
[ˋstorɪdʒ]
必

All of the office furniture and equipment will be placed in storage at a public **storage** facility until the renovation project is complete.

(n.) 貯藏，保管
辦公室所有的家具和設備都會貯藏在公共貯藏區域，直到修繕工程完成為止。

0073

store

[stor]

必

The supermarket chain plans to open at least twelve **stores** in the San Francisco Bay Area over the next year, many in areas that other grocery stores have long overlooked.

(n.) 百貨店

那個連鎖超市計畫明年在舊金山灣區至少開設十二間店面，其中有很多會開在長期以來都被其他雜貨業者忽略的地區。

0074

strategize

[ˋstrætəˌdʒaɪz]

必
名 **strategy** 同 scheme
形 **strategic**

The marketing director called a meeting of the marketing team to **strategize** about how to strengthen the company's presence on the Internet.

(v.) 定策略

行銷主管召集行銷小組成員開會，擬定策略來加強公司在網路上的能見度。

0075

strategy

[ˋstrætədʒɪ]

必 聽
同 **scheme**

As part of its overall **strategy** for enhancing shareholder value, the high-tech company set the goal of increasing its annual revenues by $90 million.

(n.) 策略

那間高科技公司訂下目標要將年營收提高九千萬美元，是提高股東價值這整體策略當中的一環。

0076

strength

[strɛnθ]

必
反 **weakness**
動 **strengthen**
　　同 fortify, toughen
　　反 weaken

The **strength** of our brand, combined with our commitment to providing top quality products and services, has enabled us to capture leading market share.

(n.) 實力

我們的品牌實力，加上致力提供最高品質的產品和服務，已使我們拿下領先的市占率。

0077

strict

[strɪkt]

必 聽 讀
同 **rigorous, harsh, severe**
反 **easy-going**
副 **strictly**
名 **strictness**同 stringency

All products are manufactured in **strict** adherence to internationally recognized standards and specifications, and come with a 60-day unconditional money back guarantee.

(a.) 嚴格的,徹底的
所有產品的製造均恪遵國際認可的標準和規格,且附有六十天的無條件退款保證。

0078

strictness

[ˋstrɪktnɪs]

必
同 **stringency**

The **strictness** of accounting standards has increased significantly over the past several years in response to the recent string of corporate accounting scandals.

(n.) 嚴格
為了因應近年來一連串的企業會計醜聞,過去幾年來會計標準的嚴格程度大幅提高。

0079

strong

[strɔŋ]

必
同 **acute, muscular, tough, sturdy, stout, stalwart**
反 **weak**
副 **strongly**
名 **strength**
動 **strengthen**

In view of Greg's **strong** desire to become a supervisor, demonstrated aptitude for supervisory work and high performance ratings, management decided to promote him to the position of assistant manager.

(a.) 強烈的
有鑑於克雷強烈想成為主管、對管理工作展現出才能,以及績效評等很高,管理階層決定升他為副理。

0080

stylish

[ˋstaɪlɪʃ]

同 **chic, fashionable**
反 **unstylish**
副 **stylishly**
副 **stylistically**
名 **style**

The director of the fashion division was a very **stylish** lady who always managed to stay on top of the latest fashion trends.

(a.) 時髦的,有型的
時裝部門的主管是一位非常時髦的女士,她總是走在最新時尚潮流的尖端。

0081

subcontractor

[sʌb͵kən`træktɚ]

動 subcontract

After winning the bid for construction of the new library, the construction company hired **subcontractors** to handle the electrical, plumbing, heating, and air conditioning work for the project.

(n.) 轉包商，分包商
在贏得新圖書館工程的招標案之後，建設公司雇用下包商來處理建案中的水電及空調工作。

0082

subject

[`sʌbdʒɪkt]

必
同 dependent
片 be subject to... 易受…影響

Prices listed in our catalog are **subject** to change without notice, and do not include shipping and handling charges or applicable taxes.

(a.) 易受…的，常遇…的
我們型錄上所列的價格隨時可能有變動，恕不另行通知，並且不包含運費、手續費或相關稅金。

0083

subjective

[səb`dʒɛktɪv]

必
同 prejudiced, biased
反 objective
副 subjectively

While qualitative research relies on **subjective** information like customer surveys and focus groups, quantitative research builds on existing information like census demographics or industry analysis.

(a.) 主觀的
質的研究取決於主觀的資料，好比顧客調查和焦點團體；而量的研究則建立在現有資料上，好比人口統計資料或產業分析。

0084

submission

[sʌb`mɪʃən]

必
同 submitting, handing in
動 submit
　同 surrender, yield, hand in, present
形 submissive
副 submissively

The paper **submission** deadline for the 3rd International Conference on Technology Management has been extended from July 25, 2008 to August 25, 2008.

(n.) 提交，呈遞
繳交第三屆科技管理國際研討會報告的最後期限，已經從二〇〇八年七月二十五日延長到二〇〇八年八月二十五日。

0085

submit

[səbˋmɪt]

必 讀

同 comply, yield, hand in, present

When you **submit** a patent application, you must include not only a written description of your invention, but also patent drawings illustrating how the invention works.

(v.) 呈交

當你呈交專利申請書時，不但必須附上發明物品的文字描述，還要有說明該項發明運作原理的圖畫。

0086

subscribe

[səbˋskraɪb]

必

名 subscription

名 subscriber

I **subscribe** to the belief that coworkers should work together to accomplish company goals rather than wasting time working against each other for personal benefit.

(v.) 同意，訂閱

我贊成同事應該合作來達成公司目標，不要為了個人利益而浪費時間彼此競爭。

0087

subscription

[səbˋskrɪpʃən]

必

The magazine **subscription** will run out this November, and the publishing company is asking if we are interested in renewing.

(n.) 訂閱

雜誌的訂閱將於今年十一月到期，出版社問我們是否有興趣續訂。

0088

subsidiary

[səbˋsɪdɪˏɛrɪ]

聽

同 division, branch

形 subsidiary

　　同 subordinate, underling

相關字彙

　　headquarters 總部

　　affiliated company 關係企業

　　branch office 分公司

This office is a **subsidiary** of our main office, which is located on Broad Street in Manhattan's financial district.

(n.) 子公司

這個辦公室是我們總公司的子公司之一，坐落於曼哈頓金融區的大通街上。

subsidize

[ˈsʌbsəˌdaɪz]

同 **fund, finance**
名 **subsidy** 回 stipend

It is clear that low-income families cannot afford health insurance without some assistance, and various federal and state programs exist to provide or **subsidize** health insurance for people with limited means.

(v.) 補貼，補助

若無協助，低收入戶顯然無法負擔健保費用，而許多聯邦與州級方案的存在，都是為了提供或補助健保給資源有限的人。

subsidy

[ˈsʌbsədɪ]

讀
同 **stipend**

While proponents of agricultural **subsidies** argue that they help increase agricultural production and drive down food prices, others insist that these subsidies actually hinder economic growth.

(n.) 補助金

雖然倡議農業補助的人，主張補助有助於增加農產量並降低食物價格，但其他人堅持這些補助金其實會阻礙經濟成長。

substance

[ˈsʌbstəns]

必
同 **material**

While this drug is available over the counter in pharmacies in this country, it is a controlled **substance** in many countries.

(n.) 物品，物質

雖然這種藥物在這國家的藥局裡不需處方箋就可購買，但在很多國家都是管制品。

substantial

[səbˈstænʃəl]

必
同 **significant, considerable**
反 **small**
副 **substantially**

All capital raising activities require companies to devote a **substantial** amount of time, effort, and resources in order to be successful, and an initial public offering is no exception.

(a.) 大量的

所有募資活動均需公司投入大量時間、努力與資源才能成功，首次股票公開發行也不例外。

0093

substitute

[ˈsʌbstəˌtjut]

必
同 **alternative**
名 **substitute** 同 replacement
動 **substitute** 同 replace
名 **substitution**
    同 commutation, exchange

If for any reason an employee is unable to work a scheduled shift and cannot find a **substitute** worker, management must be notified no less than two hours before the shift is scheduled to begin.

(a.) 代理的，替代的

如果員工因故無法依排定的工作時間上班，卻又找不到代班的人，最晚一定要在該班次預定開始前兩小時通知管理部門。

0094

substitution

[ˌsʌbstəˈtjuʃən]

同 **exchange**

Product **substitution** occurs when goods or services not strictly meeting contractual requirements are delivered to the customer without approval, and there was prior knowledge that requirements were violated.

(n.) 替換

當未完全符合契約要求的物品或服務，在客戶未同意前便送達，而且在事前便得知其違反要求，就要更換產品。

0095

subtract

[səbˈtrækt]

必
同 **deduct, take off**
反 **add**
名 **subtraction**

If the repair costs less than $100, you may tell the landlord that you will have the repair made yourself and **subtract** the cost from your rent if the landlord does not make the repair within 14 days.

(v.) 減去

如果房東十四天之內沒有維修，而維修費用又不到一百美元，你可以告訴房東說你會自己處理，再從你的房租減去這筆金額。

0096

succeed

[səkˈsid]

必
反 **miscarry, fail**
名 **success** 同 triumph, victory
            反 failure
形 **successful**
    同 victorious, triumphant
    反 unsuccessful
副 **successfully**

To **succeed** in the world of finance, you have to have a great head for numbers and be able to perform at peak level under pressure.

(v.) 成功

要在金融界成功，你一定要具備很棒的數字能力，還要能夠在壓力下達成最佳表現。

success

[sək`sɛs]

必
同 triumph, victory
反 failure

High search engine rankings are essential to the **success** of e-commerce sites, because high rankings make the products sold on them more accessible to online shoppers.

(n.) 成功

電子商務網站若要成功，在搜尋引擎占有高排名是必要的，因為高排名能讓線上購物顧客更容易看到這些網站上銷售的商品。

successive

[sək`sɛsɪv]

必
同 sequential, consecutive
副 successively

The struggling automaker has lost market share in the United States for ten **successive** years, and is now in danger of bankruptcy.

(a.) 連續的

那間苦撐的車商在美國的市占率已連續十年下滑，如今正面臨破產危機。

sufficient

[sə`fɪʃənt]

必
同 ample, enough
反 insufficient, deficient
名 sufficiency

We have gathered a **sufficient** amount of information from all of our area managers, and can now start compiling the annual sales report.

(a.) 充足的

我們已從所有的區域經理那邊蒐集充足的資訊，現在可以開始彙整年度銷售報告書。

suggest

[sə`dʒɛst]

必
同 propose, advise
名 suggestion
  proposal, recommendation

Can someone **suggest** a way for us to improve productivity without sacrificing quality or increasing labor costs?

(v.) 建議

誰能建議我們一個既能提高產能，又無須犧牲品質或提高勞力成本的方法？

0101

suggestion

[səˈdʒɛstʃən]

必

同 **proposal, recommendation**

Anna's **suggestion** that employees be allowed to work from home several days a week did not meet with approval by management.

(n.) 提議

安娜提出員工一週可以在家工作幾天的提議，並未受到管理階層同意。

0102

suit

[sut]

必

動 **suit** 同 **fit, accommodate**

Male employees are required to wear **suits**, dress shirts, ties, and dress shoes on every day except Friday, when they are permitted to wear casual shirts and pants.

(n.) 西裝

男性員工被要求每天穿著西裝襯衫、打領帶以及正式皮鞋，只有週五除外，這一天他們可以穿著休閒襯衫和長褲。

0103

suitable

[ˈsutəbl]

必

同 **appropriate, suited, fitting**

反 **unseemly**

副 **suitably**

動 **suit**

　同 fit, accommodate

In your résumé, you should present yourself as the most **suitable** candidate for the position you are applying for.

(a.) 適當的，合適的

在你的履歷中，你應該把自己描述成最適合你所應徵職位的求職者。

0104

sum

[sʌm]

讀

同 **total**

反 **fraction, part**

Although the computer manufacturer spent an enormous **sum** of money developing and marketing the tablet laptop computer, in the end it was a failure in the marketplace.

(n.) 總數，合計

雖然這家電腦製造商耗費鉅資來發展及行銷平板筆記電腦，最後在市場上仍宣告失敗。

0105

superior
[sə`pɪrɪə]

名 **superior**
　同 higher-up, superordinate
形 **superior**
　同 condescending, haughty, disdainful
　反 inferior
名 **superiority**　反 inferiority

Michael asked his **superior** for a raise, and while his superior approved, he said that he didn't have the authority to make that kind of decision and would have to take it up with the department head.

(n.) 上司
麥可向上司要求加薪，儘管他的上司同意，卻說自己無權做這種決定，必須向上呈報給部門主管。

0106

superior
[sə`pɪrɪə]

讀
同 condescending, haughty, disdainful
反 inferior
片 be superior to...,
　 be superior than...

While our products are **superior** to those of our main competitors, their strong distribution networks have made it difficult for us to gain market share.

(a.) 優於…的
雖然我們的產品優於我們的主要競爭對手，他們堅強的經銷網卻讓我們很難增加市場占有率。

0107

supervise
[`supəˌvaɪz]

必　聽
同 oversee, superintend
名 **supervisor**
　同 superintendent
名 **supervision**

Alan was asked to **supervise** a team of twelve for a new project, and while he was a little nervous about taking on this level of responsibility, he knew that this was a good chance to prove his abilities.

(v.) 監督，管理
艾倫被要求去管理一個負責新企畫案的十二人小組，雖然他對於承擔這種層級的責任有點緊張，但他知道這是證明自己能力的好機會。

0108

supervisor
[ˌsupə`vaɪzə]

聽
同 administrator

My **supervisor** called me into his office last week to inform me that a branch office manager's job had opened up in Germany, and that I was a shoo-in for the position.

(n.) 監督人，管理人，上司
上星期，我的上司把我叫進他的辦公室，告訴我德國有一個分公司經理的職位出缺，而我十之八九會得到那個職位。

0109

supplier
[sə`plaɪɚ]
讀
同 **provider**
動 **supply**　同 provide

If you are unable to ensure that deliveries arrive on time and resolve the quality issues that we have raised, we may be forced to switch to a new **supplier**.

(n.) 供應商，供應者
假如你無法擔保貨物會準時送達，並解決我們提出的品質問題，我們也許會被迫換用新的供應商。

0110

supply
[sə`plaɪ]
必 聽
同 **provision**
反 **demand**

The **supply** of plastic goods that we had in stock at the beginning of the year was insufficient to cover all of our clients' needs for the entire year.

(n.) 供應（量）
今年初我們庫存的塑膠品供應量並不足以應付我們客戶一整年的需求。

0111

supply
[sə`plaɪ]
必 聽
同 **provide**

To assure our ability to **supply** customers with quality, reliable, price-competitive products, we are currently reorganizing our production, distribution, and marketing systems.

(v.) 供應
為確保我們有能力供應客戶品質優良、可靠又有價格競爭力的產品，目前我們正在重整我們的生產、配銷和行銷系統。

0112

support
[sə`port]
同 **sustain, foster**
名 **support**　同 help, aid
形 **supporting**
形 **supportive**
　　反 unsupportive

We will be sorry to lose such a valuable member of our staff, but at the same time we fully **support** your decision to go back to school and get a higher degree.

(v.) 撫養，支持
我們會遺憾失去了我們員工當中可貴的一員，但同時，我們也完全支持你重回校園取得更高學位的決定。

0113

surrounding

[sə`raundɪŋ]

讀

同 circumferent, encompassing

名 surroundings
　同 environment, setting

動 surround

After opening up a successful shop in the downtown area last year, the coffee shop chain decided to open four more shops in the **surrounding** area over the next several years.

(a.) 周圍的

去年在市中心開店成功後，這間咖啡連鎖店決定在未來數年內於周邊地區再多開四家店。

0114

survey

[sə`ve]

讀

同 research, review, inquiry

動 survey

名 surveyor

片 conduct a survey

After conducting a market **survey**, the company came to the conclusion that there was no room for growth in their current market, and that they must attempt to expand into new market niches.

(n.) 調查，民意調查

進行一次市場調查後，公司得出了結論，也就是他們目前的市場已沒有成長空間，必須嘗試打入新市場。

0115

sustain

[sə`sten]

聽 讀

同 maintain

名 sustainability

形 sustainable

All hopes of **sustaining** the business for another year or two faded when it came to light that the boss had been embezzling company funds.

(v.) 支撐，維持

當老闆盜用公款的事曝光後，所有支撐公司多營運一、兩年的希望盡皆消退。

0116

sweep

[swip]

聽

同 brush

名 sweep　同 expanse

形 sweeping

Although the Republican candidate was consistently ahead in the polls in the run-up to the election, the Democrats ended up **sweeping** the elections with 79 percent of the vote.

(v.) 橫掃，大勝

儘管共和黨候選人在選前的民調持續領先，民主黨最後卻在選舉中拿下七成九的選票而獲得大勝。

system

[ˈsɪstəm]

必
同 **structure**
形 **systematic**
　同 methodical, efficient
反 **unsystematic**
副 **systematically**

The online retailer put new **systems** in place to manage periods of peak demand and smooth out the operational glitches that had frustrated its customers.

(n.) 系統
線上零售商使用新系統來管理尖峰期的需求，並消除讓顧客感到挫折的操作毛病。

systematic

[ˌsɪstəˈmætɪk]

必
同 **methodical, efficient**
反 **unsystematic**

The government undertook a **systematic** overhaul of financial and banking systems, downsizing the overcrowded banking sector, enhancing the transparency of banking operations and further liberalizing capital markets.

(a.) 有系統的
政府對於金融及銀行體制，進行了有系統的通盤檢查，縮減過度氾濫的銀行業，加強銀行營運的透明度，並進一步讓資本市場自由化。

systematically

[ˌsɪstəˈmætɪklɪ]

The reason our products are so successful in the marketplace is that they are **systematically** conceived, designed, produced, and distributed based solely on the preferences of consumers.

(adv.) 有系統地
我們的產品在市場上如此成功，是因為它們完全根據客戶的喜好、有系統地加以構思、設計、生產和配銷。

New TOEIC 990 新多益高分關鍵字彙

New
TOEIC
990

新多益高分關鍵字彙

990

T

Group

0001

take advantage of

[tek əd`væntɪdʒ əv]
聽 讀

In order to **take** full **advantage of** marketing opportunities, it is essential for marketing executives to be aware of the external business environment and changes in the marketplace.

利用
為了完全利用行銷機會，行銷主管必須瞭解外在的商業環境和市場的變化。

0002

take back

[tek bæk]
必

My wife bought a new vacuum cleaner last week, but it turned out to be defective, and when she **took it back** to the department store to exchange it for a new one, they told her that it was out of stock.

退還，退貨
我的妻子上星期買了一台新的吸塵器，結果卻有瑕疵，當她把它退還給百貨公司想換一台新的，他們告訴她已無現貨。

0003

take notice of

[tek `notɪs əv]

Consumers are starting to **take notice of** how well businesses protect their personal data, and are more willing to do business with companies that have good security practices.

注意到，關注
消費者開始注意公司行號對他們個人資料的保護程度，也更願意和安全措施良好的公司做生意。

0004

take out

[tek aut]
必

In Hong Kong, employers are required to **take out** insurance policies to cover employees, both full-time and part-time, who are injured or die in accidents that occur in the workplace.

申請取得（貸款、保險）
在香港，雇主被要求投保以支付因職場意外而受傷或死亡的全職與兼職員工。

0005

take part in

[tek pɑrt ɪn]

必

Although Cassandra **took part in** every office event that was held since she joined the company, her boss still couldn't remember her name.

參與

雖然卡珊卓參與了從她進入公司後所舉辦的每一項辦公室活動，但她老闆仍然記不得她的名字。

0006

take steps

[tek stɛps]

讀

We are **taking steps** to make sure our suppliers understand and respect our business code of conduct, and that they must abide by this code if they desire to continue doing business with us.

採取步驟

我們採取措施以確保我們的供應商瞭解並尊重我們的生意守則，他們若想跟我們繼續做生意，就必須遵守此守則。

0007

takeover

[ˈtekˌovɚ]

讀

動 take over

相關字彙 takeover bid
　　　　 公開出價收購（TOB）

When Kualtech Systems announced the **takeover** of Techutrade Inc. last year, the company warned that it could be cutting up to 3,000 jobs worldwide, and closing several Techutrade production facilities.

(n.) 接管，接收

當 Kualtech Systems 去年宣布接管 Techutrade 公司，便預告將在全球裁減最多三千名員工，並關閉幾處 Techutrade 的生產設施。

0008

target

[ˈtɑrgɪt]

必

同 goal, aim

Sales representatives who meet their annual sales **targets** will receive a bonus of 10 percent of their current salary package at the end of the year.

(n.) 目標

達到年度銷售目標的業務代表，年底將得到他們現有薪水配套百分之十的紅利。

0009

taste
[test]

必
同 penchant, fondness
動 taste　　同 sample
形 tasteful
　　同 refined, elegant, cultured
　　反 tasteless
形 tasteless 同 flavorless
形 tasty
　　同 palatable, delectable
名 tastefulness

The annual music festival offers a wide variety of musical genres to appeal to all **tastes**, from opera and classical music to pop and jazz.

(n.)口味，愛好
這個年度音樂節提供廣泛多變的音樂類型，從歌劇和古典樂到流行樂和爵士都有，以吸引各種口味的人。

0010

tax evasion
[tæks ɪˋveʒən]

The man was arrested for **tax evasion** and incarcerated, leaving his two sons to run the family business in his absence.

逃漏稅
這個男人因逃漏稅被捕入獄，留下兩個兒子在他不在時經營家族事業。

0011

tax exemption
[tæks ɪgˋzɛmpʃən]

Generally, you are allowed one **tax exemption** for yourself and, if you are married, one tax exemption for your spouse.

免稅
一般而言，你自己可以有一項免稅額，若你已婚，配偶也有一項免稅額。

0012

tax return
[tæks rɪˋtɜn]

If you're asking voters of this country to elect you as President, it's reasonable and rational that your **tax returns** be made public.

報稅單
假如你要求這個國家的選民選你當總統，公布你的報稅單是適當且合理的。

0013

tax revenue
[tæks `rɛvə,nju]
 聽 讀

Seeking to enlarge the tax base and increase **tax revenues,** the new administration has been considering a number of new tax policies, including a capital gains tax on securities.

稅收
為了擴大稅基和增加稅收，新政府考慮一些新的租稅政策，包括證券交易所得稅。

0014

technical
[`tɛknɪkl]
必
 technological, skilled, specialist
副 technically
名 technician

After some **technical** difficulties with the projector were resolved, Kara was able to carry on with her presentation and managed to finish within the allotted time.

(a.) 技術性的
解決了投影機一些技術困難後，卡拉能夠繼續她的報告，並得以在指定的時間內完成。

0015

tedious
[`tidɪəs]
必
 long-winded, boring
副 tediously
名 tedium

After many long hours of **tedious** work, the R&D team finally completed the prototype of the new digital stereo system.

(a.) 冗長乏味的
經過許多冗長乏味工作的日子之後，研發小組終於完成新款數位立體音響系統的原型。

0016

telescope
[`tɛlə,skop]

A **telescope** was placed on the top floor of the office building so that employees could enjoy the surrounding scenery during their breaks.

(n.) 望遠鏡
一架望遠鏡被放置在辦公大樓的頂樓，以便員工能夠在休息時欣賞周圍的景致。

temporarily

[ˈtɛmpəˌrɛrəlɪ]

讀
反 for good, permanently
形 temporary
同 passing, transitory

We will have to **temporarily** disconnect our system from the Internet between two and five today, so please take care of any important e-mail before two.

(adv.) 暫時地，臨時地
我們今天兩點到五點必須暫時中斷我們網路系統，所以請在兩點前處理好任何重要電子郵件。

tempt

[tɛmpt]

必
同 draw, allure
名 temptation
同 enticement, lure
形 tempting
同 tantalizing, alluring

Paula woke up with a cold and was **tempted** to call in sick, but she realized that if she missed a day of work she would fall hopelessly behind on her project.

(v.) 引誘，很想要做
寶拉早上醒來時感冒了，她很想打電話請病假，但她知道她如果少工作一天，她的企畫案進度就會無可救藥地落後。

temptation

[tɛmpˈteʃən]

必
同 enticement, lure

Although we have met our quarterly sales goals, we must resist the **temptation** to rest on our laurels, because the competition is constantly striving to steal market share from us.

(n.) 誘惑
雖然我們達到了季銷售目標，但必須抗拒志得意滿的誘惑，因為競爭對手不停地努力從我們這邊奪取市場。

term

[tɝm]

必 讀

When writing advertising copy, it is best to avoid technical **terms** and highlight the key features that will distinguish the products or services from those provided by other companies.

(n.) 專門術語
寫廣告文案時最好避免專門術語，並強調出產品或服務勝過其他公司的主要特點。

0021

term
[tɜm]

I believe that the **terms** of the contract are very clear, but should you have any concerns or questions, please don't hesitate to call me.

(n.) 條款
我相信合約的條款非常清楚，但若你有任何顧慮或問題，請不要猶豫，打電話給我。

0022

terminate
[ˈtɜməˌnet]
同 end
名 termination
　同 expiration, expiry

In a sale by installment payment, when the buyer fails to make payments as they become due, if the delinquent amount has reached one third of the total price, the seller may require payment of the full price from the buyer or **terminate** the contract.

(v.) 終止
在分期付款的買賣中，當買家無法在期限內付出款項，若未付款數目達到總價的三分之一時，賣家能夠要求買家支付全額費用或終止合約。

0023

termination
[ˌtɜməˈneʃən]
同 expiration, expiry

Causes for **termination** of employment include dishonesty or other unethical conduct, demonstrated incompetence, neglect of duty and violation of laws or company policies.

(n.) 終止
終止雇用的原因包括不誠實等不道德的行為、不適任、怠忽職守以及違反法律或公司政策。

0024

theme
[θim]
同 idea, topic
形 thematic
副 thematically

The **theme** of today's meeting is, "How to derive maximum value from each customer interaction," so I hope you'll all listen carefully as the knowledge and skills you learn could help you contribute more to the bottom line.

(n.) 主題
今天會議的主題是「如何從顧客互動中衍生最大價值」，所以我希望你們全都能夠專注地聽，因為你學到的知識和技巧能幫你對公司的獲利做更多貢獻。

.0025

thorough

[ˈθɝo]

必
同 **complete, sweeping**
副 **thoroughly**
　　同 exhaustively
名 **thoroughness**
　　同 fastidiousness,
　　meticulousness

Lanie was so **thorough** in her investigation into the office information leaks that she also discovered that two of her coworkers were cheating on their spouses.

(a.) 仔細的
蕾妮在調查辦公室資料外洩是如此的仔細，以至於她還發現有兩個同事對其伴侶不忠。

.0026

thoroughness

[ˈθɝonɪs]

必
同 **fastidiousness,
meticulousness**

We were quite impressed by the **thoroughness** and professional manner of the auditors sent over by the accounting firm, and have decided to have them do all of our auditing in the future.

(n.) 仔細
我們對會計事務所派來的查帳員的仔細和專業態度印象深刻，決定讓他們處理我們以後所有的帳目。

.0027

threat

[θrɛt]

同 **menace**
動 **threaten** 同 warn, admonish

There is growing concern in Southeast Asia about the growing competitive **threat** posed by China's growing exports, exacerbated by its entry into the World Trade Organization.

(n.) 威脅
在東南亞，對於中國出口成長而導致競爭加劇的擔憂逐漸升高，並因中國加入世界貿易組織而更形惡化。

.0028

thrill

[θrɪl]

必
同 **sensation**
動 **thrill**
　　同 stimulate, arouse
形 **thrilling**
　　同 electrifying, gripping
名 **thriller**

A **thrill** of excitement ran through Joanie when she heard that she had been offered a position in the company's Rome office.

(n.) 興奮，顫動
當瓊妮得知她得到公司在羅馬辦事處的職位時，興奮到全身發抖。

0029

throughout
[θru`aʊt]
同 all through

Scientists have found that having lots of small cups of coffee during the day rather than several large cups will keep you more alert **throughout** the day.

(prep.) 從頭到尾
科學家發現，一天喝多份小杯咖啡，而非幾份大杯咖啡，會讓你一整天更能保持機靈。

0030

throw out
[θro aʊt]
必

In an attempt to make sure everyone is trying to follow the company guidelines on neatness, I would like to ask you to **throw out** any unnecessary items stored at your desk.

扔掉
為了確定每一個人都試著遵循公司對整齊的指導方針，我希望你們扔掉任何堆在你們桌上不必要的物品。

0031

tier
[tɪr]
必
同 grade, level

Our company has three different **tiers** of management: senior management, middle management, and junior management.

(n.) 階層，等級
我們公司有三種階層的管理人：高階管理人員、中階管理人員和基層管理人員。

0032

time-consuming
[ˋtaɪmkənˌsjumɪŋ]
必

Poring over the sales figures was a **time-consuming** process, but Catherine tried to remind herself that this information was vital to her work.

(a.) 耗時的
研讀銷售數字是很耗時的過程，但是凱薩琳試著提醒自己這樣的資料對她的工作極其重要。

0033

tolerance
[ˈtɑlərəns]

同 **permissiveness**
反 **intolerance**
形 **tolerant**
    同 sympathetic, open-minded
形 **tolerable**

Before putting together an investment portfolio, it is important to first determine your **tolerance** for risk.

(n.) 寬容，容忍力
在擬定投資組合之前，重點是先確定你對風險的容忍度。

0034

trainee
[treˈni]

名 **trainer**
    同 instructor, coach
名 **training**
    同 preparation, coaching
動 **train**
    同 coach, teach

After working as a **trainee** for six months in the Customer Relations Department, Selma was offered a full-time position as a customer relations representative.

(n.) 受訓者，新進人員
在客戶關係部門中受訓六個月後，謝瑪得到了客戶關係代表的全職工作。

0035

trainer
[ˈtrenə]

必
同 **instructor, coach**

Our company is currently seeking a corporate **trainer** to implement and lead training programs for our sales and marketing departments.

(n.) 訓練人
我們的公司目前正在找一個培訓人員，來實行並領導我們業務與行銷部門的培訓計畫。

0036

training
[ˈtrenɪŋ]

必
同 **preparation, coaching**

All new employees must go through three months of intensive **training** before they are allowed to handle their first account.

(n.) 訓練
新員工都必須先經過三個月的密集訓練，才能獲准處理第一位客戶。

0037

transaction

[træn`zækʃən]

讀
動 **transact** 同 handle, conduct

All **transactions** at our bank are monitored, and suspicious account activity will be reported to the appropriate authorities.

(n.) 執行，交易

我們銀行所有的交易都受到監控，可疑的帳戶活動都會呈報給有關當局。

0038

transfer

[træns`fɜ]

聽
同 **move**
名 **transfer** 同 transference
形 **transferable**

Jake asked if he could be **transferred** to the human resources department because he felt his abilities would be put to better use there.

(v.) 調任

傑克詢問他是否能夠調任到人資部門，因為他認為在那兒更能發揮能力。

0039

transferable skill

[træns`fɜəbl̩ skɪl]

Identifying your **transferable skills** and communicating them to potential employers during job interviews will greatly increase your chances of success in finding a good job.

可轉移的技術

確定出你可轉移的技術，並在工作面試時將之傳達給可能的雇主，將大大提升你找到好工作的成功機會。

0040

translate

[træns`let]

必
同 **interpret, decipher**
名 **translation**
　同 rendering, paraphrase
名 **translator**

Before the big meeting with the Mexican client, the company hired a **translator** to translate all of the relevant documents into Spanish.

(v.) 翻譯

在與墨西哥客戶的大型會議開始前，公司雇用了一名翻譯將所有相關文件翻譯成西班牙文。

0041

translation
[træns`leʃən]
必

Our **translation** agency provides high quality English-Chinese and Chinese-English translation and interpreting services, as well as website localization, all at competitive prices.

(n.) 翻譯
我們的翻譯公司以具有競爭性的價格,提供高品質的英翻中和中翻英,以及口譯服務。

0042

trend
[trɛnd]
必
同 **inclination, current, flow**
形 **trendy** 同 fashionable

The vocational school keeps a close eye on emerging employment market **trends** and adjusts its programs to quickly meet changing market demands.

(n.) 潮流
這所職業學校密切注意新興就業市場潮流,並調整課程以迅速符合變動的市場需求。

0043

troubleshoot
[`trʌbl͵ʃut]

After **troubleshooting** for several hours, the IT technician finally determined the source of the network malfunction.

(v.) 檢測問題,排除疑難
在檢測問題數小時後,資訊技術人員終於確定網路故障的源頭。

0044

trust
[trʌst]
名 **trust**
同 guardianship, safekeeping, trusteeship
名 **trustee**

The CEO hired an estate planner to help him establish a **trust** to provide for the needs of his wife and children should he pass away.

(n.) 信託
執行長聘請了一位財產規劃師來幫他成立信託基金,在他萬一去世後以備妻兒所需。

turnover

[ˈtɜnˌovə]

同 business, productivity

While last year's **turnover** was down ten percent from the previous year, surprisingly, this year's turnover has shown a twelve percent increase.

(n.) 營業額

雖然去年的營業額比前年降低了百分之十，今年的營業額卻出乎意料地增加了百分之十二。

turnover rate

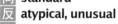

[ˈtɜnˌovə ret]

Many companies actually benefit from high employee **turnover rates** because they are able to keep their labor costs low by avoiding the pay increases associated with long-term employees.

流動率

其實許多公司從高員工流動率中受惠，因為他們能夠免於支付長期員工的加薪來壓低人工成本。

typical

[ˈtɪpɪkl]

必
同 standard
反 atypical, unusual
副 typically

According to a recent survey, the **typical** employee at a large corporation pays 16 to 25 percent of their health plan premium.

(a.) 典型的，一般的

根據最近一項調查指出，在大型企業中，一般員工要支付百分之十六到二十五的健康保險費用。

New
TOEIC 990 新多益高分關鍵字彙

New

TOEIC

新多益高分關鍵字彙

990

U

Group

0001

unanimous

[juˋnænəməs]

同 united, agreed
反 split
副 unanimously
名 unanimity

The response was a **unanimous** 'yes' when the employees were asked if they felt they were underpaid.

(a.) 全體一致的
當員工被問及是否覺得薪水過低時，全體一致回答「是的」。

 0002

unanimously

[juˋnænəməslɪ]

It was decided **unanimously** that Joe should be placed in charge of the office pool since everyone agreed that he had done an excellent job managing the last two pools.

(adv.) 全體一致地，無異議地
全體無異議通過喬應該被叫去負責辦公室合賭，因為大家都同意他在主導上兩次合賭時表現出色。

 0003

undecided

[ˌʌndɪˋsaɪdɪd]

同 unresolved, undetermined
反 definite

The troubled cell phone manufacturer has received takeover offers from three of its competitors, but is still **undecided** about which offer to accept.

(a.) 未決定的
這家陷入困境的手機製造商已收到三家對手公司的收購提議，但尚未決定要接受哪一家的條件。

 0004

under construction

[ˋʌndɚ kənˋstrʌkʃən]

Our official website is still **under construction** and should be up and running in a few weeks; if you have any questions in the meantime, please feel free to contact us by e-mail.

架構中
我們的官方網站還在架設中，應該會在幾個星期後啟用；若您在此同時有任何問題，歡迎以電子郵件聯絡我們。

0005

under development
[ˈʌndɚ dɪˈvɛləpmənt]

The pharmaceutical company has a number of new drugs **under development**, and also several products awaiting government approval.

發展中
這家製藥公司在研發一些新藥，還有幾項產品尚待政府核可。

0006

undergo
[ˌʌndɚˈgo]

Potential kidney donors must **undergo** a series of tests to ensure that it is safe for them to donate and that their kidney will be able to help the potential recipient.

(v.) 歷經
可能的捐腎人必須歷經連串測試，以確保捐贈器官對他們而言是安全的，且他們的腎臟將對可能的受贈者有所幫助。

0007

underlie
[ˌʌndɚˈlaɪ]
讀
動詞三態：
underlie, underlay, underlain

Many factors **underlie** Allan's decision to retire from managing the company and devote his time to charity work, but the main reason is the death of his wife.

(v.) 構成⋯的基礎
有許多因素促成艾倫決定退出公司的經營，將時間奉獻給慈善事業，但是主因是他太太的過世。

0008

understaffed
[ˌʌndɚˈstæft]
動 **understaff**

The office had been **understaffed** countless times in the last several years, and many of the remaining employees were tired of continually picking up the slack.

(a.) 人手不足的
公司在過去幾年歷經無數次的人手不足，許多留下的員工厭倦了不停收拾別人的懶攤子。

0009

unforeseen

[ˌʌnforˈsin]

同 unanticipated

An **unforeseen** problem halted production for two days, but once it was sorted out, everything was quickly back on track.

(a.) 未預見到的

一個沒預見到的問題讓生產線停擺兩天,但一經解決後,一切很快就回到正軌。

0010

uniform

[ˈjunəˌfɔrm]

必
同 alike, identical
副 uniformly

It is essential that all customer complaints be handled in a **uniform** manner, as this insures that all customers are treated equally and fairly.

(a.) 相同的,一致的

重點是客訴均需以一致的方式來處理,如此才可確保所有顧客都得到平等又公平的對待。

0011

uniformly

[junəˈfɔrmlɪ]

As the performance of the interviewees was **uniformly** excellent, it will be difficult to make a decision on which to hire for the management position.

(adv.) 一致地

由於面試者的表現一樣傑出,要決定雇用哪一位擔任主管將很困難。

0012

unload

[ʌnˈlod]

聽
同 discharge, disburden
反 load

The shipping container had to be **unloaded** and then reloaded several times before they were able to fit everything in.

(v.) 卸貨

貨櫃必須先卸完貨,而且要重新裝幾次貨才能把所有貨物裝上去。

0013

unused
[ʌn`juzd]
反 used

If for some reason you are unsatisfied with your purchase, you may send the **unused** portion of the product back within 30 days and receive a full refund minus shipping charges.

(a.) 未使用的
若您因故不滿意所購買的物品,可在三十天內將未使用的產品寄回,並獲得扣除運費之後的全額退費。

0014

up to par
[ʌp tu pɑr]

Jerry's supervisor told him that his work was **up to par**, but that his communication and teamwork skills still had room for improvement.

符合標準或預期的
傑瑞的上司跟他說他工作表現合格,但他的溝通技巧與團隊合作能力還有進步空間。

0015

update
[ʌp`det]
必
同 amend

You can **update** all of the information contained in your account by logging into your account and following the appropriate links.

(v.) 更新
你可以登入帳戶並依照合適的連結來更新帳戶內的所有資訊。

0016

upgrade
[ʌp`gred]
同 advance, elevate

To ensure the safety of your computer files, you should **upgrade** to the latest version of your antivirus software and make sure that your firewall is turned on.

(v.) 升級
為了確保電腦檔案的安全,你應該將防毒軟體升級到最新版本,也要確定防火牆已開啟。

0017

urge
[ɜdʒ]

必
同 exhort, press
反 dissuade
名 urge　　同 impulse

In light of the recent string of thefts at the office, we strongly **urge** employees to be on the alert and report any suspicious behavior to management.

(v.) 呼籲
基於辦公室內最近發生一連串偷竊事件，我們強烈呼籲員工提高警覺，並將任何可疑行為上呈主管單位。

0018

user-friendly
[ˈjuzɚˈfrɛndlɪ]

After switching to a more **user-friendly** operating system, productivity at our office has increased by 20 percent.

(a.) 容易使用的，考慮使用者需要的
改用更容易使用的作業系統後，我們辦公室的生產力增加了兩成。

0019

user manual
[ˈjuzɚ ˈmænjʊəl]

After consulting the **user manual**, the office manager was able to troubleshoot and fix the malfunctioning printer without having to call in a repairman.

使用手冊
參閱使用手冊之後，公司經理不用打電話給修理工人，便找出問題並修好了故障的印表機。

0020

utility
[juˈtɪlətɪ]

讀
名 utility
形 utilitarian

In the interests of protecting the environment and saving on **utility** bills, the office will be installing insulation, purchasing more energy efficient office equipment, and implementing an energy conservation plan.

(a.) 公用事業的
為了保護環境並節省公用事業費（水電、瓦斯等費用），辦公室將會安裝隔熱材料，購買更多節能的辦公室設備，並實施保護能源計畫。

utilize

[ˈjutəˌlaɪz]

同 **employ, use**
名 **utilization**

The company announced its plan to enhance shareholder value by **utilizing** excess cash to reduce debt and buy back outstanding shares.

(v.) 利用

公司宣布了增加股東價值的計畫，利用多餘現金來減少負債，並買回流通在外的股票。

utmost

[ˈʌtˌmost]

同 **extreme**
名 **utmost**

We pride ourselves on being able to assure our banking clients that their transactions will be handled with the **utmost** care, precision, and discretion.

(a.) 極度的，最大的

我們自豪的是我們會以最仔細、精確及謹慎的方式來處理銀行客戶的交易。

New
TOEIC 990 新多益 高分關鍵字彙

New
ToEIC
新多益高分關鍵字彙
990

V
Group

0001

vacant
[ˈvekənt]
同 empty
副 vacantly
名 vacancy

A **vacant** lot adjacent to the office building is scheduled to become the site of our new warehouse and storage facility.

(a.) 空著的
緊鄰辦公大樓的一片空地，預定成為我們新的倉庫與倉儲設施用地。

0002

valid
[ˈvælɪd]
必 讀
同 validated, effective
反 invalid
名 validity

An employee shall not be dismissed, whether adequate notice is given or not, unless there is a **valid** reason for the termination of employment.

(a.) 有根據的，有效的
不論有沒有預先通知，都不應解雇員工，除非有終止聘雇的合法理由。

0003

valid for
[ˈvælɪd fɔr]
讀

If you are traveling visa-free on the Visa Waiver Program and your passport is **valid for** less than 90 days, you will generally be admitted only until the date the passport expires.

（一段期間）有效的
如果你採免簽證計畫而未持簽證旅行，且護照效期不到九十天，入境許可一般只會給到護照到期那天。

0004

validate
[ˈvælə͵det]
必
同 formalize, certify
反 invalidate, nullify
名 validation 同 proof

We offer free parking for clinic patients, so if you park in the clinic parking lot, be sure to bring your parking ticket with you and our receptionist will **validate** it.

(v.) 確認，承認…為正當
我們為診所病患提供免費停車服務，所以如果您在診所停車場內停車，一定要隨身帶著停車券，我們的櫃臺人員將會進行確認。

0005

valuables

[ˋvæljʊəb]z]

形 valuable
　同 precious, expensive
反 worthless

Please lock your car and do not leave any **valuables** in your car that would encourage theft.

(n.) 貴重物品

請將車子上鎖，並不要在車內留下任何可能引起竊賊覬覦的貴重物品。

0006

value

[ˋvælju]

必

In today's increasingly competitive job market, the **value** of a university education cannot be underestimated.

(n.) 價值

在現今日益競爭的就業市場中，不可低估大學教育的價值。

0007

variable

[ˋvɛrɪəbl]

同 changeable
反 invariable
名 variability

Because of the **variable** nature of the market, investors are advised to diversify their investments across a range of assets and industry sectors.

(a.) 易變的，多變的

由於股市本質多變，建議投資人把投資分散在各個不同的資產與產業別。

0008

variety

[vəˋraɪətɪ]

同 assortment, diverseness
名 variation　同 variety
動 vary　　　同 alter, change
形 various　　同 diverse
形 varied　　同 mixed, various

The organic produce section at the supermarket offers an abundant **variety** of the freshest locally grown fruits and vegetables, as well as exotic items grown around the world.

(n.) 多樣化

超市的有機農產品區提供種類豐富、最新鮮的當地種植蔬果，連同全球各地種植的異國產品。

0009

vary

[ˋvɛrɪ]

必 讀
同 alter, change

The answers on the employee satisfaction survey **varied** widely, but the one thing everyone seemed to agree on was a need for more holidays.

(v.) 不同，變化

員工滿意度調查中的答案相當分歧，但是大家似乎都同意一件事，就是需要多放假。

0010

vendor

[ˋvɛndɚ]

動 vend　　同 hawk

Two of the key challenges for small business owners are hiring good employees and establishing and maintaining good relationships with **vendors**.

(n.) 賣主，小販

小公司老闆的兩項關鍵挑戰是，雇用好員工以及與賣家建立並維持良好關係。

0011

venture

[ˋvɛntʃɚ]

同 enterprise
動 venture
相關字彙 venture capital 創投

After selling his first high-tech company for 20 million dollars, the young entrepreneur began seeking partners for a new business **venture**.

(n.)（冒險）事業

以兩千萬美元賣掉他第一間高科技公司之後，這名年輕實業家開始尋找合夥人開創新事業。

0012

verbal

[ˋvɝbl]

必
同 oral
副 verbally
動 verbalize 同 speak, talk, utter

Although most people believe that it is always necessary to get any agreement in writing, there are cases where a **verbal** agreement is legal and valid.

(a.) 口頭上的

雖然大多數人認為凡協議就必須要以書面為之，不過也有口頭協議是合法並有效的例子。

0013

verbalize
[ˋvɝbəˏlaɪz]
必

Employees should be allowed to **verbalize** their preferences for shifts, and employers should make an effort to accommodate them whenever possible.

(v.) 以言語表述
員工應該可以說出他們排班的偏好，而雇主應該盡可能努力給他們方便。

0014

verify
[ˋvɛrəˏfaɪ]
必 聽 讀
同 **check, confirm, certify**
名 **verification**
　　同 validation, corroboration,
　　　authentication
形 **verifiable**

Before setting up a bank account, customers are required to **verify** their identity with two forms of photo identification, such as a valid passport, driver's license, or other government or employer-issued photo ID.

(v.) 證實，核對確認
開立銀行帳戶之前，客戶必須以兩種附有照片的證件來證實其身分，例如有效的護照、駕照或其他由政府、雇主核發之有照片證件。

0015

vested
[ˋvɛstɪd]
必
動 **vest**　　同 enthrone, invest

Venture capitalists who invest in a company at the seed stage take an active and **vested** interest in guiding, leading, and growing the company.

(a.) 既得的，既定的
在一間公司的種子時期即加以投資的創投家，對指導、領導與發展公司有濃厚興趣與既得利益。

0016

vocalist
[ˋvokəlɪst]
同 **singer**
形 名 **vocal**
動 **vocalize**

A **vocalist** was hired to perform at the company's year-end party, and she was well received by the audience.

(n.) 歌手
一名歌手受聘在這間公司的尾牙晚會表演，而且她大受觀眾好評。

0017

voice recognition

[vɔɪs ˌrɛkəgˈnɪʃən]

The CEO's executive assistant is no longer required to take dictation, because the CEO now has **voice recognition** software installed on his computer that can perform the same duty more quickly and accurately.

語音辨識

執行長特助不用再聽寫，因為現在執行長的電腦裝了語音辨識軟體，可以更快也更準確地執行這項任務。

0018

volunteer

[ˌvɑlənˈtɪr]

必
同 voluntary
動 volunteer 同 offer

Three days a week after work, Carol serves as a **volunteer** at the local library helping children overcome literacy problems.

(n.) 義工

每週三天下班後，卡蘿會在當地圖書館當義工，幫助孩童克服讀寫方面的問題。

New

新多益高分關鍵字彙

TOEIC

990

WY

Group

0001

wage

[wedʒ]

必
同 **pay**
動 **wage**   同 engage

The standard starting **wage** offered to recent graduates is about one-third of what an experienced employee can make.

(n.) 薪水
應屆畢業生的標準起薪,約是有工作經驗員工薪水的三分之一。

0002

warehouse

[ˈwɛrˌhaʊs]

聽
同 **storehouse, repository**

An inventory of the **warehouse** is conducted once every year to determine the number and value of all products in stock.

(n.) 倉庫
一年會進行一次倉庫盤點,以確定所有存貨的數量與價格。

0003

warn

[wɔrn]

必 聽 讀
同 **alert, admonish**
名 **warning** 同 admonition
形 **warning** 同 cautionary
副 **warningly**

Please **warn** Henley that the Marketing VP is looking for him and wants him to hand in the proposal he was supposed to have finished last week.

(v.) 警告,提醒
請警告亨利,行銷副總裁正在找他,並要他交出上星期早該完成的提案。

0004

warning

[ˈwɔrnɪŋ]

必
同 **admonition**

A recorded **warning** was broadcast over the sound system the moment the strong earthquake started shaking the building.

(n.) 警報,警告
強烈地震一開始晃動這座建築物時,音響系統便會廣播預錄好的警報。

0005

warranty
[ˈwɔrəntɪ]

聽 讀
同 guarantee, warrantee, warrant
名 動 warrant
片 under warranty 在保固期間

An extended **warranty** is typically designed to protect the consumer against any manufacturing defects beyond the life of the manufacturer's standard warranty.

(n.) 保固，保證書
延長保固的設計基本上是保護消費者，以防廠商標準保固期之外的製造瑕疵。

0006

waste
[west]

必
同 squander, blow
反 economize
名 waste
名 wastage
形 wasteful
副 wastefully

By focusing first and foremost on real customer needs, a company can avoid **wasting** precious time and resources developing products that have no chance of succeeding in the marketplace.

(v.) 浪費
透過首重顧客真正需要的方式，公司可以避免把寶貴的時間與資源，浪費在發展市場上沒有成功機會的產品。

0007

weakness
[ˈwiknɪs]

必
同 frailty
反 strength
形 weak

The new computer company is aggressively expanding its market share, taking advantage of every **weakness** in its competitors' business models.

(n.) 弱點，缺點
這間新電腦公司利用競爭對手經營模式的每一處弱點，野心勃勃地拓展其市場占有率。

0008

win-win situation
[ˈwɪnwɪn ˌsɪtʃuˋeʃən]

Trust me, this is a **win-win situation**; you will benefit from our technical expertise, and your sales channels will help us expand into new markets.

雙贏局面
相信我，這是雙贏的局面；你們將可從我們的技術專業中受益，而你們的銷售通路將有助我們拓展新市場。

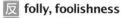

0009

wisdom
[ˈwɪzdəm]

必
同 wiseness
反 folly, foolishness
形 wise 同 foresighted, clever
　　　 反 unwise, ignorant

Theo's **wisdom** about matters of the heart made him the perfect guy for all the girls in the office to come and talk to when their men weren't acting right.

(n.) 智慧
提歐處理心事的智慧，讓他成為公司內所有女孩的另一半做錯事時，跑來訴苦的最佳對象。

0010

wise
[waɪz]

必
同 foresighted, clever

It was a **wise** decision on the part of Mr. McGillis to request a background check on the new hire because it turned out that he was wanted in three states for fraud.

(a.) 明智的，有智慧的
麥吉利斯先生要求對這位新進員工進行背景調查，是很明智的決定，因為最後證明他在三個州因詐欺而被通緝。

0011

with care
[wɪð kɛr]

Please handle this package **with care** because the items inside are very fragile and I am sorry to say that it is not packed very well.

悉心地
請小心搬動這個包裹，因為裡面的品項非常易碎，而我也很抱歉要說，它包得不是很好。

0012

with caution
[wɪð ˋkɔʃən]

Just remember to handle this client **with** extreme **caution**, because he tends to raise difficult technical questions when you least expect it.

謹慎地
千萬記住要小心翼翼應付這位客戶，因為他常冷不妨就提出困難的技術性問題。

withdraw

[wɪðˋdrɔ]

讀
同 **disengage**
名 **withdrawal**
形 **withdrawn** 圓 reclusive
動詞三態 **withdraw**
　　　　 withdrew
　　　　 withdrawn

After attempting to win this bid for two weeks and finding that everyone else has submitted a lower price, I have decided to **withdraw** my bid.

(v.) 撤回，移開
為了得標而努力兩個星期，卻發現其他人的標價都更低，我決定退標。

withhold

[wɪðˋhold]

必
同 **conceal**
反 **reveal**

Whatever you do, don't try to **withhold** information from the boss, as he somehow always seems to know everything.

(v.) 隱瞞
不管你做什麼，都別試圖隱瞞老闆，因為他似乎總是有辦法知道一切。

without notice

[wɪˋðaʊtˋnotɪs]

讀

The company closed its doors **without notice**, leaving its employees out of work and with no last paycheck.

無預警
這家公司無預警倒閉，導致員工失業且拿不到上個月的薪水。

workflow

[ˋwɝkˏflo]

Since installation of the new productivity software package, the **workflow** in our office has quickened considerably.

(n.) 工作流程
自從安裝了這個新的生產力套裝軟體，我們辦公室工作流程的效率大增。

0017

workplace
[ˈwɝkˌples]
聽 讀

Violence in the workplace has received growing attention, in part due to the increase in litigation by victims of **workplace** violence.

(n.) 職場
職場暴力越來越受到關注，部分原因是職場暴力受害者提告的案例增加了。

0018

wrinkle
[ˈrɪŋkl̩]
必
同 difficulty

Everything was going great until a little **wrinkle** in production set the delivery date back two weeks, and we are still trying to catch up.

(n.) 困難，難題
一切原本進行地很順利，直到生產過程中發生了一點困難，使得交貨要延遲兩星期，而我們還在試著趕工。

0019

yield
[jild]
必
同 profit, return

The **yield** on short-term bonds has risen steadily over the past decade, while the **yield** on long-term bonds has held steady.

(n.) 利潤
十年來，短期債券的利潤穩定增加中，而長期債券的利潤則持穩。

New TOEIC 990 新多益高分關鍵字彙

國家圖書館出版品預行編目資料

New TOEIC 990 新多益高分關鍵字彙
EZ 叢書館編輯部 作
初版，臺北市：日月文化，2010.11
368 面，17 x 23 公分（EZ 叢書館）
ISBN：978-986-248-130-1（平裝）
1. 多益測驗　2. 詞彙
805.1895　　　　　　　　　　　　　　99020874

New TOEIC 990 新多益高分關鍵字彙

作　　　者：EZ 叢書館編輯部
總　編　輯：陳思容
主　　　編：葉瑋玲
執 行 編 輯：張曉莉
文 字 編 輯：鄭彥谷・游明芳・林錦慧
英 文 主 筆：Judd Piggott・Leah Scott
英 文 錄 音：Debra Thoreson・Robert William Fher・
　　　　　　James Taylor・Clare Lear
美 術 設 計：謝靜怡・王睿穎・劉麗雪
排 版 設 計：健呈電腦排版股份有限公司

董 事 長：洪祺祥
總 經 理：胡芳芳
法 律 顧 問：林穆弘
財 務 顧 問：高威會計師事務所

出　　　版：日月文化集團 日月文化出版股份有限公司
製　　　作：EZ 叢書館
地　　　址：台北市大安區信義路三段 151 號 9 樓
電　　　話：(02) 2708-5509
傳　　　真：(02) 2708-6157
網　　　址：www.ezbooks.com.tw

總 經 銷：高見文化行銷股份有限公司
電　　　話：(02)2668-9005
傳　　　真：(02)2668-6220
印　　　刷：禹利電子分色有限公司
初　　　版：2010 年 11 月
定　　　價：350 元
I S B N：978-986-248-130-1